"*Mingo* is a realistic depictic ... a closely detailed look at the entire cuiture of coal ... re of Richmond and the Old South. Seen through the eyes of two irresistible mountain brothers, Durwood and Bascom Matney from the coal mining community of Mingo, the issues of class, race, and unionization take on real flesh and blood. Suspense and pathos mount in a plot as relevant today as ever. *Mingo* is a moving and thought-provoking page turner."

—Lee Smith, Bestselling author of *The Last Girls* and
Fair and Tender Ladies

"An unforgettable coming of age story that sets brother against brother in the 20th century coal wars. Jeff Barnes is a natural storyteller."

—Kelly Corrigan, Host of "Tell Me More," PBS, and New York Times
bestselling author of *The Middle Place and Glitter and Glue*

"In his poignant depiction of the West Virginia coal-mining war, Jeff Barnes breathes life into both the hardscrabble fictional Matney family and such outsize historical figures as local hero Sheriff Sid Hatfield, fiery labor organizer Mother Jones, brutal Baldwin-Felts strikebreakers, and courageous 'Redneck Army' strikers willing to sacrifice their lives in the fight for humane working conditions. *Mingo* is a worthy memorial to these tough times in the Southern Appalachians."

—Dean King, nationally bestselling author of *Skeletons on the Zahara* and
The Feud: The Hatfields & McCoys: The True Story

"*Mingo* is like the mining of coal itself, explosive and powerful, darkness emerging into light. Barnes has found a rich seam."

—David L. Robbins, New York Times bestselling author of *War of the Rats*
and *Isaac's Beacon*

"Family, friendship and fighting for human rights and dignity are the touchstones that bind rising talent Jeff Barnes' *Mingo* together in a classic tale from the great West Virginia coal fields. Bascom and Durwood Matney, brothers bound by blood amid the 1921 Mountain State mine war, the largest American insurrection since the Civil War, take a timeless trip through homespun heroism, heartbreak and resolution. Barnes has meticulously researched those events that captured the nation's attention a century ago and resonate still in the hearts of working people everywhere. The legendary Mother Jones, fiery Sid Hatfield, and the notorious Baldwin-Felts agency are accurately and dramatically portrayed in this classic piece of historical fiction. Barnes' first novel is a top-shelf 'page turner' which holds the reader close from the emotional opening to the final, explosive conclusion."

—Larry Hypes, Bluefield (WV) Daily Telegraph

"Full of detail and well-drawn characters, *Mingo* is a highly satisfying read wrapped in a sneaky-good history lesson."

—Paul Fletcher, Virginia Lawyers Weekly

MINGO

▼

A NOVEL

BY

W. JEFF BARNES

Published by Little Star
Richmond, VA

Mingo is a work of fiction based upon some real events and people. Drawn from
a variety of sources, including published materials, it derives primarily from the author's
imagination. The book contains fictionalized scenes and dialogue, composite and representative
characters, and time compression. The views and opinions expressed in the book are those of
the characters only and do not necessarily reflect or represent the views and opinions held by
individuals on whom those characters are based.

Contact the author at www.wjeffbarnes.com

ISBN 978-1-7358872-7-2

Book design by Wendy Daniel

Printed in the United States of America

For Tamera

Chapter 1

October 17, 1908

Mingo County, West Virginia

Rain beaded on the church windows which did little to keep out the cold. The pews overflowed in a sea of black. Durwood dug deep in his pockets and hunched. He wanted to stamp, but his feet didn't reach the floor. Though it was cold enough to see the preacher's breath, sweat beaded the man's brow. Every few minutes, the preacher paused to wipe his forehead and catch his breath. What was he so worked up about? It was Durwood's mother who had crossed over the Jordan, not his.

"Every day in heaven, sitting at the foot of our Lord and savior, Jesus Christ, is more glorious than the most beautiful day you can imagine on this here planet Earth." The spittle that clung to the preacher's lip threatened to untether.

Was Ma already in paradise? Durwood hoped the preacher was right. Ma hated dreary days worse than a toothache. A beach at sunset was her heaven.

Durwood tried to conjure a beach. The closest he ever came was the picture postcard of Virginia Beach Ma kept in her Bible. She promised to take him and Bascom one day. They would make sandcastles and swim in the ocean. Durwood didn't care if he never saw the ocean if it meant he could have Ma back.

"Can I get an Amen?"

"Amen, brother!" Cousin Cesco sat nearby.

"Can I get an Amen?"

Overcome by the Spirit, several mourners leapt to their feet to join Cesco in a chorus of Amens. Folks lined the back wall and sides of the church, more than when the Pentecostal Revival packed the house in June.

Durwood and Bascom crowded their father in the first pew, reserved for the mine superintendent's family on Sundays. Pa said it would be alright for them to sit here today. Durwood was surprised to find this pew as rough and the back as hard as the ones in the rear that he shared with Bascom and Ma on Sunday mornings and during Wednesday night Bible study.

Once, when Bascom complained after jerking a splinter, Ma responded, "We come to church to comfort our souls, not our backsides."

"It would be a sight easier for my soul to find comfort if my bottom didn't feel like a pin cushion."

Though serious about her soul, Ma hadn't been able to suppress a smile.

Pa wore a black suit with a string tie. He'd buttoned a fresh collar and cuffs on his white dress shirt. Durwood couldn't recall seeing him in a suit before. Pa said he'd worn it twice—when he married Ma and when they buried Durwood's older sister five years earlier. That also happened to be the last time Pa set foot in church. Try as he might, Durwood couldn't remember Georgie. He was only three when she died shy of her sixth birthday. Pa sat straight and clasped his hands, rough and knobby as tree roots. Durwood nestled against his arm, hoping Pa would pull him close.

Working harder than a steam engine pulling coal, the preacher led the congregation in prayer. "Our Father, who art in heaven…"

"Come on, son."

Durwood opened his eyes to the church folk standing and staring. He wished everybody would stop looking at him the same, pitiful way. Been that way ever since Ma took to the bed a few months back. The preacher waited by their pew to usher them out.

"Where we going?"

"Outside to say goodbye to your Ma."

Men from Pa's shift lifted the rough-hewn pine casket off the trusses. Heads bowed, they headed toward the door. The newspaper Durwood had stuffed into his shoes for warmth crinkled as he followed Bascom down the aisle. Over half the folks were either Matneys or Powers—his Daddy's kin. Ma had said he would meet her side of the family when they went to the beach.

In the last pew, a short, erect woman Durwood had never seen nodded like she knew him. Her smooth, ivory complexion stood out in a sea of weathered, sallow faces. Transfixed, Durwood fell off the pace. Her black dress shimmered unlike the shapeless, drab cotton and burlap of the others. Dark buttons anchored a high collar under a ring of lace. The beads of her necklace matched the buttons. Instead of a coat, a jet-black cape draped her shoulders. Even her hat, wide-brimmed with a feather, stuck out like a sore thumb. Ma wore a hat to church, but this was the first he ever saw with a feather. It seemed silly, but it looked good on her. Durwood knew every bird in the southern West Virginia mountains, but try as he might he could not place the big, wispy green one. The woman's gaze held his eyes in an odd way, as if she knew a secret.

Next to her stood a tall man in an ebony overcoat. Beneath the open coat, he wore a black, three-piece suit and necktie. His dark hair glistened with pomade. Except for a neatly-trimmed moustache, his face was supple, like a barber had shaved it that morning. Holding a Fedora, his hands were smooth, nails clean. Durwood couldn't place these folks but they weren't from Mingo County.

Pa nudged his back. Durwood began moving again as the ushers opened the doors for the pallbearers. Cold air chilled his face.

Durwood pulled on his wool cap and tugged at his collar. Trudging to the cemetery on the hill overlooking the single-room church, rain tickled the back of his neck. The trees on the ridge had shed their leaves weeks before, signaling another early winter on the mountain. Everyone gathered around the plot. The pallbearers placed Ma's casket in the freshly-dug hole, next to where Georgie lay. The flowers Ma placed the last time she was strong enough to mount the hill lay undisturbed; twine still held fast the dried stems.

"Lord God almighty, we commend this soul to your heavenly kingdom. May she rejoice in your presence and be reunited with her precious child. We ask that you provide strength and comfort to those she leaves behind. Amen."

The pallbearers shoveled dirt onto the casket when the preacher intoned, "Ashes to ashes, and dust to dust." The first few shovelfuls hit with a dull thud until dirt obscured the casket. When the shoveling stopped, the preacher led the mourners in prayer. At the last amen, Tillie McBride, Ma's best friend, sang "Amazing Grace." Her haunting voice matched the bleak mountainside. As the last note faded, the preacher thanked everyone for coming and asked them to pray for the family.

Who was going to cook? Help with his lessons and tuck him in? Who was there to hug now? When Durwood had asked if it was true, like folks said, that the good Lord needed Ma more than they did, Pa didn't hesitate:"If that's the case, son, then the good Lord ain't paying close enough attention."

The crowd dwindled. Folks shared their condolences, then headed home to their own troubles. Durwood looked for the handsome couple, disappointed that only family, the preacher and a couple of deacons remained.

"Uncle Clem, me and Maude come to pay our respects. Aunt Hope was a fine woman." "Thank you kindly, Cesco."

"If they's anything we can do, just say the word."

"I reckon we'll make do."

Cesco bent to hug Durwood and Bascom. "Family pulls together in times of trouble. Don't you boys forget that."

"Clem, unless you or the boys need me, I reckon I'll be takin' my leave."

"Much obliged, Preacher. Hope would have appreciated your kind words."

"She was a woman of faith. I hope we'll see you back in church with the boys real soon."

"Don't take no offense, but the next time you see me in church I'll be wearing a pine box. When that day comes, I'm afraid your job will be a sight harder than today. Come on, boys, there's somebody in the church I need to see to."

Pa headed downhill to the weathered, clapboard church. Durwood and Bascom shook the preacher's hand and followed. Durwood tugged Bascom's sleeve.

"Did you see them fancy folks in the back of the church?"

"Sure did. Who do you think they was?"

"Don't know, but they was all spiffed up. That lady was awful pretty."

"Dang straight. But the man looked like a dandy. That hat must've been the heaviest thing them hands ever lifted."

Pa climbed the steep steps to hold open the splintered, white-washed doors for Durwood and Bascom. The church stood empty except for the fancy couple. They had not moved from the last pew.

"Hello, Grace. Walker."

"I'm glad you sent word, Clem."

"Just done like I promised Hope."

"I can't believe she's gone. How are you all getting along?"

"Everyone has took real good care of us. Ain't nothing like death or threat of a strike to bring folks on the mountain together."

How did Pa know these people?

"Boys, this here's your Ma's cousin, Grace. And her husband, Walker. They come all the way from Richmond, Virginia, to pay their respects."

Grace extended her hand. "You must be Bascom. By the look of things, you'll be taller than your father in no time. How old are you?"

"Fourteen next week, ma'am."

"I hear you're already working in the mines with your father."

"That's right."

"Must be hard work."

"It ain't so bad."

"Let me guess. Durwood?" Grace knelt close enough that her sweet breath warmed his cheeks.

"Yes ma'am."

"Your mother told me all about you. You're in second grade, right?"

Durwood nodded as Pa stepped forward.

"I need to talk with these folks a bit. You two take a seat."

Taking Durwood's hand, Bascom returned to the first pew, their footsteps amplified in the empty church.

"What do you suppose they's talking about, Bascom?"

"Don't know. But they don't want us hearing."

"Maybe they's planning a trip to the beach."

Pa removed from his pocket a wad of cash, more money than Durwood had ever seen. He held out his hand, but Walker refused. Pa turned to Grace. She shook her head and said something. Pa grabbed

Walker's lapel, stuffed the cash in his breast pocket and turned toward the window.

"What do you think that was about, Bascom?"

"Dang if I know. But Pa done give away all our money."

"Boys, did you know I grew up with your mother in Richmond?" Grace asked as she walked down the aisle. "We were like sisters."

Durwood nodded. "She said you and her was like two peas in a pod."

"What else did she tell you?"

"Y'all played in the river during the summer and went to the beach once."

"That's right. Your mother loved the beach best of all. Never stopped talking about it. Durwood, how would you like to come back to Richmond and stay with us? We could show you where your mother grew up."

Walker moved down the aisle. "And take you to the beach."

Pa stared out the window toward the cemetery. Why wasn't Bascom speaking up? After all, he was the one who had been pining to see the ocean.

"That would be real nice, but I reckon I best stay put. Pa and Bascom will be needing me around here."

Grace said, "Your father thinks it would be a good idea if you came back to Richmond with us."

"That the gospel, Pa?"

Pa dabbed his handkerchief to his nose. Still gazing out the window, he cleared his throat. "That's right, son. Now that Bascom's working in the mines full time, there ain't nobody to care for you. Grace and Walker have a real nice home in Richmond. He's got a good job with the railroad."

"I don't want to go, Pa. I don't need looking after. And I can do Ma's chores."

"It's what your mother wanted. Why don't you read this to him, Clem?" Grace extended an envelope.

"You read it. My eyes ain't so good. Too much time underground."

Grace read the letter. Durwood was to go to Richmond where Grace could look after him and see to it that he kept up his schooling. She was trusting Grace to raise her son in a good, Christian home.

"Like Grace said, your Ma and I discussed it before she passed."

6

"What about Bascom? He needs lookin' after too."

"Bascom's almost fourteen."

Grace knelt again. She smiled like Ma before the cancer hollowed her cheeks, only prettier. "What do you say, Durwood?"

"Give it a try, son. Just 'til things settle down around here."

"Where would I sleep?"

"You'd have your own bedroom, of course," Grace said.

Bascom sat stone-faced.

"Can Bascom and Pa come visit?"

"Of course."

"I reckon it won't hurt none 'til things settle down."

Grace grasped Walker's hand. Bascom sprung to his feet. "Just like that! You're gonna up and quit your kin?"

Pa turned from the window. "He ain't quitting us. He's just accepting a kind offer to help us out for the time being, like your Ma wanted."

"It ain't like that, Bascom. Besides, you'll have a bed to yourself and my helping of supper."

"I don't want your dang supper." Bascom ran from the church.

Grace turned to Clem. "We didn't mean to upset him, Clem."

"He's just missing his Ma, is all. When are you planning on heading back?"

"On the morning train, if that suits you."

"We'll meet you at the station in the morning. Know the way back to town?"

"Yes. Thank you."

"Come on, son." Pa blew out the candles and closed the door behind them. The sky was dark.

"We taking the shortcut?"

"We'll stick to the path. Moon ain't going to be much account tonight."

"Why we walking so slow?"

"Hadn't noticed we was."

Durwood had questions, but they would have to wait until morning; Pa wasn't in a talking mood. Ma liked to say she talked enough for the both of them. He longed to hear her voice once more.

They crested the last hill. Their house lay dark.

"Where do you reckon Bascom is, Pa?"

"In bed, I suppose."

Durwood raced ahead. Pa entered behind and lit a lamp.

"You go on to bed, son. I'll see to your belongings."

Durwood slid through the curtain into their room. "You awake? Bascom?"

"Hush. I don't feel like talking none."

"It ain't like I'm going away forever. Just 'til things settle down. Besides, you heard them. You and Pa can come visit. When you do, we'll take that trip to the beach. What was it you said you wanted to eat? Them things like crawdads only bigger."

"Shrimp."

"Yeah. Shrimp."

"You must be a danged fool."

"How you figure?"

"Where do you think Pa and I are going to come up with the money to travel all the way to Richmond? Didn't you see he done give all our money away so's they'd take you in? And even if we had the money, you think the company is just gonna up and say, 'Have a nice trip. We'll hold your jobs 'til you two come back.' I ain't going nowhere except back down in that damned hole. Just like Pa. Time's passing me by."

"It ain't gonna be that way. You'll see."

"That's what Jacob thought."

"Who's Jacob?"

"You know. The Bible story about them brothers that got crosswise. Their Ma favored the younger one and sent him off to live with her rich relatives."

"We ain't crosswise, are we?"

"I don't reckon."

"Remind me what happened to them brothers."

"They didn't see one another for a long time."

"I done changed my mind. I don't want to be like that Jacob fellow."

"It's done settled. Now go to sleep."

"Promise me we'll see each other. Bascom, promise."

"Course we will."

Chapter 2

October 18, 1908

Matewan, West Virginia

"There they are, son."

Grace waved from the far end of the platform where she waited with Walker, hand-in-hand. A steamer and two large, matching leather suitcases sat at their feet. Travelers moved about the platform.

"Why they always holding hands? He afraid of losing her?"

"That's just a way of showing they care about one another."

"You ever hold Ma's hand?"

"That's different."

"What should I call them, Pa?"

"They'll let you know. 'Til then, 'sir' and 'ma'am' will do fine. Let's go. Looks like the train's running on time for a change."

Durwood carried his bundle of clothes: extra shirt, pair of socks, a sweater, and a pair of Bascom's dungarees that were still a couple sizes too big. Pa reached into Durwood's hip pocket, snagging a slingshot Bascom helped make the previous summer.

"Don't reckon you'll be needing a slingshot in the city, unless you done run all the squirrels out of Mingo County."

"Pa. Please."

"Ain't going to be party to any mischief. Best leave it with me."

Walker extended a hand to Pa. "Morning, Clem. Durwood. Bascom didn't come to see you off?"

"He cleared out of the house with his pole before sunup. Must've been itching to fish on his day off."

"Be sure to tell him we hope he'll come visit."

"All aboard the 458 for Bluefield," the station master announced.

Grace touched Durwood's shoulder. "That's us. Are you ready?"

Durwood looked up at Pa, hoping he'd call the whole thing off. Say he'd changed his mind.

"Mind giving us a minute?"

"Of course." Grace hugged Clem. "If you and Bascom ever need anything..."

"Just take care of my boy."

"We will. Walker, let's get help with our luggage." Grace turned to Durwood. "Where's your bag?"

"Ain't got one." Pa cocked his head to cast a stern look. "Ma'am."

"Here's his belongings." Pa motioned to Durwood, who handed the small bundle to Grace. Placing it on top of the steamer, she and Walker strode toward the station master.

Durwood waited until they were out of earshot. "Do I have to go?"

"We done been over this."

"What if I don't like Richmond?"

"You will. Besides, your Ma wouldn't have asked Grace and Walker to care for you if they won't good people."

"Will you come visit?"

"Soon as we can. Promise me something, son."

"Sir?"

"Make something of yourself. But don't ever forget your roots."

"What do you mean?"

Pa knelt to put his hands on Durwood's shoulders and look him in the eye. "One day, you'll understand." Pa hugged him tightly, the way Ma hugged. Durwood closed his eyes and wished he wouldn't let go.

"All aboard."

Pa relaxed his embrace to stand. Walker and Grace waited on the first step of the train.

"Write to me, Pa."

"We will."

"Tell Bascom we ain't going to be like them Bible brothers."

"Bye, son. Remember what I told you."

Durwood moved toward the train. Grace helped him up as the train started to roll. Pa shuffled away, head down. The tip of a bamboo fishing pole peaked from behind a man seated in the shoeshine stand's elevated chair. Bascom stepped from behind the stand.

"Look! Bascom."

Grace turned. "Where?"

"There."

Durwood wagged his index finger at the stand. Bent over, the shoeshine boy buffed a man's shoes. Another waited his turn. Bascom was gone.

"You sure it was him?"

"I knew he'd come. I knew he couldn't stay sore."

"What do you two say we find our berth? See the numbers over the doors?" Walker pointed. "We're in berth twenty-five. See if you can find it for us, Durwood."

Durwood moved down the narrow passageway, checking above the doors. He stopped at the third door.

"Here it is."

"You're right. Open the door."

Durwood pulled the brass handle with both hands, revealing a spacious room with four leather seats, two on each side of a big window with lace curtains tied back. A wash basin with an oval-shaped mirror above it occupied one corner. Plush towels draped over a rack beside the basin. Across from the basin, a wardrobe reached to the top of the car.

"Where would you like to sit?"

"By the window?"

Grace smiled, reminding him again of his mother.

Durwood scrambled onto the seat, hoping for another glimpse of Bascom. The train had cleared the station. Matewan slipped away.

Walker hung his overcoat in the wardrobe. "Anybody else?"

"No, thank you, dear."

"Durwood?"

"If it's all the same, I'll keep mine on."

"Of course."

"Mind if I sit next to you?"

"No, ma'am."

As Grace sat, a floral scent spilled over Durwood. Was she hiding flowers under her wrap? He tried to remember Ma's clean smell, redolent of lye soap.

Grace asked, "You don't get motion sickness, do you? I forgot to ask your father."

"Don't reckon I do."

"Have you ridden a train before?"

"Bascom and I hopped a freight car over to Bluefield once."

Walker chuckled. "That sounds dangerous."

"That's what Pa said right before he give us a licking. Bascom got the worst of it though 'cause he was supposed to know better."

"You and your brother are close, aren't you?"

"About like you and our Ma was, I suppose."

The train accelerated. The landscape blurred past. Durwood wished everything would slow. Walker removed a newspaper from his briefcase. "You like school, Durwood?" He peered over the top of his spectacles.

"Yes, sir."

"What subjects do you like best?"

"Reading and 'rithmetic, I suppose."

"Get good marks?"

"Mostly. My teacher says my penmanship ain't nothing to write home about."

"What does she say about your diction?"

"What's that?"

"Never mind."

"What do you want to be when you grow up?"

"How do you mean?"

"What do you say when people ask what kind of work you want to do?"

"Ain't never been asked that question. Suppose I'll work with Pa and Bascom when the time comes." Durwood fidgeted. "How long is the train ride?"

"We'll reach Roanoke this evening and spend two nights. Walker has some business there. We'll arrive in Richmond late the day after tomorrow. While he's working, you and I will do some shopping. Looks like you may need a new wardrobe."

Durwood glanced at the corner.

Grace winked at Walker. "Wardrobe also means clothes. What do you say we buy some new clothes?"

His folks never said anything about needing new clothes. They were clean; all the holes patched. Besides, they had worked just fine for Bascom. He had a jacket and cap for the cold and a pair of brogans. Was Grace going to spend Pa's hard-earned money on new clothes he didn't need?

"Ma says it's a waste for folks to have a bunch of clothes seeing as they could only wear one set at a time."

Grace laughed. "That sounds like her. Always the practical one."

"I think I'll take a nap. We was up early this morning." Durwood leaned his head against the window, pretending to sleep.

Chapter 3

October 18, 1908

Mingo County, West Virginia

Bascom squinted at the house from the rocky outcropping above their plot. He and Durwood had spent hours here watching the clouds by day, stars by night. A plume of smoke drifted from the chimney into the afternoon sky. The outside of the house gave no hint of the changes inside. Bascom felt alone. After a day wallowing in self-pity, he had shed his last tear. Whatever lay ahead, he'd face it head-on. Like the man everyone kept telling him he was.

Jumping to the ground, he grabbed his fishing pole. He marched across the meadow, ignoring the path he and Durwood had cut. As he stepped onto the porch to lift the door latch, the sun slid behind the peak on the far side of the hollow.

"I was beginning to think you stowed away on the train with your brother. Catch us some supper?" Pa rocked in front of the fireplace.

"No, sir. Weren't nothing biting."

"You remember how to make cornbread and beans like your Ma showed you?"

Bascom nodded.

"Better get started, then."

Pa leaned halfway out of his cane rocker to stoke the fire. Sitting back, he lifted a jug.

"You starting that again?"

"What are you talking about?"

"You think I don't remember how much you was drinking after Georgie died?"

"Don't forget your place, boy. Just 'cause you's fixing supper don't think you can act like your Ma. This is my house and I'm damn well going to do as I please from now on."

"So Ma was holding you back?"

"Ain't what I said."

"What are you saying?"

"Don't trifle with me."

"How about you give me some of that, then?"

Pa scoffed.

"I said give me some corn mash."

"You ain't man enough."

"I'm man enough to mine coal ten hours a day."

"I didn't say you wasn't old enough. I said you wasn't man enough."

"What's the difference?"

"Suit yourself."

As the jug passed under his nose, Bascom regretted his bravado. He couldn't back down. He swigged more than he intended; the whiskey burned like he imagined turpentine would. His cheeks pooched as his throat resisted the urge to swallow.

"Best not spit that out."

Bascom gulped. He sputtered, choking back bile.

"Care for some more?"

Regaining his composure, Bascom grabbed the sack of cornmeal Ma kept in the cupboard. He managed to rasp, "I'm fine." Loosening the drawstring, he sifted for mealy bugs before pouring the contents into a bowl. He added the other ingredients like he'd seen Ma do and poured everything into the skillet on top of the warm morning stove. A pot of beans from breakfast sat on the table. Lifting the lid, he sloshed the contents.

"Looks like we got enough beans from this morning. I'll warm them up and make us a new batch tomorrow."

"Suits me."

Bascom opened the stove to poke the fire. He added a log. "You reckon he's okay?"

"He'll be fine. They's good people."

Bascom stirred the beans. "How can you be sure?"

"'Cause your Ma was a good judge of character."

"Dang. Look what Durwood forgot." Bascom picked up the hickory sling shot from a coat hook beside the front door.

"He ain't forgot. I took it from him."

"Why'd you go and do that for?"

"Didn't want him getting hisself in trouble. If Walker and Grace want him to have a slingshot, I reckon they can use the money I give them to buy him one."

"Supper's ready." Bascom sliced the cornbread. He placed half on his father's plate, along with a heaping spoonful of beans. Taking a smaller slice for himself, he scooped a few beans.

"That all you going to eat?"

"Ain't too hungry."

Pa scooped the last slice of cornbread between his fork and thumb and scraped the pot of beans onto his plate. Mashing his bread, he mixed it in with the soupy beans and dug in.

"Ain't we going to bless the food?"

"You go ahead. I done experienced all the blessings I can stand."

Bascom bowed his head. He prayed that Durwood would prosper like Jacob.

Chapter 4

"What time is it, Walker?" The train swayed as it slowed.

Walker pulled his pocket watch from his vest. "Almost seven."

"How late is the hotel dining room open?

"Ten."

"That gives us time to freshen up and still make a late dinner."

"What are we going to do about Durwood?"

"What do you mean?"

"He isn't dressed for dinner."

Clothes seemed to be causing a fuss again. Durwood was hungry and didn't want to go to bed on an empty stomach because of his clothes, unsure why it mattered.

"I guess we'll have dinner delivered to our room. I'm hungry and I'm sure Durwood is, too. Right, Durwood?"

"Did you say hotel?"

"We're staying at the Hotel Roanoke the next two nights. It's a lovely hotel. One of Virginia's finest."

The train jerked to a stop. Walker put on his coat. He draped Grace's over her shoulders. Durwood grabbed his coat and cap. Walker slid the compartment door open and waited for Grace and Durwood to exit.

"Is it fancy like the Urias Hotel back home? I went with Ma once when she asked about taking in some ironing."

"Something like that." Walker winked. "You'll see."

Durwood stepped off the train behind Grace. The engine belched steam thick as early fog. Durwood breathed deeply; coal tinged the air. Where had this coal come from? Had Bascom dug it? Pa?

Grace touched his shoulder. "What do you think?"

On a hill less than two hundred yards away, silhouetted against the clear, night sky, stood the grandest structure he had ever seen. Darkness hid its details, but its size and shape dwarfed anything he knew. Stretching as far as Matewan's main street, it appeared to touch the stars. Lights shone from a hundred windows.

"It looks like a castle."

Grace leaned in. "Wait until you see the inside."

A large man in a fancy black suit, white shirt, black bow tie and top hat approached. Unlatching a gate, he stepped onto the platform and bowed. "Welcome to the Hotel Roanoke. My name is Robert. If you folks will kindly follow me, I'll show you to the hotel. Your luggage will follow directly."

Robert led the group up the walkway to the hotel. Gas lamps lit the path. Durwood wanted to run ahead but checked his gait to stay tight on Robert's heels. As they neared the entrance, the hotel's grandeur emerged—five stories tall in the center, with lower-slung wings branching off at angles for a hundred yards. A bell tower topped the hotel and flags fluttered from a first-floor balcony. Robert led them onto a red carpet protected by an awning that stretched from the front doors.

Doormen dressed like Robert swung open two massive oak portals. Durwood stopped the instant he stepped inside. This was nothing like the Urias. Multiple chandeliers, suspended from the vaulted ceiling, cast the room in a dazzling light. Light emanated from glass bulbs, fueled by neither wax nor gas. Leather chairs and couches lined the marble floor. In the center of the lobby, directly under the largest and most ornate chandelier, water sprayed ten feet from a basin in the floor. Colors flashed in the droplets. Bascom should be here to see this.

"This way to the front desk."

Lingering at the fountain, Durwood asked Grace, "You see that?"

"What?"

"They's all kinds of money in that water."

"That's because people believe their wishes will come true if they toss in a coin. Want to try?" Grace pulled a penny from her purse.

Durwood closed his eyes. Before tossing the coin, he cracked one eye. "Do I get it back after I make my wish?"

"It doesn't work that way."

"Then I reckon you best keep your money." A penny would buy a pound of flour or sugar. Pa would tan his hide if he found out he had tossed a penny away just so he could make a wish. That's what prayers were for, and they were free.

"You sure?"

"Yes, ma'am."

"Why don't you hang onto it for now?" Durwood searched his pocket for holes before releasing the coin.

"If the people what throws their money away don't get it back, who gets to keep it?"

"That's a great question. I'll bet Walker will know." Grace and Durwood moved to the front desk beside Walker, who waited for the clerk to finish helping another guest.

"Welcome back, Mr. Hopkins. How long will you be with us?"

"Two nights. I wired ahead for a suite."

"Looks like we have you and Mrs. Hopkins on the fifth floor."

"Thank you." Walker looked at Durwood. "We will need an extra bed."

The manager peered over the counter at Durwood. "Your suite has a Murphy bed. Will that suffice or should I have a bed sent up?"

"That will do just fine, thank you."

Strains of music caught Durwood's attention. Across the lobby in another room, folks danced. The preacher said close-dancing led to sins of the flesh, whatever that meant. What did tempting the devil look like? Durwood crossed the lobby to stand in an open doorway. Instead of flat-footing, men and women dressed fancier than Grace and Walker at Ma's funeral twirled around the room. Others sat at tables eating dinner, admiring the dancers. Best he could tell, dizziness was the worst thing to come of dancing. A bald, bespectacled man at a nearby table gestured at Durwood. Others looked his way. Why were they looking at him? Durwood turned to leave. Before he could take a step, a hand grabbed a fistful of collar.

"Let's go, lad."

"I ain't done nothing wrong." Durwood didn't resist as he was led toward the entrance.

"I don't know how you got in here. I do know how you're leaving."

As he was led past the fountain, Durwood regretted not making a wish.

"What do you think you're doing?" Fearing further blame, Durwood craned his neck. Grace marched toward them. Her voice had an edge; her words clipped.

"I was just showing this ragamuffin out."

Durwood dropped his head. "I'm sorry, ma'am. All I done was to watch folks dance."

"That ragamuffin is with me. I will thank you to unhand him." The grip relaxed. Durwood jerked free to adjust his collar.

Walker approached. "What's going on, Grace?"

"This man was just about to offer Durwood an apology."

"For what?"

"I'm sorry. I didn't realize he was a guest."

The manager joined the gathering crowd. "What seems to be the matter, Mr. Hopkins?"

"Seems your maître d' made an unfortunate, if honest, assumption."

"Charles, please explain yourself."

"One of the diners pointed out Master Durwood peering in the dining room. I wasn't aware he was accompanying the Hopkins."

"Mr. and Mrs. Hopkins, we are so sorry for this misunderstanding. If there's anything we can do."

"There is." Grace turned toward the dining room. "Charles, ready a table for three. We're famished."

"Grace, we already discussed this."

"We did. But I don't believe we included Durwood in that discussion. As you can see, he prefers to eat in the dining room. So do I."

Charles looked to the manager. "Sir?"

"You heard Mrs. Hopkins. They will be joining us in the dining room."

"Yes, sir."

"And Charles. We would like a table close to the dance floor."

Charles hesitated. The manager nodded before returning to the front desk. Durwood straightened his coat and moved closer to Grace.

"I know you're upset, dear, but let's not be rash. It was an honest mistake. Let's take dinner in our room as we agreed."

"Not tonight, Walker."

"But I may know some of the guests in the dining room."

"Then they're about to become acquainted with a side of you they may not have seen." Charles waved from across the room. "Let's go. Charles is ready for us."

Grace and Durwood followed Charles and Walker past gawking diners. Pulling Durwood close, Grace met the stares with a smile and a pleasant, "Good evening."

Round tables under white tablecloths fanned out on three sides from a dance floor. A band occupied an elevated platform in front of a panel of mirrors. They played a piano, trumpet, stand-up bass, drums and an assortment of violins. The music was nothing like the chaotic, foot-stomping tunes in town on summer Saturday nights. These instruments blended into a song that matched the surroundings, smooth as a river.

Charles led them to a square table on the edge of the dance floor. "My apologies, but the dining room was full. We borrowed a card table from the library."

"This will do." Grace motioned to the chair facing the dance floor. "Sit here, Durwood, where you can see the dancers." Charles held Grace's chair while she sat. Durwood hopped into his chair.

"Your waiter will be with you shortly."

Silverware surrounded a dinner plate decorated with a bright floral print. A kerchief folded like a teepee stood in the middle of the plate. Grace placed hers in her lap; Walker tucked his into his collar. Taking his cue from Walker, Durwood stuffed and fanned his own napkin.

Durwood asked Grace, "Who's eatin' with us?"

"No one."

"Then how come they brung us so many knives and forks?"

"They're for you." Walker picked up the outside fork. "This is for your appetizer. It's smaller. See? The next fork is for your entrée. Your main course. On the other side of your plate, it's the same thing. The smaller knife on the outside is for the first course. The second knife is for the main course. The spoon is for your soup and above your plate is your dessert spoon."

"Why can't I use the same knife and fork?"

"You could, but it wouldn't be proper. Just remember, start with the utensils on the outside and work your way toward your plate."

The band launched into another song as dancers filled the floor. Durwood was grateful for the distraction. Backs straight and heads erect, handsome couples glided past. Each man extended his left arm to clasp his partner's hand, while resting his right hand on her back. The women's free hands gently rested on the men's shoulders. It was beautiful, perfect.

Grace asked, "What do you think?"

"Ain't nothing like flat-footing back home."

"Tell us about it."

"Folks lower their heads, put their hands behind their backs and get to stomping to the music. But they ain't dancing with anyone. The good ones look like they know what they's doing. Everybody else acts like they's putting out a brush fire."

Grace laughed. "I'm going to have to see that for myself one day. Sounds fun."

"How is it all them folks know to do exactly the same thing without minding their feet?"

"It's called the waltz. We learn it when we're young. Your mother knew the waltz."

"She did?"

"I know because we practiced together. She was much better than I."

"Good evening. I will be taking care of you. Tonight's menu is cream of potato soup, salad, and roast duck breast. For dessert we have crème brûlée."

"Good evening, Walker. Grace." A bald man with glasses stood behind Durwood; he was the man who had pointed at Durwood in the doorway.

Walker stood. "Good evening, Wallace."

"What brings you to town?"

"Railroad business. You?"

"I have a trial starting tomorrow. Who do we have here?"

"This is Durwood Matney, Grace's cousin's child. Durwood, this is Mr. Sanders, a friend from Richmond." Walker motioned for Durwood to stand.

"Hello, sir."

"I couldn't help but notice Durwood in the doorway earlier. He fancies the dancers, I believe."

"They's something to watch, what with all them twirls and stuff." Walker raised an eyebrow. "Sir."

"I can't place the accent. Where do you call home, Durwood?"

"He's from Matewan, West Virginia. His mother recently passed. He's coming to Richmond for a while."

The waiter arrived with soup. Durwood slurped several spoonfuls before wiping his mouth on his sleeve.

"I should let you get back to your dinner. Durwood appears famished. So nice to see you, Grace. I can't wait to tell Nan I ran into you."

"Please give her my best."

"Durwood, I look forward to seeing you again. Make sure Walker brings you to the Club. You will be a hit with the boys." Wallace bowed slightly, then returned to his table.

"I told you we should have taken dinner in our room."

Grace asked, "How do you like the soup?"

"Can't say as I've had better." Grabbing the bowl with both hands, Durwood leaned forward. Before he could tilt the bowl, Walker gently pushed it down.

"We don't drink from our bowl."

Durwood reached for the bread. Walker deflected his wrist. "And we don't sop up our food."

"How am I supposed to get the last bit?"

"You're not."

What about waste not want not? These folks were hard to figure. They threw money in fountains and left food on their plates. On top of that, everyone continued to fuss over his clothes. One day from Matewan, Durwood missed home.

The band finished and packed their instruments. The dining room thinned. Grace led the way into the lobby.

"I don't know about the two of you, but I'm ready to retire."

"Me too, ma'am. Where we headed?"

"Fifth floor."

Durwood hurried for the stairs.

"We're taking the lift."

"Ma'am?"

"The lift. We'll take it to the fifth floor." Grace and Walker stood before a wall. Durwood wasn't sure what they were doing, but he wasn't about to wander off again.

"Have you ridden a lift before?"

"What's a lift?"

"An elevator. It's like a room that moves up and down between floors."

"You pulling my leg?"

"Stand here. When the lift arrives, these doors will open."

"If these is doors, how come they ain't got knobs?"

"You're a breath of fresh air. Push this button. You'll see."

Durwood depressed the button. The grinding and thumping that came from behind the doors made Durwood step back. The commotion stopped with a thud as the wall parted. A man wearing a vest and a brimless, flat-topped cap sat on a stool inside a little room. He slid open a metal gate. "What floor?"

"Five, please." Grace and Walker stepped into the lift; Durwood didn't budge.

"You coming, young man?"

Grace stepped off the lift. "Do you trust me?" Taking her hand, Durwood entered. The attendant latched the gate. From a panel of knobs, he pulled one. Grinding began as the outer doors closed. Durwood wished he had stayed put. Without warning, the elevator jolted upward, knocking Durwood off balance. He squeezed Grace's hand.

Walker pointed. "See the arrow above the door? It tells where we are. Almost there." Eager for the ride to end, Durwood could have run up and down the steps twice in the time it took the lift to sputter up to the fifth floor.

"Fifth floor. Have a good night, folks."

Durwood stepped off into a wide, carpeted hallway. Light fixtures lined the walls. Walker opened a door and fumbled along the wall just inside the darkened room. "Where's the switch? There." With a click, the room exploded in light.

"Wondering how I did that?" Durwood nodded. "See these buttons?" Two buttons sat in a column. "If you want to turn on the light, you push the top one. To turn it off, you push the bottom one." The button clicked and the light extinguished. Walker clicked again to turn it back on.

"You ain't got to light a lamp?"

"These lights are electric."

"Can I give it a go?"

"Of course."

Durwood punched the buttons several times as Grace rummaged through the steamer. "Durwood, I don't see your pajamas."

"Ain't got none."

"What do you sleep in?"

"My woolens."

"Guess we'll be adding pajamas to our shopping list."

A wardrobe and desk lined one wall. A four-poster bed stood against the back wall. Piled high with pillows, it was too small for the three of them. On the wall opposite the wardrobe, a couch looked like it would sleep fine.

"Walker, will you show Durwood the bathroom?"

Durwood reached for his coat. "You don't need your coat. It's just down the hall." Why would anyone bring the outhouse indoors? Durwood hoped it was at the far end of the hall.

A few steps from their room, Walker stopped in front of a wooden door with smoky glass on the top half. Light shone through. Walker pushed open the door. Sinks and mirrors lined the far wall. Opposite was a long, porcelain trough adjoining several stalls with closed doors. A man relieved himself into the trough. At a sink, another man brushed his teeth, controlling the flow of water with the turn of a handle. At the nearest sink, Durwood flipped the handle. Water gushed onto his shirt. Walker turned down the water. "Brush your teeth."

"Yes, sir." After brushing his teeth, Durwood relieved himself.

"One more thing." Walker pushed open a stall, revealing what appeared to be a white chair. "Have you ever seen a toilet?"

Durwood shook his head.

"In the morning when you need to do your business, use this paper to clean yourself, then put it into the toilet." Walker dropped a square of paper into the bowl. "Before you leave, pull this chain." Walker yanked the chain. The water and paper disappeared with a flush. "Got that?"

"I reckon."

"Good. Let's go to bed."

In the room, they found Grace brushing her hair. Shorter than Ma's, it reached halfway to her waist. She wore a thick robe and shiny slippers. Even in her night clothes, Grace was the prettiest woman Durwood had ever seen.

He climbed on the couch and pulled his knees tight.

Grace asked, "What are you doing?"

"Going to sleep."

"Don't you want to sleep in the bed?"

"I don't reckon it's big enough for the three of us."

Walker reached for a handle in the wall. He tugged and a bed unfolded. "Wouldn't you rather sleep here?"

Miss Grace had been right; this hotel was a wonderland. Indoor fountains, hot and cold water that poured out of spigots and beds hidden in walls. But, he would give it all back to be tucked in beside Bascom.

"Did your mother say prayers with you at night?"

"Yes, ma'am."

"Would you like me to say them with you?"

"If it ain't no trouble."

"Of course not. Take off your clothes. You can sleep in your woolens tonight."

Turning his back, Durwood slipped off his pants and shirt as quickly as he could and slid under the covers. Grace knelt beside his bed. After blessing his mother, father and brother, she led him in the Lord's Prayer then kissed him on the forehead.

"Good night, Durwood. I hope you sleep well."

"Night, ma'am."

"Good night, Durwood,"

"Night, sir."

Durwood closed his eyes and prayed for home.

Chapter 5

October 20, 1908

Richmond, Virginia

The conductor slid open the door. "Next stop, Richmond. May I call a porter, ma'am?"

"Yes, please."

"What's a porter?"

Grace said, "A man who helps passengers with their baggage."

"Why don't folks carry their own bags?"

"It wouldn't be proper for us to carry our bags. Besides, how would the three of us manage all this luggage?"

What was proper about asking other folks to carry what belonged to you?

Sticking his fingers under his starched collar, Durwood tugged to loosen his tie.

Grace asked, "What's the matter?"

"Ain't used to fighting my shirt for breathing room. You sure this is how boys is supposed to dress in the city?"

"You look like you've lived in Richmond all your life."

"Grace is right. Trust me, you'll get used to it in no time."

The same had better be true for his shoes. The Buster Browns dug into his heels and crowded his toes. Durwood longed for the comfort of his brogans. When he fretted that the new shoes were too small to accommodate newspaper, Grace assured him he wouldn't need to stuff them. They were so tight he couldn't feel his toes anyway.

The train slowed. "What are all them brick and stone buildings?"

"Houses."

Durwood whistled. "Most of them's bigger than my schoolhouse. I wish Bascom was here to see this."

Grace nodded. "You'll have to write and tell him about it."

"He'll think I'm pulling his leg."

"Then we'll have to make sure he doesn't, won't we?"

"How will we do that?"

"Picture postcards."

"Ma had one of them of Virginia Beach. She kept it in her Bible."

"I was with her when she bought it."

As the train neared the station, the buildings grew taller and grander. Cobblestone lanes yielded to wide, paved streets. Cars chugged with horns blaring as if they were on parade, covering the few buggies in a haze of exhaust.

"Dang. Look at all them cars. Everybody in Richmond got one?"

"Not quite. They're expensive."

"Do you all have one?"

"Our car will meet us at the station."

"You have cars in Matewan. Grace and I saw one."

"They's a few. Reckon you saw the Sheriff's. It's mostly for show. Sits in front of the jail because it won't carry him most places he needs to go. Only paved road in the county is over in Williamson."

Grace pointed toward a high-rise building. "That's where Walker works."

Occupying most of a block, the brick building had more windows than Durwood could count. He sounded out writing on the side of the building.

"Nor-folk and Po-to-mac."

"Very good."

"Can I ask you something, sir?"

"Of course."

"Why don't you dress like a railroad man?"

"What do you mean?"

"Back home they wear dungarees and denim jackets. Cotton caps."
Walker chuckled.

"Walker doesn't work on the railroad, Durwood. He works for the railroad. He's general counsel."

"General counsel?"

"The railroad's lawyer. He works in an office. He prepares their contracts and represents them in court."

"That explains things."

"Explains what?"

"Bascom said your hands looked like they ain't never lifted nothing heavier than your hat."

"Walker's hands might not resemble your father's, but he's quite a sportsman. He's been club golf champion twice, and he's quite adept in lawn tennis. He'll teach you these games."

Durwood wasn't sure what lawn tennis was, but Bascom had told him about golf. Lying on the big rock behind their house, they had laughed at the thought of grown men knocking a little ball around cow pastures with mallets.

"How is it you got time to play games?"

"You'll find, Durwood, that things are quite different in Richmond. If you give it a chance, I think you will like it."

The train stopped under a canopied station. The platform bustled; Durwood had never seen so many people in one place. Everyone dressed like they were headed to church. Where were they all going in such a hurry? Several trains sat on adjacent tracks, none pulling coal cars.

Durwood turned from the window to Grace. "Do you have to be colored to be a porter?"

"Why do you ask?"

"'Cause the only ones I see carrying bags is."

Grace said, "That's just the way it is."

Walker put Grace's cape around her shoulders and handed Durwood his new overcoat, a smaller version of his. "Why don't you two stretch your legs? I'll wait for the porter."

Durwood followed Grace off the train. He marveled at the size of the station and the fact it was under roof. Birds fluttered in the rafters.

"Grace?"

"Margaret Ann. What a surprise. Hello John Randolph."

"Who's this with you?"

"This is my cousin's son, Durwood Matney. Durwood, this is Margaret Ann Claiborne and her son, John Randolph."

"So nice to meet you, Durwood."

Durwood shook her hand.

"Are you visiting?"

Durwood wasn't sure how to respond.

"His mother just passed. We brought him from West Virginia to stay with us."

Durwood added, "Just 'til things settle down back home."

"I'm so sorry for your loss. It must have been awful for you, dear."

"Thank you kindly, ma'am. We done got used to the idea by the time the Good Lord called her home."

"West Virginia. That makes you a Yankee."

"John Randolph. Be polite."

"Just stating a fact, mother. Everyone knows West Virginia seceded."

"What did you say your name was again?"

"Durwood."

"Are you a quitter, Durwood?"

Durwood spoke between clenched teeth. "Nope."

"What kind of a name is Durwood, anyway? Sounds like a Yankee name."

"They called me that after my uncle on my Pa's side. He got killed in a mine explosion. My brother, Bascom, was named for Pa's other brother."

"Bascom? You have a brother named Bascom?" John Randolph slapped his thigh.

"Grace, if you'll excuse us, we must be going. Durwood, it was a pleasure to meet you. We'll have you over to play with John Randolph's younger brother sometime."

"Bye, Margaret Ann. Bye, John Randolph."

John Randolph cocked his thumb and pointed his index finger. "See you around, Yank."

Margaret Ann tugged John Randolph's arm as they disappeared into the crowd. Durwood couldn't make out what she was saying, but it appeared to be an earful.

"I'm sorry for the way John Randolph behaved. He's usually a very respectful young man."

"Is Durwood really a Yankee name?"

"Of course not. It's a lovely family name. Don't pay any attention to him."

Walker stepped from the train.

"The porter will meet us at the car."

How would they find their way through the bustling throng? As Walker threaded the crowd, Grace and Durwood followed. Reaching the station, Walker opened the door. Eager to leave the crowd behind, Durwood crossed the threshold only to find more people compressed inside. He struggled to catch his breath. Was this how it felt underground? Taking Grace's gloved hand, he started moving again. At last, they exited the station. A line of cars with drivers in dark suits standing at attention lay before them.

"There's our car." Grace waved.

A driver nodded.

"Reynolds, this is Durwood."

"A pleasure, Master Durwood." Standing beside a large black car with a canvas top and open sides, the driver tipped his cap. He opened the rear door and extended his hand to help Grace onto the running board, then into the back seat. Durwood climbed onto the firm leather bench seat beside Grace. Walker waited until the porter loaded the luggage, then handed him money. With Walker in the front, Reynolds cranked the engine, pulled on his goggles and eased into traffic. Durwood placed his arms on the front seat to lean forward.

Walker turned. "Better button your coat. It's going to get chilly."

Too excited to care and grateful to be free of the crowded station, Durwood watched Richmond whiz by.

"What do you think?" Grace asked loudly to be heard over the engine and the rushing wind.

"Think he can sound the horn?"

"Of course."

Grace leaned forward to speak to Reynolds, who squeezed the horn mounted on the side of the steering wheel. Reynolds turned onto a wide boulevard of asphalt paving bricks. The car rumbled along, rattling Durwood's teeth. Grand houses anchored the tree-lined road. The car sped toward a towering figure rising from the middle of the street. A bronze statue of a uniformed man on horseback stood atop an ornate, granite base.

Walker turned and cupped his hands. "Do you know who that is?"

Durwood shook his head.

"General Robert E. Lee, commander of the Army of Northern Virginia. Greatest General of the modern age. True Virginia hero."

The car slowed. Reynolds eased into a circular driveway between two brick columns and pulled under a portico.

Grace placed her hand on Durwood's shoulder. "We're home."

Reynolds opened the door to help Grace from the car. Durwood jumped to the ground. The house was twice the size of the ones that captured his eye from the train. White columns supported a two-story porch. Double oak doors, highlighted by brass knockers, swung open.

A middle-aged woman in a gray uniform stepped onto the porch, wiping her hands on a white apron. "Welcome home."

Grace said, "Thank you, Hattie. It's good to be home. This is Durwood. He's going to be staying with us. Is the guest room at the top of the stairs made up?"

"Yes, ma'am."

"Durwood, this is Hattie. She's our housekeeper and cook. If you're not careful, she will fatten you up."

What did Grace do all day if Hattie did the chores and the cooking? Fearing another confusing answer, Durwood kept quiet. Hattie smiled; slight dimples dotted her cheeks.

"Welcome, Durwood. It will be nice to have a young one to fuss over. My kids are all grown."

"How do you do, ma'am?"

"You don't have to say ma'am to me."

"Why not?"

"Come on, Durwood. Let me show you your room." Grace ushered him inside.

The great hallway reached to the ceiling and led to a sweeping staircase. Sun shone through a round window over the front door, bathing the stairs in afternoon light. Grace lifted her hem to start up the stairs. Behind, Durwood counted as he went. Ten steps to the landing, another ten to the second floor. Grace opened the first door, ushering Durwood into a room nearly the size of the home he had shared with his family. Two large beds lay on either side of a curtained window. A chest of drawers bordered one wall; a secretary with a wicker chair the other. Beside the secretary was another door.

"Who else sleeps in here?"

"No one."

"Then why's they two beds? Bascom and I shared one."

"We planned on having children when we built the house."

"How come you didn't?"

"It wasn't in the good Lord's plans."

"Sounds like something Ma would say."

"How about your father?"

"He ain't much for the Living Word. Where does that door lead to?"

Grace opened it. "It's a closet. It's like a wardrobe, but takes up less space. All the new homes have them."

"What do you think about the room?"

"It's a sight bigger than I need, ma'am. I don't want to put you out."

"Nonsense. Besides, this is the smallest bedroom in the house. We'll get your clothes put away so it doesn't seem so impersonal. Now, how about some dinner? I'll show you the back staircase to the kitchen. Good thing to know if you get hungry at night like Walker."

The steep, narrow staircase lacked the flair of the front steps. It ended in a hallway on the first floor. Durwood followed Grace through a swinging door into the kitchen. Copper pots and pans hung from the ceiling; many more lay in the sink. Hattie busied herself over the stove as they passed through another swinging door. A large oak table with sixteen chairs filled the room. A crystal chandelier, centered above the table, sparkled. The table was laid with three settings—one at either-end and a third in the center. Walker pulled out Grace's chair, then tapped the middle chair as he passed to the other end. "This is your seat."

As Durwood sat, Hattie entered with a tray of food.

"What have you made us, Hattie?"

"Oysters Rockefeller. Roast lamb for the main course. Cherry pie for dessert."

"Walker's favorite."

Hattie served Grace and Walker before placing a small plate of grayish objects in front of Durwood. When he poked one, his fork clanged against the shell.

"They're oysters. Shellfish. Cooked with bacon and spinach. Hattie's Oysters Rockefeller are as good as any you'll find. Keep your guard up. Walker's been known to raid a neighboring plate."

Walker raised his fork in a threatening manner.

"What's a shellfish?"

"Oysters, clams, crabs."

Pa and Bascom should be sitting down to eat their cornbread and beans about now.

"Lobster and shrimp are also shellfish."

"Shrimp? Got any of them?"

"I'm afraid we don't."

"Would you like Hattie to bring your lamb now?"

"I ain't too hungry. Mind if I go to bed?"

"Of course not. You've had a couple of busy days with lots of changes thrown at you. Tomorrow will be another. We will enroll you in school. Walker, excuse me while I help Durwood get ready for bed."

Walker pulled out Grace's chair. Durwood followed her from the dining room and up the front stairs.

She showed Durwood to the bathroom in the hallway beside his bedroom. She pressed a button in the wall, lighting the room. A porcelain sink, toilet, and cast iron bathtub filled the room. Durwood washed his face and brushed his teeth, mesmerized by water that gushed from the spigot at the twist of a handle. Water on demand meant no trips outside to the well or the outhouse. When he returned to his room, Grace had laid new pajamas on the back of the wicker chair.

"Which bed do you want to sleep in?"

"Don't matter none."

"How about the one on the right? When I was a little girl and your mother visited, she slept on the right."

He slipped into his pajamas and climbed into bed. Grace hung up his suit. His old clothes that he had asked to keep hung on the far side of the closet apart from the new attire. Grace knelt by the bed to say the Lord's Prayer with him. She kissed his forehead.

"Good night, Durwood. Sleep tight. If you need us, we're just down the hall."

Grace turned out the light and shut the door.

Durwood felt alone in the big bed. Hopping out, he wriggled out of his pajamas and made his way in the dark to the closet. He removed his old clothes from the hanger and grabbed his brogans. He dressed, laced up his brogans and climbed back into bed. Durwood prayed things would settle down soon.

Chapter 6

October 21, 1908

Richmond, Virginia

"Time to get up." A gentle hand shook his shoulder.

Unable to place the voice that greeted him, Durwood opened his eyes. Grace sat on the edge of the bed.

"I hope you slept well."

Rubbing his eyes, Durwood froze. At the far end of the bed, his brogans tented the linens. Durwood drew up his knees and jerked the covers to his chin, hoping Grace hadn't noticed. The pajamas, which he had left puddled in the floor, were neatly folded over the back of the chair.

"Why don't you freshen up and get dressed? Your clothes are hanging on the closet door."

"Yes, ma'am."

"I know you like your new clothes, but I was thinking. Until your Buster Browns are broken in, maybe you should wear your old shoes. When we get home from school, you can wear your new shoes around the house until they're comfortable. What do you think?"

"I reckon that makes sense. Them new shoes ain't got much give."

"Are you hungry?"

"I reckon I could eat."

"Hattie's making oatmeal. Do you like oatmeal?"

"Oatmeal will do just fine, thank you." Durwood couldn't recall if he'd ever eaten oatmeal. Ma made biscuits and gravy.

He dressed and headed downstairs. Hattie ladled porridge into bowls. It looked a little like gravy, but not as dark.

"Morning, Durwood."

"Morning."

"Do you like raisins in your oatmeal?"

"Does Miss Grace?"

"Most definitely."

"Then I do, too. Thank you."

Durwoood entered the dining room to find Walker and Grace seated.

"Good morning."

"Morning, sir."

"Did the bed suit you?"

"Yes, sir."

"That's good. You've got a big day ahead of you. You want to be well rested."

Hattie brought the oatmeal. Walker sprinkled sugar in his bowl and poured cream from a pitcher. He blew on the oatmeal.

"Would you like cream and sugar?"

"Thank you, sir."

Durwood stirred in sugar and cream. He blew on the spoon and took a bite, delighted to discover his breakfast tasted as sweet as dessert.

"Are you excited to see your new school?"

"I reckon, sir."

"You will do just fine if you mind your teachers and listen carefully."

"Yes, sir."

Walker finished his coffee. "I have to leave for the office." He folded the newspaper to place under his arm. Walking to the end of the table, he patted Durwood's shoulder, then stooped to kiss Grace.

"Bye, dear. I will see you tonight."

Grace squeezed his hand.

***

Durwood sat next to Grace in front of a dark, wooden desk inlaid with leather. Stacks of paper lined the edges. On the wall behind the desk hung two paintings of bearded men in gray uniforms. A piece of framed paper with writing he couldn't decipher had been mounted between the soldiers. Bookshelves full of leather-bound volumes lined the walls. A sword sat atop one of the bookshelves, C.S.A. engraved on its sheath.

"Good morning. I am Mr. Rucker, principal of West End School."

A tall man in a three-piece suit entered the office. He had gray hair and a bushy mustache that trailed past the corners of his mouth. His right sleeve, bereft of an arm, was pinned to the side of his coat. With his left hand, he fingered a pocket watch in his vest pocket.

Grace extended a gloved hand. "Grace Hopkins."

"I am sorry if I kept you waiting."

"That's quite alright."

"Whom do we have here?"

"This is my ward, Durwood Matney. I am here to enroll him."

"Tell me a little about Durwood."

"He's eight years old. From Matewan, West Virginia. His mother, my cousin, recently passed. Before she departed, she asked my husband and me to take him in."

"Is he an orphan?"

"No, sir, I ain't no orphan. I got a Pa and a brother back home. I'll be going back, soon as things settle down." Grace patted Durwood's wrist.

"His father and brother are coal miners but presently aren't in a position to care for him. So we brought him back from West Virginia. He will be living with us for the time being."

"Very well. Does he have any formal education?"

Why was he asking Grace these questions? It hadn't been a week since they first laid eyes on each other.

"Durwood, tell Mr. Rucker what sort of schooling you've had."

"I done finished first grade. Was part way through second when Pa shipped me off."

"And what were they teaching you in West Virginia?"

"Reading, writing and 'rithmetic, mostly."

"Do you know your multiplication tables?"

"Better than most, I'd say."

"What is nine times eight?"

"Seventy-two."

"How about ten times eleven?"

"One hundred and ten."

"Well done. How about reading?"

Durwood hoped he wouldn't ask him to read the paper on the wall. "Not as good as Bascom. He's thirteen. Wait. What's today?"

Grace said, "Wednesday."

"Make that fourteen. But I reckon I read pretty good, so long as you don't ask me to read that paper with the fancy writing on your wall."

"That's my diploma. It's in Latin. Not to worry. Before you leave us, you won't have any trouble reading it. Who is Bascom?"

"His brother."

"I see. How about his comportment?"

"His mother said he's never been in any trouble."

"That's good to hear, because we have rules at West End, Durwood. We do not tolerate fighting. Will that be a problem?"

"I don't reckon."

"We do not tolerate cussing. I assume you do not swear."

"No, sir. Ma said cussing was the refuge of the unlettered."

"Your mother sounds like a wise woman."

"Smartest woman I ever knew." Durwood hoped Grace didn't take offense.

"That makes two of us." Grace winked.

"We don't permit our students to chew tobacco. Do you chew tobacco?"

"Not no more, I don't."

"I think you will do well here at West End. Any questions?"

Durwood shook his head.

"Good. Be here at eight in the morning ready to work. You will be in Miss Gordon's class."

"Yes, sir."

"Thank you, Mr. Rucker."

"Good day, Mrs. Hopkins."

Durwood and Grace exited the two-story brick building onto Main Street. Turning down a side street, they passed a playground teeming with boys at the back of the school. Durwood lingered. Younger boys played on a swing set. Others jumped on and off a large spinning platform. Older boys kicked a ball.

"What's this?"

"The school playground."

"Will I get to play here?"

"Of course."

A ball sailed over the fence. Durwood retreated several steps to snatch it out of the air while Grace continued walking.

A couple of older boys watched. "Good catch," one called. "Throw it back."

"If you know what's good for you, you'll throw it to me, Yank."

Hands on hips, John Randolph stared.

Durwood cocked his arm and threw the ball to the other boy.

"I won't forget that, Yank."

Durwood hurried to catch up with Grace.

"Looks fun, doesn't it?"

"I reckon."

Chapter 7

October 22, 1908

Richmond, Virginia

"You need to finish your breakfast, Durwood. John Randolph and Ben will be here any minute."

"Who?"

"John Randolph Claiborne and his brother, Ben. You met John Randolph at the train station the other day. With his mother."

"Why's he coming here?"

"His mother said John Randolph offered to walk you to school. I think he's trying to make up for being rude at the train station. What do you think?"

"Probably something like that."

A dull, metallic knock filled the front hallway.

"There they are. Do you have your satchel?"

"Yes, ma'am."

"Your lunch?"

"Yes, ma'am."

"You look grand."

Durwood wasn't sure how grand was supposed to feel. His new clothes itched in places, pinched in others.

Grace swung open the door. "Hello, boys."

"Good morning, Miss Grace."

"Hello, Ben. Ben, this is Durwood."

"Pleased to meet you, Durwood."

"Likewise."

"Good morning, Miss Grace."

"I think it's awfully nice that you volunteered to walk Durwood to school, John Randolph."

"Anything I can do to help him feel at home."

"How sweet. Now you boys best run along. Durwood doesn't want to be late for his first day of school."

As Durwood stepped toward the door, Grace hugged him.

Heading down the steps, John Randolph draped his arm around Durwood's shoulder. As the door closed, John Randolph squeezed Durwood tight. Releasing his grip, he grabbed Durwood's ear.

"Why didn't you throw me the ball yesterday, hillbilly?"

Durwood jerked his head, breaking John's grip. His ear stung, but he resisted rubbing it.

"That other boy asked first."

"If you know what's good for you, you won't do that again." John Randolph pecked Durwood's chest. "Got that?"

"Leave him alone, John Randolph."

"Or what?"

"He hasn't done anything to you."

John Randolph ran ahead. At the end of the walk, he threw open the wrought iron gate. As Durwood approached, John Randolph slammed it shut. Durwood stepped back quickly to avoid the bars. He lifted the latch, pushed the gate and waited for Ben, who must have fallen victim to this prank before.

"Nice shoes, Yank. Looks like they've been around since Bull Run."

"They was my brother's."

"Tell me his name again."

"Bascom."

"That's it. Didn't I tell you it was the dumbest name you'd ever heard, Ben? After Durwood, that is."

The boys turned onto Monument Avenue, following a hard-packed path that ran parallel to the road. Sheep grazed in the median.

Ben asked, "How old are you?"

"Eight."

"Me, too. John Randolph's eleven. He says you're from West Virginia. What's it like?"

"Nothing like here. They's mountains and woods all around, with lots of squirrels to hunt and berries galore. Houses ain't as nice or as big neither." Two automobiles chugged past, kicking up swirls of leaves. Ben signaled and the lead car sounded his horn; the second followed suit. "Ain't hardly nobody got cars."

Ben asked, "How come you talk differently?"

"Because he's a dumb hillbilly from West Virginia."

Ben stopped. "Why do you say that?"

"Beause everybody knows hillbillies are as dumb as they sound."

"He doesn't seem dumb to me."

"That's because you're as dumb as he is. Only difference is you aren't a hillbilly bumpkin."

"Watch this." John Randolph picked up several rocks the size of pecans.

"Mother told you to leave the sheep alone. I'm going to tell."

"You do and I'll make you wish you weren't born."

A flock of sheep grazed on the far side of the road. John Randolph drew back to throw. The rock landed harmlessly between two sheep. He took aim again. The rock struck the haunches of a ram closest to the road. Startled, it took off with the flock close behind.

"That's what you call a dead aim."

With his slingshot, Durwood could have bounced a rock off the horns if he wanted. And with a lot more power.

"What do you think, Yank?"

"Not bad."

"Think you can do better?"

"With my slingshot, I could."

"Let's see."

"Pa took it before I left home."

"Sure he did."

Durwood dropped his satchel to face John Randolph. "You saying I'm lying?"

"Easy, Yank. Don't get yourself all worked up before you even make it to school. Trust me. You'll have plenty of time to square off."

Ben grabbed Durwood's satchel and took off. "Come on. I'll

race you."

With his brogans carrying him down the path, Durwood easily caught up to Ben, who struggled under the weight of two satchels.

"I got that." Shouldering his satchel, Durwood slowed to a walk.

"Whose class are you in?"

"Miss Gordon's."

"Me, too."

"What's she like?"

"Tough as nails."

"Sounds like Miss Rasnick."

"Who's that?"

"My teacher back home. She's meaner than a striped snake."

"Come on. Let's get in a few turns on the merry-go-round before the bell rings."

***

Ben hurried to his seat. "Sit next to me."

"I get my own desk?"

"Sure do."

Instead of a rough-hewn pine bench, wooden desks on wrought iron legs lined the room in four neat rows. "Welcome, Durwood" in flowing cursive greeted him from the enormous green chalkboard on the wall behind the teacher's desk. Cardboard tiles adorned with letters and numbers covered the other walls. Bright light filled the room from fixtures suspended from the ceiling. The other students sat straight, pencils in hand, composition books open. Durwood removed his composition book and pencil from his new satchel, then stowed the bag under his seat.

"Everybody here has their own pencil and paper."

"Why wouldn't they?"

"Back home we shared writing slates."

"Writing slates? You go to school with Abe Lincoln?"

"Must get cold in the winter."

"Not really. Why?"

"'Cause they's no fireplace."

"We got radiators."

Before Durwood could ask, a tall, heavyset lady wearing glasses entered. She wore her hair in a bun, exposing a high forehead. She didn't look like she'd go out of her way to make pleasantries, but she didn't look mean either, like his Granny Matney, whose toothless mouth dribbled tobacco juice and whose hands were rough as corn cobs. "Class, we have a new student. Stand and introduce yourself, please."

Durwood stood. Unlike in Matewan, his classmates were all boys; same as on the playground. "I'm Durwood Matney." The boy on the other side of Ben covered his mouth.

"Class, please welcome Durwood."

"Welcome, Durwood." Stifled snickers broke the greeting. Durwood glanced around to identify the offenders.

"Tell us a little about yourself, Durwood."

"I come from Mingo County, West Virginia. I got a Pa and a brother back home. They's miners."

"Where's your mother?" a boy asked.

"She passed."

"We're sorry for your loss, Durwood. I'm Miss Gordon. Why don't you show us on the globe where you're from?"

Globe? Was this another Latin word? Time slowed, as everyone stared. He prayed for a clue. Ben tugged his sleeve and pointed. On the corner of the teacher's desk sat a large ball with what appeared to be a map stretched tight around it.

"Don't they have globes in West Virginia?" The boy asking the question was one of those who'd snickered.

"'Course we do. I ain't noticed where it was at 'til just now."

"I had not noticed where it was until now." Miss Gordon prompted more snickers.

"Ma'am?"

"The proper way to say it is, 'I had not noticed where it was until now.'"

Ignoring the laughter, Durwood walked to the teacher's desk. He stared at the globe, unsure what he was looking at, but certain West Virginia wasn't near the Indian Ocean.

"May I help, Miss Gordon?"

"Yes, you may, Ben."

Standing beside Durwood, Ben slowly spun the globe until Durwood found the United States.

"West Virginia's right here."

"Well done, Durwood. Are you living with family in Richmond?"

"Sort of, I reckon."

"What do you mean?"

"I'm staying with my Ma's cousin, Miss Grace, and her husband, Mr. Walker."

"What is their last name?"

The room felt close, the fancy clothes suffocating. No one had prepared him for all the questions. Why did Pa have to send him off? Miss Grace had introduced herself to the principal the day before. What was it?

"I reckon they do but I ain't bothered to ask yet."

Giggles erupted into full-blown laughter. Even Ben joined in.

"Settle down, class."

"May I sit down?"

"You may."

Returning to his seat, Durwood gritted his teeth and stared straight ahead. He hadn't cried when he said goodbye to Pa. He wasn't about to start.

Chapter 8

October 23, 1908

Richmond, Virginia

The bell rang. Eager to start the weekend, boys leaped from their desks.

"Come on, Durwood." Ben hurriedly stuffed his book bag.

"Where we going?"

"Outside. We play kickball every Friday."

Durwood placed his primer in his satchel and flung the bag over his shoulder. Walking double time down the hall, Durwood followed Ben out the back door onto the playground. John Randolph marshaled the boys into teams. Durwood and Ben stood to the side until everyone else had been picked. "I got Ben. Hillbilly, you're on the other team. Watch out, boys. Those clodhoppers might do some damage."

Durwood's captain sized up Durwood. "You ever played kickball before?"

"Not as I can recollect."

"You're in left field, then. Ball hardly ever comes out there." Durwood didn't see anything to indicate left field. "What are you waiting for?"

"What's left field?"

"For crying out loud. It's out there. You really are a hillbilly, aren't you?" He turned Durwood's shoulders and shoved his back. "If they kick it to you, catch it before the ball hits the ground. Can you do that?"

"I reckon."

"Then get out there. Batter up."

Durwood quickly sized up the game. There didn't seem to be a lot of rules. As predicted, most of the balls went elsewhere, high toward the middle of the field or they bounced on the ground to be scooped up by those in front of him. After the first few innings, he figured out the teams traded places whenever the kicking team made three outs. An out usually came from catching the ball in the air. Sometimes a team got an out by hitting a runner between the bases with the ball. The worst way to get out was to miss it three times, like Ben did.

The captain tapped Durwood's shoulder. "You're up." Durwood stood behind home plate, a piece of sack cloth tacked to the ground.

"Easy out, fellas," John Randolph yelled from center field. Ben rolled the ball toward Durwood, who ran to meet it. As the ball crossed the cloth, he planted one foot to strike it hard with the other. The ball arced high into the middle of the outfield where John Randolph waited, arms crossed. At the last second, John Randolph unfolded his arms to catch the ball. He tossed it to the second baseman. "What'd I tell you? Yanks aren't worth a hoot. Especially hillbilly Yanks."

Durwood stuffed clenched fists in his pockets. "Don't pay him any mind," Ben called. A train whistle brought the game to a halt. The boys stopped to count the cars.

"Fifty-four," one of Durwood's teammates shouted.

"You can't count. Definitely fifty-five," a boy on the other team responded.

Durwood didn't care to count the cars. What caught his eye was the coal filling them. He asked a teammate, "Where's that train headed?"

"Where do you think? The coal yard."

"Where's that?"

"Couple miles down the track."

The game resumed once the train had passed. When Durwood's team got its third out, he trotted back into left field.

Mr. Rucker exited the building holding his pocket watch. "Wrap it up, boys. Time to go home."

John Randoph replied, "Yes, sir. We're almost finished. Game's tied."

After Durwood's team got two quick outs, John Randolph stepped up to kick. "Coming your way, Yank." Durwood took a few steps back. True to his word, John launched the ball into left field, but considerably shorter than Durwood anticipated. Durwood raced for the ball. Realizing he wasn't going to make it in time, he dove. The ball hit his outstretched hands just as Durwood's elbows, chin and knees struck the hardscrabble. Before Durwood could secure the ball, it popped out of his hands. John Randolph rounded the bases as his teammates jumped up and down. Crossing home plate, he was greeted with hugs and slaps on the back.

Durwood's chin and knees stung. Ben ran to meet him. "Nice try."

"Almost had it."

"Probably a good thing you didn't. John Randolph would've been harder on you if you had made him look bad. You're bleeding."

Durwood touched his chin. Blood covered his fingertips. "It ain't too bad."

"Dang. Look at your pants." Both knees bore ragged holes the size of half-dollars. His new pants were ruined. "That elbow's going to need some patching, too." Ben pointed. "What are you going to tell Miss Grace?"

"The truth, I reckon."

"Good luck with that. My mother would kill me if I ruined my clothes playing kickball."

What would Grace say? More importantly, what would Walker say? After all, it was his money. Or was it Pa's money he just wasted?

"Let's go home. Loser carries." John Randolph held out his book satchel.

"I ain't going home just yet."

"Where you going, Yank?"

"Down to the coal yard."

Ben asked, "Mind if I tag along?"

"Now if that isn't the dumbest thing you two have thought up this week. What are you going to do at the coal yard?"

"Mine to know, yours to find out."

"Suit yourself. Come on, Ben."

"But I want to go with Durwood."

"I'm not responsible for Durwood, but I am for you. We're going home."

"See you, Durwood."

"See you."

Durwood left the schoolyard toward the tracks. Finding a hole in the fence, he squeezed through. Brush grew thick here, but most of the leaves had dropped. The view from the tracks was far different from the one he had traveling into town by car with Miss Grace earlier in the week. The further east he went, the smaller and more dilapidated the homes became. Washboards, busted wagons, broken toys and trash cluttered the yards. This looked more like home than anything he had seen since arriving in Richmond. Durwood kicked a bottle. As it clattered across the gravel, a dark string tied to its base popped out of the dirt, revealing it was connected to several cans. Partially filled with gravel, the cans rattled across the ground.

"Where you think you're going?" A scruffy boy Durwood's size popped out of a hole in the fence, followed by several others. About Durwood's age, they wore threadbare clothes and raggedy shoes.

"Coal yard."

"Didn't your mother tell you it ain't safe for a rich boy like you to wander around by hisself?"

"My Ma's dead. And I ain't rich."

"Look rich to me. Check his pockets."

A couple of the boys approached. Durwood set his feet and balled his fists. "I done told you, I ain't rich."

One of the boys assigned to check Durwood's pockets stopped. "He might be telling the truth. Them pants is tore up and I ain't never seen a rich person wearing brogans like them." Durwood held his stance.

The leader asked, "What do you want to go to the coal yard for anyways?"

"Just want to see it."

"What for?"

"My Pa and brother are miners back in West Virginia. Figure it's as close to them as I'm going to get for a while."

"What's your name?"

"Durwood."

"Durwood. Can't say as I've ever heard that name before. I believe Durwood may be telling us the truth."

"What's yours?"

"Everyone calls me Cap. Tell you what, Durwood. This is your lucky day. We'll take you there ourselves. Ain't got nothing else better to do. Right fellas?"

"Much obliged."

"Gotta warn you, though. The railroad don't like us fooling around down there. They'll run us off if they catch us."

"Why's that?"

"Let's just say they don't like sharing."

As they neared the yard, tracks split off the main line. Durwood was thankful Cap and the gang knew the way. Cap led the group down one of the spurs. In the distance, the coal train that interrupted the game an hour earlier stood idle, still overflowing with coal. Further on, mountains of coal blocked the view of downtown. "If that ain't a sight for sore eyes." Durwood started toward the mounds when a hand tugged him down from behind.

"Watchman." Cap held tight to Durwood's shoulder. Thirty yards away, a man dressed like a policeman stepped between two cars. "Wait'll he passes. He won't be back around this way for another thirty minutes." The boys huddled at the back of the last car. Twirling a billy club, the watchmen whistled past the group, never bothering to look in their direction.

"How come you know so much about the coal yard?"

"Where do you think we get our coal? Sneak down here at night to fill up sacks. Sometimes if we's got enough we sell it cheap to folks."

"Ain't that stealing?"

"Not if you don't get caught. Besides, you think they's going to miss a lump or two?"

"Why don't you just buy it?"

"With what?"

"Do your folks know?"

"Who you think sends us?"

"Why don't they do it themselves?"

"'Cause they'd get thrown in jail if they's caught stealing. Worst that happens when we get caught is they rough us up a bit."

"You been caught?'

"We all have. Ain't so bad. Let's go." Cap sprinted toward the lead car. From there it was a short distance to the piles of coal. Durwood and the others followed. Reaching the first mound, Durwood scooped a handful of nuggets. Holding them close, he closed his eyes and inhaled.

"You look like my Pa sipping whiskey. What are you doing?"

"Smelling home."

Cap turned to the others. "Let's see if we can find Durwood some West Virginia coal." Boys spread out.

Durwood laughed. "How on earth you figure on doing that?"

"The mines put scatter tags in with the coal before shipping it."

"Scatter tags?"

"Metal tags that have the name of the mine the coal comes from."

"Is this what you're looking for, Cap?" The smallest boy in the group handed Cap a thin metal disk the size of a silver piece.

"Kentucky. West Virginia starts with a 'W,' like this." Cap traced a 'W' in the dust. He rubbed the boy's head. "Keep looking, Cut Bait." Cap gave the tag to Durwood, which had "Deep Vein, Kentucky" stamped in it.

"Here's one that says West Virginia." Cap and Durwood hurried over.

"Dry Branch, West Virginia." Cap showed it to Durwood.

"That the one you're looking for?"

"No, but that mine's not far from us, over in Fayette County. Got a cousin working there. Mind if I have it?"

Cap gave the tag to Durwood who pulled a handkerchief from his pocket. Unfolding it, he laid it on the ground to put the metal emblem in the center. Carefully selecting several nuggets, he placed them in the kerchief, then cinched it up before tying the corners. Stuffing the sack in his pocket, Durwood stood.

"I reckon I should be getting back."

"You sure? We ain't found the one you're looking for."

"That's all right. This here's close enough for now. I'll be back."

"Tell us the name of the mine. We'll keep an eye out."

"Paint Lick."

"Paint Lick. Got it."

"Y'all coming?"

"No. As long as we're here we might as well do a little mining ourselves."

Standing at Cap's elbow, the little boy he called Cut Bait, asked, "How? We ain't got our satchels."

"Load up your jackets. See you around, Durwood."

"Thanks, Cap. Nice meeting you fellas." As Durwood retraced his route, the others busied themselves scooping coal into their jackets.

***

Durwood entered the kitchen through the back door. The sun had set twenty minutes earlier. Streetlights would be cutting on any minute. Hattie wheeled from the sink. "Where in God's name have you been, son? Miss Grace is wearing grooves in the floor."

"What time is it?"

"Quarter of six. Miss Grace was expecting you two hours ago. She's been over to the school and to Ben's house looking for you. John Randolph said you went to the coal yard. Sent Mr. Walker down there looking for you."

"I didn't mean to be this late."

"Let me look at you." Hattie took his face in her hands. "You been fighting?"

"I fell. Playing kickball."

"That cut needs cleaning. Let me tell Miss Grace you're home." Hattie hurried from the kitchen. Durwood fretted over his ruined clothes. Even worse, he regretted his selfishness had caused Miss Grace worry.

Grace flew into the kitchen. "I've been worried sick." Hattie followed with a bottle and a washcloth. Grace raised her hand as she approached. Durwood closed his eyes and braced himself. She couldn't possibly hit harder than Pa. Instead of a slap, Grace grabbed his arm to pull him close. "Thank the Lord you're okay."

"Miss Grace, I'm sorry. I didn't mean to…"

"Hush. We can discuss this later. Let's take a look at you. Hattie says you look like you've been in a cat fight." She gently pushed him backward. Tilting his head, she studied his chin. "How about your knees?"

"They's just scraped up. I sure am sorry about the new britches though."

"That's why we bought several pairs. We'll patch these up and you can wear them to play in. The main thing is you're home safe." She pulled him close again and kissed his head. Releasing her grip, she straightened. "Hattie's going to tend to your cuts. After she's finished, why don't you clean up and dress for dinner?"

"Yes, ma'am."

As Grace left the kitchen, Hattie moved her stool to the center of the room under the light. "Sit up here so I can get a good look at you."

Durwood hopped onto the stool. "Tilt your head back some." This may sting a little."

"What is it?"

"Hydrogen peroxide." Hattie dabbed his chin with the cloth. Durwood winced. "That hurt?"

"Not too bad."

"I'm not finished yet."

"What's a hillbilly?"

"What makes you ask that?"

"That's what the other kids call me."

"Don't you pay them no mind."

"But what's a hillbilly?"

"It's just another way of saying you're from the mountains. Don't ever be ashamed of where you come from. Now run get cleaned up like Miss Grace asked. Dinner will be ready as soon as Mr. Walker gets home."

"I'll bet he's going to be sore at me."

"Don't you worry about him. Leave that to Miss Grace. Pull this stunt again and things might turn out different. Be sure to put some of this peroxide on your knees and that elbow."

"Thanks, Hattie." Durwood took the bottle and cloth and pushed through the door to run up the back stairs.

"And bring them trousers back down so I can mend them."

Durwood pulled the Buster Brown shoe box from under his bed and placed it on top of the quilt. Removing the bound handkerchief from his pocket, he untied the knot. He rolled each lump of coal around in his hand before placing it in the box, never before realizing how many edges a nugget had. He traced the words stamped in the scatter tag. After placing it in the box, he slid it back under the bed.

In the bathroom, Durwood leaned into the mirror. His chin was raw. Black smudges dotted his face. Even if John Randolph hadn't told Miss Grace where he had been, one look would have given him away. As he washed his face and hands, coal dust drained away. He removed his pants to wash dirt and debris off his knees before dabbing them with peroxide. After cleaning his elbow, he returned to his room. He slipped into his jacket and tie and laced his new shoes. He descended the back stairs into the kitchen; Hattie sized him up as he passed through into the dining room.

"How do I look?"

"A sight better than you did. Go on in. They're waiting."

Grace and Walker sat at the dining table. "Have a seat, son, so we can bless the food."

"Yes, sir."

"Heavenly Father, bless this food and those about to partake. We thank you for watching over us and keeping us safe. Make us ever mindful of the needs of others. In your name, we pray, Amen."

"Amen." Durwood tucked his linen into his shirt. "Sir, I'm sorry for the fuss I caused today."

"Grace and I discussed what happened. We understand you're in a new place full of new adventures. But you must understand that we promised your Pa to take care of you."

"I understand."

"And we can't do that if we don't know where you are. Richmond isn't like Mingo County, where everyone knows everyone else. Where folks can be counted on to look out for each other. There are places here you don't go. One of them happens to be the coal yard. There are lots of ruffians down there. They cause lots of trouble for the railroad and anyone who doesn't belong in their neighborhood. You could have been hurt."

"Or worse," Grace added.

"All that we ask is that you let us know what you're doing. Understand?"

"Yes, sir."

"Let's eat."

❋❋❋

Durwood rinsed his toothbrush. He wiped his hands on a towel and turned off the light. Miss Grace sat on his bed. Durwood climbed under the covers.

After they said prayers, Grace took his hand. "Don't ever worry about things."

"Ma'am?"

"Ben told me you went to the coal yard because you were worried about your pants. We can always replace things. We can't replace you."

"That ain't why I went."

"It's not?"

"No, ma'am. Even though I figured you'd be sore about them britches, I went to the yard because I wanted to see where all the coal goes that Pa and Bascom digs every day." Grace squeezed his hand. "A coal train passed by while we was playing kickball. A boy told me where it was headed so I went to see for myself."

"Tell you what. Next time you want to go to the coal yard, you let Walker know. He'll take you and show you all around."

"Can I ask you something?"

"Of course."

"Did Mr. Walker mean what he said in the blessing?"

"What are you talking about?"

"That part about being mindful of the needs of others."

"Yes. Why do you ask?"

"'Cause I met some boys on my way to the coal yard."

"Listen to me, Durwood. There are some bad people who live near that coal yard. They would just as soon knock you in the head as look at you."

"Not these fellas. They was real nice. Look what they give me." Durwood hopped out of bed. Grabbing the shoe box, he opened the lid. "This here's what they call a scatter tag." He handed it to Grace.

"Dry Branch, West Virginia."

"That's the mine the coal in that pile comes from. We was looking for one that said Paint Lick, Pa's and Bascom's mine. Cap said they'd keep an eye out and give it to me next time I go to the yard."

"Who's Cap?"

"One of the boys I met."

"How does he know so much about the coal yard?"

"His folks can't afford to buy coal, so they do a little mining for themselves at night."

"Is that what they call it?"

"Yes, ma'am."

"Do you think it makes it right to take the railroad's coal because they can't afford it?"

"I don't know if it makes it right, but it don't exactly make it wrong in my mind neither. You ought to see the mountains of coal they got down there. You think the railroad might could spare some coal for those boys. That way, they wouldn't have to spend their time chasing them off every night."

"I wish it were that easy, Durwood. Tell you what. When the time's right, I'll speak to Walker about it."

"Thank you, Ma'am. Good night."

"Night, Durwood." Grace kissed his forehead and turned off the light.

Chapter 9

"Fire in the hole!"

Bascom covered his ears as the ground quivered. A rush of warm, gritty air washed over him. Eyes squeezed tight, he breathed through his handkerchief. He stayed put behind a coal slab, mindful of the rare secondary explosion that proved deadly for those in too big a hurry. The hand gripping his shoulder relaxed.

"Don't worry, son. After a while, you don't hardly notice it no more."

"How long you been digging coal, Abner?"

"Going on forty years."

"When did you get used to the blasting?"

"Just now." Abner slapped Bascom's back.

"All clear!"

Turning the knob controlling the gas, Bascom relit the carbide lamp perched on the bill of his cap and spat. Somehow, coal dust always managed to filter through his kerchief. Bascom hopped up, grabbed his pickaxe, shovel and lunch pail. He waited for Abner to gather himself.

"Let's go make hay while the sun ain't shining!" Abner flashed a toothless grin. The man's glass was always half full, despite miner's cough and a gimpy leg.

"Age before beauty."

Bascom followed Abner through the main shaft. He kept one eye on the ground, the other overhead. He found the roofing timbers especially worrisome right after a shot had given everything a good shimmy. Abner stooped to navigate the main shaft. Bascom wanted to hurry—the first to reach the blast area reaped the coal littering the ground. Busting up coal on the ground was easier than clawing it from the seam. Abner made up for his slow gait with his experience. Sheltering closer to the blast zone than most dared, they would be among the first to arrive. Abner's limp had seemed to worsen the last few weeks. "Stick close to Abner and do as he says," Pa had told him. "He'll teach you everything you need to know. Most important, he'll teach you how to stay alive."

Turning from the main shaft to a smaller one, the roof lowered, forcing Bascom to bend more. Before they reached where they had set the charge, rhythmic thumps signaled they wouldn't get the best spot today.

Bascom entered the chamber where they'd work the next few days. Two lights bobbed at the far side where the roof was highest. Coal lay scattered about, waiting to be cleaved into smaller, more manageable bits.

"Mind if we join this party?"

A man grunted between strikes, "That you, Abner?"

"In the flesh."

"Who's with you?"

"Clem's boy, Bascom."

"What're you two waiting for? Coal don't bust itself."

"Over there." Bascom stepped around Abner to tear into a three-foot seam exposed by the blast. The coal glistened as his tool bit. A stray blow struck the occasional spark.

"Why you working so hard when there's easy pickings at your feet?"

Bascom didn't let up. "Pa says I'm too soft."

"Let me tell you something, son. Being soft and showing you care about folks ain't the same thing. You'll toughen up down here just fine or die trying. But lose your kindness and there ain't no difference between you and them draft mules that hump our coal out to the scales."

"Yes, sir."

More men filtered into the room, indistinguishable shadows; human windmills in motion. Until they coughed. You could judge a man's time underground by the timbre of his hacking. In the light of day, the degree of stoop to a man's shoulders spoke volumes about his time underground, too. How long 'til folks could tell he dug coal?

"Let me tell you something else. Your Pa's a good man. He loves you." Leaning against the wall, Abner untied his kerchief from around his neck to wipe his brow.

Bascom rested his pick on his shoulder.

"Losing your Ma and little brother in one fell swoop took a toll on him. Give him time."

"It's been a year. Ain't like he's the only one suffered a loss. Besides, he's the one what shipped Durwood off. Works all day. Night time, he mostly drinks and stares at a photograph of Ma and Durwood. Like to worn holes in that picture. Hardly says a word. Don't eat much neither."

"Just because he pines for your Ma and your brother don't mean he cares any less for you."

"Be nice if he showed it every now and then."

"I been knowing Clem a long time. He's a man of few words. You said so yourself. Been my experience, the people who talk the least tend to mean it the most."

Bascom tore into the seam again.

"Don't be too hard on your Pa, is all I'm saying."

"Hey Abner. Best tell your shadow if he don't pace hisself he'll be lucky to last 'til Christmas."

Abner shouted, "Don't you boys worry about the skinny mule, you just keep loading the wagon." Turning to Bascom, he whispered: "They's right, you know. It's all about finding your pace. Remember, the coal ain't going nowhere."

A dozen more men came to labor shoulder to shoulder. No one spoke as the pickaxes kept time.

"Must be lunchtime. Mule team's here."

The clang of bells neared. Bascom leaned his pickaxe against the wall. Each mule pulled a wagon narrow enough to navigate the tight shafts. They came by twice a day, marking lunchtime and the end of a shift. Bascom gathered his coal to place in a wagon bearing a metal tag with the number assigned to him his first day on the job. Within minutes, he filled his car. Abner lagged. Bascom scooped the last of the coal he dug to fill Abner's wagon.

"Maybe your Pa's right."

* * *

Bascom sat on a slab near Abner in the dinner hole. He removed the outer lid of his dinner bucket, flipped it and placed it on the ground. Taking a clean kerchief from his pocket, he spread it in the bottom of the upturned lid. He reached into the bucket to retrieve two bread slices slathered with butter, a slab of bacon and an onion. He carefully placed them on the kerchief, trying to avoid coal dust that gave everything an earthy, gritty taste. Removing the inner compartment, Bascom popped the lid to sip lukewarm tea.

Abner asked, "What's for lunch today?"

"Same as yesterday. And the day before that. What did Eloise pack for you?"

"Let's see. Couple of sandwiches, an apple, a paw paw and a piece of pie." Abner sniffed a large pie slice and wrinkled his nose. "Rhubarb. Now that woman knows I'd just as soon go hungry as eat rhubarb pie. How about you do me a favor and take it?"

Did Abner know rhubarb pie was his favorite? That Ma made the best rhubarb pie on the mountain?

"As long as you two been married you'd think she'd be knowing that by now."

"Oh, she knows it alright. Does it just to be spiteful."

"Don't sound like Eloise. Besides, ain't you just encouraging her if you go home with an empty bucket?"

"How you figure?"

"She'll think you liked it. You want to break her from sending rhubarb pie, send it back every evening."

"You got as much to learn about marriage as you do mining, son. Good thing I'm a patient man."

"Even if you ain't a wise one," Clyde Everett chimed in. "I'm with Bascom on this one." "Mary wouldn't pack nothing I don't care for."

Abner asked, "How long you been married, Clyde? A year?"

"Eight months."

"Eight months? Mary thinks she's still in love. Soon as the honeymoon wears off and she realizes she's stuck with you for the rest of her earthly days, you best gird your loins for battle, as it says in the

Good Book."

Laughter, mixed with coughs, echoed in the cramped room lit only by carbide lamps.

"Now, back to that pie. If Eloise decides she ain't getting to me by packing rhubarb pie, she'll move on. Besides, I don't want to give her the pleasure of knowing she got the best of me."

"Tell you what, Abner, I'll split it with you."

"Deal." Abner took out his pocket knife and cut the pie, giving Bascom a slice that dwarfed the piece he kept.

A couple of miners entered the dinner hole looking for a place to sit. As youngest on the crew, Bascom stood to offer his seat to Ralph Owens and a middle-aged man he didn't recognize.

Abner squeezed to the edge of his slab to make room for Bascom. Bascom waved him off and squatted on his heels, still cradling the pie.

"Boys, this here's Kendall Vance. Just moved from Ohio with his wife and kids. Today's his first day."

Abner asked, "What brings you to Mingo County, Kendall?"

"We come to look after my wife's mother."

"What part of Ohio?"

"Massillon. Stark County."

"That's coal country."

"Shore is."

"So what do you think about West Virginia coal so far?"

"Coal's coal. Only difference is how you're digging it. And from what I've seen, I ain't too keen on how you boys are forced to dig coal here."

"How do you mean?" Abner took a bite of pie.

"I'm talking about the working conditions. You ain't got the union. Ohio's been union since '98."

"Pa says the union ain't no better than the owners. Both looking to make a buck off the backs of them that's doing all the work."

"What's your name, boy?"

"Bascom."

"I don't mean no disrespect to your Pa, Bascom, but he don't know what he's talking about."

Ralph said, "Go ahead and tell the crew what you been telling me."

Kendall asked, "For starters, how are you paid?"

Abner said, "By the ton."

"And who's weighing the coal?"

"The foreman's men."

"You allowed to have anyone watch the scales to make sure they ain't cheating you? 'Course not. In Ohio, the union cut a deal so's we get paid by the hour with regular wage increases. Can't cheat us on our pay. Clock don't lie."

The room grew still.

"How long you work each day?"

The crew continued to defer to Abner. "Ten or more. Depends on when the foreman feels like we've dug enough, I guess."

"In Ohio, the union negotiated an eight-hour work day."

Bascom asked, "What happens if you ain't done after eight hours?"

"The clock determines when you're done, not some damned foreman. How many of you live in company houses?" Most of the men raised their hands.

"Rent keeps increasing even though your pay don't, right?"

A voice called, "Damn straight."

"When I met with the foreman yesterday he told me they was reducing my pay for the cost of the dynamite we use to bust the seams open. Ain't that something? Would've charged me for tools, too, except I got my own pickaxe and shovel."

Ralph Owens spoke up. "I told him he might as well get used to it. Ain't nothing going to change around here."

Bascom asked, "They know you a union man?"

"Hell no. And if you know what's good for you, you'll keep your mouth shut."

Before Bascom could respond, Abner spoke.

"Bascom ain't going to say nothing. None of us are. But let me warn you. They catch you talking up the union around these parts and you'll be lucky if the only thing you lose is your job and your house."

"All I'm saying is they got you over a barrel. By the time they've taken all your deductions, you might as well be paying them for the right to dig coal."

A whistle sounded.

Abner pushed off the slab. "Don't know what time your clock says it is, Kendall, but mine says it's time to get back to work."

Chapter 10

August 14, 1909

Richmond, Virginia

Durwood moved the fishing pole to his other shoulder to rap on the heavy oak door. Ben's three-story stone house, the largest on Monument Avenue, occupied two lots and had turrets like a castle. A Confederate flag hung limp above the front door. The day promised to be a scorcher. It wasn't eight o'clock and already sweat pebbled Durwood's forehead. As the door cracked, Ben's Irish Setter bounded out and planted his front paws onto Durwood's chest.

"Stonewall, down. Durwood, I'm so sorry."

"That's okay, Mrs. Claiborne. Me and Stonewall is pals." Durwood rubbed the dog's shoulders.

"I hear you and Ben are going fishing."

"Yes, ma'am."

"He's finishing breakfast. Won't you come inside?"

"If you don't mind, I think I'll just sit here on the porch and visit with Stonewall."

Soon, Ben skipped around the side of the house, a fishing pole in one hand, a shiny metal tackle box in the other. "Let's go catch some fish." He wore a new fishing vest peppered with pockets. A canteen hung around his neck. His boots shone like they just came off the rack.

"Do you have the sandwiches Lena packed?"

"In my knapsack."

"You boys have fun. Be home by supper."

"Yes, ma'am."

Ben pushed open the wrought iron gate for Durwood, letting it close behind him. As they reached Monument Avenue, Durwood whistled. "You look like one of them models in the Sears & Roebuck catalog."

"What are you talking about?"

"Ain't you got no old clothes to muck around in?"

"Mother doesn't like us to wear old clothes. She says it's important to always look nice. To stand apart from the common man."

"Not today, it ain't."

"What are you talking about?"

"We ain't going fishing. Not right off, anyways."

"Where we going?"

"The coal yard."

"Coal yard? What for?"

Durwood fished around in his pocket. "See this? Called a scatter tag. Looking for one from my brother's mine. You can help. Plus, I got some fellas I want you to meet."

"Mother will be awfully mad if she finds out we didn't go fishing."

"Don't worry. We'll get our lines wet before the day's over so's you ain't got to fib."

"Who we meeting?"

"Just some fellas I run into that time I went down there after school."

"How do we get there?"

"They's a hole cut in the fence over by the school. Follow me."

***

The sun in a cloudless sky reflected off the rails. Durwood pulled his cap low. Ben stayed close by his side.

"Want me to carry that a while?" Durwood nodded at the tackle box.

"That's okay. How much farther? Seems like we've been walking a long time."

"Almost there. Let's take a break. Over there." Durwood settled on his haunches under the full branches of an apple tree that grew on the other side of the fence, thick with wisteria and honeysuckle. Careful to avoid rotting apples, Ben sat beside him and wiped his brow. He offered his canteen to Durwood.

"After you."

Ben gulped, then handed the canteen to Durwood. "You miss your father and brother?"

"Sure do."

"I'd miss my parents. Not so sure about John Randolph, though. What's Bascom like?"

"Ain't nothing like John Randolph."

"How so?"

"We's best friends. Before Ma got the cancer and he went to work the mines, we done everything together. Fished. Hunted squirrels. Skipped stones."

"What do you miss most?"

"Lying on the big rock out behind our house. We could sit for hours watching the clouds. We'd talk about everything. Or nothing."

"How do you like living with Mr. and Mrs. Hopkins?"

"They been real good to me. Given me things I ain't never had."

"Like what?"

"Everything. Plenty of food. Books. New clothes. My own bed."

"Was your house nice?"

"Was to us. You ready to get moving again?"

Ben stood to shoulder his pack.

"Hang on." Durwood took the pack and set it down. "Give me your vest."

"How come?"

"Trust me." Ben removed his vest. Durwood tucked the tackle box into the bushes at the base of the fence. After folding the vest, Durwood placed it on top of the box, careful to cover them with foliage. He laid the poles upright against the fence so they blended with the greenery. He smeared a handful of mud on Ben's boots and pants.

"What in Sam's name are you doing? These are new boots."

"Need to make them look a little worn. Take this rock and scuff the toes." Durwood flipped Ben a stone to Ben.

"You trying to get me killed, or something?"

"Not hardly. Now we're ready."

Durwood and Ben scampered back up to the tracks. As they continued east another quarter mile, the railroad bed leveled out even with the fence line.

"See that bottle up ahead?" Durwood pointed twenty yards to a bottle standing on the edge of a tie. "Pretend you's playing kick ball and give it a swift boot." Ben kicked the bottle. Within seconds, Cap popped through the fence, followed by two more dirty-faced boys.

"Hello, Cap. Remember me?"

"'Course we remember you. Durwood. Right?"

"That's me."

"Who you got with you?"

"Cap, this here's my friend, Ben. Ben, meet Cap and the boys. They's the ones who told me about scatter tags."

Cap studied Ben, who avoided his gaze. "What brings you all down to the yard?"

"Thought we'd have a look around to see if we can't find us a Paint Lick tag."

Cap spit. "Afraid that ain't possible today."

"How come?"

"Yard's crawling with security. Something must have gotten filched last night besides a few satchels of coal." Cap winked. "Anyway, try as we might, Durwood, we can't find no scatter tag that's got Paint Lick on it. We've looked hard, too. Ain't we, boys?"

Cap's little sidekick muttered, "That's right."

"You sure they ship their coal to Richmond?"

"Guess not."

"Just as well. As sweaty as you'd get today, you'd be black from head to toe. They oil that coal to keep down the dust. Ben's new duds would get ruint for sure."

Ben's face brightened. "Guess we'll have to go fishing, Durwood."

Cap asked, "Fishing?"

"We got fishing poles hid back down the tracks. Care to join us?"

"Won't be no fish biting in this heat. Tell you what. We was fixin' to go swimming at the quarry. Why don't y'all come with us?"

Durwood turned to Ben. "What do you say?"

"I don't know. Mother would be awfully upset if she found out."

Cap busied himself looking behind the brush overhanging the fence. He disappeared through the hole in the chain link and back again.

Durwood wiped his brow. "Cap, what are you doing?"

"Looking for Ben's mother. Pretty sure she ain't here, Ben. Only way she's going to find out you went swimming is if somebody tells her. I ain't going to tell her. Boys, you going to tell Ben's mother he went swimming?"

One of them said, "No, Cap."

The one called Cut Bait said, "I don't know his mother, Cap." Cap patted the back of the little boy who followed him like a shadow.

"That only leaves you, Durwood. You going to tell Ben's mother?"

"Nope."

"Then that settles it. We're going swimming." Cheers erupted as the boys followed Cap through the fence.

Durwood stopped. "Wait here. Be right back." He squeezed through the fence and raced down the tracks to where he left the poles. Grabbing a rod, he ran back down the tracks. Sweat poured from his face and moistened his clothes.

"I'm back."

Cap scratched his head. "What are you doing? There ain't no fish in the quarry."

Durwood handed Ben his bamboo rod. "Ben's mom don't know that."

Trash smoldered in a dirt patch masquerading as a yard. A plume of acrid smoke lingered in the heavy air. Moving away from the tracks, the boys passed between two homes that sat closer than the company houses in Paint Lick. Arms extended, Durwood could almost touch the rough, particle-board exteriors of both. The single-story homes had tar paper roofs and not a trace of paint, unlike those in Paint Lick which occasionally got a coat of whitewash when the company wanted to lift spirits for a week or two.

Leaving the yard, the boys stepped onto a dirt road that ran between the rows of houses, all of which appeared to be in a similar state of disrepair. Fifty yards in one direction the street dead-ended. The group followed Cap in the other. Not a single car was in sight. From the looks of things, folks here struggled the same as in Mingo County.

Durwood asked, "You live around here, Cap?"

"Whose yard you think we just traipsed through?"

Ben pointed over his shoulder. "That's your house?"

"Yep."

Durwood caught up to Cap. "How far is the quarry?"

"About a mile. Say, you fellas ain't got any money, do you?"

Ben looked at Durwood. "I got a quarter."

"Give it here."

"Here you go. All I got." Durwood handed a dime to Cap, who stopped walking. Placing his hand on Durwood's shoulder, Cap removed his shoe. Cardboard lined the insole. He separated the leather at the heel to deposit the dime between the seams. Staring at Ben, he continued to balance on one leg.

Durwood nudged Ben. "Go ahead. It's alright."

Ben removed his backpack. Sifting through its contents, Ben took a coin from a change purse. "I need this back."

"Don't worry." Cap placed the coin in the slot, pushed it down beside the dime and slid his foot back into the worn shoe. "What else you got in there?"

"Some apples. And sandwiches."

"What kind?"

"Not sure. Probably some ham and peanut butter. You hungry?"

"I could eat."

Durwood said, "Let's find some shade and see if they's enough to go around."

"I know just the place." The boys followed Cap to the next intersection. On the far side of the street stood a decrepit wooden building. Durwood could barely make out W.S. Johnson Livery across the front. Busted windows flanked a front door, slightly ajar. Cap pushed through the opening. A rat scurried away.

Ben stopped. "Are we going in there?"

Cap said, "It's our clubhouse. Ain't much to look at but it's a sight cooler than out here."

"What is it?"

"Used to be old man Johnson's livery. Went out of business when the trolley went electric."

Durwood counted the sandwiches. "Got four here. If we quarter them, they's enough for each of us to almost get a sandwich. What do you say, Ben?"

"Let's eat." Ben unwrapped the sandwiches.

"Here." Cap whipped out a pocket knife.

Ben opened the blade. Before cutting the sandwiches, he wiped it on his pants. "Got two ham and two peanut butter. Who wants ham?" Three hands shot up. Ben handed half a sandwich each to Cap and his friends. "Guess we're having peanut butter, Durwood."

"Suits me."

Cap's two friends swallowed their squares, barely stopping to chew. Cap savored his portions. "Ain't never had bread so soft. Sticks to the roof of my mouth. Where'd you get it?"

"My mother gets it at the market. What's your bread like?"

"Hard as a rock. A man could lose a tooth. Don't recall having a better meal. How about you boys?" Cap's friends nodded.

"Got half a ham left. Who wants it?" Ben held up half a sandwich.

Cap took the wax paper from Ben and handed a quarter to each of his friends. "Why don't you two chew it this time and see what ham tastes like?"

The little boy popped the sandwich in his mouth.

"You keep eating like this, Cut Bait, and maybe you'll get a growth spurt yet."

The empty, musty room smelled of hay and manure.

"Help us finish off the peanut butter, Cap." Durwood tossed a square.

"Got two apples. Want to split them?"

Cap swallowed. "Better save 'em for later. Swimming works up an appetite."

"Hello, girls. Having a nice picnic?" Four teenage boys, bare-chested under grubby overalls, towered over them, their thick arms crossed. Cap rose, but the largest of the group pushed him to the ground. "What do you got in that pack for us?"

"Afraid we done finished off the sandwiches, Mack. Got a couple of apples."

"I'll have a look for myself." Mack snatched the backpack from Ben to rummage inside. "Two stinking apples."

"You can have them."

"No thanks. What's this?" He held Ben's change purse and squeezed the ends before tossing it to the ground. "Where's your money?"

Ben looked in Cap's direction and started to speak. He hesitated long enough for Durwood to respond. "We ain't got none."

Mack nodded to his mates. "Check 'em." Two of the boys lifted Ben while the third searched his pockets.

"Nothing." They pushed Ben down.

"Your turn." Before they could grab him, Durwood jumped to his feet and turned his pockets inside out.

"See for yourself."

"Then I guess we'll be taking the backpack and rods for our trouble."

Durwood took a step. "You can't do that."

"I think we got us a hero. What's your name, boy?"

"Durwood."

"And where do you live?"

Durwood thumbed in Ben's direction. "Me and him's from West Virginia. We's visiting relatives."

"Should have had some money on you, Durwood." Mack pecked Durwood's chest. "Next time I see you two bumpkins, you better have some money for me. Got it?" Mack grabbed the poles and flung the pack over his shoulder. "Let's go, boys."

"Mack. Wait." Cap hopped to his feet. "I got a deal for you."

"I'm listening."

"Leave the pack and fishing pole and I'll bring you coal every night for a week. Free of charge."

"Deal. I expect to see the first batch tonight." Mack tossed the rod and pack on the ground, kicking up dust.

"Not tonight. Yard's swarming with security. Things should calm down in a couple of days."

"Not my problem." Mack motioned to one of his lackeys. "Get the stuff."

"Okay. We'll start tonight."

"See you girls around. You remember what I said, Durwood."

"No one dared speak until Mack and his friends were out of earshot. Durwood said to Cap. "You can't do that."

"Why not?"

"You might get caught. Said yourself it ain't safe."

"Rather take my chances with railroad security than with Mack's midtown boys. Railroad men might box our ears a little, but Mack'll beat us good."

Ben asked, "Why didn't you just give him the money?"

"Ain't mine to give, now was it?"

Ben extended his hand. "Thanks, Cap."

"Don't mention it. You and Durwood would've done the same for me if the shoe was on the other foot. Get it?" Cap slapped Ben's back. "I'm ready for a swim. Let's get out of here."

Chapter 11

October 1, 1909

Mingo County, West Virginia

Bascom finished cleaning up after supper. He sat at the kitchen table and adjusted the kerosene lamp so it wouldn't cast shadows on the paper. Pa rocked by the fire, sipping from his jug. The photo of Ma and Durwood rested in his lap. Rain pattered the tin roof and pinged a bucket in the corner.

Pa stopped rocking. "When are you going to patch the roof? A man can't think with all that dripping."

"Soon as this rain lets up, and I have a day off."

"Lot of good that's going to do me then."

"Tell you what, why don't you let the foreman know I need a day off to fix the roof so's you can think? You keep reminding me you and him was buddies growing up." What did Pa have to think about that was so pressing? Bascom didn't feel like arguing tonight.

Pa set the jug beside the rocker. "What are you doing?"

"I'm fixing to write Durwood."

"About what?"

"Ain't figured it out, exactly. I could tell him the roof's leaking again. Or the coal company's still trying to work us to death. What do you think?"

"Be glad you have work, son. How about you tell him things is settling down, and we'll be sending for him soon."

"You think that's a good idea?"

"What do you mean?"

"I don't want to go getting his hopes up until you're shore the time is right."

"And when exactly is that going to be, you reckon?"

"You been saying you was in line for assistant foreman of your crew, right? When that comes through, you'll be making steady money." Pa had been talking up the promotion since before Ma passed. Even if he'd had a shot at the job before, that window had closed as his drinking took hold, but Bascom played the game.

"That might take another year or so."

"Then I reckon Durwood can wait, Pa."

"What if they pass me over again?"

"They won't. You're due. Besides, in another couple of years we won't have to worry, 'cause Durwood'll be old enough to fend for hisself."

"It's just that I'm sure he's missing home."

"And we's missing him. But seeing as how you only want what's best for him, don't you think it makes sense to wait?"

"I reckon."

Hunched over the paper, Bascom struggled to find the words. He wanted to tell Durwood that Pa's drinking had eased, but that would be a lie. Besides, Durwood didn't know Pa drank. He would like to tell Durwood that working in the mines wasn't half bad, that he didn't die a little every time he entered the pit. But that wouldn't be true, either. Most of all, he wanted to be able to tell Durwood they were coming to fetch him soon. This was a selfish wish, which was why he'd do everything in his power to make sure it never came true.

Pa kicked a log. "Fire's petering out."

Bascom unlatched the door. Stepping onto the porch, he sidestepped Blue curled against the wall. Bascom took a knee to pet the dog. Blue stayed tucked, his tail thumping the wall. Stars peeked from behind the clouds, bringing the hope of dry weather. Durwood's favorite, the Big Dipper, wasn't showing itself.

"Ain't got all night."

Filling his arms with wood from the corner of the porch, Bascom stole another glance skyward before pushing the latch up with his knee. "Night, boy."

Bascom kicked the door shut. He rolled the logs onto the floor by the fireplace. Stoking the fire, he placed two logs on top of the revived embers. Flames leapt from the hearth. "Think you can handle it from here? I got a letter to write before I turn in."

As Bascom hovered over the paper, Pa's chin rested on his chest. The tapering rain gave way to Pa's snores.

"Let's get you to bed." Like he did every night, Bascom placed the photo on the table. He lifted the jug from between Pa's legs to set it on the floor. Draping Pa's arm around his neck, he got him on his feet and led him to his room. "Sleep well. Morning's going to come early."

Pa slurred, "Where's my jug?"

"By the rocker. Don't worry. It'll be waiting for you." Bascom laid Pa on top of the bed and pulled up the blanket. He closed the bedroom curtain and returned to the table to finish the letter.

After stuffing and addressing the envelope, Bascom filled the stove to burn until morning. Before turning in, he had one last chore. He picked up the jug. Stepping onto the porch, he poured some of the whiskey on the ground. Back inside, he replaced the whiskey with water and shook it. He returned the jug to the floor by the rocker and pushed aside the curtain to enter his bedroom. He slipped off his clothes, blew out the lamp, and slid into bed.

Chapter 12

October 20, 1909

Richmond, Virginia

The afternoon light grew faint. Durwood finished his lessons. A faint knock interrupted him.

"May I come in?"

"Yes, ma'am."

Grace entered, dressed for dinner. "Finish your work?"

"Just about."

"You received a letter today."

Durwood leapt from the desk. "Bascom?"

"Appears to be." Grace handed Durwood an envelope addressed in Bascom's swooping cursive. It had been months since Bascom had written. Durwood estimated the letter's contents by its girth.

"When you're ready to respond, let me know. I had some stationery made for you."

"Thank you, ma'am."

"May I ask you something?"

"Yes, ma'am."

"You've been with us for a year now, right?"

"Little over."

"During that time, I've never heard you refer to me in any manner but 'ma'am' and Walker as 'sir.'"

"Pa told me you would let me know what I was to call you. Guess I've been waiting for directions. Is there something else you would like me to call you?"

"That depends on you. You could call me Miss Grace, like Ben does."

"That would be fine."

"Or, perhaps, Aunt Grace. I know I'm not really your aunt, but your mother and I were like sisters."

"That would be fine too, ma'am." Aunt Grace had a comfortable sound; Uncle Walker was a stretch.

"You think about it."

"Thank you, ma'am."

"We'll be in the library before supper. Will you join us?"

"Yes, ma'am."

As the door closed, Durwood ripped open the envelope and unfolded three handwritten pages. Memories of home were growing dim, but Bascom's infrequent letters kept him connected. Fire had closed off a part of the mine, but Pa and Bascom still had work. Some Italians had moved into the county to replace strikers at another mine. The company hired them because they worked longer hours for less money. Most people hated them but Bascom said they was just trying to make a living like everyone else and the operators was using them to keep out the union. Because they didn't speak English, they kept to themselves, which made folks less welcoming. Bascom made squirrel gravy, but it didn't taste as good as Ma's. Blue was getting old but treed a raccoon on their last hunt. Durwood read the letter again, then returned it to the envelope. He slid open the top drawer of his secretary to tuck it in with several others. He turned off his light, shut his door, and headed downstairs.

Outside the library, Durwood knocked.

"Come in."

A fire warmed the room, casting long shadows on the mahogany bookshelves. It was Durwood's favorite room because it reminded him of Matewan, sitting around the fire with his family after supper. Ma knitted while Pa told stories of the days before the mines and the railroad came to Mingo County.

"Evening, Durwood. Was the news from home good?" Behind his

desk, Walker read the evening paper. Grace sat across from him in a high-back leather chair, reading a book.

"Just fine, sir."

"Finished your lessons?"

"Yes, sir. Anything in the paper about home?"

"Don't believe so."

"Do you mind if I look at the Encyclopedias?"

"Of course not. You know you don't need to ask, right?"

"Thank you, sir."

"What are you looking up?"

"Italy."

"Why Italy?"

"Bascom says some I-talians have moved into Mingo County to replace striking miners. I want to see where Italy is and what kind of folks they are."

"Italians is the way you pronounce it. Were your father and brother among the strikers?"

"No, sir. Wasn't their mine."

"I'm glad to hear that. Strikes are bad for this country."

"Why's that, sir?"

"Because they interfere with progress and bring hardship on others trying to make an honest living."

"How do they do that?"

"When miners strike, there isn't any coal being shipped. That puts decent railroad folks out of work. When that happens, shopkeepers are affected because the railroad workers don't have money to buy their goods."

"Such serious talk. Durwood, here's the stationery I ordered for you." Grace removed the lid and separated tissue, revealing white paper which bore his name and address at the top in black ink. The envelopes also had his name and address in raised letters across the back flap. "Do you like it?"

"Very much, thank you." It looked expensive. He wasn't sure why he needed fancy writing paper. Would Bascom think he was showing off? Durwood placed the box on a side table and moved toward the Encyclopedias.

Walker said, "Grace tells me she spoke with you about what you should call us."

"Yes, sir."

"What do you think?"

"Can I ask you something first?"

"Of course."

"When am I going back home?"

"Why do you ask?"

"It's just that I hardly hear from home and now I'm being told I can call you Aunt Grace and Uncle Walker. The way I figure, you wouldn't be suggesting that unless I'm staying put."

Grace closed her book. "We don't know how long you will be with us, Durwood. It depends on your father's circumstances."

"What does that mean?"

"He said he would send for you as soon as he was able."

"When I left home, Pa said I was only going to be here until things settled down. Seems to me there's been more than enough time."

"Are you unhappy living with us?"

"No, ma'am. It's just that I'm keen to get back to Pa and Bascom."

"I hope you know we consider you part of our family. No different than if you were our son."

"Yes, ma'am, I do. But we know I ain't. I appreciate what all you've done for me—taking me in when you didn't have to."

"Durwood."

"Sir?"

"What Grace is trying to say is that it doesn't appear that you will be going home soon. But we promise to see that you get back to Matewan just as soon as your father sends word. As much as we like having you live with us, it's never been our intention to come between you and your father."

"Thank you." Durwood picked up the box of stationery and turned to leave.

"What about the Encyclopedias?"

"I got a letter to write. Miss Grace."

Chapter 13

September 4, 1910

Mingo County, West Virginia

Bascom bent over the fire waiting for the iron to heat. He wore his best trousers and a clean undershirt; suspenders dangled by his sides.

"Best hurry, son. Don't want to miss the parade."

"Soon as I press my shirt."

"How many times you going to iron that thing?'

"As many as it takes."

"You're going to wear it to nubbins before you put it on the first time."

Bascom wrapped burlap around the handle before removing the iron from the fire. His new white shirt lay over the table. He guided the iron across the cotton, pushing creases toward the edges. First the sleeves, then the back. Finishing, Bascom slipped the shirt on, then slid his suspenders into place.

"Next time you wash that new shirt, you might want to hang it up right away. Helps to keep the wrinkles from setting in. Ma learn you to iron like that?"

"I seen her press enough clothes for folks in town."

"Sadie hitched?"

"Yes, sir."

"Well, douse the fire and let's go."

✳✳✳

Sunlight dappled through the trees as they wound their way down the mountain along the narrow, rutted logging trail. Reds, yellows, and oranges accented the trees, but the day promised warmth and sunshine for the holiday celebration. Entering town, Labor Day banners swayed. Red and white bows anchored by blue ribbons hung from gas lamps lining Main Street. Next to Fourth of July and election day, Labor Day was the biggest day of the year in Matewan. Now that he was working, Bascom enjoyed Labor Day the most. Folks from surrounding mountains and hollows poured into town. Dressed in their finest, they strolled along Main Street waiting for the festivities.

"Let me off here, son. I'm going to catch up with the fellas." A group of old-timers relaxed on the general store's porch. When he was younger, Bascom lingered on the porch until Ma would run him off. No point in listening to drunken lies, she told him. Now that he was old enough to join them, he had other things on his mind.

Bascom pulled on the reins until Sadie stopped. Nearby, at the train depot, fifteen Baldwin-Felts agents lurked. Cradling rifles and wearing sidearms, they scrutinized the crowd. A couple jotted notes.

"You steer clear of them, you hear?"

"Don't worry. It ain't trouble I'm looking for."

Holding the jug in one hand, Pa stepped off the wagon. "You courting somebody I don't know about?"

Bascom snapped the reins. "Let's go, girl."

After tying up Sadie just outside of town, Bascom headed to the schoolhouse where a group of boys gathered on the lawn. Some younger boys played mumblety-peg or shot marbles. The older boys shared whiskey. "Hey, fellas."

"Bascom. Ain't seen you in a month of Sundays. How's the mines treating you?" Earl Givens swigged from the communal jug.

"Okay, I reckon."

"Pretty good, I'd say. Look at that brand new shirt." Grover Ratliff let out a long whistle. "Must have set you back a couple bucks."

Bascom asked, "You still in school, Earl?"

"Sure am. Graduate next year."

"Want a nip, Bascom?" Grover offered the jug.

"Not now, thanks. You boys seen Ellen Mae?"

"No, but reckon I will when school starts up tomorrow."

"I'm talking about today, Earl. Tomorrow ain't going to do me no good. In case you ain't noticed, I ain't in school no more."

"That explains the fancy shirt." Grover leaned in to sniff behind Bascom's ear. "Smells sweeter than a whore on Saturday night, too."

Bascom pushed Grover away. "Leave me be. You boys see all them Baldwin-Felts guns at the depot?"

One of the boys asked, "What do you reckon they's up to?"

Bascom spit in his palm and slicked the back of his head. "Pa says the union is going to march in the parade. Owners brought in extra guns to make folks think twice about showing support."

Earl asked, "Is it true your Pa's a member, Grover?"

"He won't say. All's I know is he slips out late some nights. Won't never say where he's been."

Bascom added, "He's a union man, for sure."

"Either that or he's wetting his whistle down at the brothel." The group shared a laugh.

"You best watch your tongue, Earl."

"I'm only funning you, Grover. Besides, everybody knows your Pa's scared your Ma would cut it off if she caught him cheating."

"Son of a bitch." Grover placed Earl in a headlock.

"I take it back." Grover released his grip and pushed Earl away.

The beat of a bass drum signaled the start of the parade. The younger boys grabbed their knives, scooped up their marbles, and hurried off to Main Street.

"What say we go watch the parade?" Bascom led the group of teens toward the music. By the time they reached Main Street, folks were three deep. The community band passed, mainly in key, as the clarinets and drums played a military tune. Bascom leaned in toward another teen. "How come you ain't playing in the band this year, Earl?"

"Busted my lip." The boy pooched a bruised and swollen lower lip.

"Dang. How'd you do that?"

"Run into Pa's fist."

Bascom choked on his tobacco. He spit and coughed until he regained his composure. The mayor rode by in his new car, wife at his side.

Bascom whistled. "Ain't never seen a car like that."

"Pence Arrow. Bought it in Charleston. Had it shipped in on the train last week."

Anyone could march, and just about everyone did. A ragtag formation of veterans from the Spanish-American War shuffled behind the mayor's car. At the head of the column, Colonel Stephens, who boasted of having beaten President Roosevelt up San Juan Hill, maintained a crisp salute. Pa said the closest the Colonel got to action was when his pistol accidentally discharged while he was cleaning it. Unable to reject the call of free whiskey, one of the soldiers broke ranks to join the porch-sitters for a long pull from a brown jug.

Next came the ladies of the Temperance Society. Ma's best friend, Tillie McBride, took Ma's place at the head of the column, an axe across her shoulder. The men on the porch let out a chorus of boos. Only Pa held his tongue. Carrying a banner bearing the likeness of Carrie Nation, the stern-faced ladies marched with more discipline than the old troopers who preceded them.

In the middle of the parade, children marched with their teachers followed by Hungarian accordion players and Italians from the Calabria Society. The rank of accordion players grew each year, as the Hungarians passed the skill to the next generation. Bascom scanned the crowd for Ellen Mae.

The parade-watchers roared as two boys on elevated unicycles rode by, weaving in and out. The crowd held its breath as they teetered on the verge of crashing. Close behind, a bear cub and a small monkey pedaled bicycles. A trainer walked beside them, blowing into a whistle and snapping a crop. The bear, chained to the trainer's waist, wobbled and appeared ready to fall; the monkey wore a brimless hat and bared its teeth as it pedaled to stay in front of the cub. Many in the crowd left their positions to follow the animals. As they did, Bascom and his companions moved forward to the front row.

After the animals moved on, a handful of men passed in tweed suits and hats, holding a Local Union 17 banner, offering the crowd handbills. Mindful of the Baldwin-Felts agents who filtered through the gallery, most folks refused the printed material. The union men probably came from headquarters in Charleston. As the last of the group moved past, a man at the rear popped in front of Bascom.

"Mr. Ratliff." Grabbing Bascom's hand, Grover's father closed

Bascom's fist around a handbill before moving on.

Every year, Union soldiers enjoyed the honor of bringing up the rear of the parade. Wearing ill-fitting, faded uniforms, their ranks had dwindled to a couple dozen. Bascom opened the crinkled paper as the group of grizzled Civil War veterans passed. The handbill appealed to miners to stand up for their rights to organize. Without warning, the paper was ripped from Bascom's hands.

"What's your name, boy?" A broad-shouldered man in a black suit and bowler stood inches away. Tobacco and coffee washed over Bascom with each word.

"Bascom."

"Bascom what?"

"Bascom Matney."

He turned to a man behind him. "You get that?" The man nodded as he scribbled in a notebook.

"You a union man, Bascom Matney?"

"No, sir. One of them fellows in the parade just stuck that paper in my hand." Bascom nodded to the crumpled paper that lay at the man's feet. "I don't even know what it is."

"Looked to me like you two was pals."

"I know his boy is all." Bascom hoped Grover couldn't hear.

"What's his name?" Bascom fidgeted.

"Grover."

"Grover what? Ratliff ring a bell?"

"I reckon that could be it."

"Don't trifle with me, boy."

"I ain't trifling with you. I just come to enjoy the parade and see my girl. I ain't no union man."

"What seems to be the matter, Bascom?" Abner and Eloise stood arm-in-arm.

"Abner, tell this fellow I ain't no union man."

"I can vouch for him, officer. He works with me at Paint Lick. Ain't a union bone in his body."

"Better keep it that way." Pa crossed the street as the agent and his partner moved on.

Pa placed a trembling hand on Bascom's shoulder. "I thought I told you to steer clear of them Baldwin-Felts men."

"I wasn't doing nothing."

"You've got to be careful, son. Them agents got a long memory. Abner, thanks for looking after him."

"Don't think nothing of it, Clem. We just happened by."

"Can I trust you to keep your nose clean the rest of the day?"

"Yes, sir."

With the parade over, the crowd drifted in different directions. Some filled the bleachers at the end of town for a band concert. Others headed for the cake walk at the school. That was a likely place to find Ellen Mae, so Bascom set off for the schoolhouse. Crossing the schoolyard, he caught a glimpse of her blonde curls as she entered the front door.

Bascom hurried up the crowded steps to push his way inside. "Excuse me, please."

Bascom tapped her shoulder. "Ellen Mae. I been looking for you all day."

She turned, pulling Cabell Justice with her, their hands intertwined. "Afternoon, Bascom."

"What can we do for you, Bascom?" A couple of years older than Bascom, Cabell wore a fitted three-piece suit. A gold fob draped from his vest button to disappear in a watch pocket.

Why hadn't someone bothered to tell him Ellen Mae and Cabell Justice were courting? It would have saved him from looking the fool, not to mention the two dollars for the shirt from a mail order catalog.

"Didn't mean to bother you two. Just wanted to pay my respects to Ellen Mae, is all."

"What have you been up to, Bascom? Ain't seen you around."

"I told you he was working in your daddy's mine, Cabell."

"That right, Bascom?"

"Couple years now."

"How do you like it?" Only someone privileged to know he would never spend a day underground could ask such a question.

"I'm managing."

"Won't be long until I'm running things. When that time comes, look me up and I'll see if we can't find a job for you that ain't down in the pits."

"I'd be obliged."

Ellen Mae smiled. "Nice to see you, Bascom. I like your shirt."

"Thanks. I best be going. Told Grover I'd meet up with him after the parade." Bascom fought his way out of the school, starved for fresh air the same as if he were emerging from the mine.

Chapter 14

September 18, 1911

Paint Lick Mine | Mingo County, West Virginia

The last blast of the steam whistle lingered in the heavy air at the mine entrance. "Night, Abner."

"See you in the morning."

"Tell Eloise I asked after her."

Bascom waited for Pa to exit the mine. He tilted back his head to enjoy the waning daylight. Men in coveralls, black as coal, poured out. Heads down, dinner buckets under their arms, they trudged home. The sun had slipped behind the surrounding peaks. Clouds rolled in. In another week or two, it would be dark going and coming, and all day in between.

Pa emerged with his crew, stoop-shouldered. "We better hurry. Looking like rain."

Cinders crunched as they braked down the steep grade past a slate pile. At the bottom of the hill, most of the men turned onto the dirt road to the company houses half a mile away. Chimney-smoke laid over the small community. A cold drizzle began as Bascom and Pa headed in the opposite direction to climb the mountain home. Although it would take them the better part of an hour to navigate the trail, Bascom didn't envy the men who would be indoors in minutes. He relished the long walk, even in the rain. It gave him a chance to stretch his back and legs; a chance to breathe.

"You and Abner load any coal today?"

"No, sir. Started in on a new seam."

"When do you reckon you'll be digging again?"

"Day after tomorrow."

"Does it look like a good seam?"

"Don't to me."

"What's Abner say?"

"He ain't said much about the seam. His mind's on them timbers."

"How's that?"

"Says the beams ain't as thick as they call for and they's spaced too far apart."

"How far apart are they?" Pa stopped to cough.

"Ten feet between some on this run."

"How high's the roof?"

"No more than five feet."

"I wouldn't expect they'd be more than five feet between timbers in a low ceiling." Pa slowed. Walking and talking got harder each day.

"That's what Abner says."

"Has he talked to the timber crew?"

"Said he would excepting his I-talian ain't what it used to be."

"Anybody talk with the pit boss?"

"Abner tried. The boss said they wasn't nothing he could do."

"Could mean they's simply running low on timbers."

"I hope you're right, but it seems to me they's trying to save money on this puny seam like they do on everything else."

"How do you mean?"

"It'll be two days of work 'til we's loading coal again. That's two free days for doing company work. Don't seem it's too much to ask to get paid whether we's loading coal or not."

"I'm afraid it don't work that way."

"Maybe it's time it did."

"You ain't letting yourself get caught up in union talk, are you?"

"Some of the boys is saying it's just a matter of time before we get the union."

"They best get that notion out of their heads."

"How come you're so against the union? You see how the company does us."

"Let's just say I'm smart enough to know they's two sides to every coin."

"What does that mean?"

"Just what exactly do these boys on your crew know about the union?"

"The one talking it up the most moved down here a few years back from Ohio. He's a union man."

"If things was so rosy in Ohio, why'd he up and move down here for?"

"To care for his wife's ma."

"Likely story. Come down here to stir things up is more like it. What's this fella's name?"

"It don't matter."

"It does to me. I don't want this come-here filling your head with fairy tales about how great everything would be if we only had the union."

"Up there they get paid by the hour, not according to how much coal they dig."

"That right?"

"And their hours is set by the union."

"While he was talking up the union, did he bother to tell you how much his dues was?"

"No."

"Didn't think so."

"But they's helping folks."

"You think the fat cats running the union care a lick about the likes of you and me? Think you can count on them if things don't break their way?"

"I don't know."

"Well, I do. They'll cut and run in a heartbeat. Then blame it on the miners. Just like they done us in '02."

"Us?"

"That's right."

"Was you involved in the '02 strike?"

"Me and your Uncle Durwood both. You don't remember?"

"I remember Georgie's passing and the grief it brung. I remember you was gone the day she died. Don't recall much else."

Pa leaned against a tree to catch his breath. The rain picked up as darkness enveloped the mountain. "They come into Mingo and Fayette Counties signing boys up left and right. Promises flowed as free as whiskey on election day. For good measure, they brung in Mother Jones to work everyone into a good lather."

"Did you see Mother Jones?"

"See her? I saw her alright. Looked like a schoolmarm, cussed like a sailor. But everyone stood taller after listening to one of her speeches."

"What happened?"

"Things was going good at first. The strike spread. Union sent money and men to help us organize. Then the operators wised up and banded together. They hired Baldwin-Felts guns to rough up agitators and threaten families. Started kicking folks out of their houses and blacklisting union organizers, same as they's doing now. Brought in strikebreakers. Paid off judges. Then some Baldwin-Felts men murdered six miners in a strikers' camp in Fayette County. Busted down the door to their house and shot them like they was dogs. When the union leaders in Charleston figured out the companies wasn't going to back down, they lost interest and moved on. Left us holding the bag."

"I ain't had no idea you was a union man. Why'd you keep this from me?"

Pa spit a tobacco plug and replaced it with a fresh cut. "No one kept anything from you. You was old enough to know what was going on. At the same time, ain't like I went around boasting about the biggest mistake of my life. One that cost me my daughter and my brother."

"What are you talking about?

"When Georgie took sick, the company Doctor refused to help. Said he could lose his job for helping strikers. By the time Ma got her over to the Doctor in Williamson, it was too late. Whooping cough done took hold. She died in a week."

Bascom stood. "What'd the strike have to do with Uncle Durwood dying in an explosion?"

"That's what we told you boys. Found him in the woods with a gunshot to his head. Sheriff claimed it was suicide, but I know better. They killed him 'cause they knew he wouldn't stop agitating."

"What'd you do?"

"What I should've done in the first place. Started listening to your

Ma. Turned my back on the union and went back to work. I had a family to feed."

"Why ain't you ever told me this before?"

"I'm telling you now. Come on. It's getting late."

The trail narrowed, forcing them to walk single file. Bascom's mind jumbled. He had a thousand questions. Lost in thought, he tripped, pitching forward onto his hands.

"Run ahead and get supper started."

"Yes, sir."

"For God's sake, burn your lamp before you go breaking your neck."

Ignoring his exhaustion and confusion, Bascom raced ahead. He didn't mind that his lungs ached—it was fresh air that filled them. Exiting the woods, he crossed the meadow and started up the ridge, covering the last half-mile with ease. Hopping onto the porch, he slapped his cap against his leg. Coal dust splattered the floor. Pa's light bobbed in the meadow far below.

Blue crossed the porch to nuzzle his leg. Bascom sat on the steps. Rubbing Blue's head, things started making sense. Pa didn't start drinking because Georgie died. He blamed himself for her death. Maybe he was carrying the burden of Uncle Durwood's death, too. He stood up to the operators and it had cost him a daughter and a brother. He hadn't turned his back on the union; he had chosen family.

Pa labored up the ridge to the house, stopping just short of the porch. He bent over until he could catch his breath. "Ain't you supposed to be fixing dinner?"

"Why'd you go back to the mines?"

"What?"

"After what they done to our family, why'd you go back to the mines?"

"I told you. I had a family to feed."

"Why didn't you do something else?"

"Like what?"

"I don't know. Farming?"

"You know as good as me that unless rocks was to become a cash crop they ain't a living to be made on this patch of mountain. We's lucky just to feed the two of us. And that's in a good year."

"Logging, then?"

"Money wasn't much good, and after what happened to your uncle, your Ma wanted me home nights instead of off in some logging camp for weeks at a time. Trust me, son, if there was some other job that paid a decent wage I would've took it. Coal was the only job around here then. Same as now. The sooner you accept that, the better off you'll be."

"Don't it gall you to know you's working for the people what killed Georgie?"

"Dammit, boy. Sometimes you got to make choices, even if none of them is worth a damn. That's what I done. And I been living with it every day. You'll see for yourself."

Bascom spit. "Gotta be a better way."

"What'd you say?'

"Nothing. Reckon I'll fix us something to eat." Bascom grabbed a load of firewood and entered the house.

Chapter 15

September 19, 1911

Paint Lick Mine | Mingo County, West Virginia

Bascom lay twisted on his side, chipping away under the wall face with his pickaxe. The shelf needed to be deep enough that the wall would shear off in the blast. The work was tedious for a reason: pushing too fast or too deep risked a collapse. Working in a space two feet high, he closed his eyes to keep dust and flakes out. Every couple of minutes he paused to check his progress and to roll over on his back to prevent cramping. Over the past day and a half, he had cut a shelf deep enough that only his legs stuck out. Above him, the breast auger drilled into the wall face to prepare for powder and shot. He preferred no one drill above him while he worked, but the crew agreed the faster they could get the blasting done, the sooner they could get back to hauling coal and making money.

"Ain't hearing much digging. You asleep under there?" Abner kicked his foot.

"Like hell, I am. I been busting my butt while you fellas been sitting around cleaning your nails."

"How's it looking?"

"Pretty good, I think. Top seems to be holding."

"You be sure to let me know if it ain't. I don't want to send you home to your Pa looking like a flapjack."

"Think we's deep enough?"

"Looks to be three to four feet. That should be good enough for us to get a good fracture. Ready to come out?"

"Hell, yes."

"Give me a hand, boys." Bascom rolled over on his back and cradled his pickaxe to his chest. He turned his head sideways so the bill of his cap wouldn't snag. "One, two, three." Bascom's back slid across the rough floor as the crew yanked him out. He wiped his eyes. Standing to stretch, he bent at the waist to avoid striking his head.

"Let's take a break, boys."

Abner sat on a dynamite crate. Placing a leg on the crate, Bascom leaned on his knee. The other two men squatted against the wall.

Bascom broke the silence. "This is one pitiful seam."

One of the men responded, "They'll have us chase coal all the way to China if they's a buck to be made."

Bascom lifted his leg from the crate to kick a piece of slate. "Maybe they's making a buck, but we ain't hardly. Been two days since we hauled any coal."

"Let's finish drilling so's we can get to blasting some time this week. Maybe we'll find something on the other side of this wall that's worth our time." Abner stood. "You boys ready?"

Bascom and Abner steadied the auger while the other two used offset handles to crank the drill. Things moved quickly so long as they were drilling coal. Hit rock and one hole might take all day.

"How many more holes you figure we got to go, Abner?"

"Two, maybe three."

"That's deep enough for this one. Mark the next hole." As Abner spoke, a sharp crack froze the crew. Before anyone could move, splinters and coal dust showered them.

Abner screamed, "Run!"

Before Bascom could move, Abner shoved him, as chunks of roof and support timbers crashed around them. The other two sprinted toward the open shaft. Bascom covered his soft cap with his hands and ducked to run after them.

The cave-in started at the next-to-last beam, fifteen feet from the wall they were drilling. If they could get past that section, they'd be in the clear. Bascom tripped over a chunk of slate that had crashed at his feet. Six inches closer and his flight would have been over. Picking himself up, he scrambled on all fours over a pile of rubble. Running again, he cleared the next-to-last beam. He doubled over to claps on the back by the other two men who waited for him.

"We thought you was a goner. Where's Abner?"

Bascom turned. "He was right behind me."

Coal dust choked the tunnel. A faint light flickered near the base of the wall. "Abner? You alright?"

"Still taking stock. You boys go for help."

Bascom took a couple of deep breaths and covered his face with his bandana.

One of the miners asked, "What the hell you doing?"

"Going back to fetch Abner."

"You're crazy. It ain't stabilized yet. Listen." The collapse had slowed, but parts of roof continued to cleave and slam to the ground.

"I ain't leaving him behind. You boys get help. Hurry."

Retracing his steps, Bascom scrambled over the debris pile five feet in. He bent low to sprint toward the wall and the faint light. Dodging falling coal and slate, Bascom reached the wall. He knelt beside Abner who lay sprawled on his back.

"Get up, Abner. We gotta go before we's sealed off."

"What in the hell do you think you're doing?"

"Sticking by your side. Just like you done told me a thousand times."

"Now's the time you start listening?"

"Come on."

"I'm telling you to get the hell out of here, son."

"Not without you."

"I ain't going nowhere."

A slab of slate the size of a mule's head lay across Abner's thigh. A timber splinter half as thick as an axe handle stuck out of his side.

"That your good leg?"

"Used to be."

"Hold still." Bascom strained to lift the slab, but it barely budged.

Abner bit off a scream. Blood pooled beneath his leg. Perhaps they would be okay; the beam directly overhead seemed to be holding. Dust continued to fill the air. Ripping off his bandana, Bascom tied it across Abner's face.

"How about the other fellas?"

"They's clear. You just lay still. Help'll be here soon." Bascom removed his jacket. Folding it, he placed it under Abner's head.

"Can you see my dinner bucket?"

"What's left of it."

"See if they's any pie, will you?"

Bascom opened the lid and unwrapped a wedge-shaped linen. "Looks like Eloise packed rhubarb again."

"Want some?"

"No thanks. Ain't too hungry."

"Mind giving it here, then?"

"Thought you hated rhubarb pie?"

"I do. But I figure the disagreeable taste might take my mind off our predicament."

"Here you go." Bascom extended the pie. Without warning, another section of roof gave way in a deafening roar. Bascom threw himself across Abner.

✹✹✹

"Bascom? Can you hear me, son?" Muffled voices and faint thumping filled the room.

"That you, Pa?"

"Are you hurt, son?"

Bascom's head throbbed. He rubbed a knot on the back of his scalp and shook debris from his back. "Don't think so. But Abner's hurt real bad. Get the doctor."

"We's working to clear the tunnel. Gonna take us a while, but don't you worry."

"Abner? Can you hear me?"

"'Course I can hear you," Abner grunted. "You're lying on top of me."

Bascom rolled off.

"You get plunked on the head or something? Beginning to think I'd lost you for a minute." Abner's voice was weak.

"I'm all right. Got a pump knot's, all."

"How about you?"

"Been better."

"Tell them to hurry up, Pa."

"You mind setting me up? I'm getting tired of staring straight up at this widow maker."

"Course." Bascom lifted Abner's head. As Bascom helped Abner upright, Abner gasped; his back tensed.

"Sorry."

"You's fine. Now lean your back against mine. Thanks."

"They's gonna be hell to pay for this."

"What are you talking about, son? Promise me you ain't gonna do nothing stupid."

"I ain't gonna turn my back on this. You told the pit boss things wasn't safe down here and he didn't do nothing."

"You start agitating and they'll run you out of here. Or worse."

"I don't give a damn."

"That's what your uncle thought. Didn't turn out so good for him."

"I ain't my uncle."

"No, but you're starting to sound an awful lot like him." Abner tensed. "Lay me back down."

Bascom lowered Abner to his lap. "Why don't you stop yapping and take it easy?"

Voices on the other side of the cave-in grew stronger.

A rescuer yelled, "Almost there, Bascom."

"Hear that, Abner?"

"Will you do me a favor?"

"'Course, I will."

"Tell Eloise I didn't suffer none. Tell her she was on my mind 'til the end."

"Stop talking nonsense. We's walking out of here together."

"Promise me." Abner's head slumped.

"Abner? Abner?" Bascom cupped Abner's face.

Pa climbed over a breach in the wall to reach Bascom first. The rescue team followed carrying first aid supplies and a couple of stretchers.

"You okay?"

"Tell me he ain't dead." Pa moved aside as the rescue team arrived.

"Where you hurt, son?" The leader of the team knelt beside Bascom.

"Ain't nothing wrong with me. Abner needs tending to."

One of the rescuers placed two fingers on Abner's neck, then shook his head. Bascom leaned against the wall and sobbed.

"Sorry, son." Three rescuers struggled to lift the slate off Abner's leg, revealing a wound that penetrated to the bone. Bascom retched.

"Everybody pukes the first time. Ain't no shame in it. Let's get you on a stretcher."

"I reckon I can walk out."

Pa placed his hand under Bascom's elbow to help him up. A path had been cleared through the rubble. They headed toward the main shaft.

"You change your mind, we'll be behind shortly. Ain't no one going to fault you for being carried out."

"What happened, son?"

"The greedy bastards killed him."

"What are you talking about?"

"I told you them timbers wasn't thick enough and was spaced too far apart."

"Sometimes roofs don't need a reason to collapse."

"He warned the pit boss. Didn't change nothing."

When they reached the portal, a crowd waited on the other side in bright sunshine. Bascom had barely seen the sun in a week, but it didn't ease the pain. Moving through the crowd, men patted him on the back; some clapped. Eloise stood off to the side by herself, as if she knew. Pa relaxed his grip. Bascom moved toward her, afraid to look at her, afraid not to. Covering her mouth, she didn't make a sound.

"I'm so sorry."

Eloise grabbed him around the waist to pull him close. Wrapping her in his arms, she buried her face in the crook of his shoulder.

"He didn't suffer none. Your name was the last word to cross his lips."

"What happened down there?"

Three feet away, the pit boss stood next to the foreman. Their clean clothes reflected the sunlight.

Bascom smashed his fist into the pit boss's face. "Son of a bitch." Before he hit the ground, Bascom pounced. Strong arms tried to pull him off, but Bascom landed blow after blow.

Eloise's soft voice implored, "Stop. You want to honor Abner's memory, you'll stop this right now."

Bascom pulled his last punch. His hands dropped to his side.

"Clem, get your boy out of here now before I have him arrested."

The foreman bent over the pit boss. "Somebody get the Doctor."

Pa helped Bascom to his feet. "Let's go home, son."

Chapter 16

September 20, 1911

Paint Lick Mine | Mingo County, West Virginia

The office looked much bigger from the outside. The foreman sat behind a small oak desk. Pa's age, he looked ten years younger. Metal filing cabinets topped with a thick black layer of dust lined the back wall. The only personal item visible, a grainy photo of the foreman with his wife and four kids, sat atop one of the cabinets. Rolled-up mine maps filled every corner. Several lay unfurled across the desk, red grease pencil marking the seams being mined. Bascom strained to identify the tunnel that claimed Abner. A phone sat on the edge of the desk, nearly lost in a sea of papers. Windows were closed in a futile effort to keep out the coal dust.

Standing next to Bascom, Pa cleared his throat. "How's Tate?"

"Still in the hospital over in Williamson. Broke his nose and cheekbone, lost a couple of teeth."

"We're sorry to hear that." Pa turned to Bascom. "Ain't we?"

Seventy-five yards away, an idling train sat under the tipple. Coal rushed through the chute into an empty car, clanging against the sides like marbles filling a coffee tin. The train belched steam and inched forward as the process repeated.

"Ain't we?"

"That's right. Didn't intend to put him in the hospital."

"Well, you did, and now we have to decide what to do about it."

"What about what he done to Abner?"

"Don't get me wrong, son. I'm real sorry about Abner. We all are. I know you think it was Tate's fault, but mining is dangerous work. Plain and simple. Nobody knew that better than Abner. The fact there was an accident don't make it Tate's fault."

"I reckon Tate didn't tell you that Abner pointed out them roofing timbers was an accident waiting to happen."

"After the beating you put on him yesterday, Tate didn't come to until late last night. I haven't had the chance to discuss it with him. But I will."

"Good."

"You know how many men I got working for me here?"

"Not exactly."

"Two hundred fifty, not counting the men running the tipple." He nodded toward the window. "You know how many complaints we get every day about this or that problem?"

"No."

"About two hundred and fifty. Point is, we do the best we can with what we got to run a safe operation. It don't benefit nobody to lose a man. Results in down time and a drop in morale. Just the same, every time there's an accident, folks are eager to point out that more could've been done. Truth of the matter is, sometimes accidents just happen."

"Tell that to Eloise."

"Son, the only reason we're even having this discussion is 'cause your daddy and me go way back. I'm doing this for him, not you."

"And I sure appreciate that, Ben."

"I'm trying to keep you out of jail, which is where Tate's family thinks you ought to be. I'm trying to figure out a way we can satisfy them short of involving the law. Do you understand?"

"I reckon."

"Good. Tell you what I'm going to do. You can keep your job, provided you pay off Tate's medical bills, plus fifty dollars. We'll dock half your pay each month 'til it's paid off. The harder you work, the quicker it'll be done."

"But..."

"There ain't no buts. That's the deal. Take it or leave it. Don't much matter to me."

Pa shook the foreman's hand. "We'll take it. Much obliged."

"One more thing. You'll be working with your Pa's crew. Clem, I expect you to make sure he don't step out of line no more."

"Don't worry."

Bascom hurried from the office, put on his cap and trotted down the steps. The train left the siding and headed to market. Tipple workers shoveled spillage into an empty car. When they filled it, they would hook it to the next train and pull an empty car to start all over again. As Bascom reached the ground, the tipple operator leaned on his shovel to tip his cap. The two-man crew followed suit. Breathing heavily, Pa eased down the steep stairs.

"Appreciate your support back there."

"You should be grateful, son. He just kept you out of jail."

"For what?"

"Almost killing a man."

"At least I almost killed a man what deserved it."

Pa's backhand caught him by surprise. "You listen good. Abner's gone. And it don't matter if you's right, 'cause they make the rules. So long as you work here, you will do as they say. Understand?" Mindful of the eyes still on him, Bascom resisted the urge to rub his cheek. "Do you understand?"

"I understand. But let me tell you one thing. As soon as I pay off this debt, I'm done with the mines. I'd leave right now except I know these bastards would take the money out of your paycheck."

"And what do you think you're going to do?"

"Hell if I know, but one thing's for certain. They ain't going to get the chance to work me to the bone 'til I ain't no more use, then turn me out so the bottle can finish the job."

Pa's jaw clenched. Regretting the rebuke, Bascom braced for another backhand.

"You better get to work. You're already an hour behind."

Chapter 17

March 15, 1912

Mingo County, West Virginia

Bascom placed Ma's dog-eared dictionary on the table. Moonlight filtered through the window. Beans simmered while cornbread browned on the stove. Pa's hunched figure in his rocker cast a long shadow on the rough-hewn wall.

"Why's Grace writing you?"

"I sent her a letter asking if it'd be okay if I took her up on her invite to come to Richmond for a visit."

"You really gonna quit, then?"

"Done worked off my debt and have a little extra to boot. Plan to tell the foreman first thing in the morning and collect my pay."

"How you plan on getting to Richmond?"

Bascom stirred the beans and poured another cup of coffee. "Train."

"What're you gonna do once you get there?"

"Ain't figured that part out."

"Maybe Walker can get you on with the railroad."

"Or maybe I can finish my schooling."

"You be sure to earn your keep. Don't want Ma's kin thinking I've raised no freeloader."

"I ain't never took a handout. Don't intend to start now. I just want to see Durwood and try to get a fresh start. Far away from here."

"What's she say?"

"Hold your horses."

Bascom moved the candle close. He teased open a corner of the envelope; a hint of Miss Grace's perfume escaped. When Durwood left home, Bascom had labored to read Miss Grace's elegant cursive. While he no longer struggled to make out the words, their meanings sometimes eluded him.

"She says they would be delighted for me to visit."

"Bet your brother is tickled."

"They ain't sharing the news with Durwood until my arrival is imminent." Bascom reached for the dictionary.

"How's your brother?'

"Doing good. Continues to get high marks in school."

"At least one of you is acting like you got some sense."

"Says he misses us, as always." Durwood had spent a third of his life in Richmond now. He was so young when he left, Bascom wondered how much of home Durwood remembered. Though their correspondence was infrequent, Bascom tried to write about things to help his little brother remember home: Blue, Pa, holidays, the mine.

"What else she got to say?"

"Got a room ready for me."

"Sounds like you's set, then."

"Who's going to fix you supper when I'm gone?"

"Reckon I will."

"Think you can manage?"

"You been doing it. How hard can it be?"

Bascom sipped his coffee. "Why don't you come with me? You could see Durwood."

"Who'd look after this place?"

"Nobody's saying you'd be staying. I'm just talking about going for a visit. It would do you some good to get out of these mountains for a spell. Besides, it would mean a lot to Durwood."

"And what about my job?"

"Your buddy would hire you back on."

"And what if he don't?"

"You know good as I do you can't hardly spit without hitting a mine around these parts. Somebody's always hiring, even if Paint Lick don't take you back. Fact that you speak English gives you a leg up."

Cradling his jug, Pa stopped rocking and stared into the fire.

"Sleep on it. You ain't got to decide now."

"Reckon I best stay here. Your Ma wouldn't forgive me if I let this place go to seed after all the hard work she put in to make it our home. Besides, her birthday's coming up. If we's both gone, who's gonna take her and Georgie their flowers?"

Bascom set the pot of beans and iron skillet brimming with cornbread on the table. He laid out two plates and forks and filled the tin cups with coffee. "Let's eat."

Chapter 18

March 16, 1912

Paint Lick Coal Camp | Mingo County, West Virginia

"Here you go. Ten, Twenty, Thirty, Forty-Five and fifty cents." The paymaster slapped the thin, yellow bills bearing the Paint Lick logo on the counter, topping the stack with a tin token.

"Wait a minute. This here's scrip. Can't use it at the general store over in Matewan."

"No. But last I checked it works just fine at the company store down the road."

"They ain't got what I need."

"Now that ain't my problem, is it?" The paymaster pushed the currency toward the edge of the counter.

"I thought when a man took his leave he was to be paid in cash."

"Just following orders."

"Whose orders?"

"Pit boss. Sent word down here to say you'd quit and that you was to be paid in scrip."

Bascom scraped the bills and token into his hand and left the office, slamming the door. Blackened snow piles lined the edges of the mud-covered road. Off to one side, a stream of meltwater ran dark downhill toward camp before it flowed into Lick Creek. A smaller stream on the other side of the road flowed into a ditch that ran in front of the first row of identical, slapdash company houses, three deep above the road.

His plan to buy fancy new clothes for the trip at the Matewan general store had been derailed. The company store only carried over-priced work clothes. His white dress shirt was a couple of years old and hugged tight, but he could make do. With his scrip, he could pick up a new pair of overalls and boots, which would be better than what he had on. At least he could buy some hardtack and jerky for the trip and some licorice whips and horehound sticks for Durwood.

"Morning, ma'am." Twenty yards away, a woman knelt on a rock at the edge of the creek washing clothes.

"Halo," she replied in a thick accent. Italian? Maybe Hungarian.

Placing wet clothing on the rock, she spot-scrubbed stains with lye soap, then rubbed the material together to bust the grime. As dirty as the water was from the mine run-off, she was likely washing more stains in than she was getting out. Fish hadn't been seen in the creek since a few years after the mine opened when Pa was a boy. Besides rainwater people collected in barrels, the creek provided the camp's only source of water. Folks had to boil it to bathe and cook. Before drinking, they strained it through cheesecloth. Even then, it was impossible to take a drink without chewing grit. Things must be awfully bad where they come from to make them cross the ocean to settle here.

Near the end of town, Bascom climbed the steps to the company store. Unlike the small, single story, company-owned houses, the store, which doubled as the post office, had two floors and a fresh coat of paint. Reaching the door, he scraped the mud off each boot with the opposite foot. For good measure, before entering he whisked the boots and hem of his pants with a broom leaning beside the door.

"Morning, sir." The store was empty except for a couple of women making groceries. Picks, shovels and assorted hand tools hung from one wall. Mining caps and leather work gloves lined a table; shiny dinner buckets crowded beneath the table. Bascom recalled the excitement when Pa brought him to get outfitted before his first day of work, four years before, and how fast it left him when he learned how long it would take to pay off the privilege of toiling in the dark six days a week.

"Morning, Bascom. Haven't seen you in a while."

"No, sir."

"How come you aren't working? Everything okay?"

"Better than okay. Gave my notice this morning."

"Got big plans?"

"Headed to Richmond to see my brother. Hoping you can fix me up with some new clothes for the trip."

"What did you have in mind?"

"I need me some pants that look like they was made for something besides the pit."

Behind the counter, half the shelves contained trousers; the other half shirts. A ladder on rollers angled to the floor. The clerk slid the ladder toward the middle before climbing to rifle through a stack of pants. Unfurling a pair, coal dust dispersed as he patted the fabric. "How about these? They look like they should fit."

"Let me have a look."

The clerk descended to hand the dungarees to Bascom.

"I reckon they'll do. Sight better than what I got on."

"What else you need?"

"Pair of boots."

"Right over here." Cardboard boxes stacked eight feet high occupied one corner of the store. "What size?"

"These are tens, but my toes is a bit cramped."

The clerk handed Bascom a pair of brown, leather boots. "Try on these elevens."

Bascom sat. He tugged off his boots, slid on the new pair and took a few steps. "Feel good. I'll take 'em."

"Anything else?"

"How much does Pa owe you?"

"Let's see." From behind the counter he pulled a ledger to add some figures. "Four-fifty."

"I'd like to pay that off. And some hardtack and jerky for the train."

The clerk retrieved a tin of biscuits from under the counter. "The jerky is over there in the jar by the door. Get what you need."

Bascom reached into the jar for a handful of jerky.

"Is that it?"

"Just about. Need some licorice and horehound for my brother."

"That's on the house. Don't tell anyone."

Bascom glanced at the women who were inspecting a bolt of cloth.

The clerk shook his head. "They ain't got the foggiest notion what we're saying."

The bell over the front door clanged. Two Baldwin-Felts agents in suits, string ties and bowlers entered tracking mud. Both wore sidearms; one shouldered a shotgun. They had been hanging around the paymaster's office when Bascom cashed out. He figured they were hired to guard the payroll.

"I'll be with you gentlemen in a minute."

"Why if it ain't Gentleman Jim Corbett himself," the man carrying the shotgun said as he stepped toward Bascom. Several inches taller, his barrel chest strained the buttons of his vest.

Bascom stepped around the agent to set his purchases on the counter. "What do I owe you?"

"Ain't you going to speak to us, Gentleman Jim?"

"You must be mistaken. My name's Matney. I don't know no Jim Corbett."

"You hear that? He don't know the former heavyweight champ. You need to get out from under that rock you've been hiding under, boy. That's okay, we know who you are. I hear you're quite the pugilist. How about you and me go a few rounds?"

"I'm just here to pick up a few things, then I'll be on my way."

Bascom laid the scrip on the table. Before the clerk could take it, the agent slammed his hand on the currency.

"Looks like we have a problem. Your privileges at this establishment ended the minute you quit the mine. I'm sure they'd love to have your business over in Matewan."

"I'd be happy to, except all I got to spend is company scrip."

"Sounds to me like you should have asked to be paid in cash when you quit."

"I did. Paymaster said the pit boss told him to pay me in scrip."

"That's not the way I heard it. I distinctly remember you demanding scrip."

Bascom placed the dungarees and jerky on the counter to turn and face the agents. "Leave me be."

The agents pressed close. "Boy, this is going to end one of two ways. Either you're going to walk out that door right now, or we're going to throw you out. Your choice."

The women dropped the cloth and hurried out the door. Bascom tensed and clenched his fists. He might be able to take one of them, but not both. If he couldn't spend the scrip here, what was he going to do?

"Gentlemen, I don't want any trouble. Bascom, do as they ask and leave."

Bascom glared at the man holding his scrip.

"I ain't leaving without my money."

"Suit yourself. Lot of good it's going to do you." The agent swept the bills into the floor. "There you go."

Bascom bent over to grab the money. He brushed by the agents. Laughter followed him out the door.

✳✳✳

Bascom started a fire to warm the house before Pa arrived. Sneaking a pour from the jug, he filled his tin cup and walked onto the porch. The sun had set, but it would be a while before Pa arrived. Each day took him a few minutes longer.

Bascom sat on the steps and pulled his collar close. Blue nudged his arm. "Gonna miss you, boy." Although spring was around the corner, patches of snow lingered. Eager to leave, Bascom wished he could see the mountain burst into bloom one more time. Bascom sipped the mash, which warmed as it went down, but tasted as bad as the first time. How did Pa drink this stuff? Pa's light grew close. Bascom tossed the mash on the ground.

Reaching the porch, Pa caught his breath. Bascom slid over. "Have a seat."

"Ready for your trip?"

"Not hardly."

"Why's that?"

"Pit boss screwed me."

"He didn't pay you your wages?"

"He paid me. In scrip."

"That ain't right."

"That ain't the half of it. When I went to the company store to buy what I could, them Baldwin-Felts sons of bitches told me I wasn't allowed in there no more, seeing as I'd quit the company. If I hadn't left they was gonna throw me out."

Pa stood to enter the house. He returned with his jug. "How much they pay you?"

"Forty-five fifty."

"That what they owed you?"

"They owed me a lot more, the way I figure it. But that's all they was obliged to pay."

"Here." Pa counted off a series of bills. "Fifty. Give me the scrip."

"That ain't fair to you and you know it. Fifty dollars is worth a hell of a lot more than fifty in scrip."

"Course it is, but I can get most all I need at the company store and still have some left over. Besides, what else am I going to use this money for?"

"That, for one." Bascom nodded at the jug.

"I get a discount for volume." Pa smiled through tobacco-stained teeth. "You go into Matewan tomorrow and get what you need. Should be plenty left over for a train ticket."

"I figure on hopping a rail car to save some money."

"Don't be a fool. Take the money."

"Pa, I can't."

"Course you can."

"I'll pay you back."

"It ain't meant to be a loan."

Chapter 19

March 18, 1912

Richmond, Virginia

Sunlight filtered through cracks in the rail car. "Richmond's next. That's where you was headed, right?"

Bascom sat up. "That's right."

Two men in soiled clothes huddled on the floor atop a bed of straw. Legs outstretched and heads covered by denim caps, they hadn't budged for hours. Eager to leave the train and the smell of filth and urine, Bascom steadied himself as the slowing train rocked. He was eager to see Durwood. Would he recognize him? "Appreciate you all letting me share your car."

"We're obliged for the food. Wish you luck finding your brother."

Bascom opened his pack to remove his cinched bandana. Unwrapping his kerchief, he handed over three slices of stale bread, two pieces of jerky. "Now that we's in Richmond, don't reckon' I'll be needing these. You fellows mind helping me lighten my load?"

The larger man took the food. "Anything to help a fellow traveler." He broke a small corner from one of the pieces of bread, then lifted the flap of his breast pocket. Whiskers preceded a small, black nose and probing mouth which snatched the morsel. "One more thing you need to know about riding the rails."

"What's that?"

"Don't be in a hurry. When the train pulls into the freight yard, they'll be lots of activity. Checking cargo. Uncoupling cars. They'll be watching for rail riders trying to sneak off. If they catch you, they'll throw you in jail. You need to wait 'til it turns dark to hop off, so you might as well settle down a few more hours."

Bascom slid down the wall onto his heels. He had hoped to find Miss Grace's home during daylight; he didn't want to arrive unannounced after dark. Where would he sleep? He'd figure that out later; maybe his companions could help. This must have been how Moses felt after finally glimpsing the Promised Land, knowing he couldn't enter.

"Lucky for you we got us some food if you get hungry before taking your leave." Next to him, the quiet man's lips pursed and his closed eyes creased. Was that a smile?

Bascom tottered to the corner to unbutton his fly. Urine trickled down the wall. The train groaned to a halt as Bascom returned to his spot. Muffled voices drifted into the car.

"Nothing to worry about," the man whispered, "so long as they ain't checking all the cars. Try to keep quiet like Jake here until nightfall."

Nobody could keep quiet like Jake. Since Bascom joined the pair in Roanoke, Jake hadn't so much as broken wind.

"Check these cars." The door of a nearby car slid open.

"Looks like luck ain't on our side today. Get ready to run, boy. Soon as that door opens, you hit the ground running." The older men didn't budge except to stuff food into their mouths. Bascom regretted not taking Pa's advice to buy a ticket.

"What about you all?"

"Afraid our days of jumping from trains is over. You're young. Get the drop on them and you might stand a chance. Run along the fence until you find a break. Squeeze through and keep running 'til you ain't being chased."

The door of the car in front slid open. "Empty." Gravel crunched outside their car. Bascom looped his arms through his pack and crouched in front of the door, ready to spring. As the door cracked, sunlight blitzed the car. Momentarily blinded, he could only see the outlines of four men. Was that a gun? Ready to leap, he froze as a shotgun pumped a round into the chamber.

"Jackpot! Come out with your hands up." Four men in blue uniforms and caps waited. One pointed a shotgun. The others rapped billy clubs in their palms.

Bascom knelt, placed his hand on the floor of the car and turned sideways to push off. As soon as he landed, he was grabbed and forced to the ground on his stomach. "Check his pack." One of the officers ripped the pack off his back. A boot pressed against his neck while handcuffs clicked into place. Gravel bit into his cheek.

The two men climbed down from the car, still chewing.

"Well, look who it is. Thought you two would've learnt your lesson by now. Who's your new friend?" The man with the gun was in charge. "Get him up." Bascom's shoulders burned as the guards jerked him up by the cuffs.

"Go easy on the boy. Only thing he's guilty of is wanting to see his little brother. They been apart four years now. Traveled all the way from West Virginia."

"Well, ain't that sweet."

"He's right." Bascom took a step.

"Did I say something to you, boy?" The officer pointed the shotgun.

"I was just fixing to tell you I ain't trying to cause no trouble."

"Shut him up, will you?" A billy club crashed into Bascom's forehead.

❋❋❋

Cold water splashed his face. Bascom sputtered. "Can you hear me?" A firm hand gripped shook his shoulder. "Wake up, boy."

Bascom fluttered his eyes to focus. Sitting up, he swung his legs off a bench. His head throbbed. His pack sat on the bench next to him. Two officers stood over him. One held a bucket, the other an envelope. Several other police officers milled about the whitewashed office. Radiators popped and hissed. Bascom placed his head in his hands.

"Where'd you get this?" the one holding the envelope asked.

"What is it?"

"Envelope you had in your pocket. Where did you get it?"

Bascom patted his breast pockets. He focused on the man's silver badge and name tag: Captain Miller, Richmond City Police.

"It was sent to me."

"Your name Bascom Matney?"

"That's right."

"Who sent it to you?"

"What's it say on the envelope?"

"Don't get smart with me, boy."

"Miss Grace Hopkins sent it to me, like it says."

"How do you know her?"

"If you'd done read the letter, you'd know I was on my way to pay my brother a visit. He's been living with the Hopkins."

"Why is he staying with them?"

"Miss Grace was cousins to our Ma. When Ma died, the Hopkins took Durwood in. Ain't seen him since '08."

"How about Mr. Hopkins. Know him too?"

"Met him once."

"I suppose he knows you're coming."

"I reckon. You got my money?"

"What money?"

"That envelope you's holding in your hands had forty dollars cash in it."

"There's no money in here. We'll have to check your paperwork, but I don't recall seeing anything about railroad security finding money on you." The captain nodded at the deputy, who put down the bucket. Pushing past a swinging gate, he disappeared on the other side of a large wooden desk.

"You know it's against the law to hop a train? Punishable by a year in jail?"

"Didn't see no harm in it. Railroad wasn't using the car."

"That isn't the point. If you had forty dollars on you, why didn't you just buy a ticket?" The second cop returned. He handed a folder to the captain, who thumbed the file. "Inventory says one envelope with letter, a pack with a slingshot and the clothes on your back. No money."

"Well, that's a lie." Bascom peered inside the pack and removed Durwood's slingshot. "Besides this, had a buck knife and a clean shirt."

"Are you saying railroad police stole from you, then lied to cover it up?"

"I ain't in the policing business like you, but that's the way it looks to me."

"Well, we'll see."

"Where are those fellows what was with me on the train?"

"Behind bars, where you're going to wind up if your story doesn't check out. I'll be back shortly. How's your head?"

Bascom rubbed a knot in the center of his forehead. "Hurts."

"Must have been some fall."

"Fall?"

"Report says you tried to jump from the car and landed on your head."

"That proves it."

"Proves what?"

"They's lying. I ain't never fell. Standing up with my hands hogtied behind me when I got bashed in the head with a billy club."

"Son, if you aren't telling the truth, you're just digging yourself in deeper. Do yourself a favor while I'm gone and don't go telling anybody else that the railroad police hit you in the head so they could rob you. Keep an eye on him." The captain left the room.

"Got any water?"

The officer looked at the empty bucket. "That wasn't enough for you?"'

Bascom shook his head. "To drink."

"Someone bring us a cup of water over here."

"What's going to happen to those other men?"

"Fined fifteen dollars each."

"What if they can't pay?"

"They'll spend a year in jail. This is the third time we've caught them free-loading. Judge won't have any patience this time."

"Here you go." An officer offered a cup.

"Thanks." Bascom tossed back the water.

Bascom laid his head against the wall, hoping to ease the throbbing. How would he get word to Miss Grace that he was in jail? What was he going to do without his savings?

***

Bascom woke to voices; a group of men stood before him. The Captain and the deputy who'd been sitting with him were joined by two of the railroad security detail who arrested him and a tall man with a cropped mustache in a three piece suit. An overcoat draped over his arm.

114

"That him?"

"Bascom?"

"Hello, Mr. Walker."

"Don't know that I would have recognized you."

"I'm mighty glad to see you, sir."

"Are you okay?"

"I'll be fine soon as the drum in my head lets up."

"The officers tell me you were caught riding a freight car. Is that true?"

"Yes, sir."

"You know that's against the law?"

"They done filled me in."

"How much is the fine?" Walker opened his wallet.

"Normally, five dollars first offense. But seeing he is who he says he is, we won't be pressing charges."

"Thank you, officer. Bascom, let's go." Bascom stood. He faced the Captain.

"How about if I want to press charges?" Everyone stared at him.

The Captain cocked his head. "How's that, son?"

Bascom pointed at the railroad officers. "Them two beat me for no reason, then stole my money and belongings."

One of the railroad officers stepped forward. "About that. When we heard you were missing some money, we went back to check the freight car you stowed away in. Found your money and shirt. Must have fallen out of your pack before you jumped. Here you go." The officer held out several bills in one hand, shirt in the other.

"Thank you, officers. We appreciate your diligence." Walker shook their hands.

Bascom thumbed the money. "They's only thirty dollars here. Where's the rest?"

"Rest? That was all we found. You sure those bums didn't steal it while you were sleeping?"

"I'm shore. Wish I could say the same about you." Bascom took the shirt and stuffed it in his pack. "Sorry I ain't your size. Don't suppose you found my buck knife neither?"

"Can't say we did." The railroad officer shrugged. "Mr. Hopkins, we're sorry for arresting Mr. Matney. If we'd had any notion he was an acquaintance of yours, we would have called you straight away."

"There's no need to apologize for doing your jobs." Walker tapped Bascom on the shoulder and headed for the door. "Let's go, Bascom, before Captain Miller changes his mind."

Bascom turned to the deputy. "How much you say the fine was for them other two fellows?"

"Thirty dollars."

"It gets paid and they go free, right?"

Walker released the doorknob. The assistant looked to the Captain, who shook his head. "That's right."

Here you go, then. Thirty even." Bascom handed the money to Captain Miller. "I'd like a receipt."

The Captain nodded at the deputy, who produced a pad from his pocket. He scribbled a receipt.

Walker moved away from the door. "Think about what you're doing."

The assistant ripped the paper from the pad.

Bascom grabbed the receipt. "Ain't nothing to think about."

He opened the door to leave. Walker followed down the steps to the street. Light from a nearby gas lamp cast the sidewalk in a soft glow. A stiff wind blew in their faces. Walker slipped into his overcoat.

"Why didn't you believe me back there?"

"What makes you think I didn't?"

"Then why didn't you say so?"

"What good would it have done? Your word against that of two sworn railroad law enforcement officers and you'd just been caught hiding in a freight car. It wasn't going to change things."

"What about standing up for what's right?"

"You're young. You have to learn to pick your battles."

"You sound like my Pa talking."

"Take those two hobos you just bailed out."

"What about 'em?

"You just threw away all the money you had to get them out of jail. You think they're going to change?"

"I don't know."

"Well, I do. They're criminals."

"Way I see it, only thing they's guilty of is not having two nickels to rub together."

"When you get to be my age, you'll understand."

"Afraid I ain't got that luxury."

"What do you mean?"

"Waiting until I might feel different about things."

"Tell you what. There's been enough excitement for one day. Let's go home and get you settled."

"Sounds good. Sir?"

"Yes."

"Sorry for the trouble I caused. This ain't how I planned it."

"The important thing is you made it. Durwood is going to be so excited to have his big brother around."

"How is he?"

"Growing like a weed."

"Been looking forward to this day."

"I hope you can wait one more day."

"Why's that?"

"Durwood's in bed. He has school in the morning. Will you do me a favor?"

"What's that?"

"Don't tell him you got arrested."

"Wasn't planning on it."

"Good. Let's go home."

✳✳✳

"Here we are."

Walker cut the motor. The house lay dark except for a light over the front door and a bright moon. He'd heard tales of mansions in Charleston and Bramwell, but couldn't imagine they were grander than this home, which paled in comparison to several he'd spotted on the drive. He followed Walker up the front steps.

"After you." Walker pushed open the door. Stepping inside behind Bascom, Walker threw a switch to light the cavernous hallway.

Bascom let out a soft whistle.

"You hungry?"

"I reckon I can wait 'til morning."

"Come on. I could use a snack. Let's see what we can find."

A plate of cookies sat on the kitchen counter under butcher paper. "You like oatmeal?"

"I reckon."

"Nothing better at bedtime than Hattie's oatmeal cookies with milk." Durwood had written of Hattie's good food.

Walker removed two plates from the cabinet. "Will you get the milk?"

Bascom scanned the kitchen. "Where's the pitcher at?"

"Ice box."

Ice box. Bascom didn't know what to look for. The kitchen was nearly the size of his house. He hardly recognized a thing besides the pots and pans hanging from the ceiling. He reached for a handle and pulled.

"That's the electric oven. Over there." Walker pointed to the wooden cabinet with brass fixtures that stood four feet tall. Bascom lifted a latch to open the door. A blast of cool air greeted him. Removing a pitcher, he joined Walker at a small table. Bascom filled the glasses.

"You all eat in shifts around here?"

"We eat in the dining room through that door. This is where Hattie takes her meals." Bascom sipped. The milk tasted as fresh as if it had come straight from the cow, except it was cold. Walker dunked his cookie before taking a bite. Bascom followed suit. "You ever had a better oatmeal cookie?"

"Can't say as I have."

"Didn't I tell you? A word of warning, though. Don't let Grace catch you dunking your cookies at the dinner table."

"Why's that?"

"It isn't proper etiquette." Bascom wished he'd packed Ma's dictionary. Walker dunked the last bit of cookie. "Ask Durwood. The only time we partake of this heathen ritual is after Grace has retired. Our little secret. Now you're in on it. Finished?" Bascom stabbed the few remaining crumbs, licked his finger and chased it with the last sip.

"Am now. What do you want me to do with these?"

"Nothing. Hattie will take care of them in the morning. How's your head?"

"Better. How's it looking?"

"Like you got bashed in the head. Need a powder?"

"I reckon a good night's sleep is all I need."

"Okay. Let me show you to your room."

Walker led the way up the back steps. At the top, Walker whispered,

"This is your room." Walker turned on the light. A bed was flanked by a chest and a dresser with an attached mirror. A desk and chair faced a lace-curtained window. The four-poster bed dwarfed his bed at home. "Second door on the left down the hall is the bathroom. Need anything else?" Bascom couldn't imagine ever needing a thing in this house.

"Can't think of nothing. Thank you for everything, sir."

"You're welcome. See you in the morning. Going to be tough to get Durwood to school once he sees you're here."

Bascom sat on the edge of the bed to unlace his boots. Lying back, he stared at the ceiling which was divided into squares by thin, wooden panels. He checked his pocket watch: 9:30. Had Pa gotten himself to bed or was he spending nights in his rocker? Was he getting enough to eat? Leaving home was selfish. He should have stayed to look after Pa, figured out something besides mining coal. Lost in thought, Bascom caught a whiff, a raw smell that reminded him he had spent two days in dirty freight cars. He hopped off the bed. Checking the white cotton spread for dirt, he lightly brushed it to remove a few pieces of straw. Where were his companions spending the night? Wherever it was, one thing was for sure—they weren't staying in splendor like this. But, they weren't in jail, either.

Bascom crept down the hallway to the bathroom. He punched a button on the wall like he'd seen Walker do. A light over the sink blazed. He slid the suspenders off his shoulders to remove his shirt, unbuttoned his woolen top, slipped his arms out and let it fall to his waist. Turning on the spigot, Bascom moistened a washcloth and grabbed a bar of soap from a dish. Softer than Ma's gritty lye soap, it smelled like spring. He washed the grit off his face and upper body. Drying quickly, he slipped into his top, shut off the light and returned to his bedroom, eager for the soft bed.

Chapter 20

March 19, 1912

Richmond, Virginia

Bascom's room lay dark except for a thin light from a street lamp between the curtains. He opened the door; faint noises drifted up the back stairs. He slipped his new flannel shirt over his head and buttoned the plackets. He stepped into his pants and laced his boots. Tiptoeing to the bathroom, Bascom listened outside the bedroom door next to his. Was Durwood in there? He grasped the knob. After the trouble he caused last night, he couldn't afford to sneak into the wrong room. He'd waited four years. A few more hours wouldn't kill him.

Bascom shut the bathroom door, turned on the light and faced the mirror. The pump knot had gone down but a swath of purple covered the middle of his forehead. He combed his hair but his short bangs offered little cover. After relieving himself, he pulled the chain. Water thundered from the bowl. Durwood had been right—bringing the outhouse inside was a great idea.

Bascom eased down the back steps. Reaching the bottom, he pushed open the kitchen door. A short, woman in a white apron and bonnet busied herself over the stove. "Durwood, honey, what are you doing up so early?"

"It ain't Durwood. I'm Bascom."

Hattie dropped her ladle and spun around. "Lord, God, child. You trying to give me a fright?"

"No, ma'am."

"Why, you aren't ten feet tall. To hear the way Durwood carries on about you I was expecting a giant. Come here. Let me have a look at you. What in God's name happened to you?"

"On the way here, train braked sudden for a cow. Only one more surprised than the cow was me."

"You need some petroleum jelly on that bruise. Does it hurt?

"Not no more."

"Sit here." Hattie rummaged in the cabinet under the sink. "Here we are. Drop your chin a bit." She dabbed salve on his bruise. "You took quite a wallop."

"Shore did."

"I heard talk you were coming to visit, but I didn't realize it would be so soon. Durwood know you're here?"

"No, ma'am."

"You don't need to say ma'am to me."

"Why's that?"

"Your brother asked the same question when he arrived. He's adjusted. It's not the way things are done around here."

"What do you mean?"

"I'm colored."

"Ain't proper etiquette?"

"That's right."

"Where I come from, manners is manners."

"I don't know how things are done in West Virginia, but you're in Richmond. Don't forget that."

"Don't seem right to me."

"Maybe not, but for my sake, please do as I say. I'll know you'll be thinking it even if you aren't saying it. Deal?"

"Yes, ma'…Deal."

"I better get back to work. The others will be up shortly. Why don't you have a seat in the dining room."

"Anything I can do to help? I done all the cooking for Pa and me."

"The last thing I need is to have some young man show me up in my own kitchen. Then where would I be? Looking for a job is where.

121

I'll have some bacon ready in a few minutes and you can get started on that. Coffee?"

"If it ain't no trouble."

Bascom pushed through the door into the dining room and turned on the light. Sixteen chairs surrounded a large table. How many folks lived here? Durwood never talked about no one besides Miss Grace and Mr. Walker. If it was just the three of them and Hattie ate in the kitchen, why did they need such a large table? A man could grow weary walking from one end to the other. A low-slung, silver bowl full of apples, oranges and bananas sat in the center of the table. Bascom had seen bananas at the general store in Matewan a couple of times, but didn't know anyone who could afford them. He picked one up, breathing in a faint, pleasant aroma. His thumb dug into the soft peel, curious to know what it looked like underneath. Returning the banana, he fingered an orange. Pa had brought oranges home for Christmas dinner once before Georgie passed. Sweetest thing he ever tasted.

Bascom ran his hand across the edge of a long wooden sideboard. Held up by six legs and fronted with two rows of four drawers each, its dark wooden border was offset by a lighter wood that matched the table. Four silver candlesticks occupied one corner; a mirrored, silver platter with handles that rose from its base the other. A clear glass bottle half-full of a deep red liquid sat in the middle of the platter, surrounded by six glasses etched with the letter "H." A silver label with "Port" engraved on it hung from a chain around the bottle's neck. Bascom removed the glass-topped cork to sniff. Earthier and less harsh than Pa's mash.

"Do you like wine?"

Bascom fumbled the stopper before seating it in the bottle. "Miss Grace. Uh, no ma'am. Well, truth is I ain't never had no wine before."

"You'll have to try some port with dinner."

"I've tried Pa's mash, but it's a taste I ain't acquired."

"What does mash taste like?"

"Turpentine with lye added for flavoring."

"Sounds dreadful."

"Pa don't think so."

"I think you'll find port more agreeable."

Grace was shorter than he remembered. And prettier, even in a robe. "We've been praying for this day for years. Do you mind if I give you a hug?"

"No, ma'am."

Bascom closed his eyes for his first embrace by a woman since Eloise hugged him the day Abner died. Grace's touch was lighter than Ma's, with none of the desperation of Eloise's clutch.

Relaxing her grip, Grace held his arms as she looked into his face. "I see Hattie has already applied her healing touch."

"Yes, ma'am."

"I'm sorry about your introduction to Richmond."

"Makes two of us. I ain't mean to cause embarrassment and inconvenience to you and Mr. Walker."

"Nonsense. I just wish you had let us know you were coming. We could have sent a ticket."

"Couldn't let you do that, ma'am. As it is, me and Pa can never repay you for what you's done for Durwood."

"Nonsense. We're the ones who have benefitted. He's brought much joy to our lives."

Hattie entered carrying a platter and a cup of coffee. "Bacon?" Bascom grabbed a slice from the platter and swallowed it whole. Hattie's eyes widened.

"Sit here." Grace motioned to a chair. "Durwood will be down soon. I can't wait to see his reaction."

Bascom sucked his fingers and wiped them on his pants before pulling out the chair. "Ain't never had nothing taste so good, Hattie. Durwood wrote you was the best cook in Richmond. Now I can see he won't pulling my leg."

"Thank you, Mr. Bascom." Mr. Bascom? Hattie winked.

"Hattie spoils us all."

Hattie placed a cup on the table and put a couple more slices on Bascom's plate. "Ma'am?"

"Not just now, Hattie. But I will take some coffee. You can leave the platter in case Bascom would like more."

"Yes, ma'am."

"How's your father?"

"He's managing. At least he was before I up and left him."

"And you?"

"Doing fine, I reckon. How's Durwood getting along?"

"He's doing very well. It took him a while to adjust to life with us. He kept thinking your father would send for him. Once he realized that wasn't imminent, he settled into a routine here. He's a top student, you know. And he's proving to be quite a sportsman. Walker has been teaching him golf and tennis at the club."

"Ain't never doubted he'd do good at anything he set his mind to. Takes after Ma."

"And you? Whom do you favor?"

"Pa, I reckon."

"When do you have to return to work?"

"Quit the mines. Ain't going back."

"So you've come to live with us, then?"

"Not exactly. Ain't here to impose on your kindness."

"Nonsense. You're family."

"That's mighty nice of you. But I only plan to visit a spell."

"Then what?"

"Find work. Continue my schooling."

"What kind of work?"

"Not sure. Only thing I know is digging coal. But I ain't afraid of hard work. Figure they must be something I can do above ground."

"Does Walker know about this?"

"No, ma'am. We was a little caught up in the goings on of last night. We never got around to discussing my plans."

"Talk to Walker. I'm sure he'll be able to help you find work. In the meantime, you're our guest and I'm going to make certain you enjoy your visit."

"Much obliged."

"Good morning, Aunt Grace." Durwood entered the dining room carrying several books lashed together under his arm.

Aunt Grace? Had he taken to calling Walker uncle? Nearly a foot taller than when he left home, Durwood dressed like a little gentleman— brown tweed coat buttoned over a white shirt and tie, and matching knickers with black leggings and ankle-high boots. He parted his dark, oiled hair slightly off center. Before he left home, a comb would've sacrificed several tines in the struggle to make a pass through his mane.

Bascom pushed back his chair to stand. Durwood froze. Slack-jawed, breathing neither in nor out.

"Durwood, do you see who's come to visit you?"

Dropping his books, Durwood leaped into Bascom's arms. He buried his face in Bascom's chest to hide his tears. Hardly a day had passed in the previous four years that Bascom hadn't longed for this moment. Now that it was here, he wished it would never end. More than that, he wished Pa were here.

Bascom released his grip to step back. "What's all this fuss about? You're carrying on like you wasn't expecting to ever see me again. Let me get a good look at you." Even through tears, Durwood's deep-set eyes looked like Ma's. Had her strong chin, too. "I do believe Hattie has put some meat on your bones. And Miss Grace has worked miracles taming that mop on your head. I feared you was going to have to shave it off and start all over, Miss Grace."

Grace smiled. "Almost. But not quite."

"Why didn't you tell me you were coming?"

"Then it wouldn't have been a surprise!"

"When did you arrive?"

"Got here late last night. Mr. Walker picked me up at the station." It was the truth, even if it had been the police station.

"Did you stay at the Hotel Roanoke like I did?"

"Didn't want to delay. Slept and ate on the train."

"Wasn't the train ride something?"

"You could say that."

"What happened to your head?"

"Like I was telling Hattie, train stopped sudden for a cow on the tracks."

"Where's Pa?"

"Somebody had to stay behind to tend to the home place. He wanted to come. He misses you something awful."

"How's Blue?"

"Getting up in years. Ain't much at chasing squirrels no more, but he'll let you rub his ears all day."

"Better eat your breakfast, Durwood. Ben will be here shortly for school."

"Do I have to go today? I want to stay with Bascom."

"'Course you have to go to school. One of us has to get some schooling and make Ma proud. I'll be here when you come home."

"Tomorrow is Saturday. You can spend the entire day together."

"What do you want to do, Bascom?"

"Up to you. These is your stomping grounds."

"Great. I've got just the place."

A knock on the door echoed in the front hall.
"There's Ben now, dear. Get going. Here, take a biscuit."
"Bye, Aunt Grace." Durwood pecked her cheek.
Durwood embraced Bascom again. "Bye, Bascom."
"See you when you get home, little brother."

Chapter 21

March 19, 1912

Richmond, Virginia

Durwood fidgeted. School had been a blur, his mind clouded by Bascom's unexpected arrival. He checked the clock above the blackboard—fifteen minutes until dismissal.

When the teacher turned her back to write on the chalkboard, Ben slipped Durwood a note. Durwood unfolded the paper beneath the desk. "Got your mitt?"

Durwood scribbled his response before passing it back. "No. Going straight home to see Bascom."

When the bell rang, Durwood hopped out of his seat to stow his books and papers in his satchel.

"If you aren't playing, who's going to pitch for us?"

"You, I guess."

"You know I can't throw like you."

"Don't have to. Just get it across the plate and make them hit you."

"What are you and Bascom going to do today?"

"Catch up. Saturday I'm going to take him to the coal yard."

"Why on earth do you want to do that?"

"Figure he'd like to see where all his coal goes."

"See you around."

"Tell the fellows I'm sorry I can't make it today."

Durwood hurried through the crowded hallway. He pushed open the heavy front door and took the cement steps two at a time. Durwood raced home, eager not to lose another second with Bascom.

"I'm home." Durwood burst through the kitchen door. Hattie kneaded dough.

"Miss Grace and Bascom are in the library. Here." Durwood snatched an oatmeal cookie as he reached the door. "Milk?"

"Not now."

"Get one for your brother." Durwood grabbed a second cookie.

He deposited his satchel in the hallway outside the library before knocking.

"Come in."

A fire warmed the room. Grace and Bascom sat before the fireplace.

"Hattie said to give you this." Durwood handed Bascom a cookie.

"I thought you had a baseball game today, dear."

"You play baseball?"

"He's the pitcher."

"That right?"

"Who do you think is better? Christy Mathewson or Walter Johnson? Ben says Mathewson is better."

"Can't say as I know much about baseball. What do you think?"

"Johnson. Uncle Walker took me to Washington to see the Senators last year. Saw him pitch against the Yankees. Threw a two-hitter. Got his autograph after the game. You want to see it?"

"Maybe later. Don't you want to play in your game? I could come watch."

"That's okay. By the time we'd get there, the game would be winding down. Besides, it might be good for them to play a game without me."

"Say, I almost forgot. I got something for you. Wait right there." Bascom left the library.

"Are you going to buy Bascom some new clothes like you did for me, Aunt Grace?"

"That's up to Bascom. But I doubt he would agree."

"Why's that?"

"He's proud. He doesn't want to feel like he's taking advantage of us."

"Did I take advantage of you?"

"Of course not."

Entering the room, Bascom handed Durwood a slingshot. "Remember this?"

"Sure do. Pa took it from me just as I was about to board the train."

"One thing's for sure. You was a dead aim. Miss Grace, won't no squirrels in Mingo County safe when Durwood took to the woods."

Durwood studied the rough-hewn hickory branch. The crude initials he etched into the handle then burnished with a hot blade remained legible. "Looks different."

"Rubber dry rotted so I replaced it with strips I scavenged at the mine. Took the tongue out of a pair of old boots to fashion the pouch. What say we go out and see if you still recollect how to use it?"

"Would that be okay, Aunt Grace?"

"I don't see any harm so long as you don't aim it at anyone or hit any houses."

"I won't. Let's go."

"Supper's at six. Don't be late."

"Yes, ma'am."

Pushing through the swinging door, Durwood headed for the stairs.

"Where you going?"

"Change clothes. Aunt Grace prefers I don't play in my school clothes. Come on. I'll show you my room."

Durwood scurried up to his room. He opened the closet and slid a dozen coat hangers full of clothes to one side before selecting pants and a shirt. Removing his tie, he draped it over the doorknob, on top of two others. He hung up his jacket, followed by his shirt and knickers.

"All them duds yours?"

"Of course." Durwood slipped into a pair of corduroy pants with knee patches Hattie had sewn inside for reinforcement, and a linen shirt. He laced up a pair of shoes that bore a couple of scuff marks on the toes. Even his play clothes were nicer than Bascom's dungarees and flannel shirt. At least his work boots looked new.

"What in the world do you do with all of 'em?"

"Wear them, of course."

"How come you got so many?"

"They're for different occasions. Some are for school. Others for church. Some are just for playing in. Pajamas. Bath robe."

"I don't think I want to wear pajamas."

"You get used to it."

"Not shore I want to."

"Afraid you're going to turn out like me?"

"Ain't what I said."

"Didn't have to."

Bascom studied the books on the shelf beside Durwood's secretary. "You read all them?"

"Yes."

"What's your favorite?"

"Three Musketeers. Alexander Dumas wrote it. He was French."

"You know French?"

"No, but I'll study it in high school. The book is in English."

"What's it about?"

"Four swordsmen who were the French king's guards."

"Then why ain't it called the Four Musketeers?"

"Good question. The fourth isn't one of the king's guards originally, but he becomes one after proving himself."

"Is it a true story?"

"No, but it tells about a real time in history. Some of the characters are real. It's set in France during the 1600s."

"How come you like it if it ain't real?"

"It's full of sword fights. It's about the loyalty the musketeers had for each other and for their king. Without them, the king would have been overthrown or worse, killed. They had a saying that I like. 'One for all and all for one.'" Durwood pulled the book from the shelf. "Why don't you read it?"

Bascom flipped through the thick book. "Them musketeers must've been doing lots of fighting."

"What's your favorite book?"

"Can't say as I read much outside of your letters. Only books we got at home now is the Bible and Ma's dictionary. Pa gave the rest away."

"You read the Bible?"

"Not no more."

"How come?"

"Busy, I guess. By the time Pa and I get home from our shift and eat supper, ain't a lot of time left for reading."

Durwood hurried to lace up his shoes. Bascom moved to the bedside table and picked up a leather-bound book. "What're you reading now?"

"Put that down, please. That's my journal."

"Journal?"

"Like a diary. I write things in it."

"Like what?"

"Things I did. Things I'm thinking about."

Bascom returned the book to the nightstand to pick up a photograph in a silver frame. "Who's this?"

"Guess?"

"Miss Grace?"

"And?"

"Don't know."

"That's our mother. The time they went to Virginia Beach."

Bascom studied the photo. "Ma shore was pretty back then. You been to the beach?"

Bascom sounded funny, like Cap and the boys. How would John Randolph react if he met Bascom? How would Bascom react to being called a Yank? Worse yet, a hillbilly? Hopefully, Durwood could keep them apart, at least until Bascom got some new clothes. It's one thing if trouble finds a man. Another to go asking for it.

"Sure have. We go for a week each summer." Durwood removed a photo from the dresser to hand to Bascom. "This was taken at the Cavalier Hotel last summer."

"What's it like?"

"Makes the Hotel Roanoke look plain."

"I'm talking about the beach."

"Wonderful. In the mornings, Uncle Walker and I get up early to look for seashells." Durwood grabbed a jar from his secretary and handed it to Bascom. "These are just the ones I found last summer. Take a look."

Bascom unscrewed the Mason jar's lid. He pulled out two halves of a black shell joined together.

"That's a mussel. It's like a clam, only smaller. Mussels have little bits of meat inside. Hattie cooks them up in a broth with fish, shrimp, and clams. Hardly anything better than her seafood stew."

"You've ate shrimp?"

"Sure."

"You like it?"

"You bet. Tastes really good cold and dipped into a spicy sauce.

Maybe Hattie can fix some for us."

"Did you get in the ocean?"

"Of course."

"What's it like?"

"Some days it's as smooth as that windowpane. Other days, the waves are so big they can knock you down."

"Is it salty like they say?"

"Sure is."

"What's sand like?"

"Gritty. Gets in your hair, and your ears, and down your shorts."

"Sounds like coal dust."

"I guess. But you can build sandcastles. Last summer me and Ben – he's my best friend – took turns burying each other up to our necks. On really hot days, sand gets so hot you can't walk barefoot. Away from the water where the sand is thickest, it's like walking in a snowbank."

"You 'bout ready?"

"Yes."

"Let's go, then. I done missed a lifetime of pretty days tucked away in the mines."

They trotted down the steps. Durwood grabbed a tweed coat and cap from the front hall closet. "You want a coat? You can wear one of Uncle Walker's. He won't mind."

"That's okay. Ain't too cold compared to home." Bascom grabbed the newsboy cap out of his back pocket.

"Suit yourself."

***

Buds dotted the maple trees along Monument Avenue. A few more weeks of mild weather and the dogwoods and azaleas would burst in whites, pinks and reds. It felt good to walk beside Bascom, whose dark hair, deep-brown eyes and high cheek bones reminded Durwood of Pa, at least what he could remember. But Bascom seemed taller, stronger, straighter than Pa. Dark stubble covered his face.

"Do folks say you resemble Pa?"

"Those that knowed him when he was my age say I'm his spitting image, only bigger."

"Thought so. My memory's kind of fuzzy, though. Who do I resemble?"

"You take after Ma. In more ways than just looks."

"What do you mean?"

"You're smart."

"So are you."

"I ain't book smart. Not like you."

"That's because they pulled you out of school."

"They pulled me out of school because my back showed more promise than this." Bascom pointed to his head.

"You're eighteen now, right?"

"That's right."

"How old's Pa?"

"Forty."

"Same as Uncle Walker. I figured Pa was older."

"Mines'll do that to a man. Make him old before his time."

"That explains things."

"What are you talking about?"

"Why you look as old as Methuselah." Durwood punched Bascom and raced out the door and down the steps.

Catching up to him, Bascom grabbed Durwood around his neck. He rubbed his knuckles across the top of Durwood's head.

"How long before you have to go back to work?"

"Don't. Give my notice and cashed in before I left."

"How come?"

"Let's just say I ain't see eye to eye with the pit boss."

"So you've come to stay?"

"I'm going to visit a spell then find work."

"In Richmond?"

"If I'm able."

"Then you can stay with us? We've got plenty of room."

"Miss Grace offered. But like I done told her, our family is already indebted. Pa wouldn't much care to hear I'm freeloading."

"Who's going to tell him?"

"That ain't the point."

"What is the point? I don't want you to leave."

"I ain't going nowhere just yet. Even if I do, I'll be nearby so we can see one another on a regular basis."

"Promise?"

"Promise. Now show me if you can still shoot that thing."

"Come on. There are always a bunch of squirrels over in that stand of trees across the street. Race you."

"You're on."

Chapter 22

March 23, 1912

Richmond, Virginia

Mounds of coal lay just beyond the end of the tracks. Fog obscured the tops of the tallest piles, nearly two stories high and bigger around than a house. Two trainloads of empty cars occupied adjacent tracks. Seven other sets of tracks were empty. Bascom had never seen so much coal in one place.

"What do you think?"

"I come to Richmond to get away from coal. What'd you bring me here for?"

"Thought you'd like to see where all the coal you dug ends up."

"How'd you know about this place?"

"Followed a coal train when I first came to Richmond. Met some fellows who told me about scatter tags. Used to come to see if I could find one from your mine."

"What on earth did you want with a Paint Lick tag?"

"I thought it would get me a little closer to home. Found one from Dry Branch where Cesco worked. See?" Durwood pulled a tin tag from his pocket. "It's as close as I got."

"Worked in the mines four years and ain't never seen one myself.

They put 'em in after the coal reaches the tipple." Bascom turned the tag over before giving it back. "Ain't we trespassing?"

"I haven't been caught yet."

"They's always a first time."

"What do you suggest?"

"Let's get out of here. We can come back another day and I'll help you look for that tag if you's still keen on finding one."

"That's okay. Having you here is better than any scatter tag. What would you like to do?"

"I ain't seen Richmond yet. Why don't you show me around?"

"How about Forest Hill Park? We can take the trolley there."

"What's Forest Hill Park?"

"It's an amusement park. They got all kinds of things to do. Carousel, Dip-a-Dip, a penny arcade. There's a lake with boats. And a beach for swimming."

"What's a Dip-a-Dip?"

"A roller coaster."

Bascom shook his head.

"It's like a bunch of mine cars hooked together that go up and down and around a track real fast. Rode it ten times last time I went with Ben."

"Think I'll pass. But the carousel and penny arcade sounds fun."

Bascom and Durwood retraced their steps a quarter mile. Bascom unbuttoned his jacket as the late morning sun chased away the early chill. Without mountains in every direction, a man could enjoy the sunlight any time of the day. Durwood lifted some vines draped across the fence, revealing a hole. "It's a shortcut. After you."

Bascom stooped to duck walk through the gap. "You's doing your best to make sure I don't forget my mining days any time soon, ain't you?" As Bascom straightened, a group of boys approached. About Durwood's age, their tattered clothes and smudged faces reminded him of Paint Lick, as did their houses, dilapidated and tiny with hardpan yards and outhouses.

The tallest one said, "You're trespassing on private property, Mr. Gonna cost you fifty cents." Holding a baseball bat, he was smaller than Durwood, but the way he carried himself suggested toughness, like the Italian kids back home.

"That you, Cap?" Durwood popped up beside Bascom.

"Durwood? Ain't seen you in over a year. Figured you'd done forgot about us."

"How've you boys been getting along?"

Cap swept his hand around the ramshackle neighborhood. "If we was to do any better they'd be sure to pass a law against it. Who's your bodyguard?"

"This is my brother, Bascom. Bascom, this is Cap. He's the one I was telling you about who helped me look for the scatter tag."

Bascom extended his hand. "Pleased to meet you, Cap."

"You the miner?"

"Used to be."

The boys behind Cap wore denim pants and ill-fitting, woolen jackets. They cinched their pants with rope, bailing twine laced their brogans, tape wrapped around the toes. "Cap says we's miners, too."

Cap spit. "What Cut Bait's trying to say is at night we help ourselves to a little coal when nobody's looking. We figure a slice off a cut loaf ain't missed."

"Sounds like it's dark, dirty, and dangerous work," Bascom offered.

"That's about the size of things, Mr. Bascom," Cut Bait replied.

"And no matter how hard you work, you ain't got nothing to show for it."

"That'd be us for shore."

"Sounds to me like what you's doing is mining, alright. Ain't never figured to meet coal miners in Richmond, but it shore is a pleasure."

Cap turned to Durwood. "So where you two headed?"

"Bascom wants to see Richmond. Thought I'd take him to Forest Hill Park."

"Bascom asked, "You fellows care to join us?"

"Wish we could."

"What's stopping you?"

"Afraid they don't let the likes of us in the Park."

"Why not?"

"Look at us."

"What does that have to do with anything?"

"We're bad for business. Upset the proper folk."

"That true, Durwood?"

"'Course it's true." Cap stared at Durwood. "Even if he don't want to admit it."

"What makes you think I would know?"

"'Cause you's living high on Monument Avenue."

Fists clenched, Durwood stepped within inches of Cap. "You been spying on me?"

"We was curious. We followed you and Ben home the last time you was down here searching for tags. Nice house."

Before Durwood could react, Bascom stepped between them. "Don't reckon it matters no how. I ain't got no money to get us in. Train ride to Richmond done busted me good."

Durwood said, "I have money."

"Where'd you get money?"

"Uncle Walker gives me a weekly allowance."

"For what?"

"Making my bed. Shining my shoes."

Bascom whistled.

Cap said, "My Pa allows me to sleep under his roof so long as I keep his coal bin full."

Bascom laughed and slapped Cap's back. "Your Pa sounds like mine."

"You mean like ours." Durwood marched toward the street.

"Where you going? Wait up." Bascom turned to the boys. "Hope I'll be seeing you fellows around."

Cap called after him, "You's welcome anytime."

Bascom put his hand on Durwood's shoulder. "Where you going in such a hurry?" Durwood jerked away. "Your skin's a little thin, ain't it?"

"Trust me, I'm used to being made fun of. My skin's plenty thick. Guess I wasn't expecting my brother to jump on the bandwagon."

"What are you talking about?"

"The kids I go to school with used to make fun of my name. And yours. They teased me about the way I talked, the way I dressed, where I was from. I get tired trying to figure out who I'm supposed to be, is all."

"Sorry."

"I'm not finished. You and Pa sent me away. Said it'd be a little while. A little while turned into years. I decided to make the best of it. So don't fault me for trying to fit in."

"I ain't faulting you. I'm proud of what you's done. What say we go see this Park of yours and put this behind us?"

"Don't do me any favors."

"I'm not doing you any favors. I want to go to the Park."

"Okay, then."

"Be sure to keep track of what we spend so's I can repay Mr. Walker."

"You don't have to. This is my money."

"Whatever you say, little brother."

***

The trolley crossed the trestle high above the James River. Men fished along the banks, while boys hopped the boulders dotting the river. South of the river, the trolley chugged uphill. Passing through an arch announcing "Forest Hill Park," the trolley stopped to discharge passengers in front of a sturdy, two-story cut stone building. Surrounded by a porch, the building's second floor dormers were adorned with green striped awnings. Cap was right, he wouldn't be welcome here. Men dressed in dark three-piece suits and carrying walking sticks strolled with women in pastel dresses and broad-brimmed hats. Children, dressed as if they were headed to church, sprinted between attractions. Down by the lake, families tossed breadcrumbs to swans and ducks.

"Them ladies are using umbrellas. It ain't raining."

"It's for shade. They're parasols."

"Why on Earth would somebody do that?"

"Only working folks have tans."

"White as I am, you reckon folks will think I ain't a working man?"

Durwood surveyed Bascom from his boots to his newsboy cap. "Not unless they're blind."

"I reckon we's even."

"And deaf." Bascom gently shoved Durwood. "Now we're even."

"What are we going to do first?"

"Let's ride the carousel."

The boys crossed the lawn. The carousel sat on the far side of the stone building. Beyond it, four wooden carts hitched together puttered along an elevated wooden track two stories high. Boys' and girls' heads were barely visible above the sides.

"Don't look so bad."

Suddenly, the lead cart pitched forward pulling the others as it hurtled down the first incline. Screams filled the air, as several arms shot skyward.

"Why ain't they holding on?"

"Showing off so the girls won't think they're scared. Still think it doesn't look too bad?"

"Forget I said that. I didn't travel all this way to meet my maker in a runaway mine car at a fun park. Carousel's more my speed."

"Two, please." Durwood handed the attendant two nickels. Why did he have to give all his money away? Maybe he should have listened to Mr. Walker.

Durwood handed one ticket to Bascom. Together, they hopped onto the platform.

"Which horse do you fancy?"

Durwood pointed. "That blue one over there."

"I'll take the orange one next to it, then. Hurry up before somebody else gets them."

Unlike the carousels in Williamson at the County Fair, this one had horses that looked brand new. Intricately carved and freshly painted, they were as perfect as the people gathering to ride them. Bascom and Durwood hopped on their horses. Why had Ma ever left Richmond for West Virginia? Why had she given this up to work herself to death trying to make a home with Pa on the side of a cold, lonely mountain?

"What are you thinking about, Bascom?"

"Wondering what Pa would make of all this."

"Think he'd like it?"

"Shore he would."

"How about our mother?"

"'Course. Probably come, don't you think?"

"Park didn't exist then. Aunt Grace says she would have enjoyed it. Particularly this ride."

Music played as the carousel started to spin. A couple moved toward the horses in front. Bascom tipped his cap. The man frowned, grabbed his escort's hand and turned to find horses on the other side of the carousel.

"How come you call her mother?"

"People in Richmond don't say 'Ma' and 'Pa.' They made fun of me when I did."

"You still think about home?"

"Of course. Your letters help. Now that you're here, I don't need reminding."

"Good. Always remember where you come from."

Before the carousel stopped, Durwood slid off his horse and hopped to the ground.

"Come on. Let's give the Penny Arcade a go. You ever seen a kinetoscope?"

"What is it?"

"A moving picture box. Come on. You'll love it."

Chapter 23

October 12, 1912

Richmond, Virginia

Bascom woke before sunrise while the rest of the house slept. He slipped into a pair of new woolen trousers and cotton shirt he bought with money earned working in the N&P mail room, a job Walker had secured for him in June. The work was easy, clean, and safe. Bascom couldn't believe the railroad paid him a dollar fifty a day to sort and deliver mail to workers in Walker's building. Besides the clothes, he had saved enough to send some money to Pa and still managed to bank twenty dollars. Soon he would have enough to move out on his own. After lacing up his new shoes, he eased down the back steps. He enjoyed his mornings with Hattie.

"Morning."

"Look at you. The single ladies better watch out today."

"I reckon they's safe. According to Durwood, there ain't much interest in a hillbilly Yankee around here."

"Their loss."

"How come everybody's so worked up over this celebration, anyway?"

"You'll see. There's nobody more loved in Richmond than General

Lee. Around this time every year, white folks get all sentimental over the way things used to be."

"How's it make you feel?"

"I keep my feelings to myself. You go have fun."

"I'll try."

***

Reynolds exited the driveway onto Monument Avenue for the short drive to the Lee Monument. Durwood and Bascom squeezed into the back with Grace. Walker sat up front. Maples lined the street on both sides of the grassy median. In a couple of weeks they would blanket the azaleas in a mosaic of red, yellow, and orange. Squirrels gathered acorns from the occasional oak. Wind blowing through the car threatened to unseat Walker's old fedora perched on Bascom's head. Bascom felt like a costumed circus bear in Walker's tie, vest, hat and waistcoat that Grace insisted he wear. The best thing about the day so far was that the fever of August and September had finally broken, ushering in moderate days and tolerable nights. Good thing the General passed in October instead of July. Richmond's differences from Mingo County were too numerous to count, but none had been harder to get accustomed to than the stifling summer.

A line of cars queued in front of the statue. "We'll get out here, Reynolds. Meet us back here at four o'clock, sharp. We're having guests for dinner."

Reynolds eased the Kline to a stop and cut the engine. He grabbed a footstool from the floorboard and hopped out. Placing the stool on the ground, he opened the back door to offer Grace a hand. She picked up her parasol and took Reynolds's hand. A rose-colored, translucent scarf wrapped around her beige straw hat to tie in a bow under her chin. It seemed she and Walker had different hats for every occasion, if not every day.

Grace opened her parasol. "You look handsome, Bascom. You're almost a perfect fit for Walker's clothes. I'm so happy to have something to do with the things he no longer wears."

"Thank you, Miss Grace. Didn't expect to be needing so many clothes. Then again, didn't know how hot a place could be. You look pretty, as always." He regretted never telling Ma she looked pretty.

"You're kind."

"That a new hat?"

"Nice of you to notice."

They moved toward the crowd milling on the lawn around the statue. Like most men in attendance, Walker dressed in standard formal attire, except for a short piece of coarse, discolored, braided rope affixed to his lapel, its frayed ends lashed together with ribbon.

Bascom nudged Durwood. "What's he wearing that rope for?"

"Back in 1890, the statue was shipped in three giant crates from France. Men pitched in to haul them here from the train. They cut up pieces of the tow ropes to give to those who helped. Uncle Walker got a piece of the rope to show he did his part."

"He that attached to Lee?"

"Everyone is."

"How about you?"

"I guess. We study him in school."

Bascom squinted through the sunlight reflecting off General Lee, trying in vain to see what all the fuss was over a losing General. Best he could tell, the General looked like a lonely man on horseback trying to recall where he laid his hat, unaware it was in his hand.

A group of older men dressed in Confederate grays gathered beneath the monument. Few could button their jackets. Several used crutches to compensate for missing legs.

A wooden stage with two rows of chairs had been constructed at the base of the monument. Children playing follow-the-leader ducked under the red, white and blue bunting. Off to the side, near the Confederate veterans, a brass band played Dixie. Several men huddled on stage beside a podium.

"Who are them fellows?"

"Politicians. The one in the top hat is the Mayor. He's friends with Uncle Walker. He and his wife are coming for dinner tonight."

Newspaper boys raced about handing out miniature Confederate flags from canvas bags slung over their shoulders. Bascom declined. Durwood took one.

People began moving toward the stage, as dignitaries climbed the platform to take their seats. The band stopped as the Mayor raised his hand behind the podium.

"Come on. Let's get up close where we can hear what he's saying."

"You go ahead. I think I'll hang back a bit and see if I can't make my way over to that tent. Looks like they's got some food that's about to go to waste."

"You sure it's your stomach motivating you?"

"How do you figure?"

"You've been eyeballing Belle Johnston for the last five minutes." Durwood nodded toward the tent.

"I'm hungry, is all. Wait, you know her?"

"We go to the same church. You'd know that if you came once in a while."

"Ain't you hungry?"

"You go ahead. Meet you back here." Durwood disappeared into the crowd as Bascom turned toward the tent. Several tables held the picked-over remnants of fried chicken, deviled eggs, baked beans, potato salad and watermelon. A pretty girl with flaxen hair stood beside a woman on the far side of the serving tables. The woman barked directions to a stooped-shouldered man.

"Hurry up, Henry. We need to put more food out. The crowd will be coming back as soon as the speeches are done."

"Yes, Miss Nettie." The old man limped toward cars parked on the street.

"Looks like folks took a shine to your spread." Bascom tipped his hat as he smiled at the women.

The older one asked, "Would you like something?"

"Don't mind if I do." Bascom filled a plate with deviled eggs, beans and chicken.

"You look familiar. Do I know you?"

"I ain't from around here."

"No, you aren't, are you? Just the same, I feel like I know you. What's your name?"

"Bascom Matney."

"Can't say that I know any Matneys. Where do you live, Bascom?"

"I'm staying with the Hopkins down Monument a piece."

"Walker and Grace Hopkins?"

"Yes, ma'am."

"Hope Wickman was your mother?"

"Shore was."

"I heard you had joined your brother in Richmond."

"You knowed our mother?"

"Yes, I did. We went to school together."

"What was she like?"

"Very pious."

"Pious?"

"Took her religion seriously."

"That'd be Ma, alright."

"But fun. Had a twinkle in her eye. Loved to laugh. And pretty as a songbird. I was quite fond of your mother." Pious sounded right. But fun? Loved to laugh?

"I was sorry to hear of her passing. I lost track of her years ago when she moved after your grandfather got transferred. I heard she eloped with a man in West Virginia. Is that where you're from?"

"Yes, ma'am. Mingo County."

"How about your father? Is he still alive?"

"Yes, ma'am."

"What profession is he in?"

"Coal."

"He owns a coal mine?"

Bascom choked back a piece of chicken. "Not hardly. He works in one, though. So did I."

Bascom finished his plate and set it on the table. Henry moved toward the tent, struggling under the weight of several stacked boxes.

"Pardon me, ladies. Looks like Henry could use a hand."

"Nonsense. He can manage."

Bascom trotted to Henry. "Here, let me help you."

"No need to trouble yourself, sir."

"Ain't no trouble. Let me have one of them boxes." Bascom scooped the top box and returned to the tent ahead of Henry.

"Where would you like this, ma'am?"

"Just set it down. Henry will take care of it."

"I best be catching up with my brother."

"It's a pleasure to meet you, Bascom."

"You, too…"

"Nettie Johnston. This is my daughter, Belle."

Bascom tipped his hat. "Pleasure's mine, Mrs. Johnston, Miss Belle. I'll be shore to tell Miss Grace we met."

"Please do."

"Won't you have some more?" Belle asked.

"Afraid I might founder. Besides, I'll be back for seconds with my brother after the speeches. Thank you for the grub, I mean food." Belle lowered her eyes, but not before a slight smile escaped.

***

The Mayor removed his napkin from his collar, wiped his mouth and placed it on the table. "Grace, that was a lovely dinner. Don't know when I've eaten so well."

"Thank you, Mayor. Eleanor, how about you? Did you get enough?"

"Heavens, yes. My compliments to Hattie."

"Shall we retire to the parlor, Earl? Bascom, would you care to join us?"

"I'd be obliged. What about Durwood?"

"Please, Uncle Walker."

"You're a little young. Earl, what do you say?"

"I don't see why not. When I was his age I was dodging bullets at Cold Harbor."

Walker led the way into the parlor and turned on the lights. Except for Sunday afternoons following church when the family gathered to read, or when entertaining, the room sat empty. A piano Grace played on special occasions occupied one corner beside a floor lamp with a beige tasseled shade. A green and brown velvet sofa filled the space between two windows facing Monument Avenue. A low-slung, tufted footstool sat in front of the couch, an accommodation for Grace's short legs. Across from the piano a tall mahogany cabinet reached nearly to the ceiling. Three upholstered high back chairs and one cane chair beside the piano completed the room. A dark red oriental rug covered the hardwoods.

"Brandy, Earl?"

"Don't mind if I do."

"How about you, Bascom?"

"I ain't much for drink, but I reckon." Walker poured three tumblers.

"What about me?"

"I'm afraid not, Durwood. Your Aunt Grace would have me sleeping on the couch for a month if I served you brandy."

"Just a sip?"

"Not unless your brother sneaks you one while I'm not looking. Cheers."

After clinking glasses, Walker and the Mayor sipped. Bascom followed suit. The brandy warmed the back of his throat, but didn't burn.

"What do you think?"

"Not bad. Tastes like pear, maybe apple."

"Pretty good," Walker said. "It's pear brandy. Anyone care to join me in a cigar?"

The Mayor eased into one of the high back chairs. "I would enjoy one."

As Walker turned to the cabinet for cigars, Bascom slipped the tumbler to Durwood. Rushing to taste, Durwood gulped, then lapsed into a coughing fit. Bascom slapped him on the back.

"Why, Durwood, I hope you're not coming down with something." The Mayor winked.

"No, sir," he sputtered.

Walker said, "Maybe I should tell Grace to ready a dose of Castor Oil."

"Won't be necessary, sir. Just a tickle."

Walker held open a box of cigars. "I hope you enjoy Cubans."

"Indeed, I do. Thank you." The mayor snipped the end of the cigar before rolling it gently under his nose."

"Bascom?"

"Don't mind if I do."

Walker lit the cigars.

"Want to try?" Walker offered Durwood his cigar. The color had yet to return to his cheeks.

Durwood coughed. "No, thank you."

"If you change your mind, let me know."

Walker sat next to the Mayor and placed his glass on the marble-topped table between them. Bascom joined Durwood on the couch.

The Mayor exhaled. "Walker tells me you're attending night classes, Bascom."

"Yes, sir."

"How do you like it?"

"Still trying to knock the rust off."

"What do you want to do? Banking? Law?"

"Ain't figured that out, exactly."

Durwood offered, "He's good with ciphers."

"Lucky for me I got a tutor in the room next door." Bascom put his arm around Durwood's shoulder.

"How about your job?"

"Pretty good, I reckon."

"Pretty good?" Walker nudged the Mayor's arm. "His supervisor tells me he's the best worker in the mailroom and he's only been at it a few months. Says he due a promotion." Walker sipped his brandy. "Like I've told him, if he completes his schooling the sky's the limit. I've got big plans. For both of them."

"Here's to big plans." The Mayor raised his snifter. "Cheers."

"Cheers."

"Bascom, if the folks at the Norfolk and Potomac ever take your talents for granted, you be sure to look me up. We can always use a good man at the bank."

"Bank?"

"In addition to his mayoral duties, Earl is President of Farmers and Merchants Bank on Broad."

"Your Uncle's right, you know. An education, hard work, and a willingness to take risks are the only things a man needs to succeed in today's world. Take me, for example. After the War, I went to work in a foundry beside my father. Didn't take me long to realize there was no future in risking my neck working hard so others could make money off my sweat. So I saved enough to finish school. Started the bank when I was thirty-five. It's provided me with a pretty good living."

"What the Mayor isn't telling you is that Farmers and Merchants is the leading bank in the Commonwealth."

The Mayor leaned forward. "I understand you worked in the mines."

"Going on four years."

"Miss it?"

"'Bout as much as a canary misses his cage."

"That's how I felt about the foundry. Sounds like you made a wise decision to come to Richmond and are taking all the right steps. Keep it up and one day you can live in a beautiful home like this."

"That's what I'm aiming to do, sir."

"So what do you think about the troubles in West Virginia?"

"They's always a strike going on somewhere in the coalfields. According to what I seen in the paper, this time just happens to be over in Kanawha County."

The Mayor turned to Walker. "You haven't told him about the mayhem?"

Walker flicked his ashes in the tray next to his glass. "Didn't see the need. The troubles aren't in Mingo where his father mines."

Bascom focused on Walker. "What's so bad about this strike?"

"This one's not some local dispute. Labor unions and socialists are pushing this strike to gain a foothold. They've brought in guns. Lots of them. Things took a turn in late July when some miners ambushed guards at a place called Mucklow. Six guards were murdered. Owners had to rush in more guards to keep the mines running. We've had to increase protection for our trains. Fortunately, things have calmed down since the Governor took our advice and declared martial law."

"What are socialists, Uncle Walker?"

"Troublemakers, Durwood. People who don't believe in our way of life. They preach that businesses shouldn't be privately owned."

"Who would own them, then?"

"Great question. The way I understand it, the community would collectively own them, how ever that would work."

"What your Uncle is trying to tell you, Durwood, is that it makes about as much sense as letting the inmates run the asylum."

Bascom asked, "How come I didn't read about all this trouble in the paper?"

Walker stood to pour more brandy. "Two reasons. First, I convinced the editor that reporting on this strike would only encourage this behavior among the working class here. Second, he's smart enough to know that as long as people are getting coal to heat their homes, a strike in West Virginia doesn't sell papers."

"Any miners been killed, Uncle Walker?"

"A few. But they've got no one to blame but themselves."

"Is Dry Branch in Kanawha County, Bascom?"

Bascom nodded.

"Think Cesco's okay?"

The Mayor asked, "Who's Cesco?"

"Our cousin."

Walker blew a smoke ring. "I'm sure he's okay, Durwood. If he's related to you and your brother, he's too smart to be led astray by the likes of Mother Jones."

Bascom straightened. "Mother Jones?"

"Socialists brought her in to rile up the workers."

"The press calls her the most dangerous woman in America." The Mayor knocked back the last of his brandy. "You've lived and worked in the coal mines, Bascom. What do you think about all this talk of unions and socialists?"

Bascom pulled his watch from his vest pocket while he weighed his thoughts. He wanted to say the folks back home were only interested in earning a living wage and politics didn't matter. He wanted to tell them about Abner's death. Even if he could manage to get it out, now wasn't the time or place. "I hope you'll excuse me. Didn't realize it was this late. I've got some schoolwork to do before I go to bed. Besides, I'm not sure anything I have to say would be worth listening to." Reaching the doorway, he pivoted to look at Walker.

"If you don't mind my asking, how come you know so much about the goings-on in West Virginia?"

"N&P's got a lot riding on the coal mines. It's my business to know. I get dispatches from men we've placed throughout southern West Virginia."

"Think I might get a look at them dispatches after you've done read them?"

"Afraid not, son. The information is confidential."

"It was a pleasure to meet you, Mr. Mayor." Bascom shook his hand.

"Good night, Bascom."

"Night, Mr. Walker."

"Good night."

"Come on, Durwood. Tell your Aunt Grace good night."

Durwood hugged Walker and ran toward the library. Bascom climbed the stairs to his bedroom.

He entered his room, pulled the chain on his desk lamp and sat. Retrieving a pocket notebook from a slot in the secretary, he wrote "mayhem." The notebook's pages were full of words he'd learned since he began corresponding with Miss Grace. Opening the dictionary Grace had loaned him, he found mayhem and wrote, "Violent or damaging disorder; chaos." He closed his eyes and repeated the definition until he had it committed to memory. He grabbed a sheet of paper. Things must be bad in Kanawha. As rough as the strikes got, he'd never heard of ambushes and martial law. Sounded worse than what Pa described in '02.

A soft rap interrupted his thoughts. "Come in."

In his pajamas, Durwood jumped on the bed. "What are you doing?"

"Writing Cesco."

"You think he's okay?"

"That's what I aim to find out. Now, it's time for you to go to bed."

"I'm not tired."

"You will be in the morning. Run along."

"Night. Hope you have sweet dreams. About Belle." Durwood ran from the room ahead of the pencil that pinged off the door.

Chapter 24

October 13, 1912

Richmond, Virginia

"Morning, Miss Grace. Mr. Walker." Bascom descended the steps to join them in the foyer.

"Good morning." Grace touched his arm. "You look tired."

"Had trouble getting to sleep."

"Something troubling you?"

"Just thinking about schoolwork. Where's Durwood?"

"Morning," Durwood called from the parlor.

"What's he doing in there?"

Walker opened the hall closet. "Reynolds is getting the car ready. Durwood's watching for him to pull out front."

"If I didn't know better, I would say you were dressed for church."

"Figured I'd give it a whirl, Miss Grace."

"We're so delighted to have you join us. I think you'll love the Reverend's sermons."

"Durwood says they's a picnic after the service."

"He's right. Unfortunately, we can't stay. We're meeting friends at the Club for lunch. Won't you join us?"

"If it's all the same, I think I might stay for the picnic."

"Of course."

"Say, I forgot to tell you that I met Miz Nettie Johnston yesterday at the celebration. She sends her regards."

"That's very nice of her."

"That's not the only person he met." Durwood stuck his head around the door jamb.

"Did she tell you she and your mother were friends?"

"Said they went to school together."

Walker helped Grace into her coat.

"They were close. Almost as close as your mother and I."

"She said Ma and Pa run off together."

"That true?" Durwood popped into the doorway.

"That ain't the way we heard it. Ma told us they met in church."

Reynolds entered the house. "The car is ready."

Grace said, "We'll discuss it when we have more time. How about that?"

"We'd be obliged, Miss Grace."

✸✸✸

Bascom gawked at the entrance to St. James's Episcopal Church. Six white columns rose more than two stories under the ornate triangular portico. High above, a green-topped spire reached skyward. Parishioners flowed into the church. Entering, Bascom's gaze was drawn to three stained-glass windows at the far end of the sanctuary behind the pulpit. The one in the middle, larger and rounded at the top, bore an image of Jesus. Smaller windows lined the first and second floors of the sanctuary, depicting biblical scenes in brilliant colors. Bascom struggled to recall his Bible lessons. Ma would be disappointed. Light poured in, reflecting off the white interior into the vaulted ceiling. Row upon row of finely dressed congregants stretched from front to back, enough to accommodate all the church-going folk in Mingo County and then some. Soft music filled the church, like notes from a piano but fuller, richer.

Grace held the arm of an usher who led them down the center aisle to the front pew, the same place the mine foreman and his family sat in Bascom's church back home.

"She's over there, couple rows back." Durwood nodded to the pews on the other side of the aisle. Craning his neck, Bascom locked on Belle

154

who returned his gaze. She sat between her mother and a younger girl. A man Walker's age with a dark, cropped beard sat on the other side of Belle's mother.

Durwood knocked his knee against Bascom's. "Stop staring."

"Where's that music coming from?"

"Behind us. In the balcony."

Gold pipes of various sizes stretched from one side of the balcony to the other. A man in a white robe hovered over the keyboard of the largest piano Bascom had ever seen. Off to one side in tiered rows sat a chorus of men and women in red robes, sheets of music on stands in front of them.

"What are all them pipes for?"

"It's a pipe organ."

The organ stopped. Everyone stood when a white-robed preacher with a gold-embroidered collar that draped below his waist moved behind the pulpit.

"This is the day of the Lord. Let us rejoice."

The congregation responded. "Thanks be to God." Durwood reached for a red book tucked into a rack on the back of the pew in front. He pointed to another one, which Bascom took.

"What page?" Durwood tilted his book toward Bascom, then nodded to a wooden plaque on the wall beside the pulpit that had three rows of numbers. "Hymns are listed up there." Strains from the organ and voices washed over Bascom. Never before had he heard anything so powerful and beautiful at the same time. As the song ended, Durwood returned his hymnal to the rack and reached down to pull a padded bench forward, striking Bascom's shin.

"What'd you do that for?"

"Shh." Everyone knelt, bowed their heads and leaned forward. Bascom knelt as the minister launched into prayer. Unlike the preachers back home, this man remained calm and steady without a bead of sweat. He talked to God instead of shouting at him. The prayer passed without a single "Amen" from the congregation.

Bascom spent the service following Durwood's lead. Unlike the spontaneous church services of his youth, this was like an elaborate dance. He seemed the only one who didn't know the steps. Bascom tried to listen to the sermon but his mind wandered to the last time he was in church for Ma's funeral, on a cold, bleak day four years before. A day when hope seemed as elusive as the sun. A day when God seemed to abandon his family.

Things were looking up. Bascom not only had hope but, more importantly, opportunity. He was deep in thought when the minister said "Amen" and made his way down the center aisle.

Music filled the church as folks filed toward the vestibule. Bascom exited the row and waited for Durwood, Walker, and Grace to join him. Halfway up the aisle, Belle glanced back. Arm close to his side, Bascom raised his hand waist high so only Belle would see.

Grace asked, "What did you think?"

"Never heard nothing like that."

"You liked the music?"

"Yes, ma'am."

"So did your mother. She loved the organ." Bascom tried to imagine how difficult it must have been for her to go from a magnificent church like this to the bare, white-washed chapel that clung to the mountain, its only music provided by the weary voices of a handful of worshippers.

Near the door, Walker and Grace shook the preacher's hand. "Wonderful message, Reverend."

"Thank you, Walker."

"I'd like you to meet Bascom Matney, Durwood's brother."

The reverend shook Bascom's hand. "Welcome, Bascom. So glad the Lord led you to worship with us today."

"Thank you, sir."

"Will we see you again, Bascom?"

"I reckon so."

"Are you all joining us for the picnic?"

"I'm afraid the three of us have plans, but I believe Bascom is planning to stay."

"The gathering is on the lawn behind the church. Just follow the crowd."

"Thank you."

They exited into bright sunshine, closer to summer than winter.

"I hope you enjoy the picnic."

"Thank you, ma'am."

Durwood asked, "Is it okay if I stay instead of joining you and Uncle Walker for lunch?"

"If Bascom doesn't mind."

"I don't see why not."

"Want us to pick you up on our way home from the club?"

Bascom shook his head. "That's okay. I reckon we can walk."

Bascom followed Durwood to where a crowd gathered on a shaded lot. Plates in hand, church members fanned out among tables spread across the yard, while others ate on blankets. Kids too excited to eat played tag. Bascom scanned for Belle. Maybe she went home, or to the Club. In a far corner of the yard, boys tossed horseshoes.

"Come on. That's Ben and John Randolph. We can eat once the crowd dies down." Bascom recalled John Randolph from Durwood's early letters. He picked on Durwood for being from West Virginia, for the way he talked, for being a Yankee. For everything, and nothing at all.

"Hey, Ben."

"I thought you all weren't coming."

"Uncle Walker and Aunt Grace went to the Club for lunch. We decided to stay. Ben Claiborne, this is Bascom."

"Hey, Bascom."

Bascom shook Ben's hand. "Pleasure, Ben."

"Well, I'll be. I finally get to meet the infamous coal miner, Bascom Matney. Heard lots about you."

"Afraid you's got the jump on me."

"Bascom, this is Ben's brother, John Randolph."

John Randolph was younger than Bascom—maybe sixteen. Not quite Bascom's height, he was half again taller than Durwood and Ben. But like most boys Bascom had met since coming to Richmond, he looked soft. "Ain't he the one you used to write me about? The one who was so welcoming when you first come to Richmond?" John Randolph's hand disappeared in Bascom's. Bascom squeezed, resisting John Randolph's attempt to break free. "I've been looking forward to this for a long time. Pleased to meet you, John."

"Randolph."

John Randolph's face pinched. Bascom relaxed, allowing him to reclaim his hand. "Now you's confusing me, Randolph."

"John Randolph."

"Which is it?"

"It's John Randolph."

"Ain't your last name Claiborne, Ben?"

"That's right."

"I got it now. You two got different daddies."

"They have the same father. It's just that..." Bascom caught Durwood's eye and winked.

"We have the same father, you hill... My name is John Randolph Claiborne. The Second."

"All them names is too much for me to handle. How about we make this easy? I'll just call you J.R. Had me a pal back in the mines called J.R. You remind me of him, except he didn't have no teeth. That okay with you?"

"Whatever."

"J.R., it is."

"You two want to play some horseshoes against Ben and me?"

"Is there many rules?"

Ben picked up a couple of shoes from the pit and handed them to his brother. "It's easy. You'll figure it out in no time. Durwood and I'll take the other end."

John Randolph removed his coat, folded it and laid it on a stump while Durwood and Ben stood five feet behind the far stake.

Bascom asked, "Mind if we take us some practice throws before we get started?"

"You go ahead. I don't need any practice."

Wrapping his thick hand around the center of the horseshoe, Bascom took several quick steps in the pit and tossed. Releasing the shoe late, it headed straight for the younger boys' heads. The boys ducked and the errant toss thudded behind them.

"Ain't as easy as it looks. You two okay?"

"We're fine," Ben responded. "Why don't you try again?"

John Randolph handed Bascom another shoe. "Another thing. You have to release the shoe from behind the stake. You were three feet past it last time, so your toss wouldn't have counted."

Still in the pit, Bascom lined up just behind the stake. Tossing flat-footed, the shoe sailed wide and landed five feet short of the sand.

"How was that?"

"Better. You ready?"

"Ready as I'll ever be. Good thing we's just playing for the heck of it, J.R."

"What fun is that? How about a friendly wager among brothers?"

"You think it's right gambling on church grounds?"

"This isn't gambling. This is a wager based on a sporting endeavor. It takes skill. Gambling is betting on cards or some other game of chance. See the difference?"

"Not really."

"Trust me."

"If you say so."

"How about two bucks?"

"That's more'n I make in a day."

Bascom pulled open his change purse and poured two silver dollars and a quarter into his palm.

John Randolph said, "You've got enough there. What do you say?"

"I reckon just this once." The two shook again.

"Boys, J.R. and I have agreed to wager two dollars on this… what did you call it?" "Sporting endeavor."

"That's it. Sporting endeavor."

Durwood returned the horseshoes. "I'm not sure that's a good idea, Bascom."

"Done shook on it."

"I hope you know what you're doing. What are we playing to?"

John Randolph banged the shoes together. "How about first to twenty? I'm hungry. Shouldn't take long."

Bascom flipped a silver dollar. "Call it."

"Heads," John Randolph barked before it landed.

"Heads it is."

"Let me show you how it's done." John Randolph stood in the grass beside the pit. He tossed the first shoe. The shoe spun, hit the sand and skidded to within an inch of the stake. He lined up and let the second shoe fly. It slid neatly onto the stake.

Bascom's first toss landed just inside the pit; his second hit the edge of the pit and rolled out.

"Too bad." John Randolph slapped Bascom on the back. "Four to zero."

"Come on, Durwood. Help your big brother out."

Durwood's first throw stuck in the sand and leaned against the stake. It became a ringer when his second shot knocked it home. Ben's two tosses made the pit, but failed to score.

Durwood announced, "Four to three."

John Randolph's next shot hit in the pit and skidded before collaring the stake. "Ringer. Let's see you beat that." His second shot fell short.

Bascom readied his next toss.

John Randolph suggested, "You might do better if you threw from the grass."

Bascom stepped out of the pit into the lawn. "Like this?"

"Yeah."

Bascom's toss glanced off the stake and flew out of the pit. "Might be something to that." His second toss landed on top of John Randolph's ringer.

Durwood whistled. "Way to go, Bascom."

"Lucky toss." John Randolph rubbed sand off his hands.

"What'd I do?"

"You just landed a ringer on top of John Randolph's. Canceled his out. No points."

Ben and Durwood tossed again. Durwood knotted the score.

The afternoon sun breached the thinning treetops. Bascom resisted the urge to shed his coat. His stomach growled, and he was eager for some tea.

John Randolph tossed again, placing his first shoe near the pole.

"You mind showing me that fancy way you hold it?"

"Why not?" John Randolph lightly held the shoe near one end so Bascom could see. His second toss landed deep in the pit. "Your turn."

Imitating John Randolph, Bascom fingered the shoe near one end before flinging it. The shoe hit the stake on the fly and spun around twice before settling in the sand. "Either you's a good teacher, J.R., or I just got lucky again." He placed his second toss inches from the pole.

Durwood shouted, "Eight to four."

John Randolph loosened his tie and unbuttoned his vest. "Aren't you hot?"

"Nope."

Two more points on Durwood's next turn put them up ten to four. After six more rounds the score stood at seventeen to ten. John Randolph fidgeted as he prepared for his next toss.

"Why, hello, Miss Belle." Bascom tipped his hat. Next to her was the girl she sat beside in church. They stood in the shade of an oak. "This your sister?"

Belle nodded. "This is Eunice."

"Pleased to meet you, Miss Eunice. That shore is a lovely dress."

"Thank you."

John Randolph said, "Afternoon, Belle."

"You look like you could use some refreshment, John Randolph."

John Randolph wiped his brow and stuffed his kerchief in his pocket before returning to the pit beside Bascom.

"Who's winning?"

"They are," John Randolph muttered. "But I believe my luck changed the minute you arrived. Watch this." John Randolph's shoe struck the top of the stake and skidded into the grass. His second toss buried itself in the sand less than an inch from the pole.

"Too bad, J.R. Thought for sure you had yourself a ringer." Bascom lined up to toss. His shoe deflected off John Randolph's second toss and slid tight against the pole.

Durwood leaped in the air and ran toward Bascom. "Ringer. We won. Pay up."

Belle and Eunice clapped. "Well done."

"Thanks, Miss Belle. I got lucky is all. Right, J.R.?" John Randolph snatched his coat from the stump and brushed past Bascom.

Belle asked, "Would you like to get some ice cream?" She wore a serious expression that made her prettiness seem handsome. Cinched tight at her slim waist, Belle's high-collared dress hid her neck.

"That'd be real nice."

"Come on, Bascom, let's eat."

"You and Ben go ahead. I'm going to have an ice cream with Miss Belle."

"Alright. See you later." Durwood and Ben ran toward the buffet table.

"Durwood said 'pay up.' Were you all gambling?"

Bascom suddenly felt hot. Beating John Randolph should have been enough. After all, he wasn't going to pay up. But that wasn't the point.

"Were you?"

"I know it ain't right on church grounds and all, but…"

Belle turned toward Bascom. "Let me guess. It was John Randolph's idea."

"He thinks it was. I might've planted the seed."

"How much did he lose?"

"What?"

"How much did John Randolph lose?" "Two dollars."

Belle laughed. "Serves him right. Good luck getting your money."

"You ain't mad?"

"Why would I be mad?"

"Cause we was gambling on church grounds."

"Heavens, no. That's between you and God. I think it's wonderful you took him down a notch. He isn't used to losing."

"He seems sweet on you."

"I've known John Randolph my whole life. He's only interested in me because I don't return his attention."

"Why not?"

"Because he's like every boy I know. They believe everyone and everything exists for their benefit." The crowd had thinned. Across the lawn, the minister moved from table to table.

"Is that your Ma waving?" Bascom tipped his hat. Belle nodded but kept moving toward the church. "Shouldn't we go pay our respects?"

"Not unless you're prepared to endure a thousand questions from my father."

"What kind of questions?"

"Where you're from? Did your family come over on the Mayflower? Who is your father? What line of work is he in? Do you support Taft or Roosevelt? Wilson's not an option, by the way. What college do you attend?"

"Let's go get that ice cream you was talking about. I'm afraid he wouldn't care none for my answers." Bascom removed his hat as he entered the church behind Belle. In the center of the fellowship hall, tables held tall cylinders of ice cream.

"Well, hello, Belle."

"Good afternoon, Mrs. Anderson."

"What would you and your friend like?"

"Chocolate and vanilla for me."

"Young man?"

"The same, please."

Bascom took the cones. "Thank you kindly." He turned for the door. "Let's find us some seats."

"I've got a better idea." Belle headed toward the front of the church. Reaching the main entrance, she sat in the shade of the portico. Leaning back against one of the columns, Belle smoothed her dress. "It's cooler and quieter here."

Bascom sat beside her. Back against the column, he stretched his legs and licked his ice cream.

"Can I ask you something?"

Bascom wiped his mouth with his kerchief. "I reckon."

"Yesterday at the celebration. Why did you help Henry?"

"What do you mean?"

"You helped him carry those boxes. Why?"

"'Cause he looked like he could use a hand. Something wrong with that?"

"He's colored."

"I may have my shortcomings, Miss Belle, but poor eyesight ain't one of them."

"In case you haven't noticed, white folks in Richmond don't exactly treat coloreds with kindness. But you did. I'm trying to figure out why."

"The man was struggling and I ain't had no excuse not to lend a hand." Belle's hand brushed Bascom's. He held his ground. "When I was in the mines, I worked with colored folks. Italians, and Hungarians, too. Know what I come to learn?

Belle shook her head.

"Down in the dark, you can't tell nothing about a man's skin. Only thing mattered was if you could count on him. That make sense?"

"Does to me. But you keep it between the two of us. Folks around here haven't been in the mines."

"There you are." Durwood arrived breathing heavily. "Been looking all over for you."

"What's the matter?"

"Belle's family is ready to go. They've been looking for her. They saw her walk off with you and her father's hot under the collar. Sent me to find you."

"Come on, Belle, we better go put your folks at ease."

"No. You and Durwood go on home. I'll tell them I was practicing the piano."

"But that wouldn't be the truth."

"Guess we've both got some things to work out with the Lord." Belle pecked Bascom's cheek. "See you, Bascom Matney."

Chapter 25

November 1, 1912

Richmond, Virginia

Bascom kept his coat buttoned in the basement mail room. The pale green, windowless room buzzed with activity as sorters in fingerless gloves routed mail to wheeled bins for the first of two daily mail runs. Bascom circulated among the sorters, checking their progress. Heads down, they sorted envelopes. Bascom checked his pocket watch.

"Almost time, boys." Bascom moved to the end of the row of sorters, boys in their early teens. Cap scrutinized an envelope. Bascom thumbed through a stack of mail on the counter by Cap's elbow. A manila envelope marked 'Confidential' lay at the bottom. "How's it coming, Cap?"

"Sometimes I get slowed trying to make out the fancy handwriting. Don't look like English."

"I understand. Give me fits when I started. Gets easier with time. Be sure to ask if you ain't sure."

"Don't want to bother you."

"Ain't no bother. Remember, we's a team."

Bascom checked his watch as Cap deposited the last of his mail into bins—five minutes behind schedule already. "Time. Let's get rolling." Boys tossed off their coats as they hustled toward the freight elevator.

Bascom grabbed the largest cart to head toward the main elevator for his express trip to the executives' floor. Normally, Bascom shed his coat as soon as he headed upstairs to deliver mail to the sixth floor where the radiators worked.

"Bascom." Cupping his pocket watch, the supervisor moved toward the elevator as the doors began to close.

"Sir?"

"I need to speak with you when you finish your route."

"Yes, sir."

The operator closed the gate; the lift churned upward. "Sixth floor. Have a nice day."

The operator slid the gate back as the doors opened. Warm air rushed into the compartment.

Bascom pushed the cart into an alcove in the dimly-lit, empty hallway. He removed an empty manila envelope he had clipped to the inside of his cart and grabbed the Confidential envelope from the accounting manager's mail slot. He lifted the back of his coat to tuck both into his belt. Skipping several offices, including the accounting manager's, Bascom knocked on the first vice president's door.

"Come in." Bascom entered the outer office. The secretary looked up from her typewriter.

"Morning, ma'am." Bascom coughed.

"Good morning, Bascom. Why are you bundled up? Not sick, are you?"

"Feeling a little under the weather, is all. Here's the vice president's mail." Bascom handed her a stack of envelopes. "Can I ask a favor?"

"Of course."

"Will you mind the mail cart long enough for me to use the toilet? Don't want to leave it unattended in the hall."

"That would be fine."

"Much obliged."

Bascom hurried to the men's washroom. Already late, he needed to move quickly. Entering, he bent as if to adjust his shoelace, making sure the stalls were unoccupied. He slipped into the last stall, latched the door and hung up his coat. Removing the envelopes and his pocket knife, Bascom unbuckled his trousers to sit. He placed the envelopes on his knees, slipped the blade under the seal and worked carefully to coax the flap open without tearing it. He'd reseal it with adhesive from the supply room. Prying loose the last edge of the flap, Bascom opened the hasp to remove the single-spaced, two-page report stamped "Confidential" in red ink,

Night classes had improved Bascom's reading, but plowing through the report from railroad spies embedded with the strikers would add to the mail's delay. But this was his opportunity to find out what was really going on in the West Virginia mines. He didn't know when, or if, he might get another chance. As Bascom read, the gravity of the situation became apparent. During a march on Charleston, Mother Jones threatened the Governor. Unless he rid the area "of these goddammed Baldwin-Felts mine-guard thugs, there is going to be one hell of a lot of bloodletting in these hills," she predicted. Ambushes and gunfights had led the Governor to declare martial law. Evictions swelled the tent camps where disease and starvation threatened to do what the Baldwin-Felts thugs couldn't. While efforts by the operators and the railroad to demonize the union were scoring points with the legislature in Charleston, they had had little effect on the miners who seemed hell-bent on holding out until they got improved benefits and union recognition already conferred on miners in the northern coalfields of Ohio and Indiana.

A man entered the bathroom to relieve himself. Bascom froze.

"That you, Bob?"

"No, sir."

"Who's there?"

"Bascom, sir."

"You need to do your business on your own time. I was expecting my mail ten minutes ago." Was that the accounting manager?

"Sorry, sir. Heavy load of mail set us back today."

"Where's your cart?"

"Left it with the vice president's secretary."

"You skipped my office? I'll just go down there and get my mail while you finish up."

"You can't do that, sir."

"Excuse me?"

"What I meant is we got some new faces in the mailroom who's still learning the ropes. Reason I skipped you was when I was fixing to deliver your mail, I noticed your slot was empty. I needed a minute to sort things out when nature called. Soon as I finish up in here, I'll take care of your mail first thing."

"Make it quick."

"Yes, sir."

Footsteps receded into the hallway as the door closed. Bascom wiped his forehead, then returned the report to its envelope. He dipped his knife into a small tub of rubber adhesive to place a thin ribbon of paste on the underside of the flap. Pressing it tight for a few seconds, he wiped the flap clean and returned the envelope to his waistband. Exiting the stall, Bascom tossed the other envelope into the waste basket.

He entered the vice president's outer office. The secretary continued to type.

"Feeling better?"

"A little." Bascom grabbed the cart. "Sorry for the trouble."

In the hallway, he removed the envelope from under his coat to return to the accounting manager's slot. Bascom knocked before entering. His secretary was gone. The manager stood by her desk.

"Here you are, sir." The manager grabbed his mail and tore into the confidential envelope. "Now if you'll excuse me. We've got a meeting this morning."

Bascom returned to the hallway. He checked his watch; more than ten minutes behind schedule. Others would also be looking for their reports. By the time he finished his route, sweat soaked his shirt and brow.

Returning to the mailroom, Bascom removed the rubber adhesive from his coat pocket. Making sure no one was looking, he placed it back on the counter.

One of the young sorters called out, "Supervisor wants to see you."

"Thanks." Bascom hung up his coat and headed for the office.

"You wanted to see me, sir?"

The phone rang. Bascom made to leave. Grabbing the phone, the supervisor gestured for him to remain. "Mailroom. Morning, Mr. Hopkins. Bascom and I were just getting ready to discuss it. I'll take care of it. Yes, sir. Today. Won't happen again, sir." The supervisor hung up.

"Third call this morning. Folks are worked up their mail was late again. Cap isn't cutting it. You know that, right?"

"It ain't his fault. I got delayed on my rounds once I got upstairs. Had to relieve myself."

"Complaints weren't just from the sixth floor. And this isn't the first time. Listen, I know what's going on. If it weren't for you helping Cap do his job, our mail runs would be late every day."

"I'll work with him some more 'til he gets it."

"I admire what you're doing. Boys like Cap ain't got much chance without someone like you lending a hand. But folks here depend on us to make sure they get their mail on time. If we can't make that happen, you and I will be looking for work. Understand?"

Bascom nodded. The room felt close and cold.

"We got to let him go. I'll meet with him this afternoon."

"Best if he hears it from me." Bascom's selfishness had put the final nail in Cap's coffin. He should be the one to break the bad news.

"You sure?"

"Yes, sir."

"Tell you what. I'll ask around to see if there's some other job for him. Maybe we can find something for him at the yard. Or delivering coal. You let him know we'll work on that, okay?"

"I'd be obliged."

Bascom returned to the mail room. Boys tidied up or rested. The afternoon mail would arrive in fifteen minutes and the sorting process would begin again. Bascom grabbed his coat, hoping some fresh air would clear his head. Just outside the front door, Cap leaned against the wall smoking, staring at his shoes. The gray sky had a heavy feel, like before a snow.

"Ain't you cold out here?"

"Feels good. Ain't used to being cooped up inside. Maybe if I'd gone to school like Durwood it'd be easier staring at four walls."

"Afraid I got some bad news."

"Let's hear it."

"We gotta let you go."

"You do?"

"I'm mighty sorry. It's all my fault."

Cap embraced Bascom.

"You ain't upset?"

"I been wanting to quit for a couple of weeks but no way I was going to let you down. Not after you stuck your neck out to get me this job. Ain't no one ever done that for me. We both know I ain't cut out for this."

"Supervisor says he's going to see about finding you another job.

Delivering coal or a position at the yard."

"Maybe they'll make me a security guard. That'd be something, wouldn't it?"

"One thing's for certain. You'd be the best damn one the N&P ever had. After all, you know all the tricks there is for pinching coal."

"Ain't it time for the afternoon sort?"

Bascom checked his watch. "Just about."

Cap flicked the butt to the ground. "Well, let's get to it then." He skipped ahead into the building.

✳✳✳

Reynolds opened the car door as Bascom approached. "Much obliged, Reynolds." He didn't like riding home in Walker's car, so he made sure the mailroom had emptied each evening before he left the building.

"Good evening, Mr. Bascom. How was your day?"

"Had better."

"Appears Mr. Walker's running late. I'm gonna shut the door so you don't catch cold." Reynolds remained stationed at the door. What would happen to Cap if there wasn't another job? How long would it be before he got caught stealing coal and landed in jail?

The back door opened. Walker sat. He tossed something on the seat next to Bascom. "Know anything about this?"

The manila envelope Bascom had thrown in the executive washroom waste basket lay partially unfolded, alongside the original envelope.

"Grace told me you borrowed her typewriter the other night."

"I got a right to know what's happening back home."

"Perhaps. But what you don't have the right to do is countermand me and violate company policy. You realize your selfish behavior cost that boy, Cap, his job, don't you?"

Was Bascom any different from Cap in Walker's eyes? If it weren't for Ma and Miss Grace being cousins, would Walker even notice him on the street? "The supervisor said he was going to have to let Cap go anyway."

"You can believe that if it makes you feel better, but the fact remains he had a job this morning and now he doesn't. Actions have consequences, son."

"This mean I'm fired, too?"

"Reynolds, take us down to the docks."

"17th Street?"

"Yes."

What were they going to do at the docks? Nothing but trouble happened down there this time of night. "I've got class, sir."

"Not tonight, you don't."

"I didn't mean no disrespect. It's just I got folks back home I care about."

"You have people here you should care about."

"I do."

"You've got a funny way of showing it. We'll have plenty of time to talk once Reynolds drops us off. For now, I would appreciate some quiet."

Bascom stared out the window as they left the business district and headed east. There was little on this side of town besides warehouses, bars and brothels. It was where the boys in the mailroom bragged of losing their virginity. For most, that was no more than wishful thinking. Descending toward the river, the car slowed on the cobblestones. This part of town lacked streetlights, but an occasional flaming barrel illuminated pockets of men in woolen caps and work clothes, passing a bottle.

"This will do." The car pulled in front of a row of low-slung wooden buildings.

Light shone through grimy tavern windows. Reynolds opened his door.

"Stay put. We'll let ourselves out."

"Want me to wait here, sir?"

"Come back in a couple of hours. Tell Miss Grace we had to work late."

Bascom exited behind Walker, who headed down the street a couple of blocks and stopped in front of a tavern. The sign said, "The General."

"Stay close." Walker shouldered the heavy door. Men fresh from the docks stood shoulder to shoulder or leaned against thin counters that ringed the perimeter of the dark-paneled tavern. Trapped by the low ceiling, smoke hung above the crowded room, reminding Bascom of being underground. The smell of beer and cigarettes did little to soften the warm, musky room. A fire roared in a corner fireplace. Walker pushed toward the bar. A hazy portrait of Robert E. Lee astride a white horse adorned one wall. Men stopped mid-drink as the well-dressed Walker and Bascom parted the crowd.

"You boys lost?" A bearded man in a stained cable knit sweater and dark sailor's cap stepped in front of Walker. Bascom readied his fists as the crowd closed around them.

Walker leaned around the man to shout, "Mick."

The bartender slammed a bottle on the bar. "Well, I'll be a sonofabitch. Where the hell you been keeping yourself, Walker? Let 'em pass." The big man stepped aside as the bartender leaped across the bar to embrace Walker. "Who's this?"

"Mick, I'd like you to meet my wife's cousin, Bascom Matney."

Mick extended his hand. "A pleasure. Let's go over here where we can talk." Mick shooed a couple of men from the edge of the bar, put his arms around Bascom and Walker and leaned in close. "What can I get you fellows?"

"The usual."

Mick slipped back behind the bar. He poured two beers and three shots of whiskey. Keeping a shot for himself, he placed the others in front of Walker and Bascom.

Walker and Mick faced Lee's portrait. "To the General." They clinked glasses before tossing back the shots. Bascom downed his shot and coughed. Several men hovered, no doubt as confused as Bascom about what he and Walker were doing there.

"Round of drinks on me, Mick." Walker slapped several bills on the bar.

Mick raised a long, thick piece of wood; rough and splintered on one end, the grip as smooth as a bannister. He pounded the bar. The room grew quiet. This was not the first time Mick had called The General to attention.

Walker said, "Mick's a fan of Teddy Roosevelt's. That's why he always carries a big stick."

"My good friends here have bought a round of drinks for the house. Line up. If I catch anybody trying for a second, you'll be banned for a month."

Cheers erupted. Men slapped Walker's and Bascom's backs. Walker tipped back his mug.

"What's on your mind?"

"Trying to figure out how it is you know Mick."

"Met him in '90 hauling General Lee's statue. We were the only two who made the first tug on the ropes and were still pulling at the last. Gave him one of my gloves. By the end of the day, we both had a hand worn nearly to the bone. Been friends ever since."

"How often you come down here?"

"Rarely these days. But every now and then it's nice to get away from work to rub elbows with these care-free fellows."

Is that how he saw these men? Like Pa, they lived payday to payday, drinking to temporarily forget the pressures that threatened to crush them.

"Why'd you bring us here?"

"To make sure you understand what's at stake in the coalfields. What do you see?"

"A bunch of men who've had too much to drink and want more."

"Every man in here knows how to unload a ship, right?"

Bascom nodded.

"You think because of that they have the gumption to run the docks? Of course not."

"What's that got to do with the coalfields?"

"Everything. Just because a miner knows how to get coal out of the ground doesn't qualify him to run a mine. Whether you're talking about dock workers or miners, they depend on others to relieve them of that burden. In exchange, workers get jobs so they can put food on the table and have enough left over to come down here and blow off steam."

"You all need anything?" Mick wiped the bar. A snippet of braided rope hung on his lapel.

"We're fine, thanks."

"Come on, Mick, quit jawing. We're thirsty." The men waiting in line grew impatient.

"Hold your horses," Mick drifted toward the center of the bar.

"There's a war going on in Kanawha County between the owners and the union. If we don't stop it there, it'll spread to the rest of the mines, including yours in Mingo County."

"What's so bad about the union?"

"Everything. Union claims it wants to help the miners, and maybe it did at one point. But socialists like Mother Jones have taken over the United Mine Workers. What they really want is to end private ownership."

"Where's the railroad stand?"

"Where do you think? We make money hauling coal. We're working with the mine owners however we can. If the union wins this fight, they'll be at the coal yard and down here at the docks organizing next."

"What's this strike over?"

"Started over a wage dispute. Union got involved and the demands grew."

"How much was they asking for?"

"Two cents a ton."

"Let me guess. Operators turned 'em down."

"They did."

"Don't seem fair. A miner's expected to load ten tons of coal a day. What the miners is asking for amounts to twenty cents more a day for work so hard your teeth ache. You know what a man can do with twenty more cents a day? Keep his family fed and clothed."

"That's a lot of money for small companies operating along Paint Creek."

"They more than make up for it by cheating the miners. They pay 'em for a short ton but build up the sides of the mining cars so's they hold a long ton."

"You sound like a union official, always claiming the mines are cheating the workers."

"Most of the time they are."

"Aren't you losing sight of all the other benefits the mines provide?"

"Like what?" "Housing. Education. Health Care. They do these things because it benefits the companies to take care of their workers, which makes it harder to swallow when they bite the hand that feeds them"

"You ever set foot in a company house?"

Walker shook his head.

"For the privilege of living in one, a man has to pay the company $10.00 a month. The doctor you talk about costs a miner $2.00 a month whether he sees him or not. Then they pay in scrip so a man ain't got no choice but to buy goods at the company store at prices set by the company. Some men, if they's lucky, break even at the end of the month. Most ain't. They end up owing the mines, never able to get out of debt no matter how hard they work. What you see as taking care of the miners seems more like taking advantage."

"You think the union will do a better job?"

"At least they's trying."

"How do you figure?"

"By agitating for better wages, better conditions."

"How's that working out? I'll tell you. The union helped those miners in Kanawha County like your cousin right out of their jobs and their homes, all for the privilege of paying steep union dues they don't have. You think those miners and their families living in tents without enough to eat are better off than they were before the strike started eight months ago?"

"Ma always said nothing worth having ever comes without a struggle."

"I doubt she was talking about joining the union."

"Maybe not, but folks ain't got nowhere else to turn. It's easy for you to sit here and say the miners is better off the way things is, but you ain't seen both sides of the coin. You know what drove me to Richmond?"

"No."

"Watched a friend die 'cause the company cut corners just so's they could squeeze a few more dollars out of a no-count coal seam. Would've died myself except Abner pushed me clear when the roof give way. He was weeks from retiring. Instead of punishing the pit boss for the cave-in, I got threatened with jail for putting a licking on him."

"Listen, son, running a business isn't easy. You have to make tough choices. You have shareholders counting on you to make smart decisions. You can't afford to be sentimental."

"I ain't talking about sentimental. I'm talking about treating folks decent. Like they's human. Until the operators start doing that, they will always be a struggle. In the end, the side that's doing the most for the working man will win out."

"And what do you suggest the owners do?"

"For starters, they can listen to Mother Jones and get rid of them damned Baldwin-Felts thugs. They run rough-shod over everybody for no good reason. Had my own run-ins with them."

"Mother Jones. You want to talk about Mother Jones? She should be in jail. We've told the Governor as much. As long as she's spewing her Irish venom and the Socialists keep arming the strikers, the owners are never going to disband the security forces."

"You keep talking about socialists. Miners don't care about politics. They's too busy trying to get by. Republican, Democrat, Socialist, they's just hollow labels. What matters is they get paid fair for an honest day's work and they got a company that values a man more than a draft mule. That cares whether he makes it out of the pit at the end of a shift. Whatever group can make that happen is who we'll support."

"We? You picking sides in this fight?"

"Don't have to. They was picked for me the day Abner got killed."

"Let's talk about you."

"What about me?"

"The miners and dock workers need people like us who understand the way the world works to improve their lives."

"Us?"

"Educated people of means."

"Last I checked, I wasn't neither."

"Maybe not yet. But you've been given the opportunity. To change your circumstances. Like the Mayor. Are you going to take advantage of it?"

"So's I can become part of the problem?"

"Is that what I am?"

"Ain't for me to judge."

"Doesn't matter. With your mind and drive, you can make a difference. But you have to learn to control your emotions. If you're not careful, they can lead you down the wrong path."

"What are you talking about?"

"Take that boy in the mail room. He wasn't cut out for the job and you knew it, but you gave into your emotions and got him a job."

"So helping folks is going down the wrong path?"

"Depends. It's okay to listen to your heart so long as you follow your head."

"That what you's doing?"

"It is. It may not seem like it to you, but I have compassion for these men. I'm realistic enough to know in the long run they'll be better off working for men like me than the socialists running the union."

"I hope you's right."

Mick moved to their end of the bar. "Who died? You two look like you could use another round."

"Wish we could, Mick. I'm afraid we need to be on our way.

175

Thank you."

"Nice to meet you, Mick."

"Pleasure's all mine. You listen to Walker. He's a good man."

As Bascom turned to leave, Mick grabbed his arm. "Do you know how I got the money to start this place? He loaned it to me. Walker took a chance on me when no one else would. No papers to sign. A handshake's all."

Walker leaned in. "Solely a business proposition. I recognized a good bet. And I was right. Mick paid me back ahead of schedule."

"Helped that you forgave the interest."

Mick and Walker embraced again.

Mick patted Walker's back. "Don't be strangers."

Chapter 26

December 12, 1912

Richmond, Virginia

Bascom grabbed two cookies from the kitchen then skipped up the back stairs two at a time to Durwood's room. He knocked.

"Come in." Durwood sat at his secretary before an open arithmetic book.

Bascom handed him a cookie.

"Got a lot of homework?"

"The usual. Can I ask you something?"

"Sure."

"You in love with Belle?"

"What kind of a question's that? 'Course I ain't in love with her."

"Then how come you've been spending so much time with her?"

"You jealous?"

"Heck, no."

"Yes, you are."

"It's just that we haven't been doing things like you promised when you first got here."

"Work and classes take up a lot of time."

"So does courting."

"Tell you what. What say we take the trolley over to the Penny Arcade on Saturday? My treat."

"Is Belle coming?"

"'Course not."

"Sounds good to me."

"You can invite Ben if you want."

"That's okay. Prefer it just be the two of us."

A faded handbill for a Taft rally was tacked to the wall. "You might want to take that down. In case you ain't noticed, Taft lost."

"Uncle Walker says he wouldn't have if Roosevelt hadn't split the Republican vote."

"Maybe so, but I think Wilson's going to do a good job just the same."

"Not what I hear."

"You mean, not what Walker tells you. Walker doesn't like Wilson because he's speaking up for the working man."

"Why are you so hard on Uncle Walker?"

"First of all, he ain't my uncle. Second of all, he and I don't exactly see eye to eye on who's to blame for the strike back home."

"Maybe you should listen to him every now and then. You might learn something."

"And maybe you should stop treating every word that comes out of his mouth as if it's gospel. He has his point of view but that don't mean it's always right. You need to start thinking for yourself."

"All I'm saying is he isn't your enemy. He's done a lot to help you."

"Finish your homework. I'm going to get cleaned up for dinner."

In his room, a letter leaned against the inkwell on Bascom's desk. The return address read Holly Grove. Cesco. Bascom removed the letter. With each page, his anger swelled. It had been bad enough to read the railroad dispatch, but Cesco told of unimaginable suffering he and his young family faced each day, all over two cents per ton. Bascom put down the letter, unable to finish it in the comfort of his bedroom as he prepared to eat one of Hattie's meals.

***

"You're late." Walker tapped the table.

"Sorry. Had a letter from Cesco. Lost track of time reading it. You shouldn't have waited for me."

"You know Hattie doesn't serve until everyone is seated." Walker rang the bell. Hattie appeared. "We're ready."

"My apology, Hattie."

"Why are you apologizing to her? You should be apologizing to us."

"I thought I said I was sorry."

"Walker, will you bless the food, dear?"

"Heavenly Father, we thank you for this bounty we are about to receive. Make us ever mindful of the needs of others. In Jesus's name, Amen."

Grace passed the potatoes to Bascom. "I ran into Mrs. Johnston at the market today. She went on and on about how Belle thinks you hung the moon."

"Bascom says he's not in love. But I think differently."

"Hush, Durwood. Just because I've been spending some evenings with Belle don't mean I'm in love."

"Well, there's no denying you're sweet on her."

Walker said, "Maybe that explains why your marks have dipped. Got your mind on other things."

"My mind is on other things, but it ain't what you think."

Grace leaned forward. "Then what is it, dear?"

"I've been fretting about home."

Walker sipped wine. "Tell us what your cousin said, Bascom."

"I'll tell you later. Don't want to ruin Hattie's fine meal."

"No, please tell us the latest from West Virginia."

Grace reached for Bascom's hand. "Walker, please."

"That's okay, Miss Grace. I reckon it's time we laid our cards on the table. People is dying in the camp of cold and starvation. But you already knew that, didn't you? That's the plan, ain't it? Enough of 'em die, they'll give up on the strike and get back to mining coal. Gotta take care of them shareholders, right?" Walker sat impassively. "Did you know one of them that passed was Cesco's boy, Leland? Born in the camp, died in the camp."

Grace's hand shot to her mouth too late to stifle a gasp.

"All the men's been blacklisted so they's no work to be had. The railroad refuses to let the union ship supplies to the camp, but they's running scabs in as fast as they can. Things is desperate and the worst part of winter lays ahead. Cesco says they's hope with the election of

Doc Hatfield as Governor. That is, if folks can hold out 'til he takes office in March."

"Son, like I've told you before…"

Bascom jumped to his feet. "I ain't your son. Please excuse me, Miss Grace."

Bascom tossed his napkin on the table and left the room.

He rushed out the front door, through the gate and onto the street, hoping the night air would clear his head. What started as a jog turned into a sprint. Reaching Belle's house, he slowed to catch his breath and ponder what he would say. Bascom rapped the door with the heavy brass knocker.

"Evening, Miz Johnston."

"Bascom? By the way you were banging on our door I expected to see a fire engine in my front yard. Is everything okay?"

"I'm sorry, ma'am. It's just that I was hoping to see Belle for a minute."

"It's late. Tomorrow's a school day."

"I apologize for arriving unannounced. I promise not to keep her if I could just see her real quick."

"Sounds important."

"It is, ma'am."

"Won't you come into the parlor?"

"Who's at the door, dear?" Mr. Johnston's baritone carried from the study.

"I think it best if I waited right here."

"Just a minute, then." Mrs. Johnston slipped back into the house. Still panting from the sprint, Bascom's breath clouded the cold air. Having fled without his overcoat, he blew into his cupped hands.

Belle stepped onto the porch. Clutching a shawl, her hair fell several inches below her shoulders. Bascom had never seen her auburn locks down before. Closing the door, she threw her arms around his neck.

"Why didn't you let me know you were coming? I look dreadful."

He gently pushed her away. "You're the most beautiful thing I ever laid eyes on."

"Is something the matter?"

"Come to say goodbye."

"Goodbye? What are you talking about?"

"Gotta go back to West Virginia for a spell."

"What on earth for?"

"Can't stay here when folks back home is dying."

"You're not making any sense."

"Got a letter from my cousin, Cesco. His family's been living in a tent camp since the coal company kicked them out of their house on account of him joining the strike. His youngest boy, Leland, died. Six months old."

"Oh, Bascom, I'm so sorry. What did he die of?" "Not enough to eat. Too much cold. Does it matter?"

Belle shook her head.

"What matters is my kin needs me. Worse yet, the railroad I work for bears a lot of the blame. They's working hand-in-hand with the coal companies to break the strike, even if it means starving folks."

Belle hugged herself against the cold. "I thought you loved me."

"More'n I've loved anything before."

"Then why are you talking about leaving?"

"Wasn't it you who said you loved me 'cause I was different from others?"

"Yes."

"And I was different 'cause I was always looking to help people?"

Belle nodded as tears welled.

"There you have it. If I stay, I wouldn't be helping nobody."

"What about me? Us?"

"You know what I mean. I couldn't live with myself. I've seen what happens to a man when he loses self-respect. He ends up in the bottle."

"Take me with you, then."

West Virginia was no place for Belle. Not bent over a washboard, fingertips raw from scrubbing coal dust from his clothes. Not like Ma.

"Timing ain't right. Too much upheaval. And you need to finish your schooling. Besides, soon as things settle down I aim to come back."

"When are you leaving?"

"In the morning. Day after, at the latest."

"Tomorrow?" Belle buried her head in his chest.

"Good evening." A couple walked by arm-in-arm, enjoying an after-dinner stroll. He envied them and prayed that one day he and Belle would take such simple pleasures for granted.

"Evening," Bascom replied. "I best be going before you catch your death of cold." Bascom wiped her face and kissed her forehead.

"You taking Durwood home with you?"

"Durwood's already home."

"Does he know you're leaving?"

"No. Not sure I got it in me to break it to him, neither."

Belle grabbed his hand. "Hurry back. Please."

He hesitated, before hurrying down the steps and onto the street, unable to outrun his tears.

Chapter 27

December 13, 1912

Richmond, Virginia

Walker knocked. "Reynolds is waiting."

Bascom opened his bedroom door.

"You're not dressed."

"Afraid you's going to have to go without me today. I ain't feeling so good."

"No wonder. You left without your coat last night. Where'd you go, anyway?"

"Just had to figure some things out."

"A good brisk walk always helps me see things in a different light. I hope it helped."

"I reckon it did." "Listen, I know it may not seem this way, but I'm sorry for your cousin's loss."

Bascom nodded.

"We'll work this out. You'll see."

"Yes, sir."

"I'll send Hattie up to check on you."

"Won't be necessary."

"Okay. Hope you feel better."

Bascom checked his watch: 7:30. Miss Grace wouldn't be up for another couple of hours. Sliding the curtain aside, he watched as Reynolds motored the Klein onto Monument Avenue. Bascom hurried down to the kitchen.

"What in God's name you doing up? Mr. Walker said you were under the weather." Hattie sprinkled flour on biscuit dough.

"Truth be told, I am feeling poorly. But it ain't a physical ailment."

"What is it, then?"

"I got to leave."

"What are you talking about?"

"Going back to West Virginia."

Hattie released the rolling pin. "What on earth for?"

"They's a strike going on over on Paint Creek. Just got word my cousin's boy passed. Men's been shot. Others thrown in jail for no reason."

"Your father okay?"

"Strike's a couple of counties over. I suspect it's just a matter of time."

"What are you going to do about it?"

"Ain't figured that out. But I can't stay here."

"What do Mr. Walker and Miss Grace have to say about this?"

"Ain't told them yet."

"How about Durwood?"

"Him, neither."

Hattie wiped her hands on her apron. "You aren't planning to leave without telling them, are you?"

"Won't serve no purpose trying to explain it to Mr. Walker. We'd just end up in another ruckus. I ain't got the words for Durwood."

Hattie placed the pan of biscuits on the stove top. She slumped in her chair. "This will be hard on him. He's still a boy."

"He'll be okay. I was working in the mines when I was his age."

"When are you leaving?"

"I'm mostly packed. Got a couple more things to tend to before I take my leave."

"You'll need some food for the trip."

"Don't want you to go to no trouble."

"No one's ever left this house on a trip without food before. Today will be no different."

184

Bascom stooped to hug Hattie. He pecked her cheek.

"If things go well, I'll be back before noon so's I can catch the two o'clock train for Roanoke." Bascom headed out the back door.

"Pay for a ticket this time. I won't be there to patch you up if you get caught free-loading again."

"How'd you know?"

"These walls talk."

＊＊＊

Cap's house looked more neglected than the first time Bascom had seen it. Bascom knocked, then shifted back, careful to avoid rotten boards.

The door opened. "What are you doing here?"

"I could use the help of you and your boys."

Cap stepped onto the porch. "What do you need?"

"Help finding a Paint Lick scatter tag."

"What for?"

"Gotta go home for a spell."

"When you coming back?"

"Don't know. Hoping the tag will help ease Durwood's mind some."

"I'd like to help, Bascom, but we done looked a dozen times with Durwood. Never had any luck."

"That's 'cause you didn't know which pile to look in. I'll find us the right coal if you and the boys will help me get the tag."

"What about the guards?"

"Leave them to me."

"We'll meet you by the coal piles shortly."

"Much obliged, Cap."

Bascom squeezed through the fence behind Cap's house. Stepping onto the tracks, he moved toward the mounds of coal half a mile east. Moving among the coal deposits, he found the rich smell of anthracite comforting, even if the thought of returning underground unnerved him.

"Hey, you. Stay where you are. This is private property of the N&P." A security guard hurried toward him gripping a nightstick.

"Morning."

"What do you think you're doing?"

Bascom held out his hand. "Bascom Matney." The guard didn't

budge. "I work for the N&P. In the mailroom."

"Sure you do."

"Have a look for yourself." Bascom pulled a folded piece of paper from his breast pocket.

"What's this?"

"Pay card from last month. Reads better if you turn it up this way." Bascom reached for the document. The officer jerked away and righted the paper.

"So, what're you doing at the yard? Won't find no mail down here."

"Before I come to Richmond, I worked the mines. Paint Lick mine to be exact. I promised my little brother I'd get him a scatter tag that says Paint Lick on it."

"What does he want that for?"

"Collects 'em. I got some boys coming to give me a hand. They'll be here directly. If it's okay with you, that is." Bascom removed a couple of coins from his pocket. "Trade you these Liberty ladies for a chance to find a Paint Lick tag." The guard pocketed the coins. "Deal?"

"Don't dawdle. My shift ends at noon. Next man might not be as hospitable."

"We'll be gone before then."

Humming, the guard turned away as he flipped a coin.

Bascom moved slowly through the mounds. Picking up nuggets, he rolled them in his hands, held them to his nose. A whistle caught his attention. Cap and the boys crouched behind a nearby mound. Cap held his finger to his lips and pointed beyond Bascom.

"What are you waiting on? Come on."

Cap scooted to Bascom. "Shh. In case you ain't noticed, there's a guard right over there."

"Done spoke with him. Says we need to be gone before noon."

"How in God's name did you sweet talk a guard?"

"Helps if you give him a couple of these." Bascom dropped five Liberty coins in Cap's hand.

"You ain't got to pay us to help you search for a tag."

"Just the same, I'd like to. Use it to tide yourself over until that other job comes through."

"I can't take your money."

"Then think of it as a loan. Pay me back when you can."

"You sure?"

Bascom nodded.

"Thanks." Cap dropped the coins into a leather pouch. He waved his boys over.

"Bascom's done convinced the guard not to run us off. You figured out which mound you want us to search?"

"Narrowed it down to a few. Let's start over there." Bascom pointed to the mound Cap and the boys had been hiding behind.

"How is it you know to look in these piles?"

"Spend every waking minute with something, you ain't likely to forget what it looks like, smells like, tastes like."

Cap reached for a nugget. Bascom grabbed his wrist before he could lick the nugget. "Before you boys got here I found a Hazel Mountain tag and a Smoke Tree tag. Them mines is both in Mingo County. The train that dumped them probably had a load from Paint Lick nearby."

"Spread out, boys."

After a couple of minutes, one of the boys held a tag above his head. He ran to Bascom. "This what you're looking for?"

"Let's have a look. The tin tag had a black border surrounding a red center with the words 'Red Coat' stamped in the middle. "Mighty close. That's a Mingo County mine, too."

"Where to, now?"

"The one just beyond it. There."

Surrounding the base, the group moved aside chunks of coal, careful to avoid undercutting the pile. After several minutes, another boy approached. "How about this one?"

Cap studied the tag before handing it to Bascom. "What do you think?"

"That's it, boys." Cap slapped the boy on the back.

"For your troubles." Bascom handed each boy a quarter. They hugged and cheered their good fortune.

As the boys headed toward home, chattering about what they were going to do with their coins, Bascom stopped Cap.

"Don't give up on yourself. Just 'cause you're an East End boy don't mean you ain't as good as them fellas Durwood goes to school with. You remember that, okay?"

"Whatever you say, Bascom. When are you leaving?"

"Today."

"Hope I'll be seeing you again one day."

Bascom shook Cap's hand. "'Course you will. Ain't like I'm going away forever."

Cap turned to catch up with his gang. "Wait up, fellows."

✳✳✳

Bascom finished his letter to Durwood. Dropping the scatter tag into the envelope, he laid it on Durwood's pillow. He returned to his room for one last look around. He stuffed a picture of Durwood and him at the Penny Arcade in his pack. He thumbed the notebook full of words he'd learned since arriving in Richmond before placing it in his breast pocket. Shouldering his pack, Bascom grabbed his reader before going downstairs.

"Guess this is it, Hattie. Got a lot of concerns, but eating my own cooking again is at the top of the list."

"This should tide you over." Hattie handed him a basket. "When do you think you'll be back?"

"Soon as I'm sure Cesco and his family don't need me. But I ain't so sure I'll be welcome in this house again. I left Durwood a letter explaining things. Just make sure he knows my leaving ain't got nothing to do with him."

"What's this talk about leaving?" Grace stood in the doorway. Hattie busied herself with breakfast.

"Headed home, Miss Grace."

"Were you going to leave without saying goodbye?"

"Figured it was easier that way."

"For whom?"

"Me, I reckon."

"Do you have any idea how hard this will be on Durwood?"

"He'll understand."

"Will he?"

"Ain't like I'm going away forever."

"Come have breakfast with me before you go."

Bascom slid his watch from his pants pocket.

"The strike will still be going on by the time you get there."

Bascom seated Grace and started around the table to his chair.

"Sit next to me." Grace patted Walker's chair. She clasped his hand as he sat.

188

"I know you and Walker haven't seen eye to eye, but he's a good man."

Bascom nodded.

"He does lots of good things for people."

"I know. He took me to a bar down at the docks the other night. The owner said Walker loaned him the money to open up."

"That's one I didn't know about. May have to drop in some time. What's the name of it?"

"I'm afraid it ain't no place for a lady, Miss Grace."

"The point is, just because you and Walker don't agree on who's responsible for the strike doesn't mean that you're any less a part of this family. We love you like a son. Just like we do Durwood. And after this strike is over, no matter how it works out, I want you to know there will be a room for you at the top of the stairs."

"Not sure Mr. Walker's going to see it the same way."

"You leave him to me."

"I'm grateful for all you and Mr. Walker's done. There's no way I could ever repay your kindness."

"Yes, there is."

"How?"

"Come back. I lost your mother to West Virginia. I don't want to lose you, too."

"How'd she end up in Mingo County? With Pa?"

"Your grandfather was a Methodist minister. He was promoted to superintendent and transferred to West Virginia. Right before they left, your grandmother passed away, so he and your mother went alone. She was only sixteen. Your grandfather hated it. Said the people were uneducated, uncultured. Couldn't wait for his next assignment out of there. But your mother. Well, let's just say she found the country rough but beautiful. The people hard-working and genuine—like you and Durwood. She met your father at a tent revival. He was everything your grandfather wasn't, at least in her eyes. Kind and understanding. Wanted only to please her. The harder your grandfather tried to keep them apart, the stronger their bond became, until one day they ran off to Kentucky and got married. She tried to make up with your grandfather, but he never forgave her and they never spoke again. I never saw her again. But make no mistake, she was happy with the life she chose. She loved her family."

"Here's your breakfast, ma'am." Hattie sat a bowl of oatmeal on the table. "Made some bacon and eggs for you, Mr. Bascom."

Hattie pushed through the swinging door to the kitchen.

"What happened to him? My grandfather?"

"He finally got his transfer, but further into the mountains in Kentucky, not back here. Never forgave your mother or the church. He died soon after, bitter and alone. Have you told Belle?"

"Last night."

"How did she take the news?"

"'Bout like you'd expect. Wants to come with me."

"What did you tell her?"

"Things is too unsettled."

"Good."

"Good?"

"That means you'll be coming back."

Chapter 28

December 13, 1912

Richmond, Virginia

Durwood and Ben stuffed their knapsacks, ready for the weekend. Grabbing their coats, they hurried out the door. A thick, milky afternoon sky hung close.

"Looks like snow."

"Hope not. Bascom promised to take me to the Penny Arcade tomorrow."

"You're lucky. John Randolph wouldn't take me anywhere unless mother made him. Then he'd make me regret it the rest of the day."

"Bascom's not like that."

Durwood had the weekend mapped out—finish his assignments that evening so he could spend the next day with Bascom. Then church on Sunday, followed by an afternoon of reading and playing games in the parlor with Bascom. Hopefully, without Belle.

"What's your Aunt Grace doing here?" Standing inside the gate, Grace smiled and lifted her gloved hand in a slight wave. Durwood couldn't recall the last time she had waited for him after school.

"Don't know."

"Good afternoon, boys."

"Hello, Miss Grace."

Durwood bent to kiss her. "What are you doing here?"

"I had to run some errands. Since I was nearby, I thought I'd see if you'd join me for a Coca-Cola at Collier's. We haven't done that in a long time."

"Can Ben come?"

"Maybe next time. Tell your mother hello for me, Ben."

"Yes, ma'am. See you, Durwood. Have fun at the Arcade."

"See you Monday."

Ben turned for home. Durwood and Grace headed across Main.

"What's this about the Arcade?"

"Bascom's taking me tomorrow."

"I see."

Durwood offered his arm. Grace rested her wrist in the crook of his elbow. Walking with Aunt Grace made him feel special. Wherever she went, people took notice. At times like these, he struggled to remember his mother. If she were alive, would he even know Aunt Grace and Uncle Walker? What would he be doing? Certainly not walking down a city street for a soda. More likely, he'd be trudging home from the mines with Bascom and Pa. He couldn't imagine working underground every day. Bascom always shot straight with him, but Durwood didn't believe him when Bascom said the mines weren't half bad.

"He says he isn't in love with Belle, but I know better."

"Is that a bad thing?"

"Doesn't seem like a good thing to me."

"Won't be long before you're singing a different tune. Until then, I will enjoy your undivided attention."

At the store, Durwood held the door for Grace.

Grace said, "There's a table."

"You have a seat, and I'll order the sodas."

"Here." Grace opened her pocketbook to hand Bascom her beaded change purse.

Durwood waited at the counter for the pharmacist to fill a prescription. He handed the bottle to a shop boy, who hurried out the door.

"What can I do for you, young man?"

"Two Coca-Colas, please."

The druggist reached into a red ice chest for two bottles. He popped the tops. "Ten cents. Glasses are over on the counter."

Durwood fished two nickels from Grace's change purse. "Thanks."

Durwood placed a bottle and glass in front of Grace, then sat.

Several boys spilled into the store, jostling to be first in line for a float.

"I have something to tell you." Grace poured the Coke into her glass. "Bascom returned to West Virginia today."

"What are you talking about? We're going to the Penny Arcade tomorrow."

"I'm sorry to have to be the one to tell you, dear."

"Why?" Heads turned their direction.

"He felt he was needed back home. The letter from your cousin was too much to ignore."

"Is he coming back?"

"When things settle down."

"I've heard that before."

"One thing is clear. He couldn't stay here when there's so much suffering going on out there."

Durwood pushed his bottle to the center of the table and leaned on his elbows.

"You know your brother loves you, right?"

"Sounds like he loves Cesco more."

She patted his hand. "I can assure you that's not the case."

"So why did he leave?"

"Didn't you just tell me Bascom was in love with Belle?"

Durwood nodded.

"He left her, too."

"Bet he didn't steal away on Belle without saying goodbye."

"No. He told her last night after he left us at dinner."

"Then why didn't he tell me himself?"

"As strong as your brother is, I'm not sure he's that strong. He left a letter for you."

"Can we go now?"

"Of course."

❋❋❋

Durwood folded the letter back into the envelope. He slid it into the slot in his secretary with the others Bascom had written after Durwood had left Matewan four years ago. They were filled with similar promises of being united as soon as things settled down; that nothing and nobody would ever separate them again. Things never settled down.

He held the Paint Lick scatter tag, a dinged-up piece of stamped metal. Opening his closet, he took his slingshot off its hook. Durwood tossed it and the scatter tag in the wastebasket; scooping up Bascom's letters, he dumped them in, too.

Chapter 29

December 15, 1912

Matewan, West Virginia

The train entered the station. Using his cuff, Bascom scraped frost from the window. Several Baldwin-Felts men in heavy overcoats patrolled the platform cradling rifles, looking for union agitators trying to slip into town. Beyond the tracks, several feet of snow covered the ground. Icicles tinselled the trees. Bascom flipped up his collar, pulled on gloves and donned a Fedora, grateful that Grace had insisted he keep Walker's hand-me-downs. He'd barely set foot on the platform when two agents approached. Bascom set down his suitcase.

"What's your business in Matewan?"

Bascom stiffened. Hoping to avoid a repeat of his reception in Richmond, he exhaled. "I live here."

"Don't look familiar. What's your name?"

Bascom wanted to tell them it was none of their business. This was his town and they weren't welcome. But now wasn't the time.

"Bascom Matney."

"Don't recall seeing you in town before. Whereabouts you live?"

"'Bout a mile up that away." Bascom nodded toward the mountain that rose on the far side of the station. "With my Pa."

"What's his name?"

"Clem Matney. Works at Paint Lick. Check it out."

"Oh, we will."

The second agent scribbled in a notepad.

"Them's awful fancy clothes you got on for a boy who says he lives on the mountain with his Pa."

"Been staying with kin in Richmond, Virginia, since the spring. These clothes belonged to my uncle. He's an official with the N&P."

"What brings you back to Matewan?"

"Come home to see my Pa."

"Well, ain't you the good boy." The guard stepped closer. "Let me make something clear. We don't tolerate union men in Mingo County. If you're who you say you are, we'll get along just fine. Otherwise, best thing you can do is get back on that train."

"May I go now? Got a long walk. Hoping to get there before dark."

The guard stepped aside and spat. Bascom picked up his suitcase to stride away from town.

***

Bascom hung a lantern in the root cellar. By the looks of things, Pa's harvest had been bountiful. He rummaged through bins brimming with vegetables to select the best onions, potatoes, and turnips. As he bent to fasten twine around the bulging flour sack, a click cleaved the quiet of the tiny earthen room.

"Don't move, you thievin' sonofabitch."

Bascom straightened and raised his arms. The sack tumbled, spilling tubers.

"Turn around real slow."

"Pa. It's me."

"Bascom?" Pa released the hammer. "What in God's name? You trying to get yourself killed?"

"Didn't you see I was home?"

"Last person I expected to see back on this mountain was you. Saw somebody'd been in my house. Grabbed my shotgun and followed footsteps out here. What are you doing home?"

"Let's go inside and I'll tell you."

Bascom refilled the bag. Throwing the sack over his shoulder, he followed Pa inside the small, simple dwelling that once had seemed so large.

"See the roof needs patchin' again." A bucket sat in the corner near the fireplace. Nothing besides the location of the bucket had changed.

"This house is falling apart. 'Bout like me." Pa sat in front of the fire rubbing his knees. His clothes hung from his body. What had he been eating these last nine months? Or was he just drinking? His face was gaunt—sunken eyes seemed to float atop dark rings highlighted by coal dust in the creases of his face.

"Blue?"

"Moped around for a couple of months after you left. Seemed to take an interest again by late summer. Chasing squirrels like he was a pup. Then one day I come home from work and he was gone. Reckon he went off someplace to die. Never did find him."

Bascom stood next to the fire, resting his arm on the mantle. The worn photo of Durwood and Ma leaned against the wall, its edges more worn than when he left.

"Tell me about your brother."

Bascom grabbed a tin cup from the table. Pa filled it with mash. Bascom sat in Ma's rocker before taking a swig. The caustic homebrew was a long way from Grace's port, but it warmed as it went down.

"He's doing real good. He misses you. Wanted to come with me. I told him you wouldn't want him getting behind in his schooling. He's real smart."

"Takes after your Ma."

"Favors her, too. Let me show you." Bascom rummaged through his suitcase; he handed Pa the Arcade photo.

Pa stared a long time. "That him?"

"Yes, sir."

"He's so big."

"Been gone four years, now."

"That long?"

"He's gonna be thirteen soon."

Pa's lips parted and his eyes softened. "Why, if he ain't the spitting image of Hope, I don't know what is."

"How about we set it on the mantle, next to this one?"

"Where was this took?"

"Penny Arcade at Forest Hill Park last summer. Wish you could see it. They got rides, games, food, music. A lake where you can row boats. People dressed up like they was going to church. It's Durwood's favorite place."

"They taking good care of my boy?"

Bascom poked the fire. "Like he was their own flesh and blood. Done the same for me."

"Walker a good man?"

"Yes, sir. Setting a good example."

"Tell me about Grace."

Bascom didn't know where to begin. Recalling the picture of Ma and Grace in Durwood's bedroom and the stories of his mother that Grace had shared, he wanted to tell Pa to try to remember Ma before the mountain broke her and robbed her of her beauty, charm, and grace. But these weren't words Pa needed to hear. "She's filled in for Ma best as any woman could."

"That's good to hear."

"Got anything to eat around here?"

"Pot of beans and some cornbread. Need warming up."

Bascom threw kindling in the cook stove to nurse a fire. He stirred the beans to a gentle boil. "You hungry?"

"I could eat a little." Pa filled his cup and continued to clutch the photograph.

"Come on, then."

Bascom served Pa, then put a couple spoons of soupy beans and a piece of cornbread on his tin plate. A far cry from one of Hattie's meals, this was likely better than anything Cesco and the others in Holly Grove were enjoying.

"Richmond didn't suit you?"

"Suited me just fine. Had a good job, a girl and was going to school at night."

"So what brung you back?"

"Aiming to go to Paint Creek to see if I can lend a hand to Cesco and his family. They's starving to death."

"Now that may be the dumbest thing I ever heard."

"What are you talking about?"

"You're going to throw away everything you dreamed of to come back to help your cousin? Him a grown man, and all. How is it you come to know so much about Cesco?"

"Sent him a letter when I heard about the strike over on Paint Creek. He wrote back. Things is bad. Not just for him, but for a lot of folks."

"Let me guess. He threw his lot in with the union?"

"Yes, sir. Been living in the Holly Grove tent camp since summer."

"Damn fool."

"What are you talking about?"

Pa knocked his pipe against the hearth. Spent tobacco tumbled to the floor. "Cesco come to see me after the first wave of men went on strike in the spring. Asked me what he should do. Knew what I went through in '02, I guess."

"What'd you tell him?"

"Told him to keep his head down and keep on working. Had a family to care for. Won't nothing but trouble ahead if he joined the union."

"Him and Maude had a boy, Leland, born in the camp in June. Buried him last month."

"What was it your Ma used to say? The Lord helps them what help themselves. Sounds to me like he ain't helping hisself."

"Or maybe that's exactly what he done when he joined the union."

"I guess that makes you an instrument of the Lord?"

"Ain't saying that."

"Sounds like it to me."

"When I got off the train today, a couple of Baldwin-Felts men shoved a gun in my face and demanded to know my business in Matewan. Way I figure it, union must be doing something right if it's got the mines and the railroad so riled up they's got men stopping people at the Matewan station."

"What exactly are you going to do about it?"

"In the morning, I'll hop a train to Eskdale. Buy me a wheelbarrow and as many provisions as I can at the general store and head over the mountains for Holly Grove."

"You any idea how long it's going to take you in this weather, humping a wheelbarrow over them mountains?"

"With luck, figure I can be there in a few days. Biggest problem will be finding a way past the security."

"What security?"

"The coal companies stationed men in the woods to cut off supplies from reaching the camp."

"How exactly you plan on getting around them?"

"Figure all that time I spent hunting them mountains with Cesco will come in handy. I know them trails a heck of a sight better than them agents what come here from out of state."

"Think about what you's about to do. Stop all this nonsense and go back to Richmond. If you like, I can get you back on at the mine, no questions asked. Or you can get yourself a job with another outfit if Paint Lick still leaves a bad taste in your mouth. But you get crosswise with them Baldwin-Felts agents and a job in the mines will be the least of your worries."

"I'm done digging coal. Told you that when I cut out last spring. I just come back to help out my kin. Don't plan on sticking around long enough to wear out my welcome."

"You're asking for trouble. Just like your uncle."

"I'll be alright, Pa. Soon as I know Cesco's family is okay, I aim to go back to Richmond."

Bascom grabbed the plates and a bucket of water. He stepped onto the porch to lean over the railing. Pouring water on the plates, he rubbed off dried beans. Back inside, Pa was on his knees prying loose a floorboard adjacent to the hearth. He lifted a small cloth sack from the ground and dusted it off.

"Take this. It's yours anyway." He held a stack of bills.

"What is it?"

"The money you been sending me."

"That was to repay you for the money you give me when I left."

"Told you then it won't no loan."

Bascom took the money. "You shore you don't need it?"

"Look around you. What am I going to spend it on? As much as I hate to see you piss it away on your cousin who's old enough to know better, it's yours to do with as you please."

The mines may have broken his spirit and mash weakened his body, but Pa was a good man, an honest man. Always had been. That's what Ma had known. It would have been easy for Ma to cut and run when hard times got worse. She stuck by him because he needed her, and she needed him. Bascom wanted to tell him he had done the best he could. He was as good as Walker or any other man. He had taken care of Ma and Durwood and him the best he could. Bascom wanted to hold him close.

"Sure I can't talk you into joining me? With the strike over in the

Kanawha fields, we's digging coal six days a week to fill all the orders. Could always use a strong back."

"Reckon I'll stick to my plans."

"When're you coming back this way?"

"Don't know. Depends on if I can be of any use."

"Watch your back, son."

"I will."

And tell Cesco he ain't got the sense God give a mule." Pa stood. "Reckon you best turn in if you's bound to set off in the morning. Night, son."

"Pa?"

"Yeah?"

"Night."

***

Women crowded the general store. Bascom moved through the cramped aisles gathering blankets, corn meal, beans, jerky and coffee. Adding a tarp, he placed the goods by the counter. Two wheelbarrows hung from the wall. He lifted one from its hooks.

"Can I help you?" A clerk approached from his side.

"Need some jackets."

"What size?"

"Don't know. One's for a girl about eight. The other's for a boy who's four."

"Children's clothing is over there. Let's see what we got." The clerk pulled a girl's coat from the rack. "This might be a sight big, but that way she can wear it for more than a season. A little plain, maybe."

"I'll take it, long as it's warm."

"Made of wool. As warm as there is."

"Good."

"This one ought to do the boy for a couple years, too."

"Sold."

Bascom followed the clerk to the counter. "Anything else?"

"All this, too."

"How about the wheelbarrow?"

"Yes, sir."

"You must be supplying a small army."

"Just trying to keep a family clothed and fed."

The clerk reached into a jar of candy for two sticks of peppermint. "For your boy and girl."

"Mighty kind."

Chapter 30

December 18, 1912

Kanawha County, West Virginia

The narrow, snowy trail had been cut into the mountain by Indians and settlers who roamed these hills long before. Bascom straightened his cramped, frozen fingers. The cold was tolerable so long as he kept moving. His back and shoulders ached. Fighting the downward pull of the mountain was worse than pushing the wheelbarrow uphill. Below, fires from Holly Grove dotted the valley. Another twenty minutes of easing down the mountain should get him to level ground. Twenty more would put him in the camp, but he couldn't risk it in the dark. Even if he could manage the trail at night, any Baldwin-Felts men between him and Holly Grove would be invisible if they weren't burning a fire. That meant another night on the mountain. He'd have to leave the wheelbarrow and backtrack half a mile to find a spot level enough to stretch out for the night. He removed the shovel, canvas tarp and all the blankets but one, which he used to cover the vegetable sack. Wrapping a length of rope around the uphill leg, he tied it to a tree. Bascom repeated this with the wheel. He couldn't afford to have it tip on the narrow trail during the night. He retraced his steps toward the top. After wrangling the wheelbarrow up and down trails, he found the unencumbered walk almost pleasant.

Bascom unfolded the tarp over the frozen ground, then placed blankets on top. After digging a hole in the snow for a fire pit, he lit some kindling. He leaned against a boulder, too tired to do more than chew a couple hunks of jerky he chased with an onion. As clear as his decision had been only days earlier, he couldn't help but wonder if he'd done the right thing. Questions raced like shooting stars. What was Belle doing? Could she forgive him? Had Hattie and Grace explained things to Durwood? Would Walker welcome him a second time? Bascom wrapped himself in blankets before curling up atop the tarp.

***

Before dawn, Bascom woke from a fitful sleep. He ached even worse after this second night on the ground. He brushed frost from his eyebrows. Fishing the last of the jerky from his pocket, he gathered the blankets and tarp before heading downhill. Reaching the wheelbarrow at sunup, Bascom was relieved to find it upright and intact. Leaving the provisions in place, he crept down the mountain to check for any sign of agents. For a half hour, he crouched behind a snow-covered thicket just above where the steep trail yielded to the valley. Seeing only a couple of deer so thin they'd be lucky to see spring, Bascom returned to the wheelbarrow. He dug his heels into the snowy trail to restrain the load. Keeping the wheelbarrow balanced and his feet firmly beneath him, every muscle strained as he wrestled the load downhill. Bascom's relief at reaching the valley was short-lived. Without a trail through knee-high snow, it would be impossible to push the wheelbarrow any further. Leaving it behind, he trudged through a stand of naked chestnut trees toward the tents, scuffing his boots to make as wide a path as he could for when he returned for the provisions. Snow littered the gray sky.

Twenty yards away, a man stepped from behind a tree, pointing a shotgun. An unruly beard covered most of his face. "That right there is far enough, friend." Several more bearded men with dull eyes materialized, each training a gun on Bascom. This was the second time in a week a gun had been leveled at him.

Elbows bent, Bascom raised his arms. "Ain't mean no harm. Come to see Cesco Estep."

"What business you got with Cesco?"

"We's kin. Brung him some supplies."

"I don't see no supplies."

"That's 'cause I couldn't get my wheelbarrow through this snow. Had to leave it back on the trail a piece."

The leader whispered something to a rail-thin boy who set off toward camp.

"We'll fetch Cesco and see if he vouches for you. Where'd you come from?"

"Eskdale."

"You telling me you pushed a wheelbarrow over them mountains in this snow?"

"About the size of it."

"You're either a liar or a determined sonofabitch."

"Either way, they's a load of supplies a quarter mile that away."

The boy reappeared at the tree line, trailed by two men. Neither looked like Cesco, a big, broad-shouldered man. Like the others, they were thin, bearded, under-dressed.

One of the men with shotguns asked, "What'd you say your name was?"

"Didn't."

"Bascom?"

"That you, Cesco?"

Bounding through the snow, Cesco closed the gap to wrap his once-thick arms around Bascom. "Boys, this here's my cousin, Bascom Matney. What on earth you doing here? You's supposed to be in Richmond with Durwood. Got the letter to prove it."

"Missed the mountain air. Besides, figured you and Maude could use some supplies to tide you over 'til spring."

"Says he's got a wheelbarrow full of provisions back on the trail a piece."

Cesco asked, "That true?"

"Shore is."

"Didn't think it was possible, but you's stubborner than your Pa."

Bascom turned to walk. "You gonna give me a hand or stand there jawing all day?"

***

Runny-nosed kids in threadbare clothes followed as Cesco pushed the wheelbarrow toward his tent. Along the way, young and old sat outside weathered canvas tents warming themselves over small fires.

Cesco placed the wheelbarrow outside a tent indistinguishable from a hundred others. An empty cast iron pot hung above a fire. "Maude, you and the kids come out here. Got a surprise."

Cradling a toddler, Maude parted the flap. Stooped and hollow-cheeked with sunken eyes, she was followed by two bedraggled children.

"Bascom?"

"Hello, Maude."

She flung an arm around his neck to kiss his cheek. A girl stood her ground beside Maude. A boy half the girl's age and much smaller peered from behind Maude's skirt. "Ginny Mae, Gabe, you remember Bascom? He's your daddy's cousin." Only ten years older than Bascom, Maude looked old enough to be his mother, her once plump frame lost in layers of clothing.

Bascom knelt. "Good to see you two again. Been a long time." He'd wait until they were in the tent away from prying eyes to give them the peppermint sticks.

"Who's this fellow?" Bascom touched the toddler's head.

Maude removed a pacifier. "This here's little Homer. We took him in after his Ma died. His Pa had his hands full with three other young'uns. They left camp after we buried his Ma."

Cesco and Maude were barely getting by as it was. Agreeing to take on another mouth to feed was risky. Homer squeezed Bascom's finger.

"Maude, look what Bascom brung us." Cesco unsecured the load.

"You might want to do that inside the tent." The raggedy crowd of children pressed closer.

"Ain't got no secrets here. We aim to share whatever you brung us." Cesco tossed the tarp on the ground and handed the blankets to Ginny Mae. "Take a couple of these inside for Bascom. Carry the others to Mrs. Lotito. Her young'uns could use them."

"Yes, sir." Ginny Mae took off with Gabe close behind.

"What do we got here?" Cesco lifted the bag of vegetables. "Would you look at that, Maude? You ever seen a finer mess of vegetables in your life?"

"They's from Pa."

Maude peered into the sack. She scooped several onions and potatoes."Children, run get your mothers. Tell them to bring their pots. We're going to fix us a vegetable stew for supper tonight." The children scattered.

"Got some beans, corn meal, and coffee, too. Afraid it ain't enough to go around, though."

Cesco held the coffee bag to his nose. "If they's a better smell, I don't know what it is. What do we have here?"

"Figured Ginny Mae and Gabe might could use new coats. Hope they fit. Wish I'd known about Homer."

Cesco handed the coats to Maude who buried her face to hide her tears.

"Let's get out of this wind. We want to hear all about Richmond." Cesco held the flap for Bascom. He and Maude followed.

"Take a load off. You must be exhausted." Maude removed several patchwork quilts from a cane back chair at the back of the tent and tossed them on a steamer trunk. A kerosene lamp rested on an upturned wooden crate that served as a table. A cast iron skillet and half a bag of corn meal sat beside it on the bare, cold ground. Two cups hung from a tin pail. Cesco and Maude squatted on either side of the chair.

"Maude, I'm so sorry about your boy."

"Lord's will be done, not ours. Reckon He figured this ain't no place to bring up a baby." She glanced at Homer. "Leland ain't the onliest one took before his time since we been here."

A gruff voice came from outside the tent. "Cesco, mind if I have a word?"

"Come on in, Mel. We's just catching up with my cousin."

"All the same, I'd appreciate it if you'd step out here a minute."

Cesco left the tent. Cold air rushed in. How did they deal with the unrelenting cold? The wind muffled the conversation.

Cesco popped his head inside. "Come on out here, Bascom. Want you to meet someone." Cesco held open the flap. "Bascom, this here's Mel Akers. He's a union man from Ohio."

A short man in a frayed denim jacket stood next to Cesco. Underdressed like nearly everyone in camp, Akers's only concession to the cold was a woolen cap with ear flaps tied beneath his chin. Jet-black eyes narrowed as Akers sized up Bascom. Bascom extended his hand.

"Pleased to meet you." Akers's powerful grip belied his size.

"It's cold as a witch's tit, so let me get to the point. What are you doing in my camp?"

Cesco tilted his head forward. "Now hold on, Mel. I done told you what Bascom's doing here."

"I'm asking him."

"Brung Cesco and Maude supplies."

"What for?"

"How's that?"

"Look around you. This place is hell frozen over. Nobody in his right mind is going to traipse over several mountains in this weather hauling a wheelbarrow full of supplies for a cousin he hasn't seen in several years. Unless, perhaps, he has something else in mind."

"Sounds like you done made up yours."

"All I'm saying is, it doesn't add up in my book. Protecting these people is the union's business, which makes it my business. You wouldn't be the first man that tried to sneak into our camp to spy."

"Things sounded bad from Cesco's letter, and I couldn't sit idle knowing I might could help some. If it'll put your mind to ease, I ain't looking to stay. You give the word and I'll be on my way. Tomorrow, if that's what you want."

"Now, look here, Mel. I been knowing Bascom all my life. My Ma was a sister to his Pa, who was one of the leaders of the '02 strike in Mingo. Bascom's about as likely to spy on us as you was to vote for Taft. You want to see what all he brung us?"

"Where'd you get the money to pay for all these things, anyway?"

"Earned it working in a mailroom in Richmond."

"Richmond? Thought you lived across the mountains in Mingo."

"That's where the homeplace's at. Been living in Richmond since March with my Ma's cousin."

"What brought you back?"

"Cesco's letter."

"You mean to tell me you quit a job in Richmond so you could spend your savings to haul supplies over the mountains in the freezing cold?"

"Ain't that what family's supposed to do?"

Akers turned to Cesco. "You willing to trust him with your life?"

"Ain't a man here I'd trust more. That includes you."

Akers said to Bascom, "Let's say I was to believe you. Would you be willing to make a few more supply runs for us? We got a lot of folks in need."

"Afraid I done spent all my money."

"Union's got money. All we're lacking is someone with balls enough to run the blockade."

"Hold on, Mel. Bascom's done more'n we had reason to expect. Ain't right to ask him to risk his neck for a fight that ain't his. Not when he's done got out of here and started over in Richmond."

"I'm not asking him to join our fight. But since he's come all this way, I'm just asking if he'd be willing to stick around long enough to make a few more supply runs."

"That's enough, Mel. Now that he's done seen that we's making do, he'll be on his way tomorrow. His girl'll be expecting him. Besides, now that he's blazed the trail, I reckon I can bring us supplies."

Akers extended his hand. "Didn't mean to put you on the spot. I appreciate what you've done. Thanks to you, folks will be eating good for at least one night." Akers shook Bascom's hand.

"Pleasure to meet you."

"Sorry to have interrupted your reunion." Akers walked away.

"Maybe he's right, Cesco."

"Never should have wrote you that damned letter. Might've known you'd go and do something foolhardy. You're going back, all right, even if I have to put you on that train myself."

"You'd a done the same and you know it. You was the one who told me family sticks together in times of trouble."

"Now that you done seen we's getting by, you can do us all a favor and get your ass back to Richmond." Cesco cuffed Bascom's neck and led him back into the tent. "Now tell us about this girl of yours. I ain't meaning to be the man who got in the way of true love."

Chapter 31

December 20, 1912

Holly Grove Tent Camp | Kanawha County, West Virginia

"She's a coming, she's a coming." A young boy shouted as he sprinted past Bascom's tent. Exhausted from the journey and several nights of sleeping on the ground in freezing temperatures, Bascom pulled the blanket tight and rolled over.

"Get up, Bascom, or you're gonna miss her." Ginny leaned close. Standing at the foot of his cot, Gabe shook his leg.

"What are you talking about?"

"Mother Jones is coming."

"You sure?"

"Cross my heart, hope to die." Ginny Mae traced a cross above her chest. Ever quiet, Gabe mimicked her.

Bascom sat up to tousle the boy's hair. "Don't you worry none. You'll talk again when you's good and ready. You two run along. I'll be there directly." Bascom checked his watch. Almost noon.

Gathering the blanket around his shoulders as he sat, Bascom placed his stocking feet on the ground. Frost lined the inside of his tent. Using the handle of his buck knife, he cracked the ice in the water bucket to splash his face. Jolted awake, he threw on his clothes.

In the center of camp where they had celebrated his haul the night before, a crowd gathered four deep. Gray skies and a light snow didn't dampen their enthusiasm. A loud, high-pitched voice with a strange accent caught his attention before he ever glimpsed her. A diminutive woman wearing wire-rim glasses and dressed from head to toe in funeral black paced atop a makeshift stage of foot lockers and wooden crates. Coarse white hair spilled out from under her hat as she implored the crowd to stand firm in the face of government-aided capitalist oppression. Decrying martial law declared by Governor Glasscock, or "Crystal Peter" as she called him, Mother Jones hailed the successes of Socialists in the November election. Pointing out that nearby Eskdale had elected a Socialist mayor and marshall and Socialists had swept elections in the Cabin Creek District, she hailed the miners as the vanguard of a labor movement that would sweep the country and fulfill the promises guaranteed to all in the Constitution. This strike was about more than improving wages. It was about striving for the equality that led America's founders to break from England. If America was going to live up to its ideals, the workers responsible for its successes must be rewarded with pay equal to their efforts and a say in the decisions that dictated working conditions. Mother Jones was equal parts preacher and politician. Bascom had never witnessed such passion nor such foul language from a woman.

For two hours, she railed against the railroads, the mine owners and their enforcers. She condemned the government for protecting the capitalists getting rich off the backs of labor. She encouraged the audience to arm themselves and kill every damned mine guard, to blow up the mines and drive every scab from the valley. Above all, she demanded they stand with the Union—Black, White, American, Italian, Hungarian, didn't matter. They were all in this together. She was mesmerizing. The press had it wrong. Mother Jones wasn't the most dangerous woman in America. For those in power, she was the most dangerous person in America.

When her speech ended, the energized crowd dispersed. Bascom returned to his tent to gather his belongings for the trip back over the mountains to Pa's place. Ginny Mae and Gabe reappeared.

"What are you two up to now?"

Ginny Mae twirled. "Thanks for my coat, Bascom. It's the prettiest I ever seen." Gabe tugged her sleeve. "Gabe loves his, too."

"I'm glad you fancy them. Sorry they's a bit big."

"Ma says that just means we got room to grow." Ginny Mae twirled again. "Oh, yeah. Mr. Akers wants you to come to his tent. Says it's real important." Ginny Mae's hands rested on her hips. Gabe struck a similar pose.

"Why didn't he come hisself?"

Ginny Mae and Gabe shrugged. "We don't know. We's just doing what we's asked." They started to leave the tent.

"Hold your horses. You all need to show me which tent's his."

Bascom hurried to keep up with Ginny Mae and Gabe. Children played with gifts Mother Jones had brought from Charleston. Passing the clearing, several National Guardsmen warmed themselves by a fire. Governor Glasscock had dispatched a detail to ensure Mother Jones's safety, because the only thing worse than having her agitate would be for her to get injured or killed on his watch.

"That's it." Ginny Mae pointed before sticking her fingers in her ears. Gabe followed suit. A torrent of high-pitched expletives spilled from the tent. Women nearby shooed their children.

"Thanks. Tell your folks I'll come to say goodbye before I set off for home."

Ginny Mae and Gabe ran off.

Standing outside Akers's tent, Bascom called, "You wanted to see me?"

Akers stuck out his head. "Come on in." Bascom stepped inside. Mother Jones sat, sipping from a tin cup. Her scuffed shoes barely touched the ground.

"Bascom, this is Mother Jones."

Bascom removed his hat to dip his head. "It's an honor, ma'am. My Pa met you during the '02 strike in Mingo County."

"What was his name?"

"Clem Matney."

"Can't place him."

"Had a brother, Durwood."

"Him I remember. A real firebrand. If we'd had more like him things might've turned out different."

"Got hisself killed for it, Pa says."

"Your Pa's probably right. But don't fool yourself. You don't have to take up arms against those in-bred capitalist bastards to earn a Baldwin-

212

Felts bullet. Just sympathizing with the union'll do it. They'd kill every damn last one of us, including all these children here, if they thought they could get away with it." She pointed outside the tent. "Are those no-good bastard soldiers eavesdropping?"

"No, ma'am. They's in the clearing by the fire."

"Don't take offense. I'm real sorry about your uncle. But we don't have the luxury of mourning our fallen."

"None taken."

"We're aimed at keeping folks alive so we can grow our membership. Your Pa still living?"

"Yes, ma'am."

"What's he doing?"

"Mining coal."

"Is he a union man?"

"Not since '02."

"What about you?"

"No, ma'am."

"Why the hell not?"

"I'm done with the mines. With West Virginia."

"You've got a strange way of showing it. Must take after your uncle."

"How's that?"

"Takes courage to do what you did, risking your neck to smuggle supplies to these folks."

"Wasn't thinking of it like that. Just looking out for my kin."

"Maybe it's high time you did. This isn't just about this strike on Paint Creek. Everywhere you look, there's a fight for the soul of this country. So long as the capitalists are given free reign to run things, the working man is always going to have to scratch and claw to earn a living wage. For safe working conditions. Even if things improve for these folks, it won't change a thing for the miners in Colorado. Or, for that matter, across the mountains where your Pa mines in Mingo County."

Mel held up a jug. Mother Jones extended her cup. He poured until she raised her finger.

She winked. "Touch of rheumatism."

"Either way, you did a good thing, lad. You filled their bellies for a night. More important, you gave them hope. Takes a while, but a man can grow accustomed to an empty belly. Go too long without hope and he gives up."

Akers stood. "She's right, Bascom. Three families left us last week. More were planning to leave today. Thanks to you and Mother Jones, folks are singing a different tune."

"Glad I could help."

Mother Jones asked, "When are you leaving?"

"Figured on heading back over the mountains to spend some time with my Pa before going back to Richmond. If I leave soon and the weather holds, I can be there in a few days."

"I need you to stick around a while longer."

"What for?"

"These folks need more supplies and you've proven the ability to get around the Baldwin-Felts bastards. If the strike doesn't end soon of its own accord, Governor Hatfield promised me he'll put an end to this bullshit when he takes office in March. Without supplies, a lot of these folks won't make it 'til spring."

"She's right, Bascom. They'll be more Lelands laid to rest unless we get these folks some relief."

"The union will pay you for your efforts. Right, Mel?"

"Won't be what you were making in Richmond, I'm sure, but we'll make it worth your while."

"It ain't about the money."

Elbows on her knees, Mother Jones leaned forward. "Then what is it about?"

Would Belle be waiting on him in three months? If her father had his way, she'd find a proper suitor. A Richmond boy. Not some undereducated coal miner. Belle was strong. Like Ma. She'd wait. Wouldn't she?

"He's got a girl in Richmond."

"You afraid your girl won't be pining for you after a couple months?"

Bascom shrugged.

"Does she love you?"

"Says she does."

"Then she'll wait. And if she doesn't, she's not worth your time. Meanwhile, honor the memory of your uncle and do something for these people. Your people. Make five, no six, more runs. That's all I'm asking. If we send a few men with you to increase the haul, six more trips will see these families through winter. Then you can get back to that girl of yours with your head held high. Besides, what will she think of you if you turn your back on these families?"

Mel offered Bascom the jug. He shook his head. "What do you say, Bascom?"

Belle would understand. Pa, Cesco, and Walker were a different story.

Bascom stood. "Who's going to tell Cesco?"

"You leave him to me." Mother Jones reached into her bag for a pamphlet.

"What's this?"

"Latest issue of the *Labor Star*. Read it. I guarantee it will open your eyes to how important our work here is not just to strikers in Kanawha County, but to workers in every industry and every state of this country."

Bascom tucked the magazine under his arm. "Thank you, ma'am."

"Call me Mother."

Chapter 32

January 18, 1913

Kanawha County, West Virginia

A ramshackle house like Pa's stood on the far side of a clearing. Wisps of smoke from the chimney disappeared in the twilight. A scrawny hound lifted its head from the porch, its ears pricked.

Bascom asked, "Who'd you say these folks was?"

Cesco shifted under the weight of his pack. "Clyde Eastridge. Can't hardly recollect his wife's name."

"How is it you come to know them?"

"Clyde and me worked the hoot owl shift at Dry Branch a few years back."

"He still mining coal?"

Cesco nodded.

"Then what makes you think he's going to be willing to help us out?"

"He's a good man. Just 'cause he chose different when the call come to strike don't mean his sympathies ain't with the union. Lots of folks still working are on our side. Plus, he could use the money, just like everyone else we talked to." Cesco strode into the clearing; Bascom followed. The hound leapt to its feet and howled. Bascom fished in his pocket for a hunk of jerky.

The front door cracked. A double barrel preceded a burly man the size of Cesco before the strike.

"State your business."

"Clyde. It's me, Cesco Estep. This here's my cousin, Bascom Matney, from Mingo." Eastridge kept the shotgun leveled.

"What brings you here, Cesco? Heard you and Maude was holed up at Holly Grove."

"That's right. Got a business proposition to discuss. Might we come inside?"

"I reckon. Afraid we ain't got enough to feed the both of you." Eastridge lowered the weapon.

"We didn't come to eat."

Bascom's stomach growled. Except for some hardtack and jerky, the two hadn't eaten since they left Holly Grove the morning before. The packs on their backs were stuffed with food to sustain the striking families, not them.

Bascom and Cesco moved closer to the house; the dog's howls became more guttural. Eastridge backhanded the mutt. "Hush your yapping." Slinking to the far side of the porch, the dog whimpered and lay down. "Come on in. He won't bother you none."

Stepping onto the porch, Bascom flipped the jerky and whispered, "For your troubles."

The house was dark except for the fire in the hearth. Unlike Pa's house, there were no bedrooms. A loft over the back half of the room held the couple's bed. What would they do when they got too old to climb the rickety ladder? Maybe that was just wishful thinking. A woman wearing a burlap dress, sweater and a bonnet sat in a rocking chair darning socks. She clenched her teeth around an unlit corn cob pipe. Cesco and Bascom eased the packs from their backs.

"You remember Gaynelle?"

"Evening, Gaynelle. Sorry to intrude."

Head down, Gaynelle nodded.

"Have a seat." A bench ran along one side of a hickory table. "What is it you fellows want?"

Cesco cleared his throat. "Folks is starving in the tent camp."

"Winter's been hard on us all, Cesco."

"Baldwin-Felts men keep a tight watch to keep supplies out. They's hoping to starve us out. Trains pass through every day, but the railroad won't let nobody bring us nothing. Bascom here is pretty good about working his way around the blockades. Trouble is, now they got guards watching all the general stores in the area. When they see a bunch of men buying a load of supplies, they stop us before we can get out of town. That way, they ain't got to wait to try and catch us sneaking back into camp. Confiscated thirty dollars worth just last week."

"Sounds like a predicament, all right." Eastridge lit a pipe. "What's it got to do with us?"

"We figure folks like yourself can buy supplies without drawing attention."

"You mean working folks who ain't on strike."

"Exactly. Decent folk like yourself are pitching in."

"What makes you think if I didn't strike to begin with that I'd be willing to risk everything for the union now?"

"'Cause it's the right thing to do."

"And we'd pay you." Bascom stood to reach into his pocket. He pulled out some bills and a piece of paper. "Here's ten dollars. Once a week, all you got to do is have the Missus make a trip to the general store in Eskdale and buy what's on this list. Ain't enough to arouse suspicion, even if the strikebreakers could get a man into Eskdale to keep tabs. Bring it back here and we'll come of the evening to take it off your hands. For your troubles, one dollar of every ten is yours to keep. Bet you ain't clearing that in a week risking your neck digging coal."

Eastridge eyed the cash and took a long draw. His wife stopped darning.

Bascom continued. "If you like, you can use scrip to buy these supplies at the Dry Branch company store. In which case, money's all yours. We care about the provisions, not where they come from."

"Me and the Missus will speak on it. We'll give you our answer next time you's passing through. You say other folks is doing it?"

Cesco nodded. "That's right."

"Who else?"

"We ain't sharing names. For your own protection."

"Sounds like you done thought of everything."

"Bascom here's the brains."

"Say you're from Mingo County?"

"That's right."

"What're you doing on strike in Kanawha County?"

"I ain't."

"What'd you mean?"

"Let's just say I'm doing my part to help Cesco and the other families. Same as we's asking of you."

"What's in them packs?"

"Supplies for the folks in the camp." Bascom unlashed his pack. He pulled a sack of coffee to hand to Eastridge. "For letting us into your house and lending an ear."

"Sounds like folks over to Holly Grove could use it more'n us." Bascom returned the coffee to the pack.

Cesco stood to join Bascom. "Clyde. Gaynelle. We appreciate your hospitality. Don't want to trouble you no more tonight."

Eastridge opened the door. The hound stayed put.

Bascom jogged down the steps into the yard. "See you next week." Eastridge nodded.

As they neared the woods, Bascom broke the silence. "She's in."

"What do you mean?"

"Didn't you see the look on her face when we told 'em one dollar was theirs free and clear?"

"She looked mighty down in the mouth when he give us back the coffee. Going to be a long, cold night for Clyde, I'm afraid."

***

As Bascom and Cesco reached the clearing, Akers poked the fire with a charred stick. Sparks launched before flaming out. The nearly full moon shone bright—no snow tonight. Akers stood and turned. "Things work out like you planned?"

Bascom sat on one of the stumps ringing the pit. Despite wearing everything he had, cold knifed through to his skin. Cesco sat, arms folded, unfazed by the cold. Bascom insisted the three meet in the clearing to discuss plans, in case Holly Grove harbored a spy. Although the tents offered some relief, they afforded little privacy.

Bascom rubbed his hands. "Except for one fellow who cussed us out and took a pot shot for good measure, everyone else was real cordial. Two folks said they had to sleep on it, but we's pretty sure they'll join in. Hard to turn down the money."

"How many signed on?"

"Twenty. Twenty-two if we count the ones we figure are in."

"Can I see the list?"

"Ain't one. Me and Bascom's got it in our heads. Well, mostly Bascom does."

Akers tugged his cap to cover the bottom of his ears. "How many you figure you need to get the supplies back here?"

"Six. Won't that the number, Cesco?"

"That's right."

"Sure that will be enough? Twenty-two people can buy a lot of supplies."

"Maude and a couple of her lady friends is sewing us packs so's we can carry a load on our backs as well as our chests. Can almost double a man's haul."

"Anybody ever tell you you married up, Cesco?"

"Maude does. Some days twice."

"Decided who you want to join you on the runs?"

"Cesco knows the men better'n I do, so I'm leaving that up to him."

"You got it figured out, Cesco?"

"Pretty much. Bascom says we want single men. Don't want no widows."

Akers looked at Cesco. "What about you, then?"

Bascom shrugged. "I'll let you try to talk some sense into him."

"Bascom's got a point, Cesco."

Cesco stretched his legs. "Hell with his points. He's got more of 'em than a sow's got teets. I'll be damned if I'm going to sit on my ass with Maude and the kids while Bascom's risking his neck. Only reason he's still here is 'cause you let Ma Jones strongarm him behind my back. Besides, so long as he refuses to carry a gun, he needs me. I aim to send him back to Richmond in one piece."

"Cesco's got a point, now. You need to carry a gun, Bascom."

"I come to help folks, not shoot nobody."

"See what I mean, Mel? For all his smarts, he ain't got a lick of common sense."

Akers stoked the fire. It did little to warm Bascom—the night was as cold as it was clear.

Bascom stood to stomp his feet. "If Ma Jones is right, this'll all be over soon enough. Reckon I can manage in the meantime. In any event,

I got deadeye here watching my back."

"When's the first run?"

"In a week. That'll give everyone time to get the provisions. Can you get us more cash by then? We aim to drop off the next payment when we pick up the supplies."

"I can make that happen."

Bascom stood. "Good. Now if you two don't mind, I'm going back to my tent to thaw out my privates. They's frozen plumb solid. "Night, Mel. Cesco."

Chapter 33

January 25, 1913

Kanawha County, West Virginia

Heavy snow fell. Bascom raised his hand. The men behind him stopped. The full moon made traveling easier but provided less cover. Bascom untied the belt that held the double satchel in place and lifted it over his head. Big enough to carry thirty pounds on his back, Maude's design was counterbalanced in the front by a pouch that could manage twenty. Bascom squatted. Elongated tracks intersected their path in the deep snow. They led thirty yards toward the edge of a ravine where the hill fell away to the railroad bed. Bascom and his men wouldn't be able to cover the last two miles to camp along the railroad bed as planned. If Baldwin-Felts agents were on patrol, the first place they'd check for smugglers was the tracks. Bascom's men would have to slog it out in the woods where drifts topped six feet.

Cesco joined Bascom at the head of the group. "What's the matter?"

Bascom pointed. "Couldn't have passed by more'n fifteen minutes ago. Five, maybe six. Tell the boys to stay quiet and keep an eye peeled."

Cesco whispered to the four men, who shouldered their packs. Staying parallel to the railroad bed, Bascom led through snow three feet deep. The run had gone smoothly until now. Everyone who had agreed to purchase supplies had come through—their packs were full. All Bascom could think about was sleep. Rerouting would add two hours to their trip.

Shots rang out. A man behind grunted. Bascom hit the ground. Wriggling free of the pack, he maneuvered behind it. A slug slammed into the pack, pinging off a tin inside.

"Cesco. You hit?"

"No. Gordy's winged." Shots whizzed overhead and plowed into the snow, kicking up puffs. Muzzle flashes placed the gunmen at the edge of the ravine. Bascom regretted not listening to Mel's advice to carry a rifle. He didn't really believe they'd try to kill him, but he'd been wrong. The others, less foolhardy, returned fire.

Bascom turned. "Gordy? You fit to walk if someone carries your pack?"

"Reckon I can make it. It ain't too bad."

"Pass me your rifle."

Cesco shimmied beside Bascom. "Here you go. Extra bullets, too."

"Tell Junior to push his pack up here next to mine. We'll lay down fire so's you can help Gordy and the boys retrace your steps to the woods. Junior and me'll follow soon as it's safe. Think you can do that?"

"I ain't leaving you here like no sitting duck."

"Nonsense. Junior and me'll be fine. You need to get Gordy and the other boys back safe, then send a party out to meet us to make sure these bastards don't cut us off from camp. Besides, you's the only one strong enough to carry two packs. We'll see you back at camp soon as we can."

"Dammit, Bascom. This ain't your fight."

"Tell that to them fellows shooting at me. Hurry up, now." Cesco patted Bascom's shoulder. Pushing his pack, Junior slithered beside Bascom. "Count of three, Junior, I'm going to fire my rounds. When I'm done, you pick up the slack while I reload. Got to lay down a steady fire so Cesco and the boys can get clear. Got it?"

Junior spat tobacco juice. "Yep."

Bascom placed the Springfield on top of his pack and fired. Sliding back the bolt, he chambered another round. He couldn't see his targets but knew where they were. After firing five times, he rolled on his back to reload. On cue, Junior began firing. After several turns alternating shots, the return fire slacked.

Bascom whispered, "They's either getting tired of eating snow or they's trying to flank us. Either way, it's time we got a move on. You lay down another round, reload and start backing out while I cover you."

"What about you?"

"I'll move back to where you's at while you cover me. We'll keep it up 'til we can reach the trees. Gonna be light soon. We best be long gone from here by then. Ready?"

Junior spat.

"Go." Junior fired his five rounds and reloaded. Bascom covered him while he duck-walked backwards, dragging his pack. As soon as he was ready, Junior began firing again. Bascom slithered backwards. Like inchworms, they made it to the trees as sunlight sliced the forest. Bascom stood behind a thick locust. His clothes were soaked. "We're going to keep leapfrogging one another 'til we's sure they ain't following. You go and I'll follow."

Junior pushed into the woods fifty yards and stopped behind a tree. Seeing no sign of the Baldwin-Felts men giving chase, Bascom made his way to Junior. Hands on his thighs to catch his breath, the pack felt twice its weight after being dragged through the snow. Chills racked his body. "We best keep moving before we catch our death of cold. You okay?"

"I will be as soon as I get out of these wet clothes. Let's go."

Bascom straightened. "I'll take point. You watch our backs."

They trudged in silence. The snow that had been falling when the ambush began yielded to the blessing of a soft blue sky. Bascom lost track of time as he put one foot in front of the other, certain of his direction because of the red droplets dotting the snow.

"Give 'em a hand, boys." A figure stood from behind a rock. Bascom blinked, trying to focus. Cesco? A number of armed men materialized from the woods. Bascom fell to one knee. The pack was lifted from his shoulders.

"Put your arm around my neck." Cesco supported Bascom as they followed the path to camp. Chills racked his body.

"How's Gordy?"

"Had to carry him the last mile or so. Lost a lot of blood."

"Followed his trail. He's gonna make it, ain't he?"

"Time'll tell. He's being tended to."

"Where is he? I want to see him."

"You need to warm up and rest, first."

Reaching Bascom's tent, Cesco threw open the flap. Maude stirred a pot over the fire. A pile of blankets lay on his cot.

Maude handed him a steaming tin cup. "Drink this broth."

Bascom pecked her cheek. The broth lessened the shivers.

"Slip out of your clothes, thermals and all, and get under them blankets. We'll dry them while you rest."

"Turn around."

"You think I ain't seen a man naked before? I ain't got time for your modesty. Give me them pants and thermals."

Bascom finished undressing. He lay on the cot and pulled the blankets over his nose. Sleep came before Maude left his tent.

✳✳✳

Bascom raised to one elbow. Grabbing a stick under his cot, he pushed open the flap. The sun hung low. His clothes were neatly folded on his chair. Had he slept all day? Gordy. He wrestled into his thermals while still under the covers. Finished dressing, he slipped into his overcoat and hat and left the tent.

"Cesco? Maude? Anybody home?"

"Come on in."

Cesco sat on his cot dragging a stick across the dirt floor. Akers sat in the chair.

"How's Gordy?"

"Doc says he's going to make it. Maude's tending to him." Cesco didn't look up.

"Well that's good news, ain't it?"

Akers said, "It isn't all good, I'm afraid."

"What do you mean?"

"Had to take his arm."

Bascom turned to Cesco. "You said he was only winged."

"He was. But Doc said the bullet nicked an artery. Done everything they could, but he'd lost too much blood. Woulda bled out if they hadn't took it."

Bascom struggled to breathe. Even if the strike ended tomorrow, Gordy's mining days were over before his twentieth birthday. As were his prospects of finding a wife he couldn't provide for.

Bascom demanded, "What are we going to do about it?"

"Come again?" Akers looked up from under the bill of his cap.

"There must be something we can do, Mel."

"What do you suggest?"

"Go to the Sheriff."

"What's he going to do?"

"Arrest them that's responsible."

"And just who might that be? Don't suppose they happened to introduce themselves while they were shooting at you?"

Bascom shook his head.

"Even if they had, who do you think pays the sheriff's salary? Not you and me. Not Cesco and the other folks freezing their asses off. Coal operators, that's who. Same people who pay the guns who tried to kill you last night. You go trying to get the law involved and you'll find yourself looking out from the wrong side of a cell. If you're lucky."

"What about the Governor?"

"Did you listen to a word Ma Jones said last week?"

"There must be something."

"That's what I'm trying to tell you. There isn't. Sorry, son."

"It ain't right."

"Of course, it ain't. That's what we hope to change by striking. Things'll change if we can unionize."

"You really think so?"

"I do."

"Then I reckon we got to see this through."

"You're starting to sound like a union man."

"I'm going to see after Gordy." Bascom pushed through the flap.

Akers followed. "Bascom?"

"Yeah?"

"I'm going to tell you like I told Cesco. This isn't your fault."

"Sure feels that way. After all, we's the ones who recruited him."

"And he chose to do so of his own accord. You didn't make him. Only people to blame are wearing badges that say Baldwin-Felts. Don't you forget that."

"I'll try."

Chapter 34

February 7, 1913

Holly Grove Tent Camp | Kanawha County, West Virginia

"There's fixing to be trouble tonight."

Akers addressed a group huddled around a fire in the camp's clearing. The sun had already dipped behind the bare mountaintop. Bascom weaved among the men, silently taking count. With miners randomly drifting in, a precise number proved elusive. There were between seventy and eighty—nearly two thirds of the men in camp. Men was a relative term. A handful weren't shaving yet. More than a couple had fought as boys for the Union in the War. Regardless of age, not a one had proper clothing for the deep freeze that had taken hold in December. That included Akers, whose denim coat needed patching worse than most. With the exception of Akers and Bascom, the men shared a common bond—eviction from company-owned houses for swearing an oath to the United Mine Workers' Association.

"Why's that?" An old timer asked.

"There was a fight over in Mucklow again today. Some of our boys ambushed a group of Baldwin-Felts agents. Killed a couple."

A round of clapping and back-slapping erupted. Akers waited for quiet. "They'll be wanting revenge."

A teenager leaning on a shotgun asked, "What do you figure they got planned?"

"Bascom?"

Bascom stood beside Akers. "When we was making our run yesterday, couple of folks buying supplies for us said they'd heard talk the railroad outfitted the Bull Moose Special with quarter-inch plating and machine guns."

Akers said, "We figure they're going to use that train to attack our camp."

Spitting tobacco juice, an old-timer asked, "When?"

"My guess is tonight."

"Why tonight?"

"They've been looking for an excuse. We gave it to them."

Another miner shouted over the growing din, "They planning to use machine guns against women and children?"

"If they think they can break the strike that way, then that's what they'll do. After what we started in Mucklow today, they know the law'll give them free rein, at least for tonight."

"So what in God's name are we going to do?"

"First off, we got to get your families out of the tents. Move 'em to higher ground as far from the tracks as possible. Leave your fires burning so as not to give away we're on to them, but make sure the women understand once they move to the mountain they can't light any fires. Tell them to take their bedding and anything else they have to keep warm."

"What about us?"

"After you see to the women and children, meet back here in two hours with every gun and all the ammunition you can lay your hands on. Hurry up."

✳✳✳

Bascom pulled back the flap of the tent. "Didn't see you at the meeting, Cesco."

"Been helping Maude tend to the kids. Homer's sick again. Can't shake his fever." Worry creased Cesco's forehead. Fever had taken Leland. Although they placed their faith in the Lord, losing another child, even if it wasn't their own, might be more than Cesco and Maude could handle.

"Bascom!" Ginny Mae leapt into his arms.

"Why if you ain't a sight for sore eyes. I swear you've grown just in the last couple of days."

Gabe tugged at Bascom's pant leg.

"And who might you be?"

"You know," Ginny Mae said. "It's Gabe."

"Can't be. Gabe wasn't knee high to a grasshopper last time I laid eyes on him." Bascom wrapped an arm around the boy.

"Will you all excuse me while I speak to your Pa a second?"

Handing the toddler to Maude, Cesco exited the tent ahead of Bascom.

"We gotta move the women and children up toward the ridge."

"When?"

"Now."

"You done lost your mind? They's freezing as it is, but at least the tent cuts the wind."

"Got no choice. Strike-breakers is headed our way loaded for bear."

"Bastards. Why can't they just leave us be?"

"Couple of their men was ambushed over at Mucklow. They's bent on revenge."

"These women and children ain't had nothing to do with it."

"I'll start up the hill with Ginny Mae and Gabe. You and Maude follow behind with Homer and your bedding. Men is meeting in the clearing in two hours."

Bascom ducked back into the tent. "Who wants to play pioneer?" Both kids' arms shot up. "Okay. I'll be the wagon." Bascom scooped up Gabe, then knelt. "Hop on board, Ginny Mae. Hold tight." Cesco wrapped a blanket around Ginny Mae. With his free hand, Bascom gathered it close around Gabe. "Wagon ho!"

Bascom picked his way up the mountain, mindful of his precious cargo. Snow and ice made the rocky trail slippery. A long, steady line of folks stretched back toward camp. Reaching the ridge, Bascom set Gabe on the ground and swung Ginny Mae off his back. In the moonlight, a handful of families prepared for a long, cold night.

"Evening, Mrs. Deskins."

"That you, Bascom?"

"Yes, ma'am."

"Who's with you?"

"Ginny Mae and Gabe. You mind keeping an eye on them 'til their folks arrive? They should be up directly."

"'Course not. You kids come over here and get under the blankets with the other children."

"Much obliged. Guess I better go see to other folks."

Bascom hurried down the narrow, scree-filled trail, frequently jumping off to make way for families trudging up the narrow path. Several times he sank to his knees in drifts. He was almost past Cesco before he recognized him.

"Cesco?"

"Where's the kids?"

"At the top. Mrs. Deskins is minding them. The men are gathering at the clearing as soon as everyone is safe. See you there."

"After I get Maude and Homer up top, I'm headed back to my tent."

"What in God's name for?"

"Them Baldwin-Felts scoundrels forced me out of one house with only what we could carry. I ain't going to let 'em get away with it a second time. I'm staying put this time and protecting what little I got left."

"You sure? Mel thinks they may fire on the tents."

"I'm more concerned they might try to sneak up and burn us out. We'll lose Homer to the cold for sure if we ain't got us a tent."

"I hope you know what you's doing."

"Thanks for all you done, Bascom. You're a godsend." Maude reached to hug him.

"I best be going. Reckon there's other folks needing my help."

Bascom helped three more families scramble up the mountain. Despite his regular smuggling forays over the mountains of Kanawha, Mingo and McDowell Counties, the night's pace challenged him. His lungs ached and his calves screamed from the steep trek up. A quick jog around camp confirmed the tents were empty, including Cesco's. Hopefully, Maude had talked some sense into him. Bascom returned to his tent to grab a blanket for the long night ahead. Exhausted, he dared not lie down.

"Anybody home?" Akers peeked under the flap.

"Come on in."

"Take this." Akers handed Bascom a rusty Colt 45.

"I thought you didn't believe in violence."

"Never said that."

"But you's always telling the men to stand down."

"What I've been saying is don't start trouble, because they outgun us. But with trouble staring us in the face, you won't hear me telling folks to turn the other cheek."

"What's your plan?"

"Post a dozen guards fifty yards apart in the woods in case talk of the Bull Moose is a diversion and they try to flank us. We'll position most of the men in the woods near the tracks to draw fire away from the camp. The rest will hide in the rocks on the far side of the clearing to give the bastards a farewell salute."

"You think we's up to it?"

"Guess we're about to find out. You know how to use that thing?"

"What's there to know? Aim and shoot."

"Let's go. The men'll be waiting."

✳✳✳

Twenty yards from the clearing and the nearest tent, Bascom knelt behind a giant fallen oak with two older men. He rapped the trunk with the butt of his pistol to make sure it was solid. Clouds obscured a sliver of moon, pitching the woods into the kind of darkness he couldn't abide underground. "It ain't so bad once you get used to it," old timers would say, ignoring the fact he didn't want to get used to it.

Fresh snow soaked through the patches of Bascom's dungarees. He set the pistol on top of the log. Wrapping the blanket around his shoulders, he jammed his hands under his armpits. What was Belle doing? Was she thinking of him?

"You fixin' to duel somebody with that thing?" The older man cracked, cradling a shotgun.

"Big talk for a man who looks like he's fixing to go squirrel hunting in the middle of bear country."

"Cut it out, you two. What I wouldn't give for a smoke. Even my insides is froze."

Bascom raised his hand. "Shh. Hear that?"

The faint huff of a locomotive cut the night.

"Moving slow," one of the others offered.

Bascom peered into the blackness. "She's going to be hard to see until she's on top of us if she's running dark."

A shot rang from the woods seventy-five yards to their left, where the first of their men hunkered. Bascom could just make out the engine's hulking silhouette. More shots followed. The Bull Moose answered with rifle fire. Maybe they weren't going to unleash the machine guns. Perhaps they were just trying to make a point, not start a war. Suddenly, the ping of bullets deflecting off the train's steel plating yielded to a deafening barrage—machine gun fire.

A gunner's nest rode squarely atop the engine room, surrounded by sandbags. The top of a helmet poked out. A second gun sat further back on the engine's spine. Rifle barrels peeked through slits in a steel wall that projected above the engine's catwalk. Bascom counted ten guns, maybe more, on this side of the train.

As the raking gunfire drew closer, Bascom yelled, "She's getting close, boys. Fireworks is about to start!" Reaching over the log, he squeezed off a couple of rounds for good measure. His shotgun-toting companion held steady.

"Aim high," Bascom yelled. "If you get lucky you might give the gunner a taste of buckshot."

With the train twenty yards away, the shotgun's discharge drew the lead gunner's attention. He swiveled his gun their way. Bascom pulled the older man down as a torrent of bullets zipped overhead, snapping limbs and exploding into tree trunks. The gunner drew a bead on their log, showering them with wood chips. The air thickened with the smell of freshly milled wood mixed with sulfur. Bascom slid to his stomach and covered his ears. For the first time since Durwood left home, Bascom prayed. Just when it seemed the assault on their position was over, the second machine gunner picked up the slack as the train moved toward the clearing and the camp.

Once the engine cleared the woods, the gunfire momentarily eased. The Bull Moose slowed to a crawl. Training their sights on the tents which ran along both sides of the tracks for a hundred yards, the machine guns roared to life again. After what seemed an eternity, the train disappeared into woods on the far side of camp. Bascom peeked over the log. Unable to see through the shroud of gunsmoke, he imagined the devastation that lay before him. Thank God Mel had insisted on evacuating the families—this would have been a massacre.

One of the old-timers broke the silence. "You boys okay?"

The other man swore as he struggled to one knee and brushed snow from his chest. "Good-for-nothing bastards. Woulda killed every last one of us if we'd a stayed in our tents."

Bascom sprang to his feet to sprint toward camp.

"What the hell you doing? Get your ass down. They might come back for a second pass."

Bascom didn't have time to explain. Running close to the tracks, shell casings rolled under his boots, threatening to cast him off balance. Many tents no longer stood, making navigating the camp in the dark a challenge. Those that remained upright bore pockmarks or gaping holes.

"Cesco," Bascom shouted as he neared his cousin's tent, which remained upright but listing at the top. "Cesco, you in there?"

Bascom pushed through the flap to find Cesco sprawled on the ground. Splinters from what remained of the cane back chair and steamer trunk, among the few possessions Cesco was determined to protect, littered the floor. Bascom leaned close.

"Guess I shoulda listened to you," Cesco grunted.

"Where you hit?"

Cesco removed his hands from his bloody gut.

"Hang in there. You hear me? Help'll be here in a minute."

"That's okay. It don't hurt none."

Bascom ran outside to yell for help. Surely the men would be returning to camp by now. Inside, Bascom placed Cesco's head in his lap, cradling him the same way he had Abner.

"Promise me something, Bascom." Blood trickled from the corner of Cesco's mouth.

"Of course."

"Take care of Maude and the kids."

"Hush that foolish talk. The Doc'll patch you up good as new."

"Promise me."

Bascom fought back tears. "You have my word. We's family."

Chapter 35

February 10, 1913

Mingo County, West Virginia

"Get up. Pa, wake up." Bascom shook Pa's shoulder until he rolled over.

"What are you carrying on about?"

"They attacked the camp."

"Who did?"

"Not sure exactly, but folks is saying it was the Kanawha Sheriff and the Baldwin-Felts gang."

"Where did you hear this?"

"Didn't have to. I was there."

"What are you talking about?"

"Some of our boys took the fight to some Baldwin-Felts agents over in Mucklow a couple of days ago. There was talk they might take revenge. Sure enough, 'bout midnight three nights ago the Bull Moose come chugging through camp. Next thing we know, they opened up with machine guns."

"Good Lord, how bad is it?"

"Could've been a whole lot worse. We moved folks out of their tents before the shooting started. If we hadn't, no telling how many would've died."

"Is that blood on your shirt? You hurt?"

"I'm fine." Bascom lowered his eyes and set his jaw. "Cesco refused to budge from his tent. Said them damned company agents shooed him from one house and they won't be running him off again. He was gut shot. Died in my arms."

Pa sat up, coughed and spit into a spittoon. His miner's cough worsened each day. "Damned fool."

"He was a good man, doing what he thought was best for his family."

Bascom stood to pull back the curtain. Light flowed into the musty room.

"You listen to me, son. You keep running around with them union hoodlums and you're gonna end up like Cesco. And your uncle."

Bascom placed the gun from his waistband on the windowsill.

Pa said, "I raised you better than that."

"No. This is exactly how you raised me. You ever been to one of them tent camps like Holly Grove?"

"You know I ain't."

"You should see it with your own two eyes. Know where they got the tents? The union. Know where their food comes from? The union."

"You know why they's living in tents and begging for food in the first place? Do you? 'Cause the union sold 'em a bill of goods, like they done us in '02. How'd that work out? Huh? No jobs, no pay and kicked out of their homes. Ain't got a pot to piss in. Or worse yet, dead."

"You sound just like Walker. Only difference is he's got skin in the game."

"What are you trying to say, boy?"

"All I'm saying is we ain't got no choice. You know they say there's more millionaires over in Bramwell than in all of New York City? New York City. It ain't right, Pa, and you know it."

"I hope you know what you's doing, 'cause you's playing with fire."

"Don't worry about me."

"That's what your uncle said."

❋❋❋

"These come last month." Pa tossed two letters on the table. Bascom fingered the envelopes. Grace's handwriting adorned one.

"Only them two?" Why hadn't Durwood written? He'd had time to send two or three letters by now.

"That's it."

Bascom turned over the second one to see Belle's embossed name.

He slit open the envelope and unfolded the beige pages. Belle's handwriting, which he had never seen, was flawless and delicate.

"Who's it from?"

"Belle."

"That your girl?"

"Guess I'm about to find out."

Belle wrote of school, cotillion, music lessons. She had enjoyed tea with Miss Grace and her mother. She saw Durwood and the Hopkins every Sunday in church—they were well, but fretted they hadn't had word from him. Everyone was anxious not knowing if he was well. Everyone except Durwood. He had taken Bascom's sudden departure hard and refused to speak of him. Belle wanted to know why he hadn't written. When was he coming home? She'd scoured the newspaper for something, anything, about the strike, but found nothing.

She ended by imploring him to write soon, to let her know he was okay and that his feelings for her still burned bright. Rejecting the notion that absence makes the heart wander, Belle assured him that in her case, it only served to make hers grow fonder. He read it again, breathing in every word.

"How's your brother?"

"Ain't read Miss Grace's letter yet."

"Read it. I want to hear about Durwood."

Bascom opened the second envelope. Everyone enjoyed good health. Walker had told her the strike was winding down and should be over by spring. She hoped that was true, because their home wasn't the same without him. His departure had troubled Walker at first—he took it personally. Once Walker saw it as an act of family loyalty, he accepted Bascom's decision. Durwood, on the other hand, had been slower to come around. He wouldn't admit it, but he missed Bascom terribly and she was eager to see them reunited. Belle had come for tea and looked lovely, but was distressed that she hadn't heard from him. She implored Bascom to write Belle and Durwood soon. A letter to them would mean more than he could know.

If Grace knew he wasn't coming back, would she still want him to write?

Tucked inside the envelope was a twenty-dollar bill. Our secret, she called it. No doubt Walker wouldn't appreciate his money going to help the strikers. She asked that he use the money to help his cousin, Cesco, and his family, to weather the strike.

"You gonna tell me what it says?"

"She don't mention Durwood except to say he's sore at me for leaving."

"That's it? Sounds to me like you best be getting back to patch things up with your brother and your girl. This ain't your fight."

Cesco's words rattled in his head. Bascom pushed back his chair to stare through the windowpane, as if answers lay outside in the snow. "If it won't before, it is now."

"Come again?"

"Those bastards killed my cousin. Would've killed me, too, a few weeks back if they'd had better aim. If I go back to Richmond, who's going to look after Maude and her young'uns? Who's going to stand up for them other folks?"

"Let the union do it. They's the ones got Cesco in this mess."

"Who do you think I am?"

"You're talking pure nonsense."

"You ever met Cesco's young'uns?"

"Can't say's I have."

"Ginny Mae and Gabe. Ginny Mae's eight. Same age as Durwood when we sent him to Richmond. Gabe's four. The boy ain't talked since they was kicked out of their house and he watched one of them Baldwin-Felts bastards shoot his dog. Maude ain't like you. She ain't got a rich relative to care for her children. On top of their own, Cesco and Maude took in another little boy after his mom passed. They didn't have to, but they did it 'cause it was the right thing to do."

"You saying I shouldn't have sent your brother away?"

"Just stating facts. Ain't passing judgment."

Pa swung his feet off the bed. "What is it you aim to do?"

"Ain't figured that out yet."

"You should've stayed where you was at. Ain't nothing for you here but heartache and trouble."

"Too late for that."

Chapter 36

June 14, 1913

Richmond, Virginia

Durwood slipped into his woolen knickers. Golfers milled about the locker room sipping coffee and stretching the truth about their last rounds. Durwood pulled his pant legs snug below his knees, careful to make sure they covered no more than the tops of his new argyle socks. Donning his two-toned golf cleats, tweed waist jacket and cap, he paused in front of the mirror, adjusted his cap and strode outside. The sun was making short work of an early fog. The day would be hot and muggy, like most since a wet May had given way to a breathless June. Durwood was glad they were getting an early start as afternoon temperatures would be into the nineties. Heading for the first tee, his cleats left wakes in the dewy, freshly-cut grass.

"There you are. Beginning to think I was going to have to face these two alone." Walker leaned on his long club. The mayor and a teenage boy stood beside him. Off to the side, four caddies shouldered the group's canvas bags.

"I see where he gets his fashion sense, Walker. Morning, Durwood." The Mayor took a drag on his cigar.

"Morning, sir. Nice to see you again."

"Durwood, this is my nephew, Charles. He's visiting from Baltimore."

Durwood shook Charles's hand. "Nice to meet you, Charles."

"Pleasure."

"Why don't you lead us off, Durwood. I understand you're quite the golfer."

"Not sure about that, sir. Still trying to take a round off Uncle Walker." Durwood turned to the caddy on his bag. "Long club, please."

"Here you go." As Durwood took the club, Cap gave him a quick wink. Durwood wanted to hug the friend he hadn't seen in nearly a year, to find out how he'd ended up at the Country Club. He'd have to wait until they were alone on the course. The Club frowned on members and caddies mixing.

Durwood mumbled thanks and turned to address the ball. Swinging with ease, as Walker had taught him, Durwood launched his drive long and straight into the middle of the fairway.

The Mayor whistled approval. "Guess I should have asked the stakes before now. What are we playing for, Walker?"

"How about a fifty cents a hole, plus two dollars for each nine?"

"Good thing I own a bank. It may come in handy before the day's over. These two are liable to hustle us, Charles." The Mayor patted Durwood's back as he passed.

Charles's shot stopped twenty yards short of Durwood's drive, but on the same line. Together they walked from the tee, followed by their caddies. Walker's and the Mayor's balls found the rough to the right, so they veered from the group as soon as they cleared the tee box. Durwood and Cap stopped a good distance from Charles's ball to create space. As Charles contemplated his shot, Cap broke the silence in a hushed voice. "You're dressed as fancy as Ben going fishing."

"That bad, huh?"

"Nah. You look good. Like a real golfer. How come we don't see you no more?"

"Guess I've been busy." School. Scouts. Golf. Baseball. They took up a lot of time. But if he were honest, he didn't want to be reminded of Bascom, which Cap and the coal yard did. "When did you start caddying?"

"Got hired in March. Finished training a couple weeks ago."

"How'd that happen?"

"Ain't exactly sure. After I got fired from the mailroom, I got on delivering coal, thanks to Bascom and my old manager. It was good work, but hard. And dirty. Then one day a note come to my house from the Mayor's office telling me I was to meet the caddy master about a job. Not sure who set it up, but I suspect Bascom had a hand in it. With tips, I can make double in a weekend what I brought home in a week delivering coal. Hours is better too. Plus, I get to wear this fancy white coverall." Cap turned a tight circle.

Charles's approach shot found a greenside bunker. "Bad luck, Charles." Durwood and Cap moved forward to Durwood's ball, perched on a tuft of grass one hundred eighty yards from the green. "Long spoon, Caddy." Cap slid a club from the bag. Durwood launched an arcing shot that hit the fringe and rolled onto the green pin high.

"Nice shot." Charles didn't sound like he meant it and didn't wait for Durwood as he hurried down the fairway toward the bunker.

"What makes you think Bascom had a hand in it?"

"He come to see me the day he left."

"That figures. He ran off without so much as saying bye to me."

"He didn't exactly come to see me. He come to ask for my help finding that Paint Lick scatter tag you've been after since the day we met. Me and the boys found one, too. Anyways, he said he was going to try to make sure I got a good job where I'd get the chance to meet people who could help me. Ain't that just like him?"

"If you say so."

"You got it, didn't you?"

"What?"

"The scatter tag we found."

"Yes."

"Got it on you? Would make a good ball mark."

"Tossed it in the trash."

"You threw it away?"

Charles turned. "What did you say?"

Durwood answered. "I said, 'You're away.'"

"I can see that. Thanks for telling me."

Durwood elbowed Cap. "Not so loud or you're going to get fired from this job, too."

Walker approached. He put an arm around Durwood's shoulder as they paced toward the green. "Looks like you're putting for birdie."

"Got a lucky bounce. How about you?"

"Afraid I'm in the sandbox with Charles."

"Where's the Mayor?"

"Off in the woods. I left him and his caddy stomping tall grass. Figured I'd head this way in case he wants to hit a foot wedge once he finds it."

On the green, the club's banner atop the flagstick yielded to a faint breeze. Durwood sank the putt to win the hole, as Charles took two tries to exit the trap. Walker notched a par, while the Mayor finished three strokes behind, not counting the foot wedge.

"Guess we're half a buck down," the Mayor said. "We'll make it up on the next hole."

Charles nodded, his lips pursed like he'd just sucked a lemon.

Durwood pulled his second drive left just beyond the trees lining the fairway that dog-legged right, hoping it would give him a chance to continue his conversation with Cap. After sizing up Charles on the first hole, Durwood figured he could afford an errant shot or two. Besides, Walker was better than all of them, so they were unlikely to lose many holes.

Buoyed by Durwood's mishit, the Mayor remarked, "What did I tell you, Charles? This is our chance to get even."

Charles placed his drive on the left edge of the fairway, fifty yard closer to the green than Durwood's ball. Walker and the Mayor landed their shots in the short grass near Charles's ball. Durwood and Cap walked briskly away until they were out of earshot.

"Why in God's name did you throw it away?"

"When my father sent me to Richmond, it was supposed to be until things settled down. Weeks turned into years. Just when I was beginning to get used to the idea I'd never see my family again, Bascom arrived out of the blue, claiming he was through with the mines. Through with West Virginia. Promised me we'd never be separated again. Didn't last a year."

"Didn't sound to me like he wanted to leave."

"Then he should have stayed."

"When's he coming back?"

"Mind if we change the subject?"

"'Course not."

Durwood's ball rested on hardpan behind a tree, making it difficult to advance toward the green unless he hit a perfect shot between two trees sitting four feet apart.

"What do you think, Cap?"

"I'd use a wooden head. Knock it down into the fairway. Still have a shot at par. Bogey at worst."

"You ever golfed?"

"Nope."

"Could've fooled me. That's the perfect shot for this lie. Let me see that club." Durwood punched the ball thirty yards into the middle of the fairway, giving him a good approach shot to the green and a little more time to talk before they rejoined the group. "I've got an idea. You willing to be on my bag next week for the junior championship?"

Cap cocked his head. "That depends."

"On what?"

"You a good tipper?"

***

"Table for four, Henry." The Mayor slipped a silver dollar to the maître d'.

"Right this way, your Honor. Good afternoon, Mr. Hopkins. Master Durwood."

Thick with cigar smoke, the men's grill bustled with golfers coming from the course or fortifying themselves for an afternoon round. These were Richmond's elite, men like the Mayor, responsible for lifting Richmond out of the dark days of Reconstruction. Men willing to take risks. "A rising tide lifts all boats," Walker liked to say. Bankers, lawyers, politicians—they were all here. Since Bascom left, rarely a week passed without Walker having Durwood join him at the Club to rub elbows with the pillars of Richmond. Walker wanted Durwood to be as comfortable here as in their parlor, because one day this would be his club.

Men stood to greet Walker and the Mayor. Before they could sit and without having to ask, a waiter brought their drinks—tea for the boys, scotch and soda for the Mayor, bourbon on the rocks for Walker. Nearby, a white-haired man with an untamed mustache and tapered goatee nodded at their party.

"Know who that is, Charles?"

"No, sir."

Returning the greeting, the Mayor raised his scotch. "Governor William Mann. Suffered grievous wounds east of here at the Battle of Seven Pines in 1862. Recovered to study law. Now he's busy building schools and closing saloons. Happily, his zeal for prohibition doesn't extend to the Club. Now it's time to settle our debt." The Mayor pulled a money clip from his pocket. He placed crisp bills on the table like he was dealing cards. Make sure that's right, Charles."

"That's right. They took twelve holes plus both nines." Charles seemed to choke on the words.

Walker slid the money to Durwood. "You earned it today."

The Mayor drained his glass and ordered another. "Now that the coal strike's over, when's Bascom coming home? I've got a job at the bank I think would suit him."

Durwood replied swiftly. "He's not."

Walker took a drink and wiped his mouth. "What Durwood meant to say is he's not coming back right away like we expected."

"What changed?" The Mayor exhaled and flicked cigar ashes in the direction of the ashtray. "I thought he was going to help his cousin out until things got back to normal. With the mines open again, what more is there for him to do?"

"His cousin." Walker nodded to Durwood. "Their cousin. Died in a gun battle with security agents. Left a wife and several children. Bascom's staying on for now to help out."

The Mayor reached for the salt. "Don't tell me Bascom's fallen in with the damned socialists."

"Durwood's aunt and I pray this is just youthful infatuation with an idea everyone at this table knows is a fairy tale."

The Mayor asked, "What about you, Durwood? You agree?"

Walker answered for him: "You don't have to worry about Durwood. He understands how the world works."

"Maybe I should hold that job open for him."

"Don't give up on Bascom yet. Give him time. He'll come around."

The Mayor took a pull on his cigar. "That boy does have a big heart, though. You know that caddy on Durwood's bag today? Before he left, Bascom sent a note asking if I could help find him decent work. I set him up with the caddy master. He's doing a great job, I'm told."

Walker muttered, "I'll be damned."

"What's the matter?" the Mayor asked.

"Now I know why he looked familiar. That's the same boy Bascom convinced us to hire for the mailroom. Some waif from down near the coal yard. Hardworker, but not cut out for office work, so we had to let him go. You'd think that would've proved my point to your brother."

"What do you mean?"

"Capitalism works precisely because of workers like that caddy. What's his name?"

"Cap."

"Workers like him have their place. And it's not running a business. Give them work they can handle for decent wages and treat them firmly but fairly, and everyone benefits. But put them in charge like the socialists demand and before you know it, nothing will work."

The Mayor raised his glass. "Cheers."

Chapter 37

August 15, 1913

Paint Lick Mine | Mingo County, West Virginia

Bascom climbed the steps to the foreman's office behind Pa. Halfway up, Pa paused to catch his breath. A whistle signaled the start of a shift. Men disappeared into the shaft. Tomorrow, Bascom would rejoin their ranks, resuming a life underground he thought he'd escaped. A Richmond-bound train pulling twenty loaded cars idled on the spur line under the tipple. It would be easy to hop on board and stowaway for the trip back to Richmond and Belle. He'd done it before. Reaching the top step, Pa rapped on the door. Bascom took a deep breath.

"Come in."

Pa entered and stepped to the side as Bascom followed.

"Hello, Clem." Leaning across his desk, the foreman shook Pa's hand.

"You remember Bascom?"

Bascom extended his hand. The foreman remained seated.

"How could I forget? Not sure I would of recognized him, though. He's twice your size, Clem."

"He's near as big as his Uncle Durwood was."

"Let's hope that's where the comparison ends." Bascom shifted his stance, trying not to let the foreman rile him.

The cluttered office looked the same as it had a year before when Bascom learned his fate after pummeling the pit boss. The photo of the foreman's family, frame caked with coal dust, still sat atop a cabinet. Rolled-up mine maps littered the room. Aided by windows shut tight to keep down the dust, the tin-roofed office baked in the summer sun. At least it was cool underground.

"What can I do for you?"

"Here to ask for my job back, sir."

"Thought you'd moved away to the big city? Done with the mines, is the way I heard it."

"Reckon things didn't work out like I planned."

"Like I always say, grass ain't always greener on the other side. Didn't take you long to figure that out."

Hands behind his back, Bascom bit his lip.

"If I hire you back on, can I count on you to abide by the rules this time?"

"Yes, sir."

"I'll say one thing for you. Your timing's good. With the mines opening up again over in Kanawha County, we're short some men. Tell you what. I'll put you to work on your father's crew. Keep an eye on him, Clem."

"I will."

"But make no mistake, son. Cross me again and it won't just be your job on the line. Your father's will be, too."

Bascom nodded. "There's another thing. I'm going to be needing a house."

"You want to rent a house?"

"That's right."

"What for?"

Bascom glanced out the window. Maude and the kids waited by the steps; next to them sat a wheelbarrow with their few remaining possessions. "For them."

The foreman pushed away from the desk to look out the window.

"By the looks of things, you jumped straight into the deep end. When'd you get hitched?"

"Ain't married."

"I don't care that you two ain't legal, but some folks in the community might not see it the same way. You understand that, don't you?"

"We ain't together, if that's what you mean. They's my cousin's family. He passed and I aim to take care of them." Bascom knew better than to tell the foreman that Cesco died supporting the union, or that they'd been living with the strikers in the Holly Grove tent camp.

"You're not going to be living in the house?"

"No, sir. I'll be staying with Pa."

"If you sign that lease, you're agreeing to be responsible to make all the payments whether you live there or not."

"Yes, sir."

"Rent'll be $10.00 a month. $2.00 for the doctor for you and them. Same as if they were your family. Deducted from your pay each month. You sure this is what you want?"

"That's right."

The foreman shrugged. "Up to you." He pulled a piece of stationery from his desk to scribble a note. He stuffed the note in an envelope and handed it to Bascom. "Give this to the paymaster. He'll sign you up and get them settled in. What's her name?"

"Maude."

"Make sure Maude understands if she breaks the rules we won't hesitate to evict her and her kids. Won't tolerate no whoring. Paint Lick is a wholesome community, and we aim to keep it that way."

Was the foreman testing him? "She ain't like that."

"Same goes for you. If you break my trust again, they're out."

"I understand."

"Then we have a deal."

The foreman stood to signal the meeting was over. Bascom hurried out the door ahead of Pa.

"What'd he say, Bascom?" Ginny Mae didn't beat around the bush. She reminded him of Durwood at the same age.

"Got to sign some papers. Then we'll go see about your new home."

"Gabe wants to know if it's a tent or a house," Ginny Mae asked.

Bascom took a knee to look the children in the eyes. "It's an honest-to-goodness house."

Ginny Mae and Gabe locked arms and jumped up and down in a tight circle.

Maude kissed Homer. "Calm down, you two. So you got your job back?"

"Like I said I would."

"You sure about this, Bascom? You told Cesco you weren't never going back underground."

"I know what I told Cesco."

***

The paymaster led them down a cinder-filled lane toward the Paint Lick coal camp. Three rows of neglected, ash-stained houses lined one side of the road, the creek on the other. Halfway down the street, he stopped in front of a single-story, clapboard building with a tar paper roof. Smaller than Pa's house, a small porch rose two steps above the ground. Anchored on the right by a cane back chair and spittoon, the railing on the left of the porch pitched forward, the corner post rotten at the base.

"Here we are."

Ginny Mae hopped on the porch. "Why's it got two front doors?"

The paymaster answered. "Another family lives in the other half. You're on the left. Number eleven."

"Who lives on the right?" Ginny Mae plopped in the chair.

"The Peduzzis. They's Italian. Mind yourself, young lady. That's their chair."

Ginny Mae hopped up just as the door on the right opened. An olive-skinned woman holding a baby against her cocked hip stepped onto the porch. She slid the chair a few inches closer to her door.

"Mrs. Peduzzi, these is your new neighbors. What did you say your name was?"

Maude answered. "Estep."

"These is the Esteps."

Maude said hello and directed the children to do the same. Gabe smiled and nodded.

"I'm Ginny Mae. That's Gabe. He don't talk none. Ain't personal, ma'am." Ginny Mae smiled and extended her hand.

Slow to accept the gesture, Mrs. Peduzzi took Ginny Mae's hand to endure a vigorous greeting. A slight grin parted her lips. She touched her chest. "Concetta." Pointing to the infant, she said, "Fabio."

"Pleased to meet you, Fabio." Ginny Mae planted a kiss on the baby's dark, fuzzy head. Pointing at Ma, Ginny Mae continued. "She's my Ma and that baby there's Homer. He ain't ours but we's caring for him just the same. That's my cousin, Bascom. Uncle Clem's his Pa."

Brow furrowed, Mrs. Peduzzi nodded slightly. Did she understand a word Ginny Mae had said? Did it matter? She didn't need to understand the language to appreciate the girl's enthusiasm and sincerity.

Maude grasped Mrs. Peduzzi's hand. "How old is your baby?"

The Italian looked to the paymaster.

Pointing to Fabio, he asked, "Quanti?"

"Ah. Uno."

The paymaster interpreted. "He's one."

"So's Homer, I think. They'll be playmates."

Gabe tugged the paymaster's coat. "Can we go inside, mister? I want to see my new house."

Maude gasped. "Thank the Lord."

Bascom patted the boy's curls. "Well, I guess you's good and ready now."

The paymaster handed Gabe a bitted, iron key. "Here you go, son. Put it in that hole and turn it."

"Thanks." Gabe inserted the key to turn it. Twisting the knob, he entered the house with Ginny Mae close on his heels. Bascom and Pa followed Maude inside.

The room was dark, the only light coming from two windows on the front wall, shaded by the porch overhang. Bunk beds pressed into a corner. A small cupboard and cook stove occupied the shared wall. In the middle of the room, steps from the front door, sat a table and three chairs. A fireplace with brick hearth occupied the left wall.

Bascom asked, "What do you think?"

"I love it," Ginny Mae said. Gabe squealed.

Bascom recalled the wonder Miss Grace's home held for him when he first saw it. The children's delight over this simple, one-room dwelling was no less.

Maude hugged Bascom and kissed his cheek. "I love it, too. Thank you. For everything."

"They's only two beds. Where you going to sleep, Bascom?" Having decided to speak again, it seemed as if Gabe was making up for lost time.

"I ain't staying here. This is your house. I'll be up on the mountain with Pa."

"But you's family. Said so yourself."

"I know I did, Gabe. But don't you worry none. I'll be checking in on you regular after my shift ends. We'll get together on Sundays, too. Okay?"

Gabe nodded.

"Now don't go quiet on me, again. You hear?"

The boy grinned. "I won't." The children flew out the door.

Bascom placed a kerosene lamp, cast iron skillet and cook pot on the table. Pa laid a stack of quilts and coats on the bottom bunk.

"Pa and I'll go to the company store to get some supplies while you get settled in. Is there anything special you need?"

Maude shook her head, unable to utter a word.

Chapter 38

May 19, 1916

Paint Lick Coal Camp | Mingo County, West Virginia

The schoolhouse erupted in applause as a line of costumed children, holding hands, bowed on the makeshift stage. The play had been a success—Pocahontas had saved John Smith from her father and found true love with John Rolfe. Dressed as the Indian princess, Ginny Mae bent at the waist. Bascom, Maude, and the Peduzzis waved enthusiastically.

Miss Peters strode onto the stage. Her shoulder-length auburn hair bounced as she walked. Turning to her pupils, the teacher said, "Please give them another round of applause." As the clapping waned, she added, "Thank you for coming out tonight. The children have worked so hard on this performance. I particularly want to thank the families who've helped us memorize lines, sew costumes, and build stages." Did she just look Bascom's way? "It was truly a group effort. Thank you and good night."

Ginny Mae and Gabe had been carrying on about Miss Peters since Christmas. When they talked about how nice and pretty she was, Bascom dismissed it as the talk of polite children. Pretty and nice didn't go with teacher. But over the course of the week as he helped build the stage, he learned the children were right on both counts. It didn't matter whether she was speaking to Ginny Mae and Gabe or one of the Italian or Hungarian kids, she treated all the same.

Ginny Mae and Gabe rushed over.

"What did you think?" Ginny Mae asked.

Bascom bent to examine her neck.

"What're you doing?" she asked.

"Just making sure your head don't need to be sewed back on. That hatchet got mighty close."

"What about me?"

"Never seen a finer soldier. You spoke your line with real authority, too. Let me hear it again."

Gabe threw back his shoulders and saluted. "Yes, Captain Smith."

"That's it." Bascom slapped his thigh and leaned in. "Your Ma's costumes was the best. Be sure to thank her."

"Thanks for making our costumes, Ma."

Fabio fingered the wooden sword Bascom had made for Gabe. Gabe removed it from his belt to hand to him. Fabio flitted away, Homer close behind.

Miss Peters approached. Her bright blue gingham dress matched her eyes. "Ginny Mae, you were the best Pocahontas since Pocahontas herself."

"Thank you, ma'am."

"You must be proud, Mrs. Estep."

"I am. And grateful to have you here. Things is much better since you come."

"That's awfully nice of you to say."

Miss Peters turned to the Peduzzis. "I hope you enjoyed the play. It means so much to have members of the community show their support."

The Peduzzis turned to Bascom. Slowly, he translated Miss Peters' words.

"Welcome," Mrs. Peduzzi said.

Mr. Peduzzi added, "I like very much."

"Me, also," said Giovanni, Mrs. Peduzzi's brother, as he winked at Maude.

Maude extended a hand. "Thank you for a wonderful night. We best be getting the little ones to bed."

Ginny Mae scooped up Nunzio, Fabio's little brother. The group headed for the door.

Bascom touched Maude's elbow. "I'll be by directly to say goodnight to the kids."

"Good. They's something I want to discuss with you."

As the door closed, Bascom and Miss Peters were alone. She broke the silence. "You speak Italian?"

"Don't know as I'd go that far. I can say a few things."

"She sat on a bench and motioned for Bascom to join her. "I think you're being modest. How did you learn?"

"Swinging a pickaxe all day is mindless work. So I figure I might as well make good use of my time. In exchange for helping them with English, the Italians and Hungarians on our crew been teaching me."

"You speak Hungarian, too?"

"Not as good as Italian, on account of Maude shares a house with the Peduzzis and they've become mighty close."

Miss Peters stood to smooth the wrinkles in her dress before returning to the bench. "You're Ginny Mae's and Gabe's uncle, right?"

"Not exactly. Their father and me was cousins."

"Ginny Mae told me yesterday her father was dead and you've been supporting them."

"I been helping out a little. Maude takes in laundry."

"Mind if I ask something personal?"

"Don't reckon."

"How did he pass?"

Bascom fidgeted. Could he trust her? Paint Lick's owner paid her salary and expected loyalty. Bascom had worked to keep his union activities a secret. He needed this job to be able to provide for Maude's family. He didn't need any complications. She held his gaze.

"You ever hear of the Bull Moose Special attack on Holly Grove?"

"Of course."

"We was there. Cesco, their daddy, got killed by the train's gunners."

"You're a union member?" She placed her hand on top of his. "It's okay. Your secret's safe."

Bascom nodded.

"You end up in Holly Grove after being evicted?"

"Not exactly. Cesco joined the strike in the summer of '12. Got evicted and landed in a tent in Holly Grove. I got word before Christmas their little boy died and they was struggling. Had to see things for myself, so I quit my job and hopped a train from Richmond."

"Richmond? I thought you lived here."

"That's a story for some other day. One thing led to another, and next thing I know Ma Jones has got me cornered and is telling me what I can do to help."

Miss Peters leaned closer. "What's she like?"

"A force of nature. Like a tornado and earthquake all rolled into one. Ain't someone to take no for an answer. Next thing I know, I'm knee-deep in union work smuggling goods to the camp. The night the train come through, I tried to talk Cesco out of going back to his tent, but he wouldn't listen. Found him shot up."

She squeezed his hand. "I'm so sorry."

"I promised to care for Maude and the kids, so I got my old job back and got them a house where I could keep an eye on them. Here I am."

"Are you still involved with the union?"

Bascom hesitated. Something about this woman made him want to tell the truth. "Can't hardly afford to be. Foreman threatened to fire me and kick Maude out of her house if I crossed the line. It's been hard sitting idle and watching the mine take advantage, but I ain't got much choice." Bascom stood to straighten a bench.

"What about Richmond? Are you going back someday?"

"That was the plan. But ain't nothing there for me now." According to Grace's last letter, Belle had finally taken his advice and moved on; she was engaged. Even though he pushed her into it, he regretted his loss. Durwood continued to ignore Bascom's letters and was moving forward with plans for adoption. Bascom was where he belonged, even if it wasn't where he imagined he would be. "I best be going so Maude can get the kids to bed. It was a pleasure speaking with you, Miss Peters."

"Call me Alma."

Bascom moved toward the door.

"Will you teach me?"

"Pardon?"

"Will you teach me Italian and Hungarian?"

"I'm afraid I ain't no teacher. Wasn't much of a student, for that matter. Only got as far as eighth grade. Besides, I can't read a lick of it."

"I don't need to know how to read it. I just want to be able to communicate with all my students and their parents."

"I'm willing to give it a go. When do you want to start?"

"How about tomorrow?"

"Deal. I'll come by after my shift ends."

Bascom stepped outside. A polka from an accordion dueled with a harmonica playing a spiritual. He had given Belle permission to move on. Maybe it was time he allowed himself the same.

✳✳✳

A kerosene lamp cast a soft glow. Maude sat at the table. The curtain Bascom installed to separate the bunk beds from the rest of the room was drawn. "Afraid the kids is already asleep."

"Cesco would have been so proud." Bascom bent to kiss her cheek. "What was it you wanted to discuss?"

Maude took Bascom's hand as he sat next to her. "Giovanni asked me to marry him."

Bascom froze. How had he not seen this coming? Ever since Giovanni joined Concetta and her husband in America nine months earlier, he seemed to show an interest in the kids. Giovanni was a hard worker and a quick learner. His English was already better than his sister's and his brother-in-law's. He would be a good provider.

"You understand I miss Cesco. Not a day goes by I don't wish he was here."

"I know, Maude. So do I."

"But Giovanni's a kind man. And he loves the kids like they was his own. They love him, too."

"How about you? Do you love him?"

"I've come to."

"Then, I'm happy for you. When's the wedding?"

"That depends on you."

"Me?"

"I'm not telling you I'm getting married. I'm asking your permission."

"I don't understand."

"If it weren't for you, Lord knows what would have happened to us. You've been like a father to the kids since Cesco left us and a brother to me. I value your judgment more than you know. If you was to tell me you didn't think it was a good idea, then I would tell Giovanni no."

"Of course, you have my blessing, Maude. You and the kids deserve to be happy."

"So do you, Bascom. You deserve to live your own life and not be tied down to a family that ain't your own. Go back to Richmond. Make a life with Belle."

"Afraid it's too late for that."

"I'm so sorry." Maude rose to hug Bascom. "You're a good man, Bascom Matney."

Chapter 39

May 24, 1918

Matewan, West Virginia

Three taps came on the hardware store's back door. Bascom responded with two taps, followed by two more from outside. Bascom cracked open the door; three colored men slipped inside. Bascom shut the door and embraced them. "This way, brothers." He ushered them into a cramped supply room where they joined a dozen others. Bascom moved to the front. Turning up a lantern, he placed it on a shelf. Panels of black wool tacked to the lone window contained the light.

"Appreciate y'all coming. This here's Mel Akers. Union sent him to help us organize."

Giovanni translated for the Italians. One of the Hungarians did the same for his countrymen.

From the back, a man asked, "How you figure we's going to get men to join us? With the war going full tilt, men's working overtime, making the best wages of their life."

Akers said, "You're right. Wages are high and there's more than enough work. That's why we aren't asking anyone to sign up now. Keep using the money Bascom's giving you to help folks out when they get in a pinch. Make sure they know where it's coming from. When the time comes to ask folks to join, we need to be sure the union's earned their trust."

Giovanni leaned into the short, compact man next to him. "Matteo asks when will that be."

"Tell Matteo I can't exactly say. What I can tell him is the war's winding down. Germany's on its last legs. When it ends, everything's going to change."

Bascom said, "When peace comes, demand for coal's gonna drop along with wages. But you know what ain't gonna drop? The high prices you been paying on rent and goods at the company store. When that day comes, men will be begging us to join."

An old-timer about Pa's age cleared his throat. "No offense, mister, but how do we know when times get tough that the union won't leave us holding the bag? It's happened before. Just ask Bascom's Pa."

Bascom asked, "How long you been knowing me?"

"All your life, I reckon."

"You trust me?"

The man looked around the room. "'Course, I do. Every man in here does."

Bascom put his arm around Akers's shoulder. "Me and Mel worked side by side in Holly Grove during the strike in '12 over on Cabin Creek. Don't get no rougher than that. Right, Mel?"

Akers nodded.

"Point is, he didn't cut and run then. And he won't now. I trust him with my life."

Another asked, "How are we gonna protect ourselves from the Baldwin-Felts guns? Soon as the operators get a whiff of a strike, this place'll be crawling with them bastards. Even if men join up like you expect, they outgun us."

"Not for long," Akers said. "Union's been stockpiling weapons."

One of the men asked, "If we aim to hurt 'em, why don't we strike now while the prices is up?"

"Fair point," Akers said. "A strike now would cost the companies a lot of money. But there's reasons we have to wait. First of all, a strike while the war's going on would violate federal law. We don't want the feds coming down on us. Second reason we can't strike now is we'd be branded traitors while we've still got boys overseas fighting. Newspapers from here to California would run headlines saying we're just a bunch of socialists looking to overthrow the government. When the time comes, we'll need public opinion on our side."

The Hungarian translator asked, "So what you want we should do?"

"Keep working hard. Don't let on like things are about to change. Be careful who you talk to, but tell the men you trust to save every penny, so they'll have a cushion when we walk out."

Bascom asked, "Any questions? Good. I'm going out to make sure the coast is clear. Then we'll leave in pairs, fifteen minutes apart. Meet again in a week."

※※※

"Morning." Alma bent to kiss Bascom. Setting his newspaper and coffee cup down, he pulled her onto his lap. "What time did you get in?"

"After one. You was sound asleep. Couldn't get so much as a cuddle out of you."

"That's what you get for staying out so late. What are you reading?"

Bascom handed her the paper.

Alma read aloud. "Go to War, Go to Work, or Go to Jail. The State Council of Defense announced last week that all employers must report the names of any workers not fulfilling a thirty-six hour work week. Workers failing to meet their patriotic duty will be subject to arrest."

"What are you going to do? Your name's going to show up on that list."

"I've got a job."

"I don't think secret union meetings count toward the thirty-six hours they're talking about. Since that Akers fellow showed up, it seems you've been spending more time with him than at work."

Bascom sipped his coffee. "You worry too much."

"One of us needs to. Lord knows you don't."

Bascom did worry. About Alma. The time was coming when his activities could put her in danger if their relationship became known. Outside of Giovanni, Maude, and the kids, few people knew. It only took one slip of a tongue for that to change. Was he being selfish to see her? Particularly when they could never share each other's company in public like a normal couple? He pushed the thought away.

"I'll be okay. Paint Lick ain't going to report me."

"What makes you so sure?"

"Who else they got to make sure the Italians and Hungarians is doing what they's supposed to? Foreman depends on me, even if he don't like it."

Scooping Alma in his arms, Bascom stood.

"Just what do you think you're doing?"

He bumped open the bedroom door with his hip, placed her on the bed and braced himself above her. "Aiming to get that cuddle you owe me from last night."

Chapter 40

June 28, 1918

Richmond, Virginia

Durwood joined Walker and Grace in the dining room. "Sorry, I'm late."

Walker asked, "Where've you been?"

Durwood handed him a piece of paper.

"What is it?" Grace asked.

"He's enlisted."

The color left Grace's rosy cheeks. Walker tossed the paper on the table.

Grace asked, "Why didn't you discuss this with us first?"

Walker straightened. "Don't worry, dear. Durwood and I'll go down there first thing in the morning and straighten things out. Explain this was a mistake."

"This is why I didn't tell you."

Walker crumpled his napkin on the table. "This war's not for you."

"Not for me? I suppose it's for boys like Cap who don't have anyone to fix things for them."

"All I'm saying is finish your law degree. Help us make Richmond prosperous so boys like Cap have good jobs to come home to when the war's over."

"Cap's dead."

Grace squeezed Durwood's hand. "I'm so sorry. Why didn't you tell us?"

"Just got word. Killed in France last month."

Durwood turned to Walker. "Why didn't you serve?"

"Born too late for the War Between the States. By the time the Spanish-American War came along, your mother and I were married and I was well into my career. Figured I could do more good right here than on some battlefield. Like I'm telling you."

Grace added. "Please, listen to your father."

"All we're saying is, think about what you're doing. You just found out about your friend's death. Don't let your grief lead to a rash decision."

"Cap was the finest boy I knew. He was all the things boys like John Randolph, boys who are going to sit out this war, are not. If I don't owe it to myself to serve, I owe it for the privilege of having Cap think I was worthy of being his friend."

Walker stood. "Don't decide anything tonight. Sleep on it and we'll talk again in the morning." He placed a hand on Durwood's shoulder before walking from the room.

Grace broke the silence. "We understand this is your decision. We just want to help you make sure it's the right one."

Durwood took Grace's hand. "Remember the day we left Matewan on the train?"

"Of course."

"My father, Pa, told me to make something of myself."

❋❋❋

Durwood placed his suitcase on the bed. A soft knock came.

"Come in."

Grace entered carrying a shoebox. "When do you leave?"

"I report in three days."

"Here." Grace offered the box.

Durwood lifted the lid to reveal a stack of letters wrapped in a ribbon; on top lay the Paint Lick scatter tag Bascom left behind and several coal nuggets Durwood collected from the yard years ago.

"How in the world?"

"I found them in your trashcan after Bascom left. I thought the day might come when you'd like to have them back. Take the scatter tag for good luck, along with this." Grace offered a piece of worn, weathered rope affixed to a pin.

"I can't take Uncle Walker's tow rope."

"Walker wants you to have it on the condition you return it after the war."

"I love you." Durwood hugged Grace. "Where is he?"

"Not tonight, dear. You can tell him in the morning."

Chapter 41

August 30, 1918

Aboard the Transport Ship "Somali" | Arctic Ocean

Waves crashed over the bow of the ship as it lurched in the heavy Arctic Sea. Leaning on the rusted railing, Durwood turned his head before saltwater sprayed him. In the distance, two ships carrying the rest of the American Expeditionary Forces tossed about like matchsticks in a stream. Since leaving England five days ago, the sun had barely shone. The weather turned colder, made worse because their British-made woolen overcoats languished in the bottom of the hold, inaccessible. Despite the frigid, wet conditions on deck, Durwood preferred it to the smelly, rat-infested spaces below. Flu had claimed several of the troops; wrapped in sheets, their bodies had been tossed overboard to roll along the crests until the ship left them behind. Many in the close quarters below were seasick.

"Cigarette?" A man with an accent Durwood couldn't place flipped open a tarnished silver case. Tall, with long dark hair swept back from his forehead and deep-set, ebony eyes, he appeared to be in his late thirties. Durwood had spotted him after they sailed from Newcastle. Since nearing the White Sea, the man spent as much time on deck as Durwood, always looking for land.

"Thanks." The man leaned close. Durwood ignited his cigarette from the flame of the other. He extended his hand. "Durwood."

"Vanya. You say 'Ivan.'" The man shook. "I am translator."

"You're Russian?"

"Yes. From St. Petersburg."

"What were you doing in England?"

"I move with family after Revolution last October."

"Why'd you leave?"

The ship dropped into a deep trough. Ivan slammed into Durwood, who clenched the railing with the crook of his elbow.

"Communists take everything. Come to my home at night. Say I don't own home anymore. State owns. Next day, four families move in. Have paper say we get one room for my family signed by commissar. My house. One room." Ivan spat into the angry sea.

"Why'd you come back?"

"To fight Bolsheviks." Smoke whisked from Ivan's nose.

"What are your plans when we reach Archangel?"

"Fight Bolsheviks with British. Same as you."

"Our orders are to guard military supplies America sent to the Czar. Make sure the Germans don't get their hands on them. We're not fighting Bolsheviks."

"But you will."

"What makes you so sure?"

"Who's in charge of your American Expeditionary Force?"

"The British."

"That's why you fight Bolsheviks."

"I don't understand."

"British fear Bolsheviks more than Germans."

"Why?"

"Bolshevik goal is for worker to rise up and put end to oppression by capitalists. Spread communism to Europe. Even to America."

"That seems unlikely."

"That's what the Czar thought. Now he is dead. Bolsheviks kill his whole family. Do not underestimate them."

"But they don't even control their own country yet." Durwood flicked his butt into the dark water.

Ivan draped an arm around Durwood's shoulder. "And together we must make sure they never do."

Chapter 42

January 18, 1919

Nizhnyaya Gora, Russia

Durwood sat on the crowded floor of a farmhouse hugging his knees. He pressed his nose into his sleeve to cut a rancid cabbage smell. The combination of body odor and foot rot was as unrelenting as the freezing temperatures. A small fire dwindled as the last bits of scavenged furniture burned. The lieutenant stepped over and around the soldiers of Durwood's platoon to pace the farmhouse seized from the Bolsheviks two days before. Durwood couldn't shake the image of the family who lived there hanging from the barn's rafters. He had wept at the sight of the two lifeless children dangling next to their parents. Despite all he'd been told, Durwood had been unprepared for the Communists' savagery.

The sergeant stood. "Hopkins, Felts, you're on watch."

Durwood double-looped a scarf around his face and tucked it into the collar of his overcoat, covering everything but his eyes. The minus-thirty degree temperature risked frostbite in minutes. Lowering his cap's lambswool earmuffs, he tied them beneath his chin and stuffed his thermos into the canvas satchel around his neck. He slipped on one fur-lined glove. Using his teeth, he pulled the other snug. Spitting fur, he asked, "You ready?"

"You bet," Felts replied.

"Douse the light." Two nights before a private had stepped outside to relieve himself. His silhouette offered the only opportunity needed by a Bolshevik marksman.

Crouching when the door opened, Durwood and Jude dashed from the farmhouse. A bullet struck the building as the door slammed. They zig-zagged toward the platoon's perimeter forty yards away. Within seconds, the bitter cold stung like a thousand bees. Snow puffed around them from snipers' guns two hundred yards away across the white field. If Durwood were hit, how long would it be before he realized it? Would it feel different from the piercing cold? Tears made it difficult to see in the predawn sky. Reaching the trench, Durwood and Jude jumped, almost landing on the translator, Ivan, and the other sentry.

"About time," Ivan's companion barked.

"What's your report?"

"Can't see a thing, but judging from the sound of things, they're bringing in more men and artillery. Ivan says they're preparing to attack."

Durwood pointed to the field glasses dangling from the soldier's neck. "Give me those." He scanned the horizon, his vision obscured by rows of barbed wire. Sunrise was minutes away. Against the horizon's lightening backdrop, he saw no movement.

"You boys go get warm. Heads down."

"Good luck." The soldier scrambled from the trench. Sniper fire hurried him on his way. Ivan lingered.

Jude asked, "You think they're coming?"

The Russian nodded.

Durwood said, "Lieutenant thinks so, too."

Jude asked, "Can you see the Cossacks? Are they still with us?"

Durwood scanned the trenchline on their flank. "They're there. Sipping tea like a day in the park."

A loud whine broke the quiet. Durwood, Jude and Ivan dove to the ground just ahead of the percussion from a shell beyond their trench. Within seconds, the Russians rained ordnance on their garrison, forcing Durwood into a tight ball, hands pressed to his ears. The onslaught was so intense he couldn't distinguish individual explosions. A continuous thunder roiled the earth, pelting him with frozen sod. The shelling raged for thirty minutes. When it stopped, Durwood wobbled to his feet and peered over the edge of the trench.

Felts asked, "See anything?"

"Nothing. But they must be coming soon. Damn it. The Cossacks left their post."

"Chickenshit bastards. Probably defected. Watch your back." Jude peered through the binoculars down the trench seventy yards.

Ivan spoke. "You're wrong. Cossacks hate Communists as much as me. They fear nothing."

"Then where the hell are they?"

Ivan shrugged. "I do not know."

Smoke from the explosions blanketed their outpost. Fresh craters dotted the farm. The barn, which housed the company's supplies, lay in ruins. Durwood gazed across the open field. Nothing moved. Maybe they weren't planning an attack after all. Maybe it was too cold even for the Bolsheviks. A whistle followed by a flare shattered that hope. Like a whitecap just offshore, an ivory wave rose from the ground rolling in their direction.

Durwood stammered. "Jude, take a look at this."

"What is it?"

"I'm not sure."

Jude pressed the lenses to his eyes. "Shit. Bolos. They're wearing all white. Hundreds of them."

"How many men we got left?"

"I don't know. Forty-five. Not enough."

"Ivan. Get back to the house and warn the lieutenant. Hurry."

"Be careful, my friends." Ivan bounded from the trench.

Durwood grabbed his rifle.

"Where you going?" Jude asked.

"To man the Cossack's gun. We got to hold this line as long as possible. God bless you, Jude."

"You, too."

Head tucked, Durwood sprinted along the narrow trench. Reaching the unmanned Lewis gun, he looked over the top of the berm just as sunlight broached the horizon. Binoculars weren't needed. Bayonets fixed, a wave of Bolsheviks advanced a hundred yards away. Many carried boards to breach the barbed wire. From the second floor of the farmhouse, the company's two Vickers machine guns roared. Durwood followed suit. Despite the number of Russians falling, the wave never faltered. Men following the leading edge grabbed weapons spilled by fallen comrades.

Durwood emptied the first pan magazine of its ninety-seven rounds. Working as quickly as his winter gear permitted, he popped off the magazine and slapped the second in place. The Bolos were close enough that he could see their heads snap as rounds tore into them. By the time he had spent the second magazine, screaming Bolsheviks were charging as fast as their horsehair boots could carry them through knee-deep snow. Durwood swung the gun left and right until he exhausted the third magazine. The wave never slowed. Reaching the outer strand of wire, the Bolos tossed boards and dead comrades across the wire to clamber over. Soon the wave would overwhelm Durwood's trench. The only question was how many Bolos could he take out first. With luck, he might have time to reload one last time. He no longer heard the machine guns from the farmhouse. He prayed the men were pulling back to the village. If so, he needed to buy them time.

Struggling to lock the new magazine in place, a rush of footsteps drew Durwood's attention. Twenty feet away, a hulking, bearded soldier dressed head-to-toe in white bore down on him. Armed with an old bolt-action rifle with a bayonet, the Russian raised it to his shoulder. Durwood pressed against the trench wall as the gun fired. The round missed. Undeterred, the Bolshevik lowered the stock of his weapon to his side to aim the bayonet at Durwood. Reaching backward for his rifle, Durwood tripped over the spent magazines,tumbling backward onto the frozen ground. His gloved hand fumbled with his sidearm's leather strap, unable to remove it from the holster. As the steel point plunged toward his chest, he closed his eyes and raised both hands to deflect the blade. He had been right—there was no pain. The numbing cold left him feeling nothing.

Jude grabbed the collar of Durwood's coat. "Get your ass up. Let's get out of here." Jude dragged Durwood to his feet. The Bolo's rifle rolled off his chest. The dead Russian lay on his back, blood seeping from a hole between his eyes.

Durwood collapsed the Lewis gun's tripod to tuck it under his arm. He stuffed his satchel full of magazines. Scrambling over the berm, he followed Jude toward the house as a wave of white broke over the trench. Durwood and Jude raced down the icy road for the village a quarter-mile away. The first weather-beaten hovels came into view.The lieutenant and Ivan stood behind an overturned wagon, waving.

"We got you covered." Machine gun fire erupted from the houses on either side of the lieutenant's forward position. Bracing his rifle on the sideboard, Ivan fired past them at the crush of Bolos in pursuit. Reaching the cover of the wagon, Durwood and Jude dropped to their knees. Durwood's lungs burned. The lieutenant shouted over the gunfire, "Glad to see you, boys." The lieutenant nodded at the Lewis gun tucked under Durwood's arm. "I need you two to set up over there to protect our flank." The officer pointed to a house on the western edge of the village. "Whatever you do, hold that flank."

Durwood and Jude scurried across open ground to the back of the nearest house. Dodging bullets from a machine gun the Communists placed in the road, they worked past two more houses before dashing through a clearing to a house on the western edge of the hamlet. Durwood shouldered open the door and flung wide a shuttered window on the front of the house. A single chair hung from a peg in the wall. Durwood placed the chair beside the window and stacked the gun's magazines in its wicker seat. He knelt to rest the Lewis gun on the sill and unsnapped the leather holster strap securing his Colt. Jude leaned the two Enfield rifles against the wall.

"Give me your cartridges."

Durwood tossed his satchel.

Jude pushed open the shutters. "There." Hunched figures massed under snow-covered evergreen boughs eighty yards away.

"Got 'em.

"I've got fifty rounds. How many magazines you got?"

"Three."

"Wait until you can't miss. I'll cover while you reload."

Mired in snow four feet deep, the Bolsheviks advanced in a line forty yards abreast. It took bravery to face a Lewis gun in open terrain. Bullets chewed into the front of the house, splintering the front door, forcing Durwood to the floor.

Jude raised a trench periscope above the sill. Lowering it, he held up three fingers. Durwood placed his hand on the trigger and coiled on the balls of his feet. As Jude curled the third finger into a fist, Durwood popped above the window sill and squeezed. He swung the blazing barrel, tearing into the front row. Forty yards away, white-clad soldiers fell. Blood dappled the snow.

"I'm out." Durwood lifted the gun off the windowsill to change magazines.

Shouldering his Enfield, Jude raised to one knee and fired.

"One down." Jude grabbed the second rifle.

Durwood clicked the magazine into place as Jude fired his last round. "Go."

Durwood shoved the gun on the window ledge. Twenty yards away, the Bolos were closing. Despite a trail of bodies, they never wavered. Durwood couldn't keep pace—ivory figures continued to pour from the tree line. One magazine remained. "I'm out."

Jude fired as Durwood grabbed the last magazine. "No time. Here." Jude tossed Durwood his rifle as the front door flew open. Jude fired, dropping a Bolo outside the doorway. As the doomed soldier tumbled backward, he opened his hand. A grenade dribbled onto the floor. Durwood scooped up the grenade in his gloved hand, like fielding a bunt. In a single motion, he flung it out the door. The blast knocked him off his feet, but he rolled to the window to grab his rifle. Bracing for the Bolos to pour through the open door, an unfamiliar bugle call rose above the din.

Instead of pressing the attack, the Bolos retreated. For good measure, Jude reloaded and fired his last rounds at the fleeing Russians. Durwood ran to the back window. "Looks like Ivan was right."

Swords drawn, Cossack cavalry galloped down the road from the next village where their battalion was billeted. A wagon loaded with two mortars brought up the rear of the column of horsemen. The two Cossacks who left the trench hopped off the back and muscled the mortars to the ground to fire rounds at the retreating Bolsheviks.

Chapter 43

March 19, 1919

Shenkursk, Russia

Durwood sat on his tick mattress across from Jude and Ivan. Rows of bunks lined the crude barracks. Laying two cards on an upturned ammo crate, Durwood removed two more from the deck.

Ivan took three, then tossed down his cards. "Fold."

Durwood asked Jude, "What do you have?"

"Pair of fours. You?"

"Two pair."

Durwood scooped a handful of cigarettes into his hat.

"I'll be damned if you ain't the luckiest bastard."

Ivan said, "Deal. I need chance to win back cigarettes."

Durwood slipped one from behind his ear to hand to Ivan.

The lieutenant entered the barracks, his sergeant beside him. Men hopped to their feet and threw back their shoulders.

"As you were." Moving to the center of the room, the lieutenant unfolded a piece of paper. "We have new orders."

Rumors had been swirling for weeks that they would be pushing south to stop the Bolsheviks from consolidating gains made during winter. Ivan was the only one eager for this, though he knew that without reinforcements they stood little chance of dislodging the Red Army.

"We're going home."

The room erupted in hurrahs and hugs; cards flew. Durwood threw his arms around Jude. Jude was the reason Durwood was going home and not resting beneath a whitewashed cross in the U.S. cemetery in Archangel. Durwood and Jude moved about the room exchanging hugs with what remained of their platoon.

One of the soldiers asked, "When, sir?"

"We leave for Archangel next week. Everyone is to be home by July. Carry on, gentlemen." The lieutenant strode from the barracks.

Jude asked Durwood, "What are you going to do when this is over?"

"Finish law school, I guess."

"Thought you didn't like law school."

"It's what my folks want. You?"

"Headed back to West Virginia to work for my uncle."

Head in hands, Ivan sat on the bunk. The unlit cigarette dangled from his lips.

Durwood touched his shoulder. "Sorry, friend."

"I knew this day must come."

Durwood bent to pick up the cards littering the floor.

Jude asked Ivan, "What will you do?"

"Stay and fight with British."

Jude crushed a spent cigarette. "Come back with me. I could get you on with my uncle. He's keen on men with military service. You'd fit right in. Coalfields are full of folks from Hungary, Italy, Poland."

"What does this company do?" Ivan asked.

"Coal companies hire my uncle to keep socialists and unions from shutting down the mines. The union will kill anyone who tries to stand up to them. Hard to say how many of my uncle's men been murdered trying to keep the peace."

Durwood asked, "What's the company called?"

"Baldwin-Felts. Heard of it?"

"Guess not."

Ivan stood to embrace Jude.

"That a yes?"

"As soon as I kill all the Bolos, I come help your uncle." Jude and Ivan shook hands.

Durwood laced up his boots.

"Where you headed?"

"Get some fresh air."

"Hurry back so's Ivan and me can get our smokes back."

Tossing on his coat and fur cap, Durwood hurried outside.

Chapter 44

May 17, 1920

Bluefield, West Virginia

Durwood checked the address. The two-story brick building took up half a block in the center of town. Seated behind a switchboard, a pretty young woman wearing a headset smiled.

"Welcome to the Baldwin-Felts Security Agency. May I help you?"

"I'd like to speak with Mr. Tom Felts, please."

"Do you have an appointment?" "No, ma'am."

"Who should I say is calling?"

"Durwood Hopkins." He handed her a card.

"Does he know you, Mr. Hopkins?"

Durwood shook his head.

"I'm afraid Mr. Felts has a full schedule today."

"Tell him I served in the Polar Bears with his nephew, Jude."

The receptionist's smile faded. Grabbing a plug, she slid it into a slot to speak softly into the headset, careful to cover the mouthpiece with her hand.

"Please, have a seat. Mr. Felts will be with you in a minute."

Durwood sat in the well-appointed office. A photo of Jude in his military uniform before they sailed for Russia hung on one wall, a black bow draping the frame. Commendations lauding the agency on behalf of grateful coal companies and law enforcement agencies surrounded the photo.

"Durwood?" A short man with swept-back gray hair entered. Wearing a black, three-piece suit and wire rims, he extended a hand. "Tom Felts. I've heard a lot about you."

"I've come to pay my respects, sir. Jude was the finest soldier I knew."

"He said the same about you. Let's go to my office."

Felts led to a spacious office dominated by a mahogany desk and a high-back leather chair. A map with colored stick pins covered the wall behind his desk.

Felts removed his coat to hang across the back of his chair. A holstered Colt rested under his armpit.

"Please." Felts pointed to a chair facing his desk. Durwood sat.

"Cigarette?"

Reaching across the desk, Durwood took one.

"I came as soon as I heard."

"Jude was like a son to me. I'm pleased to receive a friend of his, particularly one he thought so highly of."

"How could he survive the Bolsheviks only to come home and get killed?"

"If you were from around here, you'd understand what we're dealing with."

"May I ask you something?"

"Of course."

"How'd it happen?"

Felts handed Durwood an envelope from a filing cabinet. "Jude and a couple men had been working in a coal camp in Mingo County tamping down the threat of a strike." Felts faced the map. He pulled a red stickpin, then reinserted it. "They were here at Red Branch. They'd spent the day evicting union agitators from company houses. That evening, they were headed to Matewan on a handcar to catch a train back here for a weekend off. Union men ambushed them from the woods above the tracks. Never had a chance. Jude's body was riddled with twenty bullets. His rifle hadn't been fired."

The envelope held a stack of photos. Familiar with death's pallor, Durwood wasn't sure he wanted to remember Jude this way. He had to force himself to look. Jude's body lay atop the handcar, rifle by his side. One of his companions sprawled on the tracks face down, the back of his head missing.Another corpse lay next to Jude, eyes wide. Durwood returned the photo to the envelope and slid it back across the desk.

"Did you catch the men responsible?"

"No, and we probably won't."

"Why's that?"

"The law in Mingo County isn't on our side. We fight them as much as the union."

"Jude said you prefer men with military experience."

"I find they're more disciplined than most of the men we hire. That's even more the case now that so many have seen combat."

"I want to offer my services."

"I appreciate the gesture. It means a lot. But this isn't your fight. Go back to Richmond. Live your life."

What was it Walker said when he enlisted? 'This isn't your war.'

"Did Jude tell you he saved my life?"

"No. He said you watched each other's backs."

"January of last year, the Reds overran our position. Hundreds of them. Kept coming in waves. A Bolo had a bayonet inches from my chest when Jude put a bullet between his eyes."

"Sounds to me like you've been given a second chance. Take it. If Jude were here, I'm sure he'd tell you the same thing."

"That's just it. He's not."

"Do you have a place to stay?"

Durwood nodded. "A boarding house down the street."

"Tell you what. You take the night to think things over. If you're still determined to join in the morning, come see me."

Durwood shook Felts's hand. "Thank you, sir."

"It was a pleasure, Durwood. Don't take offense, but I hope to never see you again."

Durwood stepped outside. Rain clouds gathered.

Chapter 45

May 19, 1920

Matewan, West Virginia

The train jostled along the tracks tight beside the Tug River. Rugged mountains shot skyward. Redbuds and mountain laurel bloomed against the thick canopy. The flowers reminded Durwood of his mother, who loved when the redbuds ignited in pinks and purples. Long walks home from church often stretched into the evening as she admired the blooms. Try as he might to remember his mother's face, all Durwood could see when he closed his eyes was Grace.

He fingered the round detective badge encircling a star that Tom Felts pinned on his lapel just yesterday. The impenetrable foliage was so close he could grasp the leaves if he leaned out the window. It became clear how a man as careful as Jude had been ambushed.

A man seated across from him said, "Don't recollect seeing you jack-booting around these parts before."

"That's because you haven't."

"First time in Matewan?"

Durwood wasn't sure how he should answer. Fortunately, he didn't have to. The man wasn't interested in anything Durwood had to say.

"Word of advice, friend. Baldwin-Felts men ain't exactly looked on with favor in these parts."

"So I've heard."

"If I was you, I'd give serious thought to another line of work."

"Heard that, too."

The compartment door slid open. A gritty blast of exhaust preceded the conductor who moved down the aisle. "Next stop, Matewan."

Durwood checked his watch: four-fifteen. Perhaps he had time to find where Jude was murdered, but it was too late to hike up the mountain to the home place and make it back down before dark, even if he could remember the way. It was just as well—he needed a little more time to prepare himself before dropping in on his father after twelve years. The father he knew nothing about since Bascom stopped writing years ago, finally tiring of sending unanswered letters. Was their father still alive? Bascom would have written to share such news. Was Bascom still living there? Durwood would find out soon enough. He'd take a room for the night and start up in the morning.

The train slowed into the station. Grabbing his leather bag, Durwood hopped onto the platform. Across the tracks fronting Railroad Alley, a row of connected buildings stretched a hundred yards. Midway down the street stood Chambers Hardware, the only business Durwood remembered. The man on the train bumped into Durwood's back as he moved past. "Don't say I didn't warn you."

Durwood flipped up the collar on his duster to deflect a light drizzle. The street was empty save for two women holding parasols and with hems hiked as they hurried across the street toward the train. Once he had his bearings, Durwood set off for the Urias Hotel on Mate Street. Tom Felts said it was one of the few establishments that welcomed security agents. Down from the hotel, a line of men waited in the rain outside a dilapidated building. Durwood couldn't recall seeing this many people in town when he was a boy.

Entering the worn, dated lobby, Durwood approached the desk. "I'd like a room, please."

"How many nights will you be with us?"

"Just one. How much will that be?"

"We'll put it on the Baldwin-Felts account."

"That's okay."

The clerk glanced at his badge.

"I'm not on official business."

"Two-fifty, then."

Durwood placed money on the counter then looked toward the front door. "What are all those men lined up for?"

The clerk peered over his glasses. "You sure you're a Baldwin man?"

"I'm sure."

"It's union relief day. Strikers living in union camps come to town once a month for funds and supplies."

"Didn't know there were still tent camps around."

"Union's picking up steam. So is the evictions. Couple of months ago, only a few showed up. Line formed at eight this morning and hasn't let up all day."

A group of well-dressed men entered the lobby from the dining room. Wearing badges like Durwood's, several clutched rifles. A tall, good-looking fellow with pince-nez glasses strode across the lobby. He flicked Durwood's badge. "Who might you be?"

"Durwood Hopkins."

"Since when are you a Baldwin-Felts man?"

"Signed on yesterday. Start training next week."

"I'm Albert Felts. That's my brother, Lee." Felts pointed to one of the armed men by the door who tipped his hat. Jude had spoken warmly of both uncles. Good detectives, backbone of the agency run by their older brother. Like his Uncle Tom, they had helped raise Jude after his parents passed, though these two were more like brothers. "If you ain't started yet, what the hell you doing here of all places?"

Telling his new employer his connection to Matewan would only sow distrust. "Wanted to see for myself where Jude was murdered."

"Jude? You knew him?"

"Served in Russia together."

"Why didn't you say so?" Albert embraced Durwood, lifting him off the ground. "Hear that, boys? Hopkins served with Jude." More men slapped his back.

Lee Felts shook Durwood's hand, then pulled him close. "Don't you worry. We aim to set things straight."

"That's why I'm here."

Albert checked his watch. "Better get to the station. Five-fifteen's due shortly." He turned to Durwood. "You armed?"

"No, sir."

"Then do yourself a favor and lose that badge."

Durwood slipped the badge into his hip pocket.

Alfred said, "Walk with us to the station."

The men walked from the hotel with the bearing of a platoon. The rain had eased but thick clouds shrouded the mountaintops.

"Hopkins, you say? You're the lawyer from Richmond. Father's a railroad man."

"That's right."

"Jude must've liked you. He didn't talk a lot, but I heard him speak of you on more than one occasion."

As they neared the tracks separating Railroad Alley from the station, an angular-faced man with gold teeth and a worn, soiled suit approached Albert Felts, a silver badge on his lapel. "Mayor'd like a word." He turned toward the hardware store. There, a portly man waited under an awning.

Albert turned to the group. "Let me see what this fat fool wants."

Lee asked, "Want me to come with you?"

"Just keep an eye out. Seems we've attracted a crowd." Miners drifted into the alley, which had been nearly empty less than an hour before. They sat on window ledges and slouched against buildings.

Durwood asked, "Who was that fellow?"

Lee said, "Smiling Sid Hatfield. Chief of Police."

"What's he want?"

"They're pissed we were doing our job evicting union folks up at Stone Mountain today. Claimed we didn't have jurisdiction. Threatened to arrest Albert. Can't wait to see their faces when Albert tells 'em he has a warrant for Sid's arrest."

Fifty yards away, Albert drew close to the Mayor and Hatfield. No one extended a hand. As Albert and the Mayor spoke, men in coveralls and dungarees continued to pour into the alley, filling the street and doorways with angry faces. Albert handed the Mayor a paper and pointed to Hatfield. The Mayor wadded the warrant and tossed it on the ground. He stabbed his index finger inches from Albert's chest. Hatfield spat tobacco juice on the crumpled paper.

Lee chambered a round in his rifle. "Boys, let's move a bit closer. This don't feel right." On cue, twelve detectives moved in unison. Durwood started forward with them. "You stay put," Lee said. As the agents inched closer to Albert, the Mayor became more animated. Durwood couldn't make out the words, but their meaning was clear.

Hatfield held fast by the Mayor's side.

At the far end of the street, near where Albert stood, French doors swung open onto a second-floor porch. A large man in a newsboy cap dropped to one knee behind the balustered railing. What was he doing with a rifle? Before Durwood could shout, shots rang. Gun in hand, Albert stumbled backwards and fell. The Mayor clutched his stomach and crumpled to the ground. Pistols in both hands, Hatfield sprayed rounds toward the agents twenty-five feet away. Gunfire erupted from the storefronts. Too late, Lee and the other agents returned fire.

Exposed and unarmed, bullets kicked up mud around Durwood's feet. He dashed behind two wooden barrels beside the tracks and crouched. Pinned down, he peeked around one of the casks. On the porch, the rifleman trained a carbine on Durwood's position. One of the containers splintered inches from his face, forcing Durwood back onto his haunches. Guns blazed as the five-fifteen for Bluefield pulled into the station and stopped, its whistle masked by the gunfire. A woman on the train looked down at Durwood. He motioned for her to move from the window. If he could get to the platform, the hulking train would be between him and the sniper. Head tucked, Durwood scurried between two rail cars, just ahead of a bullet that pinged off the trailing car. Hopping onto the platform, he gathered himself, figuring what to do next. The station master hurried a group of disembarking passengers into the station. At the end of the line, the woman he had seen on the train motioned. "Hurry."

As Durwood reached the door, the train pulled from the station. Quiet replaced the din of gunfire. Reversing course, Durwood moved toward the edge of the platform; the sniper had fled the porch. Pockets of gunsmoke settled over the alley. Bodies littered the muddy street. Lee and several agents had fallen near Albert's body. Laughing and shouting, locals swarmed the street, toeing the fallen agents to make sure they were dead. Jude had been right—they were no better than the Bolos. These were not miners striking for better wages, but men bent on upending social order. Men that Walker and Jude had railed against. Durwood raged. He wanted to do something. But what? Unarmed he would be cut down before he could make it across the tracks. Live for another day, he told himself. A firm hand on his shoulder spun him around. Pointing a pistol at his chest, Sid Hatfield bared gold teeth.

"Where you sneaking off to? Think I didn't notice you was with them Baldwin thugs?" Durwood raised his arms chest high. With his free hand, Hatfield threw open Durwood's duster to pat him down.

The woman from the train materialized by Durwood's side. Placing her arm around his waist, she deflected the pistol with the other.

"What cause do you have to treat my husband in this manner, officer?"

"Husband?" Hatfield flashed gold teeth. "That so? Then how 'bout showing me both your tickets?"

Durwoood froze. The ticket in his coat would seal his fate. Fingering his pockets to buy time while he searched for a way out, the woman placed her hand on his and squeezed. "I have them, dear. Remember?" Unclasping her beaded purse, she removed two tickets to hand to the police chief.

Releasing Durwood's coat, Hatfield grabbed the stubs. His gilded smile faded. Returning the tickets, he looked at Durwood's muddy shoes. "If I was you, I'd demand the railroad pay for a shine. You done got all muddy on the train." Hatfield tipped his hat. "Ma'am." To Durwood, he said, "I'll be seeing you around."

The woman turned toward town. "Come along, dear. We're going to be late for dinner." Arm in arm, she led Durwood toward the hotel.

Once they were out of earshot, blood rushed from the woman's face. "Will you please tell me what just happened? There were bodies lying in the street."

"I'm not sure what to tell you. I arrived an hour ago. I met some detectives in the hotel and was walking with them to the station when for no reason, shooting started. It was an ambush. Those men never had a chance."

"Why were you with the detectives?"

"Long story, but I joined their agency yesterday. That was a pretty reckless thing you did back there."

"I had to do something. You were crouched by those barrels. Whatever was going on, it was clear you weren't involved. Was I wrong?"

"No, but it looks like I am now. Why did you have two tickets?"

"I'm traveling to Chicago with my sister."

A few paces ahead, a girl of twelve turned. "Were those men dead?"

"I'm afraid so, Miss," Durwood said. "Is there anything I can do to repay your kindness?"

The woman replied, "You could join us for dinner and share your long story."

"Not sure I have much of an appetite."

"You need to eat. Plus, it might be in your interest to keep up appearances, at least for this evening."

Reaching the hotel, Durwood rushed ahead of the women to the reception desk. "I need to place a call to Tom Felts. Right away."

"Already been done, Mr. Hopkins. Sheriff in Williamson's on his way to collect the bodies. You'd be wise to stay put for the night."

"Thank you." Durwood stepped aside so the woman could check in.

"I believe you have a reservation for Wilmer," the woman said.

"Yes, ma'am. I apologize for the unpleasantness of this afternoon. I hope you didn't find yourself in any danger, Miss Wilmer."

"No, but I'm afraid this gentleman wasn't so lucky. Can I trust your discretion, sir?"

"Of course."

"Have your register reflect that I'm traveling with my husband." She nodded to Durwood. "And show my sister staying in a separate room."

"As you wish."

"Have you decided about dinner, Mr. Hopkins?"

"Please, call me Durwood. I'm afraid you'd find me less than companionable this evening. By morning I should be more myself. What about breakfast?"

"That would be lovely. See you at eight?"

"I look forward to it, Miss."

"Erma. Erma Wilmer. This is Sarah."

Durwood extended his hand. Behind him, the front door opened. Instead of shaking his hand, Erma took it in hers and moved toward the stairs. Sid Hatfield and a couple of lawmen entered the lobby.

"Officer," Erma said. Durwood nodded. Hatfield didn't respond as he strode toward the desk.

Reaching the first step, Erma turned to address the clerk.

"I almost forgot. It's been a long day. Can you send dinner to our room?"

The clerk laid the pencil on the register and smiled. "Of course."

"Come in." Durwood opened the door.

The waiter pushed a dinner cart into the room. Starting with a fresh linen, he converted the writing desk into a dinner table. "What would you like to drink? I brought wine and bourbon."

"Leave them both."

The waiter wheeled the empty cart out the door.

Before he could sit to eat, a tap came at the door. He cracked it to find Erma standing in the hallway, balancing tins and silverware on one hand, a bottle of champagne in the other.

"Thought I'd join you for dinner. Breakfast seemed like a long time to wait for the story you promised."

For the first time since he laid eyes on her, Durwood had a moment to study the woman who had saved his life. Tall and shapely, she was striking with almond eyes and an inviting smile. Like Grace, she wore her flaxen hair up.

"Please." Durwood stepped aside. A subtle, fresh scent trailed her. "Let me help." He relieved Erma of the tins and placed them on the table before pulling up a chair opposite his. "Will Sarah be joining us?"

"No. The day's excitement was too much. She's already tucked in."

Durwood slipped into his coat and fumbled to knot his tie.

She touched his elbow. "You're fine, Durwood." He liked the way she said his name, stressing the second syllable. "As you can see, I haven't dressed for dinner, either."

She looked stunning. Durwood poured a glass of champagne and filled a tumbler with bourbon. "To my guardian angel."

Erma raised her flute, making the slightest contact with his glass. She tipped back the champagne, never taking her eyes off him.

"Good thing you didn't have that on today." She pointed at his badge.

Durwood swigged his bourbon.

"We can talk about something else, if you prefer."

"I thought I'd left death and destruction behind when I shipped home a year ago."

"You were in the War?"

Durwood nodded.

"You picked an odd line of work for somebody looking to avoid conflict."

"Wasn't my choice."

Erma set down her glass. "Forgive me, but I don't understand."

"When I was discharged last year, I came back to Virginia to finish law school. I got word last month that my army buddy was murdered a couple miles from here."

Erma reached across to touch Durwood's hand. "I'm sorry."

"He was a detective like those men killed today. And like them, he was killed by this bunch of lawless bastards. Forgive my language."

"My ears aren't as delicate as you might think. I understand you lost your friend, but what does that have to do with you becoming a detective?"

"I want to make sure the men who killed Jude pay."

"Does that mean brought to justice?"

"That was my intention. Before today."

"Now?"

"Two of those men ambushed today were Jude's uncles. Pay means pay."

Erma withdrew her hand. "Think about what you're saying."

"Thinking I could come out here and get the law to help me get justice for Jude almost got me killed. By the Chief of Police, no less."

"These lawless bastards, as you call them. Have you stopped to think what's driven them to the point they would engage in a gun battle in the middle of town in broad daylight?"

Durwood pushed away from the table.

"All I'm saying is that no matter how thin the pancake is, there's always two sides. Before you debase yourself, or worse, get yourself killed, you might want to figure out what's really going on."

"Any questions I had got answered today."

Erma stood. "It's late. I must be going."

"I didn't mean to upset you. I'm sorry."

"I'm the one who's sorry." Erma stood.

Durwood touched her arm, but she kept moving.

Chapter 46

May 20, 1920

Mingo County, West Virginia

Durwood trudged up the mountain path grooved into the wooded hillside. Shaded by thick oaks and chestnuts, the morning air thinned as he climbed and did little to clear his mind. Last night, sleep did not come. The events of the day had played in his head like a broken record. He'd lingered in the lobby after breakfast, hoping for a chance to clear the air with Erma. She never showed.

Near the top of the first ridge, Durwood crossed the spur line that ran downhill to a tipple. Empty hoppers stood beneath the idle structure. Further uphill, a gaping hole in the mountainside marked the mine entrance. Here he'd waited for Bascom and their father to appear at the end of their shift. Once he'd been eager to take his place beside them. Now, he was grateful fate had spared him.

Several buildings dotted the landscape. Armed men milled about. A sandbag bunker guarded the mine entrance. Manned by two Baldwin-Felts men, a machine gun rested atop earthen works. Durwood had returned in the midst of another war. Before continuing uphill, he tipped his hat to the wary-eyed guards. They'd probably been shot at more than once from up here.

At the top of the second ridge, the mountain opened onto a clearing. Nestled against the last rise, the home place was smaller than he remembered. The house looked empty, save for a wisp of smoke curling from the chimney. The roof had shed many shingles and one end of the porch had collapsed. Pa had always taken pride in his home before.

Durwood knocked. He stepped back to the edge of the steps. A curtain shifted, too fast for Durwood to see who watched from the other side. A minute passed before the door cracked. The bony hands of a small, wizened man wearing coveralls and a thermal top sagged under the weight of a shotgun. Wispy gray hair topped his head. A scraggly beard covered most of his face. Dark wrinkles etched what remained.

"State your business, mister. This here's private property."

"I'm looking for Clem Matney. Would you know where I could find him?"

"You's talking to him. Who might you be?"

After twelve years, the only thing familiar about his father was his name. Durwood extended a hand. "Pa, it's me."

His father wobbled backwards. Durwood grabbed the gun before it tumbled from his gnarled hands. Tears welled in the old man's eyes. Brushing aside Durwood's hand, his father pulled Durwood close. Pa's brittle arms cut into Durwood's back. Durwood bent to hug his father, whose breathless sobs made Durwood regret ever questioning the man's love. The old man pushed away to wipe his face on his sleeve. "Don't pay me no mind. Old age done turned me into a fool."

Durwood didn't know his father's exact age, but he was shy of fifty. The same ags as Walker, Pa looked like he could be Walker's father, not his own.

Durwood entered the musty home that looked the same as the day he left.

"Let me take a look at you, son." Pa turned Durwood's chin side-to-side. "Bascom's right. You favor your Ma more than when you was a young'un. Come, sit by the fire." Pa shuffled to his rocker, inches from the flames. He placed a quilt over his lap. Durwood sat in Ma's chair. Pitching forward, a deep cough wracked Pa.

"Can I do something to help?"

Pa raised a hand and shook his head.

When the coughing subsided, he spit into a spittoon. "Ain't nothing to be done but let it run its course. Hand me them pictures." Durwood removed two photos from the mantle.

Holding a photo of Durwood and his mother, Pa asked, "You remember this?"

Durwood studied the faded photo. "Ma and I went to Matewan to have it done, not long before she got sick."

"She was already sick. You boys didn't know it. That's why she had the picture took. She begged me to bring Bascom so's the photographer could take one of the whole family."

"Why didn't you?"

"'Cause I was pig-headed. Figured if I ignored it, everything would be all right."

"Hand me the other one."

Durwood passed him the photo of Bascom and him taken at Forest Hill Park eight years ago.

"Is he still here?"

"When he ain't with his woman."

That explained why he had cut Belle loose. "Who is she?"

"Schoolteacher in Paint Lick. Name's Alma Peters."

"You like her?"

"She's a good woman."

"Then why doesn't he marry her?"

"Asked him that myself dozens of times."

"What's he say?"

"He shrugs. Says it's better this way."

"Better for him?"

"Reckon that's something you'll have to ask him."

Durwood replaced the photos on the mantle. Bascom always did things the hard way.

Pa patted Durwood's hand. "I prayed to God I'd get to lay eyes on you one last time."

"I don't recall you ever praying."

"Things come into focus when a man ain't got nothing to do but sit around all day waiting for the end. You picked a bad time to come home, son."

"That's why I'm here."

"What are you talking about?"

"Came to pay respects to the family of an army buddy."

"You was in the War?"

"Russia." Durwood stooped to put another log on the fire.

"How'd he die?"

"Ambushed. Like those men yesterday."

"What men?"

"Baldwin-Felts agents. We were walking to the train station. Before I knew it, we were being shot at by dozens of men."

"We? What was you doing with Baldwin-Felts men?"

Durwood pulled back the flap of his duster to reveal his badge. Pa rose firmly to his feet.

"You need to leave. Now." This was the father Durwood knew as a boy.

"What are you talking about?"

"If your brother sees you with that badge he's liable to kill you. And if he don't, someone else will. You need to get on back to Richmond. This ain't no place for the likes of you. Not now." There it was. Bascom was still involved with the union.

"That's what everyone keeps telling me."

"This friend of yours. Was he Baldwin-Felts, too?"

Durwood nodded.

"Why's he so important?"

"He saved my life."

"I'm grateful for what he done, but this ain't like the War in Russia."

"What do you mean?"

"Things ain't black and white. I reckon in the War it was easy to spot the enemy."

Durwood nodded.

"Here, ain't nobody wearing uniforms. Everybody looks the same. Worse yet, both sides is guilty of the same things they accuse the other of. They's just too blind to see it."

"Seems pretty clear to me. They murdered my friend and his uncles."

"Don't fool yourself. Baldwin-Felts's men done just as much killing, maybe more."

The door opened. A large man in coveralls and a woolen newsboy cap entered carrying a carbine. He removed his cap and leaned the rifle next to the door. "Why if it ain't Jacob hisself. Come home after living the good life all these years."

"Bastard."

Durwood lunged.

Bascom side-stepped him. Durwood raised his fists.

"Whoa, little brother. What's got your knickers in a twist?"

"You know damned well. You tried to kill me yesterday."

Bascom smiled. "If I had tried to kill you, we wouldn't be having this conversation."

Pa stepped between them. "What's this about?"

"He was part of that ambush. He was the one shooting at me. With that." Durwood pointed at the rifle.

"That true, Bascom?"

"I was shooting at him, but it wasn't to hit him."

"Bullshit."

"I'm not sure what you's doing here, but I recognized you with them Baldwin-Felts lowlifes. Didn't want none of our men mistaking you for part of that gang, so I was keeping you pinned down."

"So, those were your men?"

"That's right."

"You go around killing unsuspecting people?"

"Not people. Scum."

"Was Jude scum?"

"Who's Jude?"

"How about me? Am I scum?"

Pa shook his head at Durwood. "No, son."

Durwood showed his badge. Bascom grabbed the rifle.

"Let me make this easy on you." Durwood turned his back. "This is how you like to do it, right? Kill a man when he doesn't see it coming?"

Pa spun Durwood around to face his brother. "Put the gun down, Bascom. You hear me?"

Bascom lowered the rifle. "Get the hell out of my house."

"So, it's your house now?"

Bascom stepped so close their chests touched. "Listen good, little brother, 'cause I'm only going to say this once. Our story ain't going to have the happy ending of that Bible tale if you stick around. I ain't as forgiving as Esau. Turn in that badge and get on the next train out of here."

"Or what?"

"Next time I won't miss."

Bascom stepped aside. Durwood reached for the door and turned. "It was good to see you, Pa."

"Listen to your brother."

Durwood left the house and didn't look back.

Chapter 47

July 24, 1920

Paint Lick Coal Camp | Mingo County West Virginia

Durwood followed four agents down the muddy street where he'd played as a boy. Little had changed. Tiny, soot-covered duplexes sat in rows on the hillside across the street from the slag-choked river. Bedraggled kids flitted along the bank swearing and calling the agents names. He wished his first eviction could be somewhere else.

One of the agents flung a rock. "Go on. Shoo, you damned ragamuffins." Ragamuffin. Wasn't that what he'd been called at the Hotel Roanoke years before? Durwood hadn't known what it meant. Did these kids?

The leader stopped before a house with a crude numeral two painted above the door. "Let's get to work. I'll stand guard." He climbed to the porch and cradled his rifle.

One of the men banged on the door before throwing it open to enter the house. "Get out." A young mother emerged with two grimy children clinging to her skirt.

She pleaded with the man standing watch. "Please. We got no place else to go."

"Your old man shoulda thought of that before he joined the union.

We got people willing to work who needs 'em a house. Now get out of our way." He shoved her down the steps into Durwood, who prevented the woman and her children from tumbling into the mud. She jerked free.

Durwood asked, "What do we do with their belongings?"

"Toss 'em in the street. Everything but the bed frames, kitchen table and chairs. Company owns 'em."

The first agent to enter the house emerged with an armload of china dishes and cups. One at a time, he dashed them to the ground. Durwood joined the others, tossing clothes and linens in the mud.

They had few possessions, yet her family was willing to risk everything to join the union. Why would they do this when the company provided jobs and homes? Were Mother Jones and her ilk so persuasive these people were willing to risk ruin to join a band of outlaws bent on murder?

"Good work." The leader thumped down the steps. "Twelve's next."

The woman huddled across the street with her children. "Go to hell, all of you."

At number twelve, Durwood followed several agents into the house. An old woman sat alone at a table. A family Bible lay open before her, a grainy photo marked the page. Durwood picked up the old photo. A young man in a dark suit stood beside a girl in a white dress holding flowers. Expressionless, they stared into the camera. Was this her wedding photo? He returned the photo and closed the book to carry it outside. The old woman grabbed the Bible, pulling it tight to her chest. Durwood released his grip, as another agent grabbed the woman's arm. Lifting her onto her feet, the agent pushed the small of her back. "Out you go."

Clutching the keepsake in gnarled, weathered hands, she muttered "Grazi" as she passed.

Durwood grabbed a couple pots, the only items remaining in the house, to carry them outside. "That's it." He tossed them on the pile of possessions, even smaller than those from the first house.

"Why, I believe you're getting the hang of this, Hopkins. Two down, one to go. Let's finish and get off this mountain before dark."

The men moved down the lane, toward the last house. "Hopkins, you got guard duty."

"Is that necessary?"

"You notice ain't no men around? That's 'cause they's hiding in the woods nearby. Every now and then, they'll take a potshot at us for doing our jobs. Keep an eye peeled."

The agents entered the house to find no one home. After a couple of trips each, the house lay bare.

"Let's get out of this hell hole." The group headed up the road past the schoolhouse toward the trail back to Matewan. Hands on hips, a young woman in a blue gingham dress glared from the school's porch.

"Have a nice day, ma'am." The leader tipped his hat. The woman didn't respond. Was she the schoolteacher? Bascom's woman?

"Who was that?" Durwood asked.

"Schoolteacher."

"Friend of yours?"

"Not hardly."

"What's her name?"

"Miss Peters."

"Why don't you like her?"

"Didn't you see the way she was looking at us?"

"I haven't seen anyone who doesn't look at us that way."

"Company pays her to teach. It's clear she ain't on the company's side. We told the owner he needs to get rid of her."

"What's he say?"

"Said she's a good teacher. Folks like her. It'll only make things worse if he fires her. When he comes to his senses, I hope I get to be the one to throw her ass into the street."

Chapter 48

September 10, 1920

Mingo County, West Virginia

Bascom huddled in the woods with Giovanni and two other Calabrians. Guarded by Baldwin-Felts agents, the Red Onion mine opened three hundred yards away.

Bascom unscrewed a tin tub lid. Giovanni and the Calabrians rubbed axle grease on their faces, necks and ears, until only the whites of their eyes showed in the moonless night. "Don't forget your hands."

"Giovanni told the others, "Mani." The men lathered the backs of their hands.

Bascom asked, "What time you got?"

Givovanni disappeared under a blanket held by the Italians so a burning match wouldn't give them away. Reappearing, Givoanni said, "Twelve."

"Give me fifteen minutes to get to the far side of the mine before you start the fireworks. Remember the code?"

"One for all."

"And the response?"

"All for one."

Bascom embraced Giovanni. Donning a canvas rucksack, he bent low to creep through the woods, gun in hand.

Near the west end of the colliery, Bascom knelt behind a log. One hundred yards away, the tipple rose twenty-five feet, like a house on stilts. Held aloft by four oaken timbers, enough coal passed through it to fill a dozen rail cars daily. Disabling the tipple would cripple the mine for weeks, maybe more. Open ground lay between Bascom and the structure. Two cigarettes glowed under the tipple. As the union man working for the mine had said, two agents guarded the tipple overnight. Four more manned machine guns on either side of the mine entrance. Another three patrolled the foreman's office and washhouse.

He swigged from his canteen and placed it on the log. Bascom couldn't risk striking a match to check his watch.

An explosion signaled the plan was in motion. Gunfire erupted on the far side of the mine. The cigarette embers extinguished. The guards chatted excitedly before one hurried off. Bascom dropped to his belly. Coal and gravel bit his elbows and knees as he crawled toward the tipple. The remaining guard with his back to Bascom stood watch beneath the structure. The ground shuddered. Another explosion rocked the far side of the colliery. The guard took the bait and ran off, leaving the tipple unattended.

Bascom sprang to his feet to sprint toward the tipple's timbers. Ripping open his satchel, he removed a bundle of dynamite. Lathered in sticky pine resin, five sticks were lashed with bailing twine. He inserted wire into the charge and slapped the bundle onto one timber five feet off the ground. He knotted dark cloth around the dynamite to hold it fast to the pole. Moving to the adjacent pillar, he placed another charge.

Slipping the satchel over one shoulder, he unspooled two rolls of wire as he backpedaled toward the woods. Before Bascom could reach the trees, shots rang out, tumbling him backwards. He'd been spotted. Hopping up, he scrambled with the spools to the safety of the log where he'd left the detonator. He had to stop the guard from discovering the explosives. He leveled his bolt-action Springfield and fired twice toward the tipple. Setting down the gun, he snatched cutters from his pack to snip the wires from their spools. He fired two more quick rounds before screwing the wires into the detonator. As soon as the last screw bit, he plunged the detonator. Staggered explosions lit up the night.

Bascom ducked as splinters peppered the leaves. The tipple crashed to the ground. He raised a bandana over his mouth and nose as a wave of dirt and coal dust rolled into the woods.

Bascom tossed the spools, wire cutter and detonator into his pack. With his rifle, he raced through the woods toward Pa's house as gunfire dwindled. If he hurried, he would be home before daybreak.

Chapter 49

September 13, 1920

Bluefield, West Virginia

Sipping coffee and smoking cigarettes, Baldwin-Felts agents packed the VFW Hall, which was twice the size of the agency's conference room. Durwood milled about. Men in groups of three and four speculated on the reason for the important meeting. Tom Felts entered, trailed by a couple of his top lieutenants. The room fell silent as Felts made his way to the podium. "Take your seats."

Durwood grabbed a seat near the front.

"Three nights ago, union agitators blew up the tipple at the Red Onion mine in Mingo. Mine's shuttered until they can replace it. One of our men died in the attack. We got word more attacks are planned. If we let this cancer spread, gentlemen, it'll do more damage to production than any strike. So we're doubling security at every mine in the County. We aim to nip this in the bud right here, right now. Operators are counting on us to keep the coal moving. Mr. Neal and Mr. Bandy will give you your assignments."

The men took turns calling out names of five men at a time, followed by the mine they were assigned to protect. "Get to your mines by nightfall, if possible. You'll work with the men already there. It's imperative there be no more attacks. If your name wasn't called, stay seated. The rest of you are dismissed."

The room emptied except for Durwood and the three men on his eviction team.

Felts stood. "We're not assigning you to a mine. We want you to keep evicting strikers, but we want you to modify your approach. We're after information, so go easy on anyone who cooperates. No more broken china and destroyed furniture."

The leader of Durwood's team said, "We were just carrying out orders."

"Those orders have changed."

"What sort of information?"

"Anything that will take us to the man responsible for blowing up that tipple."

"Got any leads?"

"Matter of fact, we do." Felts motioned to one of his subordinates.

Felts's second-in-command removed an object from a bag. "Man who led the attack on Red Onion got careless. Left this behind in the woods with the detonator and several Springfield carbine shell casings." He held aloft a canteen. Durwood recognized the canteen Bascom had had since they were boys. "B.M. is carved near the top."

"Who's B.M.?"

"We think it stands for Bascom Matney."

"Know anything else about him?"

Durwood straightened in his chair.

"We think he was part of the gang that murdered Lee and Albert. Until recently, he lived with his Pa, a drunkard, on the mountain above Paint Lick mine. We're counting on you all to figure out where he's staying now. Worked at Paint Lick 'til he quit in the spring. Comes from a long line of no-good agitators. His Pa and uncle led the strike in '02. After we fought back, his old man came to his senses. Renounced the union and returned to mining. Hasn't given us any trouble since. The uncle was a different story."

Durwood asked, "How so?"

"Long after the strike ended, he continued to stir things up until he was found with a bullet in his head."

"He was murdered?"

Felts exhaled cigarette smoke and smiled. "Not according to the sheriff. Suicide was the official cause of death."

Pa never said anything about the uncle Durwood never met, the one he was named for, committing suicide. Why had Pa told them he died in a mining accident?

"What do we do if we find this Matney fellow?"

"Follow him. See who he's associating with. When the time's right, we'll snatch him so we can have a nice chat. Figure out what the union's up to."

Durwood asked, "What if this Matney fellow won't talk?"

"He will. Just like his uncle."

"Any more questions? Good luck, men."

Felts approached as Durwood headed for the door. "You still interested in finding Jude's killer?"

"Yes, sir."

"This might be your chance."

"How's that?"

"I'm pretty sure Matney killed Jude or knows who did. Find him and we've got a good chance of solving his murder."

"What makes you so sure?"

Felts removed a shell from his pocket and flipped it to Durwood.

"What's this?"

"Casings found in the woods where Jude was ambushed. Care to guess what gun they're from?"

"Springfield Carbine?"

"Exactly. Find Mr. Matney."

"I'll do my best."

Chapter 50

September 17, 1920

Paint Lick Coal Camp | Mingo County, West Virginia

Durwood paused in front of the schoolhouse steps. Like the company houses crammed on the side of the hill, the building longed for attention. Only the two-story foreman's house uphill from the miners' homes appeared as if it had seen a paint brush in the last decade.

Children's voices drifted through an open door and windows. Though it was just half past three, the sun had already dipped behind the western ridge. In the faint shadows of evening's approach, the heat of Indian summer gripped the camp. Durwood leaned on the railing, listening to eager voices recite multiplication tables. Down the hill, a woman hung diapers on a clothesline. Two months before, this house had belonged to an old woman who came to America looking for a better life. Where was she now? Was this newcomer destined for the same fate?

"Have a good weekend, children. Don't forget to study."

Bare feet descended the steps as children spilled out the door. Durwood moved into the doorway of the one-room school and knocked. A woman with brown hair to her shoulders looked up from a desk. She wore the same gingham dress she had on when he saw her months earlier.

Durwood removed his hat. "Pardon the interruption, ma'am. Would you be Alma Peters?"

"That's right. What can I do for you?"

"I need your help."

"Do I know you?"

"Where can I find Bascom?"

The young teacher stood. Tall and thin with an olive complexion, she appeared about Bascom's age. Arms crossed, she scrutinized Durwood with hazel eyes.

"Who are you?"

"His brother, Durwood."

"You were here a couple of months ago evicting folks."

"Will you help me?"

"You're Baldwin-Felts."

"They know Bascom blew up the Red Onion tipple. They found his canteen."

"Why are you telling me this?"

"Pa told me about you and Bascom."

"What makes you think I'd trust you? That badge stands for everything we're against."

"So that makes it okay to shoot anyone wearing one?"

"You don't know anything about us."

"I'm sorry. I didn't come here to pick a fight."

Alma sat. She pointed to the students' bench.

Durwood took a seat on a worn pine log that had been there since before his days at the school. Everything looked familiar except for a globe next to Alma Peter's desk.

"I see you got a globe."

"Bascom bought it."

Was it coincidence or had he told Bascom of his humiliation at not being able to locate West Virginia on his first day of school in Richmond?

Alma leaned on her forearms. "May I ask you something?"

"I guess."

"Did you come back and join Baldwin-Felts to spite Bascom?"

"Last thing on my mind was to ever set foot in this place again, much less join the Baldwin agency."

"Then why did you?"

"I may not see eye to eye with my brother, but that had nothing to do with it. Came to pay my respects to the family of a man I knew during the war. Jude Felts was his name."

"Was he a relation of Tom Felts?"

"Nephew."

"That figures."

"What?"

"Felts convinced you to join his band of outlaws."

"Just the opposite. He tried to talk me out of it. I joined to help find Jude's killers."

"Have you?"

"Been too busy dealing with the strike. As soon as things settle down, I plan to do just that."

"Where do you plan to start? There are a lot of people in Mingo County."

"What do you mean?"

"You'd be hard-pressed to find anyone here who doesn't have a grudge against Tom Felts and his agency."

"Enough of one to kill someone they don't even know?"

"What did you know about those folks you kicked out of their homes a couple of months back?"

"That's different."

"You sure? Weren't they evicted because they belonged to the union?"

"There's a big difference between evicting someone for joining the union and killing someone for wearing this badge."

"Keep on thinking that if it makes you feel better. Ask your brother about the folks who didn't survive the winter of 1912 in the Holly Grove tent camp."

Durwood stood. "Tell Bascom if he wants to talk, I'll be waiting for him day after tomorrow at three o'clock."

Alma leaned back in her chair. "Where can he find you?"

"He'll know. Thank you for your time, ma'am." Durwood donned his hat and passed onto the porch.

"Wait."

Durwood turned.

"Bascom's a good man."

"Is that why he goes around shooting at people?"

"He does what it takes to help these folks. He asks nothing for himself."

"Do you love him?"

"Yes."

"Then help me talk some sense into him before he ends up dead."

Chapter 51

September 20, 1920

Mingo County, West Virginia

Durwood waded through waist-high grass to reach the limestone out-cropping that rode the meadow like a ship at sea. Fescue lapped at its craggy edges. Hopping atop the rock, he sat on the edge. Pa's house lay quiet in the clearing far below. Hands behind his head, Durwood gazed into the heavens like he used to do with Bascom. They'd spent hours lounging on this rock. From here, the world's problems always seemed manageable. What did the clouds have to offer this day?

"Wish you had listened to me and gone back to Richmond." Bascom approached from behind. His rifle hung from his shoulder.

Durwood propped himself on one arm. "Why? You still planning to shoot me?"

"Not today, little brother. This here rock's sacred ground. Glad you ain't forgot about it."

"You come up here anymore?"

"Not since the day you left us."

"Wasn't exactly my choice."

Bascom placed his rifle on the rock and vaulted next to Durwood.

"Alma said you wanted to see me. Said it was important."

"You got careless the other night. Left your canteen in the woods at Red Onion. They're looking for you."

"They? You mean we, don't you?"

Durwood swallowed his response; he wasn't there to argue.

Bascom asked, "Why're you telling me this? Last time we met, you wanted to take my head off. Now, you're looking out for me?"

"I figure we're even now. But that doesn't mean I agree with what you and the union are doing."

"What would you have us do?"

"Do things legally. Go to court. Elect politicians who will change the laws."

"That's Walker talking. It's plain naïve."

"How so?"

"Every time we get the upper hand, coal owners go to court, to the judges they've put in office, and get injunctions forcing us back to work. Or else they get the Governor to send in federal troops to take our guns and end our strikes. This time's different. This time, we ain't backing down."

"What are you talking about?"

"You know things is coming to a head."

"All I know for sure is things are more complicated than they seem."

"Ninety percent of the miners in Mingo have joined the union since the shootout in May. Production is way down on account of the strike."

"You know as well as I do that as fast as you shut down a mine, it reopens with scab workers."

"And within weeks, most of them join the union. It's just a matter of time before all the mines go union and there won't be no need for men like Tom Felts."

"I think you underestimate the coal operators. And Tom Felts. They'll fight you every inch of the way. And they've got more firepower."

"They may outgun us, but they done lost."

"What makes you so sure?"

"The people's with us this time. In case you ain't been paying attention, Sid Hatfield's a hero. Made a moving picture about him."

"Sid Hatfield's a murderer."

"To some. But to folks up and down these hollers, he brung hope by standing up to Tom Felts's men. More important, he proved we was prepared to fight back."

"He's going to be prosecuted."

"Waste of time. No jury in Mingo County will convict him. It'll only serve to make him a bigger hero."

Durwood tossed a stone into the meadow. "Why didn't you come back to Richmond? Belle waited for you."

"You remember the day we buried Ma?"

"Of course."

"You recall what Cesco told us?"

Durwood shook his head.

"He told us family pulls together in times of trouble."

"So?"

"Before Cesco drew his last breath, I promised him I'd take care of Maude and the kids. You'd know that if you hadn't stopped reading my letters."

"What about the promise you made Belle to come back?"

"That's the one I regret ever making."

"So, you didn't love her?"

"'Course I did. Always will. Ain't never met another woman as kind and loving."

"Why didn't you come back, then?"

"Even before Cesco's death, what I seen during the last strike in Kanawha County convinced me I won't the man for her. I knew in the long run she'd be better off with someone else."

"Why's that?"

"'Cause I would've been miserable knowing they's a fight to be had. I'd ended up in the bottle, like Pa. As hard as I tried to fight it, this is where I belong."

Durwood leaned back again to stare at the heavens. "What do you see?"

"That there cloud looks like a unicorn."

"Where?"

Bascom pointed toward the horizon. Patches of clouds drifted toward the ridge on the Kentucky side of the Tug River.

Durwood said, "You're blind as a bat. That doesn't look anything like a unicorn, much less a horse."

"What do you think it is, then?"

"Just clouds heading to a better place. You love Alma?"

"I do. But it's different from Belle."

"In what way?"

"We's more like partners. When I get down, she's the one to buck me up. She's stronger than I am. She won't never give up the fight."

Durwood found that hard to believe. He'd never met anyone stronger than Bascom.

"You plan on making her an honest woman?"

"Not 'til things settle down."

"Why wait?"

"How safe you think it would be for her if Tom Felts and all the world knew we was hitched?"

"Why don't the two of you get away from here? Raise a family. Live like normal folks."

"I dream of that."

"Then do it."

"Not 'til I see this through."

"And what if you don't make it until then?"

"Well, at least I'll be able to hold my head high 'til that day comes."

"As opposed to me?"

"Not what I said."

"But it's what you meant."

"Pa told me about your army buddy saving your life. I disagree with who you choose to work for, but I understand why you's doing it."

"Do you know who killed Jude?"

"No."

"Would you tell me if you did?"

"If I thought it'd get you out of here and back to Richmond, I might. But I don't."

"So it wasn't you?"

"What makes you think it was me?"

Durwood pulled the shell casing from his pocket. Bascom took it.

"Gun that killed him matches your carbine."

Bascom laughed.

"What's so funny?"

"Every miner running around these hills has a Springfield on his back. The union bought 'em cheap after the war." Bascom returned the casing. "This ain't going to narrow your search none."

Durwood stood. "I need to be getting back before someone misses me."

Bascom extended his hand. Durwood tugged Bascom to his feet. Bascom pulled Durwood close. "Thanks for looking out for me, little brother."

"Stay away from Pa's. They've been watching his house."

"I know. Ain't a one of them Baldwin-Felts men worth a damn in the woods. You can spot 'em a mile off."

Durwood hopped off the rock.

Bascom called out. "Things is going to get ugly. Watch your back."

"You do the same, brother."

Chapter 52

March 21, 1921

Mingo County, West Virginia

Durwood craned to look out the window toward the front of the train. The engine labored up the mountain to pull cars crowded with workers fresh off the boat from Italy. The men, some barely in their teens, laughed and joked. They carried fewer belongings than Durwood had when he left for Richmond as a boy. Did they know what was in store? He'd heard employment agencies recruited impoverished Europeans with promises of housing and lucrative jobs and free passage to America. It wasn't until they arrived that they learned they would be toiling underground ten or more hours a day in a remote corner of West Virginia, far removed from the New York or Boston of their dreams.

The train approached a narrow mountain passage. Durwood motioned the men to lean forward. The steel plating reinforcing the sides of the train stopped just below the windows. When they boarded in Bluefield, they briefed the men there was a chance of trouble along the way. Did they understand the men they replaced sought to kill them? If an attack came, the passage ahead was the likely spot. Though most heeded Durwood's warning, two young men at the back remained upright. Durwood moved in their direction. Shots rang from the hillside.

Halfway down the aisle, glass shattered. Durwood dove, just ahead of a scream. Machine guns atop the train blazed. The compartment erupted into chaos as men, heads tucked between their knees, wept and cried out. Durwood didn't know if they were calling to each other or perhaps a loved one an ocean away. Some seemed to be praying, perhaps wondering if their God had stayed behind in Europe. Many clutched beads they kissed. Scrambling on all fours, Durwood reached the back of the train to find the man next to the window slumped over his friend's pitched back. Durwood pulled the young man into the aisle. Blood poured from his arm. Eyes wide, he stared through Durwood and mumbled the same phrase over and over. Durwood ripped the young man's sleeve for a better look. The slug had passed through the arm, leaving splintered bone in its wake. The man's rapid breathing whistled. Durwood raised the wounded man's arm; the bullet had entered his rib cage just below the armpit. He hoped a doctor waited for them at the camp.

Durwood rifled through his pack. Removing gauze, he packed the wound and wrapped several layers around the arm. Before Durwood could finish, the young Italian passed out. By the time the train reached the Black Panther mine in early afternoon, the scab workers had fallen silent. Sun filtered through the trees atop the rugged ridge. The camp lay half a mile down the mountain. A dozen guards eyed the mountainside, looking for snipers who preyed on disembarking strikebreakers.

"Give me a hand." Durwood placed his hands under the wounded man's arms, careful to avoid pressing against the chest wound. Two Italians grabbed the man's legs. Durwood called to the guards preparing to lead the somber group of strikebreakers toward their new homes. "Camp got a doctor?"

"'Course," one of the guards replied.

"Take this man straight away. Got a bullet in his chest." A sturdy Italian relieved Durwood as the group moved downhill.

***

The train pulled into Williamson near dusk. A rowdy crowd milled outside the courthouse. Men shared bottles of liquor and hugs like it was Fourth of July. Since Sid Hatfield's murder trial began in January, there was always activity at the courthouse. But Durwood had never seen it like this.

People sang and shouted. An occasional potshot pierced the din as a few policemen stood idle. Durwood called to a man near the depot. "What's going on?"

"Ain't you heard? Jury done acquitted Smilin' Sid. 'Bout an hour ago."

Hatfield emerged from the courthouse with a group of well-dressed men. Flashes popped as newsmen recorded the event. The press had stoked the public's fascination with tales of the lawless coalfields and the trial of the man they dubbed "Two Gun Sid." Before Hatfield could reach the street, men hoisted him on shoulders to parade through the crowd. Durwood slid into his seat. Bascom was right. The prosecution never stood a chance. Before God and half of Mingo County, Hatfield had led a mob that killed seven agents. He now walked free. If the miners had been emboldened a year ago by Hatfield's ambush, his acquittal was sure to add fuel to their fire.

Two of Tom Felts's top lieutenants entered Durwood's compartment. A half-dozen agents followed.

"Hello, sirs."

The men sat opposite him. "Where've you been?"

"Escorting strikebreakers to Black Panther."

"Any trouble?"

"Took some fire at the Narrows."

"Anyone hurt?"

"Young Italian was hit."

"Poor bastard."

Durwood turned toward the crowd. "So they acquitted Hatfield?"

"Afraid so. These inbred sons of bitches wouldn't convict the Kaiser for starting the Great War."

The whistle sounded the train's departure. One of the agents perched his rifle on the window ledge. "All you got to do, sir, is give the word. I could take him out with one shot."

The lead agent replied, "Nothing I'd like more. But not today."

"Pow," the agent said before reeling in his rifle. The train lurched from the station.

Chapter 53

July 31, 1921

Matewan, West Virginia

Bascom crept through dense underbrush to approach the house from the rear. A sliver of moon did little to cut the darkness; neither did it cast shadows. A faint light shone through the kitchen window. Hopping a split rail fence, he crouched behind a wood pile, watching for Baldwin-Felts agents. Seeing none, he slipped through the yard to mount the back porch. Bascom tapped the jamb in a series of pre-arranged knocks.

Pistol in hand, Sid Hatfield cracked the door.

"We was wondering if you'd make it."

Bascom entered the kitchen. A kerosene lamp silhouetted Ed Chambers, Hatfield's right-hand man. Chambers sat at a table barren except for a whiskey bottle and three shot glasses.

"Evening, Bascom."

"Ed."

Hatfield plopped beside Chambers. He poured a glass and pushed it in front of Bascom. "You's three behind."

Bascom drained it. "Since when did you start drinking, Sid?"

"Before tonight, ain't touched a drop in years. Shit always got me in trouble."

"Why start now?"

"Me and Ed goes on trial in Welch tomorrow for blowing up that mine in McDowell County. Figured how much more trouble could I get myself in by having a couple of nips?"

"Tomorrow? Thought it was next week."

"Judge moved it up. We's leaving in the morning on the 5:15."

"I don't like it." Bascom fiddled with his glass. "Law's in Felts's hip pocket over in McDowell County. Ain't nothing like Mingo."

Hatfield leaned back. "Tom Felts is a vengeful son of a bitch, alright. But he ain't a fool. He knows if anything happens to Ed and me he'll be biting off more'n he can chew. Our boys is looking for an excuse to cut loose."

Chambers poured another round. "Besides, our lawyers assured us everything's done been taken care of."

Bascom shrugged. "Maybe so, but can they guarantee a fair trial?"

"Working on that, too." Hatfield flashed a golden smile. Perhaps a few well placed threats here and generous bribes there might level the field some.

Bascom sipped his whiskey. Chambers said to him, "It's all your fault we's in this mess."

"How do you figure?"

"Me and Sid got the idea to attack the Mohawk mine on account of the trouble you caused last year at Red Onion. Made us realize they's a better way to shut down a mine than a strike. How long was Red Onion shut down, anyway?"

"Took 'em three weeks to get a new tipple up and running."

"We beat you by more'n a week." The men clinked and drank.

Jessie Hatfield pushed through the kitchen door. She kissed her husband's forehead.

Bascom pushed back his chair to stand. "Evening, Miss Jessie."

"Don't get up. Can I fix you boys something to eat?"

"Check back later, honey. We need to finish our meeting."

She picked up the nearly empty liquor bottle. "That's what you're calling this party? Tomorrow's going to be a long day, Sid. The press is going to be snapping pictures like you was the Queen of England. If you want to look your best, maybe you shouldn't have anymore."

Hatfield flipped over his shot glass on the table. "Whatever you say, dear."

Bascom didn't know if Hatfield had killed the Mayor so he could marry Jessie, like Felts claimed. Bascom's eyes had been locked on Durwood when the shooting started. By the time he looked up, Albert Felts and Mayor Testerman lay sprawled in the mud. Whatever the case, the couple hadn't helped themselves by trading in her mourning dress for a wedding gown in less than a week. Bascom stood. "I'm coming with you tomorrow. Make sure nothing happens."

Hatfield righted his glass. He poured three more shots. "We appreciate the offer, but in case you forgot, there's a warrant for your arrest. Jail in Mingo is already full of our boys. Besides, we need you back here."

"For what?"

"It's high time we took the battle to Baldwin-Felts and the owners."

"How?"

Hatfield downed his shot. "Me and Ed ain't exactly figured it out. That's where you come in. You're smarter than the both of us combined. While we's the guest of the McDowell authorities the next few weeks, you be thinking on it. When we get back, we'll hit 'em hard."

Bascom slapped the table. "That's it."

"Let's hear it," Chambers said.

"You said it yourself, Sid. Jail in Mingo County's overflowing with our boys arrested for organizing miners. Same's true in Logan. Who knows how many union men Sheriff Blankenship's got locked up."

Chambers spoke. "That ain't a plan."

"We'll set our boys free."

Hatfield said, "What do you think, Ed?"

"Wish I'd a thought of it first."

"You get to work on planning, Bascom. Figure out what we'll need to see it through. We'll meet back here second night after the trial's over to firm things up."

Chambers asked, "Why the second night?"

"First night's reserved for Jess."

"I best be going so you two can rest up for tomorrow."

"I'll see you out." Hatfield escorted Bascom onto the back porch.

"I don't want to worry Ed none, but I got the same concerns as you. No telling what Felts might try once he's got us on his turf. Make sure you see this through if something happens."

"You got my solemn oath."

"Men'll need someone to rally around. Don't know anyone better suited than you."

"You sure you don't want me tagging along? I can blend in."

"Nothing would make me feel safer knowing you's by our side. But this thing's bigger than Ed and me. Don't forget that."

"I won't." Bascom stepped off the porch and into the night.

Chapter 54

August 1, 1921

Welch, West Virginia

Durwood leaned out the second-floor window of the McDowell County courthouse hoping to catch a breeze. The day had dawned hot and humid. Soon people would file into the courtroom for Sid Hatfield's second trial in a year. Assigned to augment the undermanned sheriff's office, Durwood was ordered to arrest anyone trying to bring firearms into the courtroom. In the brief time he'd studied law, it never occurred to him that someone might enter a courthouse armed. But this was West Virginia, in the midst of a coal war.

People in their Sunday best queued outside. Different from the rabble that had greeted Hatfield's acquittal four months earlier in Mingo County, these were decent, law-abiding folks. The kind of folks who wanted to see justice served.

On the street below, two couples chatted as they headed toward the limestone steps to the courthouse lawn. Arm in arm, Sid Hatfield and his wife led the way like they were on a Sunday stroll. If Hatfield was concerned about another trial, he didn't show it. The other couple was Hatfield's co-defendant, Ed Chambers, and his wife.

At one corner of the courthouse, three men huddled in the shadows.

At the top of the stairs, a fourth propped his foot against the block bannister. He looked in the direction of the other men and nodded.

As the couples approached the first landing, the man removed his foot from the bannister and tipped his hat. Guns drawn, the other three rushed the stairs. Lost in conversation, Hatfield's group failed to see the gunmen approach.

Durwood cried, "Look out."

Hatfield shoved his wife to the ground. Chambers and his wife dropped to their knees. Covering her head, Chambers pulled her to his chest. Gunshots popped. "Help! Help!" a woman screamed. Rounds tore into Hatfield's chest. Spinning, he fell face down onto the landing. Chambers stood to run away from his wife. Before he could escape the steps, a gunman jumped onto the landing to fire at close range. Chambers dropped. His wife threw herself across him. "For the love of God, stop!" The shooter tossed her aside. He fired two rounds into Chambers's head.

Hatfield's wife crawled to her husband; she shook his lifeless body. "Sid. My dear Sid. Say something." On her feet, she lashed out at the nearest assailant. She pounded his chest. "Murderer. Murderer."

Still kneeling, Chambers's wife wailed. "Oh good Lord, please. No. No." Blood soaked the hem of her dress and dripped from her clasped hands.

Townfolk gathered at the bottom of the steps. Waving his pistol, Chambers's executioner shouted, "If you know what's good for you, you'll clear the area now and keep your mouths shut. Understand?"

Heads down, the group scurried off.

Durwood aimed his revolver. Hatfield's widow continued to struggle with one of the gunmen. He didn't have a clear shot. Durwood holstered his pistol to race from the courthouse, slowed by crowds in the stairwell waiting to enter the courtroom. Outside, he reached the steps before the gunsmoke cleared. The gunmen were gone, replaced by two deputies bent over Hatfield and Chambers. Durwood could have saved them the trouble—both were dead before they hit the pavement. Embracing, the wives rocked and cried on their knees.

Durwood grabbed the arm of a deputy. "Did you catch them?"

"Never saw them."

"Aren't you going to look for them?"

"Which way did they go?"

"I'm not sure. There were four of them."

"Who were they?"

"No idea."

Jess Hatfield rose. "Liar." She poked a finger in Durwood's face. "They're Baldwin-Felts scum, just like you."

"That true?" a deputy asked.

"I don't know. I've never seen those men before."

"You're a damned liar." Hatfield's widow lunged. Stepping in front of Durwood, a deputy cut her off.

"Ma'am, I swear. I tried to warn you."

"Go to hell."

"Come on, ladies, let's get you back to the hotel."

Jess Hatfield cried, "We ain't leaving our husbands."

"There's nothing more you can do for them. We'll take care of them. First, we need the two of you to come with us." A deputy reached for Ed Chambers's widow, who continued to wail and cling to her husband's body. "Come on, now," he said softly, as he lifted her.

Tearful, she locked eyes with Durwood and spat on his chest. "Bastard."

The deputies supported the grieving women down the steps. Wiping his coat, Durwood addressed the crowd above him on the courthouse lawn. "Where'd the gunmen go?" No one responded. "For God's sake, people, are you going to let them get away with murder?"

Durwood climbed the steps. He stopped before a well-dressed man. "Who were those men?"

"We didn't see a thing, mister."

Durwood scanned the blank faces. "Isn't anyone going to help?"

"Why're you asking us? Like the lady said, they was Baldwin-Felts men."

"Did you see badges?"

"Ain't got to see a badge. They was getting even for Matewan. Like the good book says, 'A man reaps what he sows.' Hatfield had it coming to him and everyone knows it."

Durwood slumped on the top step to rest his head in his hands. Getting even? Didn't these people understand there's no such thing as even in a war?

✳✳✳

Durwood stormed into the Baldwin-Felts agency and blew past the receptionist.

"Durwood, what's the matter?"

"Is he in?"

"He's not to be disturbed." The receptionist followed down the hall. "Did you hear me?"

Durwood threw open Felts's door. Hunched over his desk, Felts pored over a ledger.

"What can I do for you?"

Durwood leaned on the edge of the desk. "I thought we stood for law and order."

"That's right."

Durwood tossed his badge onto the desk."

"You mind telling me what this is all about?"

"Sid Hatfield and Ed Chambers got gunned down walking to the courthouse."

"You sure?"

"Saw it myself."

"Who did it?"

"I was hoping you could tell me."

"Did you recognize them?"

"Never seen them before."

"Then why do you suppose I know anything about it?"

"Hatfield's wife claimed the killers were your men."

"Hatfield's wife?"

"That's right. Hatfield and Chambers were with their wives when three men shot them point blank. They were executed. Plain and simple."

"Were the women hurt?"

"They weren't shot, if that's what you mean."

"What are you trying to say?"

"Are you telling me you had nothing to do with this?"

"I'm not sorry to hear they're dead. I'd be lying if I said I hadn't dreamed of pulling the trigger myself. But if you're asking me was I involved in their deaths, the answer is no."

"Who was, then?"

"Take your pick. The list of men wanting Hatfield dead is as long as your arm."

"Including you."

"Including me." Felts lit a cigarette. He leaned back in his chair. "You know what it's like to lose a brother?"

Durwood shook his head. Not to death, anyhow.

"It's an ache that won't go away. Gnaws at you. Worse in my case, because I'm responsible not just for the death of one brother, but two. And a nephew who was like a son."

"How are you responsible?"

"Albert was headed to California before I talked him into joining the agency. Lee did everything Albert did, so I had him, too. Jude never talked about doing anything else. But one thing I know. Killing Hatfield isn't going to bring them back."

"No, but it avenges their deaths."

"I suppose. More important, without Hatfield stirring up trouble maybe we can put an end to this strike once and for all. Let things get back to normal so you can do what you came here to do."

Felts didn't know Bascom if he thought things would settle down. "What if all that's been done is to poke a bear?"

"Then I'm going to need all the good men I can get. I know I tried to talk you out of joining in the first place, but if you're right about things heating up, I hope you'll reconsider." Felts pushed the badge toward the edge of the desk.

Durwood fingered it. "Jude believed in your mission. I won't dishonor his memory."

"I wouldn't expect anything less from you."

"And I have your word that you, that we, didn't kill those men?"

"You have my word."

"If I find we had anything to do with Hatfield's murder, I'll make sure my father, the press, anyone who will listen, knows the truth. Understood?"

"Of course."

Durwood scooped up the badge and left the building.

Chapter 55

August 28, 1921

Blair, West Virginia

Union banners fluttered atop a commandeered train as it steamed into the station. Mobilized by Sid Hatfield's death, men used to working in tight spaces underground crammed a dozen passenger cars. They sang union standards as they disembarked under a bright blue sky. This was the third train of armed volunteers since the night before, swelling their ranks to over seven thousand.

A half dozen men strode toward Bascom. Several in doughboy uniforms with carbines and gas masks fastened to knapsacks looked like they were headed back to the killing fields of France. Others wore overalls like they were taking a break from a morning harnessed to a plow. A couple mountaineers carried muzzle-loaders, powder horns dangling from their necks.

Bascom called out, "Where you boys from?"

One of the doughboys said, "Me and him is from Ohio. Them two boys is from Pennsylvania. They's others on the train from Indiana, Michigan, Illinois and Lord knows where."

"What about you two?" Bascom asked the men in overalls, one of whom looked old enough to have fought in the Civil War.

"Fayette County. Is it true what they say?"

"What are they saying?"

"That we get to shoot us some Baldwin-Felts men."

"Starting to look that way."

The man flashed a tobacco-stained smile and slapped his buddy on the back. "Told you."

"How about y'all waiting over there 'til everybody gets off the train. I need to say a few words."

Bascom climbed atop a railcar to address the third group in twenty-four hours. The platform overflowed with volunteers—young and old, Black and White, native and immigrant. Most were miners but many were shopkeepers, farmers, doctors, lawyers. Pity Sid Hatfield hadn't lived to see this day. Then again, would this day have come any other way?

Bascom raised an arm. "Welcome." Drowned out by the commotion, he squeezed off a round from his sidearm. The veterans were easy to identify—guns drawn, they dropped to one knee. The platform grew quiet.

"Welcome, union brothers. My name's Bascom Matney. Been standing with the union since the strike on Cabin Creek in '12. Judging by the gray in some of your beards, I suspect many of you fought with us then and we's damned glad to have you by our side again. Camp's down by the church at the far end of town. Military units is set up according to union locals. If you're not in a union, check in by state. If you're a veteran, make sure to tell your unit commander. One last thing. Pick up a red bandana over by the schoolhouse. Wear it around your neck at all times, so's we can identify you. It'd be a damn shame if you was to be mistook for one of Tom Felts's men. After you've checked in, get yourself something to eat."

Someone shouted, "What's the plan?"

"Over that mountain sits the town of Logan. Scores of our men, good men, are sitting in jail for nothing more than joining the union. It ain't right. The only rail line into town has been shut down. So we aim to go over the ridge to liberate our brothers and rid Logan County of its corrupt officials, starting with Sheriff Don Chafin." Cheers erupted, hats flew into the air. "Chafin's a rich man. Know why? For keeping the union out, he gets a cut of every ton of coal mined in the county. That's gonna end. Once we've cleaned up Logan, it's on to Mingo County to put an end to martial law and free our boys from the jail in Williamson."

A miner shouted, "'Bout time we took the fight to them."

"Damn straight," another bellowed.

"Make no mistake. We tried to avoid bloodshed. For years, all the way up to John L. Lewis himself, our leaders have worked to put an end to union busting and get us the right to organize. Just last week, Governor Morgan rejected our demands. Our patience is wore thin. If the coal owners and politicians won't give us what's ours by right, then I reckon we'll have to take it. Stain of blood will be on their conscience, not ours." Men stamped their feet and banged rifle butts on the wooden platform. Cries of "Solidarity forever!" thundered from the assemblage. Bascom shouted to the men closest to him. "Y'all lead the way to camp so we can clear this platform before it collapses." As the raucous crowd moved toward camp, Bascom descended.

Two young men shouldered machine guns. "What do we do with these?"

"Where the hell'd you come by them?"

"Liberated 'em from a company store in Sharpless."

Bascom patted one of the men on his back. "Good work. Take 'em to the quartermaster. He'll put 'em to good use."

As the men ambled off, a fellow Bascom's age in coveralls approached. Wearing a holstered Colt, he gripped a satchel with one hand. The other sleeve was pinned where his arm ended just below the shoulder. "Hello, Bascom."

Bascom struggled to place the familiar face.

"Remember me?"

"Gordy?"

"What give it away?"

Bascom embraced the man who'd lost an arm to a Baldwin-Felts bullet eight years earlier while smuggling supplies to the Holly Grove tent camp. "Well, I'll be a sonofabitch. How you getting along?"

"Doing better now that I get a chance to return the favor for this." He nodded at his armless sleeve. "When I heard you was helping lead this outfit, I knew we wasn't going to back down. Wasn't about to miss out on the action."

"You checked in with your unit yet?"

"Nope."

"Tell you what, I could use a good man like you helping me keep this rabble under control. What do you say?"

"I appreciate what you's doing. But if it's all the same to you, I'm going to be with the boys from Kanawha County when we throw open them jailhouse doors in Logan."

"Come on, then. I'll show you to your unit. You hungry?"

"I could eat."

"Follow me."

***

Bascom tacked several maps to the blackboard of the one-room schoolhouse. Unit commanders filled the chairs and lined the walls. Bill Blizzard, tapped by union officials to lead the miners' army, waited for Bascom to finish. Bascom had met Blizzard during the Kanawha County strike in 1912. Since then, they'd worked together organizing strikes and attacking non-union mines and trains transporting strike breakers. After being named leader, Blizzard's first action was to tap Bascom as his lieutenant.

Blizzard addressed the room. "Gentlemen, we now control nearly all of southern West Virginia. Sole exception being Mingo County and the half of Logan County across that mountain. We aim to fix that. We're nearly eight thousand strong. Another couple thousand men are southeast in Raleigh County. We take control of Logan and Mingo, and the right to organize the entire southern West Virginia coalfields is ours."

Men clapped; some smacked the walls with open palms. A hand shot up at the back. Blizzard acknowledged the man. "Yes."

"Word is Sheriff Chafin's dug in all along the top of that ridge with deputies, Baldwin-Felts men and state troopers. How are we going to get past all them guns?"

"Bascom's been working on that."

Gripping a stripped hickory branch, Bascom turned to the maps. "Only road over the mountain is between these two peaks at Blair Mountain Gap." Bascom slid the pointer northwest. "Chafin'll be expecting us to attack there, so we'll make sure not to disappoint him. His men know they have to defend the pass at all costs. We'll concentrate a large force opposite to keep them occupied. Meanwhile, we'll probe along the ridge with smaller units 'til we find a weak spot. They ain't got enough bodies to man the entire line. Once we break through, we'll flank 'em. Force 'em to pull men away from the pass. When that happens, we'll throw everything we got 'til we control the Mountain."

Snug in an officer's uniform from the Great War, a middle-aged man stood. "What kind of weapons they got?"

Bascom placed the hickory branch on the desk. "We ain't likely to encounter any muskets if that's what you's hoping. They got the best money can buy. But don't forget. We outnumber 'em three to one."

"When do we attack?"

"Couple, three days at most. All depends on how fast you can get your units trained in basic military tactics. That's where fellows like you who've served Uncle Sam come in. Most of your men don't know a thing about the military. It's up to you to teach 'em. Fast. Make sure every man's got on a red kerchief. Any questions? Good luck, brothers."

Chapter 56

August 30, 1921

Blair Mountain, West Virginia

Even with improvements by Chafin's men, the dirt road up Blair Mountain from the town of Logan wasn't suitable for automobiles. Chafin stopped his Model T behind several trucks, two hundred feet below the summit. From there, scores of men ferried supplies to the top. Struggling under the weight of sandbags, lumber, ammunition boxes, and jugs of water, they still outpaced Chafin who labored uphill in front of Durwood and Tom Felts.

Men in rolled-up sleeves dripped sweat as they stacked sandbags on the far side of the trench. Others shored the sides with two-by-fours and lumber scraps, reminding Durwood of Russia. How many trenches had he and Jude dug? These men were lucky the earth wasn't frozen and those on the other side weren't Bolsheviks.

Durwood addressed a man placing the sandbags. "That as high as you're going with those bags?"

"Yes."

"Leave a gap for your muzzle. Let me show you." Durwood jumped into the trench. He slid the sandbags a few inches apart. "This way, if the fire's heavy enough to part your hair, you can drop your head below

the tops of the bags and still be able to see what you're shooting at."
Durwood climbed out of the trench, brushing mud from his pants.

Chafin asked, "Learn that in the service?"

"Yes, sir."

Felts added, "He served with my nephew in Russia."

"What do you think of our defenses, Durwood? Our boys been working round-the-clock the last couple of weeks."

"Impressive, sir. We got enough guns to man the line?"

"About three thousand men. We're spread thin, though, covering fifteen miles along this ridge."

Felts asked, "Any places we're worried about?"

Chafin bit a plug of tobacco. "North of here, near Haddock Gap. Got some of my best men there, mostly combat veterans."

Felts wiped his forehead. "We got the high ground."

"Good thing, too. Word is the Redneck Army's got ten thousand men."

Durwood asked, "Redneck Army?"

"On account of the red bandanas around their necks. Our boys have got white armbands. Be sure to get one when we go back to town."

The three stood atop the earthworks. Before them, the mountain descended sharply for a mile to the town of Blair. Rhododendron and mountain laurel grew so thick the limestone outcroppings were lost in a sea of green. While the vegetation would provide the miners cover, it denied them space to rush the mountaintop. Only the narrow, rutted dirt trail could be used for an assault. Chafin was ready. Barbed wire stretched across the trail twenty feet from the defenses. Machine guns anchored the trench on either side of the trail, giving the defenders a lethal shooting alley. If the miners tried to run this gauntlet, it would be shooting fish in a barrel.

Felts asked, "How are we doing on arms?"

"We got machine guns, high-powered rifles, tommy guns, carbines. Governor of Kentucky just sent four hundred rifles, two machine guns and forty thousand rounds of ammunition."

Felts whistled. "Guess he's counting on us ending this nonsense here before union fever jumps the Tug."

"That's what I aim to do. And we've got three biplanes from the Kanawha airfield in Charleston to monitor troop movements and drop bombs."

"Bombs?"

"Pipes full of nuts and bolts. The main thing is to find their field headquarters. See if we can't kill the leaders and end this attack before it starts."

Felts reached for a water jug. "Do we know who's leading the rednecks?"

"Bill Blizzard."

"No surprise there. He's been trying to make a name for himself for years."

"Second-in-command is a young man we don't know much about. Bascom Matney. Word has it he's calling the shots."

Felts said, "We're familiar with him, aren't we Durwood?"

"Afraid so."

Felts offered the jug to Durwood. "Matney keeps a low profile. But we've known about his activities in Mingo for a couple years now. Been leading nighttime raids on mines and ambushing my men. Was tight with Sid Hatfield. Guess this is his coming-out party. Be nice if we could rid ourselves of Blizzard and Matney with a couple of those bombs."

Chafin spit tobacco juice. "That's the plan."

Durwood lit a cigarette. "When do you think they'll attack?"

"That's what we're trying to figure out. Night before last, we grabbed a couple of their boys poking around our defenses, couple miles from here. One of 'em claims he grew up with Matney. Hadn't said much else, but we're working him over for information. Just a matter of time before he tells us where Matney and Blizzard are. Men at the airfield are ready to fly, soon as we have a location. You ready to head back to town?"

Felts nodded. "Looks like you've got everything under control up here."

Durwood stared down the mountain.

Felts said, "Let's go, son."

⁂

The lobby of the Aracoma Hotel brimmed with activity. The Women's Auxiliary served sandwiches and coffee to volunteers pouring into Logan from across the state. American Legionnaires mingled with some of the six hundred volunteers from McDowell County and one hundred fifty veterans of the Mingo Legion who had been pressed into action earlier that year to enforce martial law. Near the entrance, bedsheets ripped into two-foot strips overflowed a table manned by an elderly couple distributing them to everyone entering the hotel.

"Put this on your arm, young man." The woman handed Durwood an armband.

"Thank you, ma'am." Durwood tied the cloth around his left arm as he climbed the stairs to Chafin's fourth floor headquarters. On the far side of the war room, Chafin, Felts and the State Police Commandant studied maps. Several deputies worked the phones; lines had been strung to Blair Mountain. Others connected the command post to the Governor in Charleston and law enforcement offices across the state. A man hurried into the room. Brushing past Durwood, he whispered to Felts. Durwood grabbed the arm of the nearest phone operator. "Who's that man talking to Tom Felts?" Durwood pointed at the man he first saw the day Sid Hatfield and Ed Chambers were murdered, the man who led Hatfield's executioners.

"C. L. Lively."

"What's he doing here?"

"Same as you. Works for Baldwin-Felts."

Durwood steadied himself on the door jamb. His chest tightened. Felts and Lively moved to the far side of the room to speak in private. Durwood retreated down the steps and out the front door, drinking in fresh air. Eager to do their part, ROTC cadets from Charleston High School loaded cigarettes, chewing tobacco, and sodas onto a truck bound for troops manning the front lines. A block away, on the roof of a bank, a Gatling gun manned by state troopers dominated the town's skyline. Further down the street, a machine gun threatened from the roof of a bar. Wearing white armbands, townspeople moved along the street with purpose. Unsure what to do, Durwood wandered to the bar. The saloon was empty except for the barkeep washing glasses.

"What can I get you?" The bartender wiped his hands on his apron.

"Johnnie Walker."

"That'll be thirty cents."

Slapping coins on the bar, Durwood tossed back the shot. Squinting, he tapped the bar. The bartender topped him off.

Durwood fiddled with the glass, tipping the whiskey side to side.

Felts's words about the pain of losing a brother played in his head. Said it was made worse because he felt responsible for his brothers' deaths. If Bascom died in a hail of machine gun fire leading a foolhardy charge up Blair Gap or was killed by one of Chafin's bombs, he would have no one but himself to blame. Bascom made his bed long ago. He knew what he was doing. Besides, Durwood didn't owe Bascom anything. They were even.

Tucked in Durwood's breast pocket was Grace's letter that had arrived that morning. Her scent blossomed as he unfolded the stationery.

Dear Son,

Your father tells me not to worry, but I can't help it. Each day the paper speaks of the increasing threat of civil war. I rejoiced when President Harding issued his proclamation for the union to stand down, but it seems to have fallen on deaf ears. I know you think what your brother is doing is wrong. And maybe it is. But Bascom's a good man who's only doing what he thinks is right. I keep reminding Walker of that and so I will remind you. I pray fervently for the safety of you and your brother. I also pray for your reconciliation, just as I have every day since he left our home. I know how much he hurt you, but set things straight. The only thing worse than regretting something you did is regretting something you didn't do. You know who taught me that? Your mother. It's what allowed her to forgive your grandfather when he forsook her for marrying your father. If she could find it in her heart to forgive him, can't you do the same with your brother?

Your father sends his love. We are eager for your return.

With adoring love and affection,

Mother

Stuffing the letter in his pocket, Durwood spun from the bar.

"Mister, what about your drink?"'

Durwood threw open the door to sprint down the busy street to the jail. Before entering, he paused to catch his breath, to compose himself.

A heavy-set deputy in a faded uniform sat behind a desk. Another leaned on its edge. A key ring hung from his belt. "Afternoon, deputies."

The one behind the desk asked, "What can we do for you?"

"I need to see the union man we picked up night before last on Beech Creek."

"Who are you?"

Durwood flashed his badge. "Durwood Hopkins. Just left the

Aracoma. Tom Felts and Sheriff Chafin sent me over here to talk to the prisoner."

"Sheriff didn't say nothing to me about it. Besides, you ain't one of the interrogators."

"Exactly. Seems their tactics aren't producing results. I had experience interrogating prisoners during the War. You boys serve Uncle Sam?"

The men's eyes dropped as they shook their heads.

"Anyway, they figured it wouldn't hurt for me to have a go."

"Reckon we should check with the Sheriff first."

"Of course. Better safe than sorry, right?" Durwood slouched in a chair opposite the jailer. He put his feet on the edge of the desk.

The jailer lifted the earpiece from its cradle.

"I might get ready for an ass-chewing, if I was you. Sheriff wasn't exactly in a charitable mood when I left the hotel. Things are a bit tense in the war room."

The deputy placed the earpiece back on its hook.

"How long you gonna be?"

"Five, ten minutes at most."

"Reckon that'll be alright, then." He nodded at the other jailer. "Let Mr. Hopkins in to see Ratliff."

Ratliff? Grover Ratliff was one of Bascom's best friends when they were young. Could he be the man behind bars?

"What's the prisoner's first name?"

"Grover."

Durwood followed the jailer down the hall. Dozens of union men crowding cells on both sides of the hallway jeered as Durwood and the jailer passed just beyond arm's reach. At the end of the hall, the jailer slid his key into a steel door. As it swung open, a foul mixture of urine and vomit wafted out. Devoid of any furniture, a single bulb hung from the ceiling of the tiny cell. Curled in a corner, Ratliff didn't move.

The jailer pinched his nose. "Be quick," he said on his way out.

Durwood knelt to touch Ratliff's shoulder. The prisoner recoiled and buried his face deeper in the crook of his arm.

"You can beat me all you want, but I ain't got nothing to say."

"I'm not going to hit you, Grover. I just want to talk."

Bascom's old friend lifted his head to peek through swollen eyes. Dried blood caked under a displaced nose.

"You hungry?" Durwood handed him a chocolate bar. Grover struggled to open his puffy, purple lips enough to nibble.

"What do you want?"

"I need to know where I can find Bascom."

"Go to hell."

"I know what you're thinking, but I'm here to help."

"Ain't no Baldwin-Felts man ever done nothing to help a union man."

"What if I told you I was Durwood Matney."

"I'd say you was lying through your teeth. Durwood's been gone from here since their Ma died years ago."

"That's right. Pa sent me to Richmond. But I'm back now and I need to know where I can find Bascom."

"If you're who you say you are, tell me the name of your dog that used to hunt squirrels with us."

"You mean Old Blue? How about the time he got sprayed by that skunk and Pa made us wash him with lye soap? We practically rubbed him to the bone trying to rid him of that smell."

"That really you, Durwood?" Grover touched Durwood's arm.

Durwood squeezed his hand. "I'm sorry for what's been done to you."

"That's okay. I ain't told 'em nothing. If you're here to help Bascom like you say, why're you wearing that badge?"

"It's a long story. Let's just say time's come for me to set things right. Now tell me where Bascom is."

"He's down the mountain planning the attack on Logan. Gonna bust us outta this shit hole."

"Where exactly is he?"

"He set up headquarters in the Blair schoolhouse. You ain't fixing to go there, are you?"

"Yes."

"How you figure on doing that? Bascom's got sentries all over Blair Mountain. They'll cut you down sure as we're sitting here."

"Not if you give me the password."

"I don't know, Durwood. If you ain't telling me straight, I could be getting my boys in a lot of trouble."

"I swear on my mother's grave, Grover. I'm trying to save Bascom."

Ratliff straightened. "'Where are you going?' is the first challenge.

'To Mingo' is the response. Second challenge is 'How are you coming?'"

"What's the reply?"

"I come creeping."

Durwood embraced his old friend. "You hang on until we can get you out of here."

"I'll try."

Durwood stood. "Guard."

"Wait. You'll need this." Grover untied the red bandana from his neck.

The door opened. Durwood stuffed the bandana into his back pocket.

"Learn anything?"

"Hell no. Man's more stubborn than a draft mule."

The guard slammed the door. "Smells like one, too."

Durwood hurried from the jail. Outside the hotel, a truck belched exhaust as its engine turned over. Durwood dashed across the street in front of the truck.

"Where you headed?"

The driver said, "Top of Blair."

"Mind if I bum a ride?"

Crates filled the front seat. "Ain't got room for you up here."

Duwood jumped onto the running board as the truck pulled away from the hotel.

"Hang on."

Chapter 57

August 31, 1921

Blair Mountain, West Virginia

Stars freckled the sky, framing a half moon. Weary from a night checking the lines, Durwood leaned against a log. With dawn hours away, he had time for a quick nap if he was going to be on the other side of the line when the sun broke. After surveying the trench and breastworks within five miles on either side of Blair Gap, Chafin's concerns proved justified. Even with two machine guns, holding Haddock Gap posed his biggest challenge. Aided by high ground and a cache of weapons, unless the miners knew where to attack, the defenders could easily withstand a weeks-long siege. Durwood jotted troop strength and machine gun placements on the back of Grace's envelope. Tucking it into his pocket, he leaned back to close his eyes.

A kick to Durwood's foot startled him. Silhouetted by the moon, a state trooper in a wide-brimmed hat stood over him. "Come on."

Durwood sat up. "What's going on?"

"Rednecks are massing for an attack. We've been ordered to Blair Gap."

"And leave this line undefended?"

"Nobody in his right mind would mount an attack here."

Durwood stood. "Which is why we should assume they'll do it."

The trooper jumped into the trench. Durwood hung back.

The trooper asked, "You coming?"

"Go ahead. I'll stay behind a while to be sure you're right."

"If you get lonely, you know where to find us."

Durwood scanned for movement. As expected, all was quiet. On the far side of a twenty-foot wide rocky swale, charred tree trunks were all that remained of a mountaintop scarred by a lightning strike and brushfire. The trooper was right. There would be no attack here.

Durwood checked his watch. Five o'clock. Dawn was less than an hour away. It was time. He slipped the white band from his arm. Unclasping his badge, he placed it, with the armband, on top of a sandbag. Removing the red bandana from his back pocket, he tied it around his neck. He slipped a canteen over his shoulder, grabbed his gun, and scrambled over the top of the trench. Durwood scrambled over rocks until he reached the far side of the swale. Taking a knee, he checked the tree line ahead for any sign of Rednecks. Satisfied, he navigated the bleak landscape, dodging saplings and taking occasional cover behind blackened tree trunks to catch his breath. After fifteen minutes of careful movement, he reached the tree line.

The moon and stars retreated, giving way to a pale sky infused with pinks and oranges. In the same way, the nighttime quiet yielded to the rumble of battle several miles south. Even from this distance, the roar of machine guns flushed birds from their roosts. Durwood picked his way down the mountain, hoping he was loud enough not to startle a nervous sentry. He prayed he wouldn't be shot before he had a chance to recite the password.

Bushes rustled, a gun cocked. Durwood tensed. "Don't shoot."

"Stay where you're at. Put down the gun."

Durwood placed his gun on the ground and raised his arms.

"Where you going?"

"To Mingo."

"How are you coming?"

"I come creeping."

Guns drawn, two figures popped up behind a mulberry thicket ten yards ahead. An older wiry man who could've passed for Durwood's Pa stepped forward and motioned to his younger companion to lower his weapon. Stroking a sparse beard, he rasped, "What the hell you doing all the way up here by yourself?"

"Scouting lines."

"Nobody told us we had any men up here. Ordered us to shoot anyone coming down the mountain."

"Lucky for me, you didn't listen."

"Damn straight. Where you headed now?"

"Over to Blair Gap. Sounds like our boys could use a hand."

The younger sentry, still in his teens, spoke. "That's where I'm headed." Pointing at the older man, he said, "He drew the short straw."

"Didn't they send both of you up here to stand watch?"

"That's right."

"Don't you think you had better follow orders?"

The young man spat. "Wasn't it you who just said it was a good thing we ain't followed orders?"

"You got a point."

"You ready?" he asked Durwood. "We better hurry or we're going to miss out on all the fun."

Durwood had all the fun he wanted in Russia. Once they reached the fighting, he would slip away down the mountain. If he was lucky, he'd reach Bascom before Chafin launched his planes.

Durwood followed the teen. Traversing the mountain, they fought their way through dense underbrush. Thorns tore at them. Durwood pulled Ratliff's crusty bandana around his face. An hour after setting out for Blair Gap, they reached the northern flank of the Redneck army. Forced by gunfire to crawl the last fifty yards, they reached a miner tucked behind a log firing a bolt-action rifle at the trench above. Even on the battle's edge, rounds whizzed overhead, caromed off rocks and splintered bark. The staccato of machine guns made it hard to think.

Next to him the teen fired wildly. "Ain't you gonna shoot?" the boy yelled. If the defenders were shooting between the sandbags like Durwood instructed, the miners were wasting ammunition. The only chance they had of hitting a defender was if he was dumb enough to stand. The miners, on the other hand, weren't so lucky. The cries of the wounded rose above the battle.

Durwood squeezed a couple rounds from his carbine into the berm below the trench.

"Can't see the bastards," the teen cried as he raised on one knee to fire.

"Get down." Durwood reached for the boy, who gasped and tumbled backwards ten feet down the mountain.

"You hit?"

The teen mumbled something Durwood couldn't make out.

He scooted to the boy. Blood oozed from the kid's shoulder, spreading across a white thermal top. "We need to get you off this mountain." Durwood pointed to a group of boulders thirty yards downhill. "If you can make it to those rocks, we should be able to walk from there. Think you can do that?"

"I'll try."

The boy propped himself on both arms, but immediately collapsed, unable to support any weight with his bad arm.

Bullets tattooed the earth around them. Exposed, they had attracted the attention of a defender finding his range.

"We need to move. Climb on my back."

"You sure?"

A bullet slammed into the boy's pack at his side.

"Hurry up, dammit." Durwood laid on his stomach.

The teen groaned as he pulled himself atop Durwood's back with his good hand.

"You on?"

"Yep."

Durwood slid his rifle ahead ten feet. Pushing onto his forearms, he wriggled downhill, straining to go ten feet without stopping. Reaching his rifle, he repeated the process, bullets nipping at his heels. Head down, he made the last push for the boulders, ignoring the pain from his knees and bloodied forearms.

Collapsing onto his stomach, Durwood rested his forehead atop crossed wrists. "You can get off now." The boy didn't budge.

"You hear me?" Durwood didn't know the boy's name. He raised on one arm. The teen rolled onto the ground. Eyes wide, he stared into the canopy, seeing nothing. Durwood closed his eyes. He turned the body over. Blood stained the middle of his back.

Durwood leaned against the rock to sip from his canteen. Did this boy leave a family? How many others like him would there be at day's end? Men foolish enough to think war was a turkey shoot.

Durwood hopped up. He needed to move fast if he was going to find Bascom before Chafin did.

Chapter 58

August 31, 1921

Blair, West Virginia

Bill Blizzard stood in the schoolhouse doorway. "Any word from our recon teams?"

Bascom paced in front of the blackboard. "Not yet."

"Men tell me we're taking a beating at the Gap. Think we should pull back some?"

Bascom stopped pacing. "You know we can't do that. We've got to keep the pressure on Chafin's men 'til we can breach their line somewhere else. Anything short of that and they win."

"We're losing some good men."

"I didn't take this job to make a point. I took it to win. Let me do it or relieve me of my command."

"Coming through." Blizzard moved sideways as stretcher bearers carrying another wounded fighter entered the schoolhouse. They moved to the far end of the room where Alma tended casualties. Desks had been moved outside to make room. "Where do you want him?" Blizzard was gone.

Head down, Alma said, "Put him next to me."

A man rushed to Bascom holding his side.

Bascom asked, "What's the matter?"

The man stammered. "We caught us a Baldwin-Felts man wearing a bandana. He was snooping around the farmhouse up the road. Asking a lot of questions about you and wanting to know where the schoolhouse was."

"What makes you think he's Baldwin-Felts?"

"One of our boys seen him evicting folks at Paint Lick."

"Take him to the holding pen. We'll deal with him later."

"That ain't all of it."

"Well, let's hear it."

"Says he's your brother."

"Where is he now?"

"Up by the farmhouse."

"Bring him to me."

"I tried, but the others think it's a trick. They aim to beat the truth out of him, first."

"Bring him here. Now. Tell them others not to lay another hand on him."

"Yes, sir."

Alma finished sewing a wound. She straightened her back to rub her belly. She should be home resting until the baby was born, not tending wounded in a field hospital. Bascom had a better chance of dislodging Chafin's men from their trenches atop the mountain than he had convincing Alma she needed to be resting at home. "You think it's really Durwood?"

"Yes. But what's he doing on our side of the lines?"

Chapter 59

August 31, 1921

Blair, West Virginia

Two miners pinned Durwood's arms behind his back. A third landed blows to his body and face.

"What was you doing sneaking around pretending you was a Redneck?" The man crashed another fist into Durwood's bloodied face. "You'd make things easier on yourself if you'd tell the truth."

"I did."

"Leave him be."

Durwood couldn't see his benefactor, but it didn't seem to carry any weight. Another blow sunk into his ribs. Doubled over and gasping, Durwood braced for another.

"Bascom said not to lay another hand on him. You hear?"

Thank God. He wasn't too late.

"Bascom wants to see him. Now."

The attacker spit in Durwood's face. "Let's go."

The men set off down the gravel road holding Durwood between them.

"Where you taking me?"

"Schoolhouse."

"How far is it?"

The man who had interceded said, "Quarter mile down this road."

"We need to hurry."

The leader of the group said, "I ain't taking orders from no Baldwin-Felts man. Now shut the hell up before I smack you again."

The faint hum of propellers drifted into the valley. Durwood craned to look for the planes, but the sun was too bright. He struggled to free himself, but the men's fingers dug into his biceps.

"Let go of me."

"For the last time, you ain't the one giving orders."

The drone grew louder. "You hear that? Those planes are headed this way. They're going to bomb the schoolhouse."

One hundred yards away, a small wooden schoolhouse with a bell tower came into view. Unable to free himself, Durwood began to scream. "Bascom. Get out of there."

Bascom appeared in the schoolhouse doorway, cupping a hand over his brow.

Durwood yelled again. "Get out of there. Now."

Over Durwood's shoulder, two biplanes dove toward the valley from Blair Mountain. Passing low, a passenger in the lead plane peered over the side as the plane sped toward the school. Seconds later, the other plane buzzed past. "Run." Bascom didn't budge. Durwood's scream was lost in the roar of the engines. Durwood braced for an explosion. Nothing happened. The planes nearly clipped the belltower, banked and faded into the distance.

Durwood's tormentor said, "Told you he was a liar."

Bascom strode toward them. The men continued to restrain Durwood.

"This man claims he's your brother. I done told him ain't no way Bascom Matney's got kin working for Baldwin-Felts."

"Let him go."

The men released Durwood's arms. He pitched onto his hands and knees.

Bascom tugged at the bandana around Durwood's neck. "What the hell you doing here dressed like one of my men?"

"You know him?"

Bascom ignored the question.

Durwood winced as he stood. "We've got to get you away from here."

Another of Durwood's captors said, "He claimed those planes that done passed by were going to bomb the school. The man's a liar."

Durwood got to his feet. "Chafin's hired planes to bomb your headquarters. Heard him say so myself."

"Slow down, little brother. You're not making sense. How did you know where to find me?"

"Grover Ratliff. He's in jail in Logan. He gave me the bandana, too."

"Let's get you to Alma. You ain't looking your best."

"Where is she?"

"Tending to wounded in the schoolhouse."

"We need to get her out of there." Durwood turned to the man who had beaten him. "Keep Bascom here."

"I done told you, I don't take orders from you. Them planes you keep harping about flew off."

"He's right, Durwood. The planes are gone. I think you've been fed misinformation."

Durwood crashed a fist into Bascom's jaw. Caught off guard, Bascom landed on his back. Ignoring the pain in his ribs, Durwood sprinted toward the schoolhouse.

In the back of the room, Alma was bent over a soldier. "Come on, Alma. We got to get you out of here."

Alma straightened to face Durwood, a hand supporting her belly. What was she doing here in that condition? By the looks of things, the baby would be here soon.

Alma stood. "Come here. Let me take a look at you."

"We don't have time. We've got to get out of here."

"What are you talking about?"

"Planes have been sent to bomb the schoolhouse."

"Planes just flew by."

"They'll be back."

"I'm not leaving these men."

"Tell you what. You go ahead and I'll bring them." He pulled Alma to her feet.

"Where's Bascom?"

"Outside waiting for you. I'll explain later. Please, hurry." Durwood rushed to the door, Alma in tow. When they reached the lawn, he pushed her toward Bascom and the others. "Run. Don't stop until you get to

Bascom. Go." In the distance the drone of planes returned. Durwood rushed back inside.

Three men lay on the floor. One raised on an elbow, a sling cradling the other arm.

"Can you walk?"

The man nodded.

"Then on your feet. Fast."

The man got up to walk toward the door.

"Hurry." The man trotted outside. "Run, dammit."

Two men remained on the floor, one unconscious. Durwood bent to pick up the other. "Sorry. This is going to hurt." The Redneck groaned as Durwood scooped him in his arms to stand. The groans increased as Durwood staggered outside. Fifty feet from the school, Bascom met them.

"How many more are there?"

"Just one."

"I'll get him."

"Like hell. For once in your life, listen to me. Here." Durwood slid the wounded miner into Bascom's arms to race back to the building. On the horizon, the planes headed for the school.

Inside, Durwood knelt beside the unconscious miner. "Your turn." Durwood threw the man over his shoulder. Determined to beat the bombs, he struggled toward the door. The whir of propellers filtered through open windows.

Chapter 60

"Take him." Bascom passed the patient to one of his men. In the distance, the planes headed for the school. A third had joined the formation. Head down, Bascom ran.

In the open schoolhouse door, Durwood struggled under the weight of a man. Bascom shouted, "Hang on. I'm coming," his words lost in the whir of propellers.

As the first plane bore down on the bell tower, several small cylinders fell. Explosions ripped through the schoolhouse, spewing wood and dust in all directions. The blasts knocked Bascom down. He was still on the ground when the second plane launched its cannisters and banked. Louder than the first two explosions, the bombs shook the ground. Bits of wood pattered around him. Bascom covered his head, waiting for the third plane to strike. Buffeted by the second blast, the third nosed straight up short of its target and joined the others in the distance.

Bascom pushed to his chest. The school's facade had buckled, its bell tower gone. He rushed to what remained. A map fluttered to the ground. He teetered over wood littering the gaping hole where the door had stood. Dust choked the air. Pulling up his bandana, he shouted for Durwood, but heard only his own ragged breath.

Inside the door, boots protruded from beneath fractured boards. Muttering a prayer, Bascom scrambled to the body. Tossing aside splintered wood, he rolled the man onto his back. A dead Redneck stared up at him.

"Durwood? Answer me, little brother."

A muffled cough came from the other side of the doorway near where the copper bell lay. Fingers pushed through the rubble. Bascom clambered over the bell tower's oak timbers. Covered by a pile of broken planks, Durwood lay on his back. Half of the bell's lip rested atop debris pressing on Durwood's chest. Bascom grabbed the top of the bell to pull it toward him. It wouldn't budge. He tried again, but the bell held fast.

Bascom cupped his hands. "Somebody give me a hand." He knelt to grasp Durwood's free hand. Bascom removed his bandana to wipe grime from Durwood's ashen face and half-opened eyes. A jagged gash traced from his temple to his jaw line.

Durwood grunted, "Was that you I just heard praying to the Lord?"

"Don't try to talk."

"Ma would be proud." A wan smile faded to a wince.

Alma entered the dilapidated structure with one of the miners who had detained Durwood. "Jesus," the miner uttered.

"Help me get this bell off him."

Together, the men tugged. Durwood gasped as the bell clanged on its side. Bascom removed the remaining wood and debris covering Durwood. "Want me to set you up?"

Durwood grunted. "I think my back is broken. Can't feel my legs."

Alma asked, "How is he?"

"Get a stretcher. And find a doctor. Hurry."

Alma and the miner disappeared.

"You'll be okay soon as we fetch a doctor."

"I'm sorry, Bascom."

"What for?"

"For getting crosswise with you."

"You ain't still stuck on that Bible story are you?"

"A woman once told me no matter how thin a pancake might be, there are always two sides. Took me a while to figure out what she meant."

"Hush. We can talk about this later."

Durwood wheezed. Blood trickled from a corner of his mouth. "Things were always black and white in Richmond. Russia too. But out here, it's nothing but greys."

"You don't belong here."

Durwood squeezed Bascom's hand. "Felts had Hatfield killed. Same as he did Uncle Durwood."

"Don't waste your breath on Felts."

"Reach in my pocket."

Bascom removed an envelope bearing Grace's handwriting.

"Turn it over."

"What's this?"

"Information on Chafin's men. Gun placements." Durwood labored to whisper. "Couple miles north of Blair Gap, line's undefended. You'll know it because the area's burned out." Durwood gasped. His eyes pinched. "That and Haddock Gap are your best bets to breach the line."

"Why are you telling me this?"

Durwood squeezed Bascom's hand. "Tell Pa I didn't forget where I'm from."

"You can tell him yourself, soon as you've mended."

Durwood's eyes fluttered. His grip relaxed.

"Durwood!" Bascom shook his shoulder. "Why did you have to come back, little brother?" For the first time since he said goodbye to Belle, Bascom wept.

Alma picked her way inside with two miners on her heels bearing a stretcher.

Bascom waved them off.

Dog tags dangled from a beaded chain around Durwood's neck. Between the tags hung a stamped metal disc with faded red paint. Bascom unclasped the chain. He slipped off the Paint Lick scatter tag. Bascom resecured the dog tags around his brother's neck. He rose, placing the scatter tag in his pocket.

As he scrambled from the building, Bill Blizzard and two lieutenants hurried down the road, stopping in front of the ruins. "Holy shit. Damned lucky you weren't in there."

"Luck ain't had nothing to do with it. Let's go. I know where to attack."

Chapter 61

September 3, 1921

Blair Mountain, West Virginia

Bascom led one hundred men, a mix of Calabrians and Great War veterans, up the mountain. Close behind, a draft mule labored to pull a Gatling gun over the steep terrain. The fighting ran heavy at the Gap several miles away, but the forest ahead lay still. Bascom imagined himself a boy hunting these mountains with Cesco. As they neared the top, a scout reported that Chafin had reinforced the burned-out mountaintop with a machine gun and more than a dozen men. An assault over the open terrain that Durwood had described would turn the rocky swale into a killing field. Bascom's men pressed on, hoping for a better report on Haddock Gap.

Planes buzzed, visible through gaps in the foliage. Unlike the private planes that bombed the schoolhouse, these bore U.S. Army insignia. Instead of bombs, they dropped leaflets warning that federal troops were on the way. Bascom's men were instructed to lay down their weapons and abandon the assault. Anyone firing on U.S. troops would be treated as enemy combatants. Time was running out.

The scout returned, sweaty and out of breath. "Haddock Fork's a quarter mile ahead. They've got a machine gun and they's a bunch of men all dug in, but it sits on a point. We can attack from three sides. Two of them sides sits higher than their earthworks."

Durwood was right.

"Almost there, boys. Y'all take a rest while I get a look."

Bascom crept to a fallen tree a hundred yards from the earthworks. Through binoculars, he surveyed the enemy line. Fifty men, maybe more, armed with automatic weapons, occupied a reinforced trench. Above the trench, a machine gun tucked in tight among rocks. On this side of the line, the left and right flanks enjoyed higher ground. These men would be hard to dislodge, but Bascom didn't have a choice. He needed to move fast if they were going to punch through to Logan before federal troops arrived to halt their attack. If they seized Logan, Bascom would be in position to demand recognition from the companies before U.S. troops forced his men to disarm. If he got lucky, he might get to deal with Chafin himself.

Returning to his men, Bascom split the force into thirds. He spoke to Giovanni and another lieutenant. "I'll take the Gatling gun and go straight at the point of their line. You two lead the men on the right and left flanks. Ground is higher for you, giving us the advantage. Get in place and draw fire to give us cover while we set up the gun. Need to make sure their big gun is occupied while we wheel ours into position. We'll concentrate fire from three sides 'til we run out of ammunition or force those bastards to retreat. See you boys in Logan."

Bascom untied the mule and stroked its forehead. "Good work, girl. We'll take it from here." Bascom removed the scatter tag from his pocket. "Thanks, little brother." He kissed the tag.

Gunfire from his flanks signaled Giovanni and the others were in place. Bascom pointed at several of the men. "You three stay behind with me to move the gun. I want the rest of you to get as close as you can to lay down fire until we maneuver the Gatling gun into place in that stand of trees."

As the advance team crept forward, small arm rounds answered them. Chafin's machine gun continued to concentrate on Bascom's flanks.

"Let's go." Bascom and another miner pushed the gun from behind. The other two took up positions by the gun's wheels to provide cover as they advanced. Nearing the trees, one of the riflemen crumpled. "Keep going," Bascom yelled. "Almost there."

They pushed the gun until its wheels were flush against a couple of trunks. The gun's muzzle extended past the trees. Exposed except for the bit of cover provided by the trees, Bascom readied the big gun. Bullets zipped the air. Aiming at the machine gun across the way, Bascom laid down fire. If he could knock out their gun, his men stood a chance.

Over the roar of the rotary cannon, a soldier sidled up to Bascom to shout, "Let me take the gun, Bascom. You find cover."

"Like hell. Go back to check on him," Bascom nodded at the man behind them on the ground.

"He's dead."

"Then find you a spot behind that log and start shooting." The man hesitated. Rounds slapped the trees in front, splintering bark.

"All due respect, Blizzard told me to make sure you didn't go and do something stupid." Several rounds ricocheted off the Gatling gun.

"Blizzard ain't here. Now get the hell out of my way." Bascom continued to fire toward the opposite gun; sparks flew as bullets stitched the rocks sheltering the gunner. Bascom tried to move the gun to adjust his aim, but a tree sat tight against the muzzle. Off to his side, another miner slumped behind the log. Ever-thickening smoke blanketed no man's land. Soon the gun across the way would be veiled. Bascom tugged on the gun's hitch to pull it free of the trees for a better aim. The gun wouldn't budge, its wheels rutted in the soft ground. As he ran around the trees in front of the gun, Bascom shouted, "Keep laying down fire." Ignoring the other gun, Bascom dug his heels in the soft ground and pressed his shoulder against the underside of the barrel to push. Caroming off the gun's barrel, a round nicked his arm. Undeterred, Bascom rocked the big gun several times before the wheels popped free. Returning to the other side, he lifted the hitch to move the gun several feet to the left. The other gunner was in his sights. Bascom fired a barrage of rounds that tore into the opposite gun's redoubt. As he paused to reload, the other gun fell silent.

Rebel yells from his right and left filled the forest. The men on the flanks were charging. Bascom ran back to the fallen soldier to grab his rifle. "Come on, boys!" He hurdled the log to sprint toward the trench. His men followed, screaming. They were shooting as they advanced, but the enemy didn't return fire—they were in retreat. Several bodies littered the trench. Bascom's men regrouped on Chafin's side of the line, their ranks thinner by half a dozen.

One of the miners shouted, "They ran toward Blair Gap,"

"Let's go after them," another responded.

Bascom said, "Let 'em go. We're headed down this mountain 'til we get to Logan."

***

Bascom signaled his men to stop. A couple hundred yards ahead, Logan lay quiet, several buildings visible through the dense forest. The men took a knee to catch their breath and learn Bascom's plan for the assault. "They're sure to have plenty of guns in town. We need to take it slow 'til we know what we's dealing with. Giovanni, take a couple men and circle 'round back of town and see what's going on. Find out where their big guns are. We'll wait here. Any questions?"

An amplified voice broke through the trees. "This is Colonel John Brady, United States Army. By order of the President of the United States, you are commanded to lay down your weapons and come out with your hands up. Anything other than unconditional surrender will be treated as a hostile action and you will be considered enemy combatants. You have five minutes."

Bascom hung his head.

A young miner broke the silence. "We ain't going to quit now, are we? We got men in jail on the other side of them trees we promised to set free. We can lick them soldiers same as we did them men on top of the mountain."

Bascom left his rifle on the ground. "Boys, we ain't got a quarrel with Uncle Sam. Even if we did, that's a fight we can't win. We may have fallen a bit short, but make no mistake. Chafin and the companies he's protecting ain't got no choice but to deal with us or next time things will be different."

Giovanni stood, weapon at his feet. In Italian, he addressed his men who released their guns. The rest followed until all the Rednecks had disarmed.

Bascom addressed them. "Put your hands on top of your heads and follow me."

Once his miners were lined up, Bascom shouted, "Colonel, we've dropped our guns and are coming out like you directed. Tell your men not to shoot."

Bascom checked his watch. A minute remained on the Colonel's ultimatum. "We ain't coming out 'til I hear you tell your men to stand down."

Colonel Brady barked over the bullhorn, "Stand down, men. They're coming out."

"Let's go, boys. Hold your heads high."

Chapter 62

September 8, 1921

Richmond, Virginia

Passengers crowded the aisle, waiting to depart the train. A boy chattered and tugged his mother's arm. Gazing out the window, Bascom remained seated until the compartment emptied. It had been nine years since his first trip to Richmond, tucked into a freight car with two down-on-their-luck strangers. How different life had been, so full of promise. He grabbed the bag and stepped onto the platform to walk toward the caboose. Near the back of the train, men loaded a wooden casket into a hearse by the tracks. Next to the hearse, Grace and Walker stood hand-in-hand. They wore black, a veil covering Grace's face. Bascom slowed, unsure what to say.

As he neared, Grace spoke. "Thank you for bringing him back to us."

"This was his home. It's where he belongs."

"Does your father agree?"

Bascom lowered his head. "He would have. Buried him next to Ma a couple days back."

Grace squeezed Walker's hand. "Dear God. Losing Durwood must have been too hard on him."

"That's just it. He didn't know. Found him in his rocking chair clutching a photo of Ma and Durwood."

Doors slammed as the hearse's engine revved. A man approached from the back of the funeral wagon. "We're on our way to the parlor, sir."

Walker nodded. "We'll be along in a minute."

"I got his things from the boarding house." Bascom extended the bag. "There's a letter in there he hadn't posted."

Walker took the bag. Grace released Walker's other hand to throw her arms around Bascom's neck. "Oh, Bascom." Tears cooled his cheek.

Bascom wrapped an arm around Grace's back. Eyes closed, he let her fragrance wash over him one last time. "I'm so sorry for your loss, Miss Grace," he whispered. "He loved you like you was his mother."

Grace placed her hands on Bascom's cheeks. "We all lost someone special. He loved you, you know?"

Bascom nodded, resolved not to shed any more tears, especially in front of Walker.

"His service is the day after tomorrow. Will you stay with us until then?"

Expressionless, Walker stood back clutching the bag.

"Thank you, but I've got to get back."

"Why the rush?"

"Things is still unsettled."

"What he means, Grace, is he's still agitating. Bascom, can't you see it's over?"

"Walker, please."

"It's just a shame President Harding waited to send troops in until after you had managed to get your brother killed."

"Walker. Stop it."

"That's okay, Miss Grace. He's right about one thing. The army took our guns. Well, some of them. But it ain't over. Not so long as men like you don't recognize the working man."

"Are you still peddling that socialist tripe? If it weren't for the men you're so quick to condemn, your people would still be wandering barefoot in the mountains lucky to survive another winter. We've provided jobs, housing, and education, only for them to be led astray by people like Mother Jones. And you."

"Keep thinking you're in the right, if it makes you feel good.

Durwood finally figured things out, you know. It's why he's dead. Killed by bombs dropped from planes hired to kill me. You know who hired those planes? Men your railroad and mine owners been paying to keep the union out. That's on you."

Walker's eyes narrowed. "Don't try to blame his death on me, son. It was your war that got him killed."

"Know what Durwood told me with his dying breath? Told me where to attack the men dug in on Blair Mountain. Would've worked, too, if the troops hadn't arrived."

"Now, you're lying. Durwood returned to Mingo to oppose men like you. We've got letters to prove it."

"You're right. He did. But in the end, he figured the men hiding behind badges were worse than men like me. You know why? Because they's only in it for the money. Just like you."

"I don't believe you."

Bascom stepped close to Walker. "Tell the truth. You're more upset that Durwood died opposing everything you've built your life around than the fact he's dead, ain't you?"

"Come on, Grace. I've heard enough."

Bascom reached for Grace's hand. "I'm sorry, Miss Grace. You're a good woman. You don't deserve this. Last thing I intended was to upset you."

"Goodbye, Bascom."

Walker led Grace to a shiny new Ford. Bascom moved toward the ticket window.

"May I help you?"

"One-way ticket to Matewan, West Virginia." Bascom slid a bill under the window and collected his change and ticket.

"I'd be careful, if I was you, mister."

Bascom slipped the change into his wallet. "How's that?"

"Haven't you heard? The coalfields are full of wild-eyed Reds looking to overthrow the government. Took Uncle Sam to bring them to heel."

"Thanks for the tip. I'll be sure to keep an eye out."

"Platform eight. Leaves in thirty minutes."

"Thanks."

Chapter 63

Bascom and Bill Blizzard sat in wobbly chairs in a cramped holding cell. Their cuffed hands rested on a worn table. Harold Houston, the union lawyer who had successfully defended Sid Hatfield for the Matewan shootout, entered. "Court's ready to resume."

Bascom asked, "Alma give you my good luck charm?"

Houston handed Bascom the Paint Lick scatter tag. Bascom kissed the tag.

"You boys realize this is the same courthouse where John Brown was convicted of treason sixty-three years ago?"

Bascom shook his head. "That your idea of a pep talk?"

"Don't worry. To convict you of treason, the prosecution must prove beyond a reasonable doubt that you intended to levy war against the State. You heard it. Their case was weak. What little credibility they had, we undermined with our witnesses."

Bascom stood. "What are you trying to say?"

"I think it's best we rest without calling you."

Blizzard said, "I'll go along with whatever you think, Mr. Houston."

"Bascom?"

"I want to take the stand."

"If you do, you're opening yourself up to cross-examination. I counsel against it."

"If I don't, can you tell me we'll win for sure?"

"Well, no. I can only give you the benefit of my professional experience. But you understand, if convicted you could be sentenced to death."

"I ain't got nothing to hide. I'll take my chances."

***

"All rise."

The Judge entered the courtroom to take the bench. "Mr. Houston. Call your next witness."

"The defense calls Bascom Matney."

Bascom stepped into the witness box below the judge. Placing his hand on the Bible, he swore to tell the truth.

The judge peered down. "Be seated."

The packed courtroom lay quiet, except for the beat of the clock on the wall. Shoulder to shoulder, people pressed into the benches. Reserved for the press, the front rows were full of men sketching and scribbling. Twelve jurors, men older than Bascom, greeted him with blank faces. Near the back of the courtroom, Alma's eyes flashed beneath a hat cut low to her brow. Would she have advised him to testify? Didn't matter. That ship had sailed.

"Tell us your name."

"Bascom Matney."

"Are you a member of the United Mine Workers Union?"

"Proud member."

"Can you tell us when you joined?"

"February 8, 1913."

"How is it you remember the day?"

"Because the day before my cousin, Cesco Estep, was murdered by a bunch of lawmen and mine agents run amok on the Bull Moose Special. Wasn't enough they forced Cesco and his family from their home to live in a tent during the coldest winter in memory. They had to kill him, too. Would've been a lot more dead if we hadn't got the women and children to safety before they opened up with machine guns."

"You were living at Holly Grove?"

"I was."

"But before that day, you weren't a union member?"

"No, sir."

"So, why on earth were you living in a union relief camp if you weren't a union member?"

"Got word that Cesco and his family was barely scraping by and their youngest had died due to the conditions. Decided I had to do something to help. Took a train back here."

"Where were you living at the time?"

"Richmond, Virginia, sir. Me and my little brother was living with my Ma's cousin and her husband."

"How old were you?"

"Eighteen."

"Did you have a job in Richmond?"

"I did." Bascom grinned. "A girl, too."

The remark produced scattered snickers. The judge reached for the gavel. Bascom stole a glance at Alma, hoping she'd forgive him for bringing Belle into the case.

"Once you got to Holly Grove, how were you able to help?"

"Smuggled food to the families. They was in a bad way."

"Were you paid for your troubles?"

"They offered, but I figured that money was better spent on supplies."

"Other than your cousin, did you have any relatives in Holly Grove?"

"No, sir."

"Any acquaintances?"

"No, sir."

"You mean to tell these good men of the jury you gave up everything to risk your life for a bunch of folks you didn't even know?"

"Let's just say I did what needed to be done and leave it at that."

"Once the 1912 strike ended, did you return to Richmond? To your job? And your girl?"

Bascom shook his head. "No, sir."

"Why not?"

"Promised Cesco before he died I'd take care of his wife and kids."

"How many did he have?"

"Two, plus the baby they took in after its ma passed."

Before a rapt courtroom, Houston led Bascom through the journey that culminated in his command of the Redneck Army and the charges that landed him in handcuffs in John Brown's courtroom. Bascom told his story. If convicted now, so be it.

"Answer any questions the prosecution has."

The prosecutor grabbed his notes and moved to the podium. Tossing his papers on the lectern, he muscled it closer to Bascom.

"You were present in Matewan on May 19, 1920 with Sid Hatfield and his men when Albert and Lee Felts and five other Baldwin-Felts agents were gunned down, weren't you?"

"I was."

Houston leapt to his feet. "Objection. This line of questioning isn't relevant to the charge before this court."

The prosecutor responded. "Your honor, we aim to show the origins of Mr. Matney's treasonous acts. To do that, we must have a little latitude. After all, Mr. Matney chose to take the stand."

"Overruled."

"You were armed?"

"I was."

"And you fired at those men who were killed, did you not?"

"No, sir."

The prosecutor scoffed and leaned across the lectern at Bascom. "You expect us to believe you didn't fire your weapon that day?"

"Wasn't what I said. I said I didn't fire at them Baldwin-Felts men, though I sure would have liked to. They had it coming."

"So you admit you went to Matewan that day with the intent to maim or kill?"

Houston was on his feet again to object. Again, the judge overruled the objection. Bascom fidgeted. He had said too much. Houston had warned him. "I went there to do what needed to be done."

"And that was to maim or kill those Baldwin Felts agents, was it not?"

"I reckon."

"Can you speak up, please?"

"I said, 'I reckon.'"

The prosecutor turned his back before pivoting back to the podium. "So tell us, Mr. Matney, if you didn't fire at those agents, who did you fire at?"

"My brother."

"Your brother?"

"That's right."

"Enlighten us, please." The prosecutor stepped away from the podium, crossed his arms and leaned against the jury box.

"Just before the firing started, I recognized my little brother was walking with them agents toward the train station. Keep in mind, I hadn't laid eyes on him since I left Richmond for Holly Grove in 1912. So I pinned him down behind a barrel with my carbine."

"Why'd you do that?"

"To keep him from being mistaken for a Baldwin-Felts man and getting hisself shot like them others."

"And that's because you knew 'them others' were to be executed, isn't that right?"

"I knew there was going to be a fight. They had guns. Turns out, we had more for once."

"And where is your brother now?"

"Killed at Blair Mountain by one of Mr. Chafin's bombs intended for me."

"So, your brother was an insurrectionist, too?"

"No, sir. He was a Baldwin-Felts man who finally saw the light."

"I thought you said he wasn't an agent of the Baldwin-Felts company."

"Turns out he was. I just didn't know it at the time. Good thing, too."

"Why's that?"

"'Cause I wouldn't have been aiming to miss."

Laughter drew a rebuke from the judge.

"Your hatred for the State runs so deep you would've killed your own brother?"

"My quarrel was with the companies and the guns hired to lock out the union. The State ain't done nothing wrong. In fact, the State ain't done nothing at all."

"And that was a problem in your eyes, wasn't it? The State wouldn't help your cause, so it was time to take matters into your own hands and overthrow the lawful government of the State of West Virginia?"

Bascom looked for help. Head in hand, Houston didn't look up.

"Wasn't what I said."

The reporters scribbled notes as fast as they could.

The prosecutor stepped away from the podium to consult his co-

counsel, before resuming the examination.

"You admit you led the rebellion in August and September last in Logan County?"

"I admit to leading a group of miners fed up with being denied the right to organize. Men determined to free their brothers who'd been jailed in Logan and Mingo Counties for union activities. I don't see it as a rebellion."

"And why is that?"

"As I understand the word, rebellion is an unlawful activity against lawful authority."

"You admit that you were opposing the lawful authority of the Sheriff of Logan County whose troops lined the top of Blair Mountain?"

"See, that's where the problem lies, ain't it? Just because a man's got a badge don't make his activities lawful anymore than that tailored suit of yours makes you handsome." Laughter erupted.

The judge slammed the gavel. "Order in the court."

"Take that man for example." Bascom pointed at Tom Felts in the front of the courtroom. "He's got a badge on. And he's been breaking laws at the bidding of the coal operators practically since the railroad laid the first tracks in southern West Virginia. And he's gotten rich doing it."

"Mr. Felts is not the one on trial, Mr. Matney."

"By God, he should be. He's responsible for the death of my uncle, not to mention Sid Hatfield, Ed Chambers and countless others."

The courtroom erupted. Several men in the back of the courtroom leapt to their feet and clapped. The judge rapped his gavel.

"Sit down. One more outburst like that and I'll clear the courtroom. Continue."

The prosecutor dabbed his forehead. "Isn't it true, Mr. Matney, that you knew the force opposing you at Blair Mountain was led by the duly elected Sheriff of Logan County, Don Chafin, and included members of the West Virginia State Police? In other words, you led an attack on the lawful authority of Logan County?"

"It's true that Don Chafin was sheriff and he was running the show for the coal companies, like he's done for the better part of a decade. Like Mr. Felts there, it's made Mr. Chafin a rich man. But lawful? No, sir, I wouldn't agree that his authority was lawful."

The prosecutor appealed to the judge. "Your honor, will you instruct the witness to answer the question?"

"Mr. Matney, answer the question."

"Do you want me to repeat the question?"

"I reckon there were all sorts of men, including deputies and state troopers, standing with Chafin on top of that mountain."

"And the Sheriff and his men were there to protect the State from the marauding, murderous army you assembled to assert your authority over the offices of the State in Logan County, isn't that right?"

"Chafin and his men were there to protect the interests of the coal companies and, in turn, his own financial interests. He don't give a damn about the State anymore than you care about hearing the truth."

The judge again banged his gavel. "That's enough, Mr. Matney. You will answer the questions and stop giving speeches."

The prosecutor leaned on the podium. "Mr. Matney, do you deny leading an armed force against the lawful authority of the Sheriff of Logan County?"

Bascom faced the jury. "If you consider Don Chafin's authority to have been lawful, then I guess you could consider my actions illegal. But we weren't levying war against West Virginia or the United States. No, sir. When Uncle Sam's boys arrived, my men laid down their arms like they was told and went home peacefully."

"You're a socialist and a communist sympathizer, aren't you, Mr. Matney?"

"My sympathies lie with the union."

"Let me show you this telegram from Governor Morgan to United Mine Workers President John L. Lewis. He accuses the union of ties to the Bolsheviks in Russia. Do you deny that, Mr. Matney?"

"I don't deny the Governor wrote that telegram, but I deny the accusation. It's true there's some in our ranks who think we'd be better off if Socialists was running things, but we got plenty of Democrats and Republicans, too." Bascom shifted in his seat. "This ain't about politics. Never has been. This is about fair wages for an honest day's work."

The prosecutor implored the judge. "Your honor, will you direct the witness to answer the question?"

"I believe that's what he's doing. Continue."

"It's about safe working conditions and an eight-hour day. The operators know they can't win that argument, so they try to frighten honest, law-abiding men into thinking the union wants to change the government. They do that by trying to tie us to the Communists. At the end of the day, we don't care who's in office so long as the working man gets a fair deal."

The prosecutor paused to flip through his notes.

"Do you have any more questions for this witness?"

"Nothing further, your honor."

"You may step down, Mr. Matney."

Bascom returned to his seat. Bill Blizzard patted his knee. "Good job." On the other side, Harold Houston sat quietly.

The judge read instructions to the jury, concluding with the charge: "Gentlemen of the jury," the judge intoned, "even though you may find the actions of the defendants constituted violence contrary to the laws of the State, not every act of forceful resistance to officers of the State carrying out their duties constitutes treason. It is only when those forceful actions are committed with the intent to undermine the government can they be considered treason. You may retire to the jury room to deliberate."

※

One by one, the jurors filed into the courtroom to take their seats in the jury box. A tall, bespectacled man with inscrutable eyes held a piece of paper containing Bascom's fate.

The judge asked, "Have you reached a verdict?"

The man stood. "We have, your honor."

The foreman handed the verdict to the judge, who unfolded the note. He jotted some notes. Bascom rubbed the scatter tag between his thumb and forefinger.

"The defendants will rise."

Houston nudged Bascom. He and Blizzard rose. Bascom clenched tight the scatter tag.

The judge read, "We, the jury, find the defendants not guilty on the charge of treason."

The gallery erupted in chaos. Reporters dashed from the courtroom to call in their stories to newsrooms all over the country. Bascom and Blizzard hugged each other as best they could in handcuffs. Houston patted their backs. The judge banged his gavel. He waited for decorum to return.

"Are there any motions?"

Quick to his feet, Houston said, "No, your honor."

The prosecutor shook his head. "Not at this time, your honor."

"Mr. Blizzard, Mr. Matney, you're free to go. Sheriff, remove their cuffs."

Outside the courtroom, newsmen pounced, eager for a quote from Bascom. Bascom had said all he was going to say. He referred the press to his attorney, who was more than happy to oblige, then slipped away from the crush of reporters. He waded through the crowd of well-wishers eager to hug and slap his back. In a corner of the lawn, Alma stood alone bouncing an infant on her hip.

Bascom hurried across the grass. As he approached, she held the baby toward him. "Give your daddy a hug."

Bascom scooped up the child and tossed him into the air. "What did I tell you, Durwood? Truth was on our side."

Bascom grabbed Alma's hand and pulled her close. "Let's get out of here."

"Where we going?"

"Going to Mingo, Mrs. Matney."

THE END

Acknowledgments

Perhaps more daunting than writing a book is trying to thank everyone who played a part in making the book a reality. That is certainly true in my case. What follows is a feeble attempt to acknowledge a few folks who deserve special mention.

To Iva Dean, Larry Hypes, and Kathy Epperly: it was in your English classes over forty years ago that I first dreamed of becoming a writer. Admittedly, I'm a slow learner, but I hope that I have acquitted myself in your eyes.

To my late brother Frank, whose love of Southwest Virginia – coal country – and interest in my progress motivated me as I spent weekends hunched over the keyboard. My biggest regret is not being able to put a copy of the book in your hands.

To my friends and fellow writers, Pam, Jim, Lisa, and Patrick, thanks for your support and deft editing touch during the book's formative stage. Special thanks go to my many beta readers, especially my brother John and good friends Mark, Ritsu, and Helen, who read *Mingo* one agonizing chapter at a time, gutting it out with me for a full three years, no doubt wondering all the while if it would ever end. To David L. Robbins, a big man with a bigger heart and robust editing pen: thank you for your guidance and friendship. Finally, to Joni Albrecht, my publisher, publicist, editor, and friend, and her wonderful team of Cathy Plageman and Wendy Daniel at Little Star: working with you has been a joy. Every author who has ever complained about the publication process should have the privilege of working with you.

And, of course, this book would have never been written without the encouragement, patience, love, and support of my wife, Tamera, and daughters Carly and Maggie. Let the record reflect, however, that I was correct: writing a book is a lot harder than writing a Christmas letter!

Too many books, articles, and documentaries were instrumental in the creation of this novel to list them all. The works that most informed the history and events conveyed in these pages are: *The Devil is Here in These Hills*, by James Green; *Bloodletting in Appalachia*, by Howard B. Lee; *Matewan: Before the Massacre*, by Rebecca J. Bailey; *The Battle of Blair Mountain: The Story of America's Largest Labor Uprising*, by Robert Shogan; *King Coal*, by Stan Cohen; *Gun Thugs, Rednecks, and Radicals: A Documentary History of the West Virginia Mine Wars*, edited by David Alan Corbin; *The Blair Mountain War: Battle of the Rednecks*, by G.T. Swain, and *The Polar Bear Expedition*, by James Carl Nelson. Another indispensable resource and inspiration was John Sayles's 1987 film *Matewan*, a movie that has rattled around in my head for decades. Finally, the 1985 documentary *Even the Heavens Weep: The West Virginia Mine Wars*, and the PBS series, *The Mine Wars*, provided invaluable insight.

A final acknowledgement goes to the West Virginia Mine Wars Museum in Matewan, West Virginia, whose work to educate the public about the Coal Mine Wars and memorialize the men and women who sacrificed so much for the right to organize is a public treasure. To learn more, visit www.wvminewars.org.